VISIONS

VISIONS

RICHARD A. LUPOFF

MYTHOS BOOKS LLC

POPLAR BLUFF

MISSOURI

2009

Mythos Books LLC
351 Lake Ridge Road,
Poplar Bluff,
MO 63901
United States of America

www.mythosbooks.com

Published by Mythos Books LLC 2009

FIRST EDITION

ISBN: 0-9728545-4-1

Set in *Cataneo BT* & *Adobe Jenson Pro*.

Cataneo BT by Bitsream.
www.bitstream.com

Adobe Jenson Pro by Adobe Systems Incorporated.
www.adobe.com

Typesetting, layout and design by PAW.

Sources

"Hebrews Have No Horns"

Original to this collection, Mythos Books, 2009.

"There Are Kings"

Original to this collection, Mythos Books, 2009.

"Steps Leading Downward"

Original to this collection, Mythos Books, 2009.

"Tangaroa's Eye"

Original to this collection, Mythos Books, 2009.

"Ankareh Minu"

Originally appeared in *The Anthology of Dark Wisdom*, Elder Signs Press, edited by William Jones, 2009.

"Petroglyphs"

Originally appeared in *Strange Tales*, Wildside Press, edited by Robert M. Price, 2007.

"Brackish Waters"

Originally appeared in *Weird Shadows Over Innsmouth*, Fedogan & Bremer, edited by Stephen Jones, 2005.

"A Freeway for Draculas"

Originally appeared in *The Berserkers*, Trident Press, edited by Roger Elwood, 1974.

"The Peltonville Horror"

Originally appeared in *It's that Time Again* Volume 2, Bear Mountain Media, edited by Jim Harmon, 2007.

"Simeon Dimsby's Workshop"

Originally appeared in *NecronomiCon Program Book*, 2001.

"Villaggio Sogno"

Originally appeared in *The Mammoth Book of Sorcerers' Tales*, Robinson (UK), Carroll & Graf (US), edited by Mike Ashley, 2005.

"Snow Ghosts"

Originally appeared in *Spirits of Christmas*, Wynwood Press, edited by David G. Hartwell & Kathryn Cramer, 1989.

CONTENTS

Introduction

Peter S. Beagle

Adding things up, I have known Richard A. Lupoff for something close to thirty-three years, on and off. He has known *me* for thirty-three years. This makes a total of sixty-six years, and brings us back to 1943, when I was four years old, and already knew that I wanted to be a writer. Okay, no—make that a storyteller. I didn't yet know how to write down the stories I was already making up; I still had to have my mother do that. But I knew that nothing in the world *contented* me in as deep a way, as hearing a story did, and thinking about it afterward. I'm advised that I was a tractable, amiable child who rarely threw fits or had tantrums—but missing a bedtime story would do it. I'm sure it's true.

A few years later, obsessively literate, scrawling stories about Tarzan and the Lone Ranger in the back row of my second-grade class (God bless you, Mrs. Margaret Butterweck, for quietly encouraging me!), I knew that I wanted to spend my life in this place I went to when I was writing. More than that, I wanted to grow up and *know* writers, hang around with writers, move in that world that seemed even more heady and glamorous than the world of movie stars and cowboys. (I don't think I discovered baseball until I was nine or so.) It really did hit that early.

Today, given a choice, I hang out with musicians.

My dour view of writers as a group does not extend to Dick Lupoff, who happens to be one of the sweetest, least malicious people I've ever known. I stress that second quality, because writers in general are as malicious a collection of people as you're likely to encounter. (Poets are by far the worst, but that's somebody else's foreword.) We're a spiteful, envious lot, with *schadenfreude* in our DNA: Shakespeare himself speaks of

> "...desiring this man's art and that man's scope,
> With what I most enjoy contented least..."

And Willie the Shake has nothing on any modern-day writer

who sees a contemporary winning a Pulitzer or a National Book Award, selling a novel to Hollywood for the approximate GNP of Burkina Faso, or signing a three-book contract with a major house (which to most of my little circle means a publisher whose books actually get into the stores and don't fall apart while you're signing them, on the off-chance anyone should ask.) We acclaim a colleague's success; we praise, we congratulate, we extol—and then we go home and get together and settle down to serious bad-mouthing. It's the way we are; mostly we don't mean any harm. Mostly.

Dick Lupoff's not like that. Maybe it's because he doesn't have to be, having nothing to prove—the man's published more books, in more fields, than I ever expect to—but I don't think that's it. He's just alarmingly *decent*, and endlessly imaginative along with it, which is an absolutely lethal combination. You could scream.

He does something in the assemblage of stories you are about to read that touches me deeply on a personal level, by including several stories about a turn-of-the-century psychic investigator named Abraham ben Zaccheus. With his spade beard, his stocky stature, and his astonishing erudition, Abraham is an alternate-universe version of Dick's late friend and mine, the uniquely marvelous writer Avram Davidson. It doesn't matter at all to the stories themselves whether you happen to be acquainted with Avram or his work; but it matters to me that Dick, out of his gift and generosity, has crafted a world in which *this* Avram gets to be a wise, powerful and triumphant hero. And with an admiring and vigorous Watson of his own, yet! This is nothing but justice, and I would have loved *Visions* for that alone if it contained nothing of value but those tales of Abraham ben Zacchaeus and his splendid chronicler John O'Leary. Happily, this is a long way from being the case.

Visions shows off a number of Dick's characteristic strengths, from his gift for weaving absurdist terror out of as homely a thing as a middle-class commuter waiting outside his suburban home for his ride ("A Freeway for Draculas"), to his poignant sense of the way time and history and love and stupidity devour us all ("Snow Ghosts") to the fearful Lovecraftian doings of "Simeon

Dimsby's Workshop" and the Abraham-and-John adventure, "Steps Leading Downward." Dick has always had a truly astonishing mimetic bent—as any reader of *The Compleat Ova Hamlet* knows—and his pastiches, even of the pulpiest pulps become something other than mere parodies because of the tenderness for the original that always informs them. Personally, I think he often does Lovecraft better than Lovecraft did—but not *too* much better. That's the whole point.

For all his skill at evoking the thoroughly contemporary (as witness his delightful Bay Area-based mystery novels featuring the even more unlikely team of Hobart Lindsey and Marvia Plum), Dick's deepest heart plainly lies with the popular literature of the 1930s and 1940s. It's instructive that he and our usual lunch-and-bitching companion Michael Kurland recently collaborated on a book on how memory works and what to do about improving your own. Memory of times and styles and superheroes past is never too far from the surface of his work: he has not only edited Edgar Rice Burroughs' uncollected stories, but also written two fine biographical studies of the creator of Tarzan and John Carter. Then there are the two classic collections of essays on the great and semi-great comic-book heroes, *All in Color for a Dime* and *The Comic-Book Book* (both co-edited with Don Thompson.) Not to mention *The Great American Paperback,* which covers the history of paperback publishing in this country from 1837 on. I often wish he'd write a book concerning baseball, our shared passion—he actually saw Willie Mays as a 19-year-old minor-leaguer—but you can't have everything, even from Dick.

He knew this stuff in his bones long before it was officially labeled Popular Culture or American Studies—before you could get doctorates in it. Because of the respect with which he has treated his sources, as any artist must, they have steadfastly yielded up true art to him over the years. I've always thought of Dick Lupoff as the professional's professional, meaning it as my best professional compliment; but reading the stories in this collection has made me realize once again just how much more he is.

Peter S. Beagle
Oakland, California

Richard A. Lupoff

My friend Stanley Sargent is at least indirectly responsible for these four stories. My wife and I were strolling through San Francisco's Tenderloin district with Stan when he raised the subject of finding fresh ideas for stories. We happened to be standing opposite a block that had been cleared to rubble pending new construction—all except for one rather decrepit building, clearly of pre-quake vintage. It was boarded up and covered with graffiti, but still it stood, surrounded by desolation. I asked Stan, "What do you think is going on in that building?" Then I asked myself the same question. The answer led to "Hebrews Have No Horns." That story led to two sequels, "There Are Kings" and "Steps Leading Downward."

With that, I thought the series was complete . . . until the day that another San Francisco-based psychic detective popped into my mind. She was none other than Abraham ben Zaccheus's granddaughter, Rebekkah. She was as much a shock to me as was her story. To date, "Ankareh Minu" is the only Rebekkah ben Zaccheus case, but one never knows.

Hebrews Have No Horns

When I was an altar boy back in Kilkee, Father Phinean warned us to watch out for Hebrews who would try and steal our immortal souls. Failing that, their favorite trick was to steal good Christian babies and grind their bones to make their *matzie* crackers and drink their blood at their Passover *sadie* parties. I once asked the Father if Our Lord hadn't told his blessed disciples to eat His Holy Flesh and drink His Holy Blood at the last Passover *sadie* He attended in Jerusalem.

For an answer Father Phinean fetched me one on the ear that made my head ring for a week and left me with a cauliflower ear that's been my blessing ever since I came to America. That was the last time I saw the inside of St. Padraic's Church, you can be certain, and the last that St. Padraic's would ever see of John O'Leary. Ah, but with my cauliflower ear all I need to do is stroll into a saloon and swagger up to the mahogany and the boys all think I'm a pugilist and my drinks are on the house or else somebody decides to show he's a better man than I am and I get to engage in a lovely brawl and then I have my drinks afterward.

But the day came when I had to leave Kilkee in a hurry and wound up in Five Points in New York City just in time to welcome in the Twentieth Century. I gradually found my way across this whole wide continent and wound up here in San Francisco with nowhere farther west to go unless I wanted to visit China. Which, come to think of it, might be an interesting experience indeed, indeed. But I'm not inclined to try that out quite yet. Mayhap a few years hence.

But here it is close to Advent in this Year of Our Lord 1905 and here I am in this lovely city in this lovely country and if they miss me in Ireland as much as I miss them then they don't miss me at all. Not at all.

Which is not to deny that I had dear friends in Kilkee. I grew up fighting and playing with Shane Galloway and Rogan Doherty and Seamus McCarthy and Malachy Teague, and chasing after Glenna Lynch and pulling her pigtails and falling in love with sweet Maeve Corrigan. Sweet Maeve with her hair the color of flame and her eyes the color of Ireland's green fields and her skin like soft, virgin snow. Dear Maeve, kicked dead by an Englishman's fancy riding horse at the age of twelve. To this day I can smell the incense burned at her obsequies. If Maeve were living I'd have stayed in Kilkee forever. Stayed there with Maeve else left with her in my arms. But with Maeve dead Kilkee will see no more of John O'Leary.

What a wonderful land this America is. I worked as a fireman, of all things, in New York. I hefted barrels in a brewery in Chicago. I was a plasterer in St. Louis and I went down in a copper mine to earn my bread and cheese in Colorado. And when I arrived in San Francisco I decided to try something new. I am very fond of new things.

I picked up a copy of the San Francisco *Daily Morning Call* that some gent had left behind in a saloon shortly after I arrived in this fine city. The newspapers of any city provide a useful introduction, I have found, and this one was full of unpleasant details about assorted murders, robberies, and political scandals. Ah, well, I said to myself, so this fine town is no different from the other metropolises of the New World.

I still had a few coins in my pocket and betwixt free hardboiled eggs with my beer and a little labor picking up merchandise that fell off the backs of drays coming from the harbor I had no problem keeping body and soul together here in San Francisco. But I did have the itch, and so I turned the pages of that newspaper looking for advertisements by employers looking for workers and I found one that interested me indeed.

It was posted by one Mr. Abraham ben Zaccheus and listed an address in the neighborhood they call Rooshian Hill. Here's what it said:

> INVESTIGATOR seeks secretary, amanuensis, and general assistant. Something is happening in the Earth. Something is going to happen. Applicant must exhibit courage, strength, willingness to take risks and explore the unknown. Keen olfactory and kinetic senses vital. Room, board, and salary provided. Apply in person only.

I read the advertisement over a number of times. Courage, strength, willingness to take risks and explore the unknown, eh? Why, if that didn't describe John O'Leary, formerly of Kilkee, County Clare, Ireland, to a T, I would still be living in Kilkee, upsetting Father Phinean with my impertinent questions and getting walloped alongside my noggin for my trouble.

As for something happening in the Earth, oh, that could mean anything or nothing. Maybe there was another volcano preparing to explode. Oh, yes, we hear about such things, even in Kilkee. I once owned a book with a picture of Krakatoa in it, and a description of the eruption of that monstrous beast in 1883, a mere twenty-two years ago. Why, I was already a lad studying my letters and interrupting Father at Mass in that remembered year. And of course there was Vesuvius that buried the wicked Romans back in the year 79 *anno domini*. I wonder, now, did the lava and dust kill all the worshippers of Jupiter and the other heathen gods in old Pompei, and spare the holy Christians? I have my doubts. Ah, but the Father would be after me with his fists if he could hear me now!

I will confess that the requirement for keen olfactory and kinetic senses left me at a loss, but I know that I have horse sense, at least, and I was willing to bluff my way through those others if the need should arise.

Thus I hied myself up Rooshian Hill and located Mr. ben Zaccheus's address, which was that of a pleasant looking residence of no great pretentiousness. The windows were large and the roof was decorated with the curlicues the local folks hereabouts call gingerbread. It was distinguished, I noticed, by an odd little gadget that was nailed to the doorpost but I didn't know what it was so I went ahead and knocked on the door.

The sky had got dark and there was a cold, wet wind ruffling my hair and starting to spatter my dear cheeks, which caused me to wish that either the personage who had placed the advertisement would admit me to his august presence, or that a servant would appear to do as much.

The fellow who opened the door looked ordinary enough. He had a beard but they're commonly seen in San Francisco, although I like to keep my own face shaved so I can show it off. Not that

I'm conceited but I'll admit that I am good-looking. He was shorter than I am and did not look lean nor hungry. I saw that he was wearing a little skull-cap like the biretta a Monsignor would wear and I was thinking that he might be some kind of Greek or Rooshian Father with that skull cap and that name and that beard.

He smiled at me and said something like, "Saloon." I don't think that was what he said, but it was as close as I could make out. I said it back to him, as close as I could come, and he seemed pleased and took a step backward and made a gesture with his hand and I felt almost as if something picked me up and carried me into the house.

He closed the door behind me and gestured again and I found myself sitting on an overstuffed sofa.

First chance I got, I asked if he was a Greek or Rooshian Father. You won't believe me but I remember exactly how he replied because it knocked me for a loop.

"No," said the gentleman in question, "I am not Greek and I am not Rooshian. I am an American but before I was an American I was a subject of — "

And then he told me and it was like the sweet poetry of Ireland. I just listened admiringly at the moment, but later I asked him to write it down for me and he did. Here is what he wrote down:

"I was a subject of His Imperial and Apostolic Majesty, Franz Joseph I, by the Grace of God, Emperor of Austria, King of Hungary and Bohemia, King of Lombardy and Venice, of Dalmatia, Croatia, Slavonia, Lodomeria and Illyria; King of Jerusalem, Archduke of Austria, Grand Duke of Tuscany and Kraków, Duke of Lorraine, of Salzburg, Styria, Carinthia, Carniola and of the Bukovina; Grand Prince of Transylvania; Margrave of Moravia; Duke of Upper and Lower Silesia, of Modena, Parma, Piacenza and Guastalla, of Oświęcim and Zator, of Cieszyn, Friuli, Ragusa and Zadar; Princely Count of Habsburg and Tyrol, of Kyburg, Gorizia and Gradisca; Prince of Trento and Brixen; Margrave of Upper and Lower Lusatia and Istria; Count of Hohenems, Feldkirch, Bregenz, Sonnenberg, Lord of Trieste, of Kotor, and the Wendish Mark, and Grand Voivode of the Voivodina of Serbia."

"Holy Mother of God," I exclaimed, falling to my knees, "I didn't know, your highness."

The gentleman guffawed and put his hand on my shoulder. I thought he was going to declare me a royal knight of the kingdom but all he did was laugh at me.

"Get up," he said. "Get up, my fine man. Those titles belonged to another fellow who lives far away in Vienna, where I was born too, but in my father's humble house, not in a splendid palace like the Emperor."

"You're not a king, then?" I asked.

He laughed again and said that he was not, and would I please be so kind as to get up off his carpet and drink a glass of tea and eat some cake.

Well, I am not a great lover of that particular beverage but I did not want to offend this king. I still thought mayhap he was a king in disguise, you see, but he was not. He was, he told me, Mr. Abraham ben Zaccheus, which I already knew as that was the name in his newspaper advertisement, and he was a gentleman of the Hebrew persuasion, he told me, which I found harder to believe than that he was not a king because he had no horns, you see. Not even little ones.

Oh, I wish he had come to Kilkee so the Father there could see that Hebrews have no horns. That set me to thinking. If the Father could be wrong about one thing, he could be wrong about other things, don't you see? And if Mr. Abraham ben Zaccheus had no horns, then mayhap he did not grind the bones of Christian babies to make his *matzie* crackers nor drink their blood in his Passover *sadies.*

Oh, this New World was a wondrous place, and San Francisco was a most wondrous city!

So there I sat, don't you see, in Mr. Abraham ben Zaccheus's parlor. This was a stuffy room furnished with a horsehair sofa and chairs, with brocaded hangings and a gilt-framed mirror and photographs on the walls of people looking solemn and serious that I took it to be relatives of Mr. Abraham ben Zaccheus in whatever country it was that he came from where he was not the king.

There was one photograph of an old gent in a splendid military uniform. This one was set aside from the others and I took it to be the Imperial and Apostolic Majesty and all them other things. I didn't think he could be of the Hebrew persuasion, though. I don't think that any Imperial and Apostolic Majesties have been of the Hebrew persuasion for a very long time.

My host excused himself from the room and I studied my surroundings while I awaited his return. There was a handsome spinet piano with a woven tapestry-looking cover on it, and a golden candelabrum with as many arms as one of them octopussy beasts that Mr. Verne the Frenchie writes about. The walls, where they were not covered with portraits of splendid ladies in elegant gowns and gentlemen in uniforms or dark robes, were covered with book cases filled with leather-bound volumes. Some were stamped with titles in English; others, in foreign markings that didn't even look like good honest ABC's.

I was about to take one down when a throat was cleared behind me and there stood my bearded host with a silver tray in his hands. He set the tray down upon a table. There were two tea cups on it, each filled with a lovely looking liquid.

"You will forgive me," the gentleman declaimed, "but this is a test of sorts. Will you be so good as to tell me what each of these cups contains?"

I resumed my seat upon the horsehair sofa and lifted one cup, then the other. Ahah! Neither of them contained tea at all.

"This, sir," I told my host after sniffing the contents of the tea cup, "is Coleraine Single Malt '34' whisky, as fine a beverage as ever was created in Ireland or anywhere else upon the face of Mother Earth." I lowered the cup and lifted its companion. *Sniff! Sniff!* "And this, alas, is Glenmorangie Madeira Wood Finish whiskey, as good a drink as the barbaric Scots folk are capable of distilling. 'Tis fit for such as them to drink, I suppose."

My host grinned broadly. "Well, young man, you have passed that test with flying colors. You identified the two cups by olfactory examination alone. If you wish to drink them down, by all means do so."

Ah, well, the Coleraine was a treat indeed, and the

Glenmorangie I managed to force down solely so as not to give offense.

The gentleman disappeared once again, taking the tray and empty cups with him.

In quick time he was back, and there was a silver pot of tea on the table before me, set there by my host with his own hands, along with fresh wedges of yellow lemon and slices of a sweet, heavy cake. I sipped at the tea, which was not at all bad although it would have benefited from a few drops of that fine Coleraine or even the poor Glenmorangie, and nibbled at the cake, thinking that if I came away from this house with naught more to show for my trouble I could drop a slice in the pocket of my jacket.

Mr. Abraham ben Zacchius removed his spectacles and—I did tell you that Mr. Abraham ben Zacchius wore thick spectacles, did I not?—and polished them with a pocket handkerchief. When he had them off he had a vague look to him that made me think that he was just about as blind as a bat, and when he put them back on they made his eyes look as big as hen's eggs.

"I assume that you have come in response to my advertisement in the San Francisco *Daily Morning Call,*" Mr. Abraham ben Zaccheus said.

I admitted that such was indeed the case. I volunteered that my name was John O'Leary and that I hailed from the village of Kilkee in the nation of Ireland, English overlords be damned.

"Well, Mr. John O'Leary, are you a man of intelligence and education?" Mr. Abraham ben Zaccheus asked me.

I admitted that such was indeed the case.

"You can read and write?"

"Indeed, sir."

"And are you a man of physical prowess and courage?"

"I've never backed off from a fight, sir," I told Mr. Abraham ben Zaccheus, "nor seldom lost one."

The gentleman grunted at that, seemingly pleased to hear what I had to say to him.

"John," he said to me, which familiarity I found objectionable until he followed it with, "I hope I may call you John, and will you be so kind as to call me Abraham?"

I almost dropped my teacup, thinking that a king was asking me to call him by his Christian name, but then I realized that Abraham was not his Christian name at all, but his Hebrew name. Which of course was but little help if he truly was a king in disguise, but I said to him, "Of course, sir, Mr. Abraham."

"Just Abraham," he insisted.

"Very well, sir."

"Now, John—we do have that settled, I hope?"

"Aye, sir."

"Now, John, it will be necessary for you to understand that mine is an unusual occupation. I travel from place to place seeking to unravel mysteries that have nonplussed the usual investigators."

I thought about that for a bit of a while, nibbling at Abraham's cake, which was really very tasty and I was certain not made from the bones of Christian babies, and sipping at his tea, which was truthfully as excellent as it could be without the aid of a drop of Coleraine or Ballydoyl or Tyrconnell's Single Malt.

"Ahah!" I replied after a bit, "like that Mr. Sherlock Holmes that the good Irish Doctor Doyle writes his tales about."

"Indeed, something like that," Abraham conceded.

"And I'm thinking," I said, taking another sip of Abraham's excellent tea and wishing that it was a bit stronger than it was, "that you're after hiring a fellow to be your Doctor Watson. Is that the idea you have, Abraham?" I very nearly called him Your Majesty, or King Abraham, but I held myself back, you see.

"John" said Abraham at this moment, "you are a clever fellow and you have fathomed my intentions exactly. Of course my methods are not exactly those of the estimable Mr. Holmes, but I will need someone to accompany me on my excursions. It will be your duty to assist me as needed, and I trust to record my doings for my own referral as well as those of others, and for my posterity. For you see, John, there are times when I am not able to protect myself against—certain forces."

Certain forces indeed, I thought, although I did not say anything at the moment. I believed that I had been fortunate indeed to pick up that copy of the San Francisco *Daily Morning Call*, and doubly so that I was the first person, mayhap the only person, to respond to Abraham's advertisement.

Abraham told me that quarters were available for my use in the rear of his home, and that a most splendid and reliable woman came in each day to keep his house in order and to prepare his meals for him. This, of course, did not startle me in the very least, for if Abraham was a kind of Californian Sherlock Holmes and I was to be his new Dr. Watson, then surely there must be a Mrs. Hudson to cook and clean.

Ah, it's a good thing, don't you see, that we learn to read and write in Kilkee. Many an Irish youth there is who doesn't know his letters, but in Kilkee the Father provides a classroom for willing lads where they learn to read and write as well as to know the Sacraments and the Commandments.

Abraham was a detective, then!

I thought, *Thou shalt not kill!*

There remained a small negotiation regarding my wages, and to my astonishment Abraham proved quite generous in that regard. As I had no possessions save the clothing in which I had arrived at Abraham's house, the gentleman provided me with two silver dollars as a small advance against my first month's wages and sent me on my way to procure some changes of raiment for myself.

I took myself on foot back down Rooshian Hill, pausing first to look out across the San Francisco Bay. Ah, if ever I felt a longing for the tors and lakes of Ireland (which I did not), I knew that I need only gaze at these glistering waters and the hills beyond to soothe my soul. The dark shapes of schooners at anchor in the Bay and the white squares and triangles of sail bellied out by a late afternoon wind added spice and vivacity to the glories of nature spreading before me. The gusty mist that had wet my face a while ago had passed, although the sky remained a pearly gray rather than blue.

It took me the shortest time to reach the emporia of Market Street and purchase a good pair of Levi Strauss's canvas trousers, a warm shirt, a mackinaw and a strong set of sturdy boots to supplement my careworn brogans. I was planning to return to Rooshian Hill and settle in for the night, but I stopped first to celebrate my good fortune at a music hall where a line of lovely young ladies disported themselves most merrily to the accompaniment of a cornet and piano.

The establishment offered a tasty selection of comestibles and a tempting array of beverages to accompany the evening's entertainment, and fortunately I had sufficient change left from Abraham's advance to purchase a good steak and a small bottle of wine. I must have looked like a swell, at least to some, and I will report with pride that I resisted the temptation to avail myself of female companionship for the evening.

As I left the establishment I was accosted by a pair of toughs. They were dressed in dark outfits with pulled-down hats. One of them was a good sight smaller than the other. I think they figured me for a dipsomaniac, which I am not, whom they could roll for his pelf, of which by now I had almost none, or possibly sell to the captain of a sailing ship to serve on his return voyage to wherever he had first parted from.

For all that I enjoy a good friendly brawl of an evening, especially after taking aboard a bit of a squiff, I am not by nature a violent man. Still, these two ruffians made me feel seriously put upon. Especially as I was carefully carrying a paper-wrapped and twine-bound package containing the fine new garments and boots I had acquired through the courtesy of Mr. Abraham ben Zaccheus's generosity and good will.

Can you imagine the embarrassment I would have felt if I had lost my package and had to return to Mr. Abraham ben Zaccheus's establishment penniless and empty-handed? This good gentleman had taken me in and treated me with such kindness, I would have been mortally ashamed to do such a thing.

Well, one of the toughs was facing me. The street was not brightly lit, but I could see the villain fairly well, courtesy of some moonlight and a bit of illumination coming from the music hall I had just left. This worthy was wearing a sailor's pea-jacket and watch-cap and sported a nifty set of brass knuckles combined with a polished belly-ripper on one hand. That hand looked pretty small and slim, so slim it made me suspect I was facing a woman.

And when the ruffian spoke I decided that I was right. This was indeed a female bandit.

A scandal, thought I.

She said something which I could not comprehend, as it was in a heathenish language with which I was unfamiliar. I could not tell if she was speaking to me or to someone standing behind me. I think she spoke a name, something like *Zany,* and since I couldn't understand her I thought indeed that she was speaking to someone else.

And sure enough there was a second voice, a nasty-sounding man's voice, speaking practically in my ear. I think this fellow called the woman a villain, or some such thing.

The woman gestured with her knuckles-and-belly-ripper. I imagine that she was expecting me to back away from her. But someone—and one of the Holy Saints, I'm sure—seemed to be whispering in my ear, *John O'Leary, don't you do that!*

Instead of backing away, I shoved my brown paper bundle straight at the woman's face, at the same moment dodging to one side and dropping to one knee.

Glory be to that whispering Saint! I wish I knew which one it was.

The tough with the knuckles-and-blade on her hand had a confederate, as I've already indicated. Said confederate, as I shortly learned, was dressed similarly to the first villain, but instead of brass knuckles and blade he was armed with a ship's belaying pin which he was in the process of bringing down upon my own dear unprotected bazoo, the which I value highly and have done my level best to protect ever since I was a wee tyke lacking both hair and choppers.

Oh, it was a lovely sight I then beheld.

The female ruffian with the knuckles-and-blade found her weapon embedded in my package. The fellow with the belaying pin in his hand was already in the act of delivering his mightiest wallop, which landed squarely, but not on my own precious crown but that of his partner.

They fell to scuffling angrily, rolling on the cobblestones, growling and snapping and biting like a pair of mongrel hounds, and I could give my warrant that the female scoundrel, though far the smaller of the two, was likely to get the best of the fight. I could have sworn that she was going for her partner's jugular with her teeth, yes, like some creature out of a novel by the great Mr. Stoker.

While they went at it I retrieved my package, the brass weapon still attached to it, and made tracks as fast as my lower limbs would carry me.

A sight I must have been when I rapped once again at the door of Mr. Abraham ben Zaccheus's house on Rooshian Hill, what with my phiz all perspired and my locks in disarray. But Mr. Abraham ben Zaccheus ushered me for the second time into his home, bolting the door behind me.

I feared that my appearance might cost me my new position, and not only that, would leave me indebted in the amount of two silver dollars to my employer, but when once I had recounted my adventure of the evening such was not the result. In fact, as I narrated the past hours' events, which I did with complete accuracy and with no embellishment whatsoever, Abraham guffawed repeatedly.

This set to rest another falsehood that I had been told by the Father in Kilkee. His teaching it was that Hebrews are unable to laugh like other men, but only to emit a gleeful cackle at the misfortune of their foes, which is to say, all good and faithful followers of Our Lord. Instead, Mr. Abraham ben Zaccheus laughed heartily at the image of the two ruffians rolling around in the gutter as I made off safe and sound with my bundle, the knuckles-and-blade device still attached thereto.

Abraham drew a huge bandanna from his pocket, wiped his streaming eyes, and blew his large nose loudly. On that score, at least, the Father was correct. Abraham's nose was truly majestic. When he had regained his breath he asked to examine the weapon I had liberated from my attackers.

He turned it over in his hands, tested the edge of the blade against his thumb, and returned it to my custody. Quoth he: A good thing that you kept the weapon, John. Take care of it. We may find it useful." He then offered me a nightcap of a beverage he called *schnapps*, which I found most tasty and enjoyable, and in which he raised a toast in a language unknown to me.

Abraham did ask me to repeat the conversation the two toughs had held, both before attacking me and during their scuffle. I scratched my head to help me recall their heathenish words, then recounted them as best I could.

"You had a narrow escape, young John," Abraham said when I was finished. I studied his phiz trying to cipher his age but with no great success. Surely he was older than my own years, but I thought not by so much as to call me young. But he was the employer, you see, and I the worker, and it was not for me to challenge him on this score.

It was not as if I was back in Kilkee and he was the Father!

"Your attackers," Abraham told me, "were almost certainly Zanna and Veleno. They are two of the most dangerous street-prowlers in this city. Obviously, you did not get a good look at Zanna's face, or you would have mentioned it. She is by all reports one of the most beautiful women alive. I have encountered her before, and I can affirm that those reports are neither falsehoods nor exaggerations. As for her consort, Veleno, he is reputed to have killed no fewer than an hundred men in his native Sicily, and half again as many in America."

He paused to inhale deeply. Then he said, "You were fortunate to get away unscathed, but you not only escaped those two, you humiliated them. I am afraid, John O'Leary, that you have made two very dangerous enemies."

Abraham sighed, patted me upon the knee, and said, "There is nothing more to do this night save get a good rest. A busy day awaits us tomorrow."

And so we retired for the night, he to whatever quarters he chose to use, it being his house, and I to a comfortable room which Abraham assigned me.

In the morning we shared a hearty breakfast served by his housekeeper. Abraham's "Mrs. Hudson" was a lady of the Chinese persuasion, whose name I later learned was rendered *Xiang Xi-Mei,* meaning fragrant beautiful plum. Xiang Xi-Mei was a most pleasant person and a talented chef. She fluttered around her employer, patting him and speaking to him in her native tongue, the which, to my astonishment, Mr. Abraham ben Zaccheus must have understood, for he replied in the same language.

Next, Abraham told me we were to explore the site of his pending investigation. Refreshed and nourished, we made our way to an elegant carriage house which stood on the grounds behind

Abraham's home. He swung open the door to reveal, not the horse and buggy which I had begun to anticipate, but an odd looking contrivance of metal and wood and cloth.

The horseless carriage had yet to make its way to the village of Kilkee. Horse-drawn buggies and dog-carts serve the needs of them as can afford them. When the mighty Bishop Quigley himself arrived one time for a pastoral visit riding regally inside a steam automobile, the conveyance rather than the Right Reverend Lordship was the focus of all eyes and the topic of conversation at the pub for days to come. It was raining that day, and His Reverend Lordship stayed high and dry inside the carriage while some poor baby priest, he looked to be fresh from the seminary, sat outside in a sopping-wet cassock, driving the contrivance.

My good friend Seamus McCarthy, he was a fellow of a scientific bent, mind you, Seamus McCarthy speculated on that steam carriage. "If the boiler blows," Seamus asked, "I suppose his Grand Holiness in there would be all right, but that poor sap of a youngster riding on top would be cooked for sure and blown to bits. We'd find chunks of sanctified stew meat strewing the countryside for a fortnight, I should think."

You might infer by now that Kilkee was not the most pious of towns, and you'd not be far wrong at that.

Indeed, I saw plenty of horseless carriages in Dublin and Liverpool and the great cities of this great land America, but I must confess that I never rode in one until Mr. Abraham ben Zaccheus directed me to climb aboard his vehicle, and he sat right there in it beside me. It didn't look nor feel so different from a lovely buggy, and he was proud as punch of the conveyance.

"A Columbia Mark LX Runabout," he told me, grinning like a new dad showing off a fresh-hatched chick. I bought it at the factory and drove it across the continent myself."

I found that hard to believe, but I was not inclined to challenge the veracity of my employer, you can be sure.

He started up the machine and slid the controller handle a notch to roll it forward, informing me that the estimable Chiang Chu-Mei would see to closing up the carriage house after we were gone. We started off down Rooshian Hill, and I will admit that I was frightened for my very life and hung on as tightly as I could while the machine rolled down the sloping way.

"Did you sleep well, John?" he asked me.

"Well indeed," I told him. It took all of my powers to hold a conversation while clutching at the buggy-railing.

"And you felt nothing, nor noticed an unpleasant odor in the night?"

"I did awaken once," I conceded. "I thought perhaps I'd been dreaming, that my bed was moving about, or perhaps the whole house."

"What else?"

"Mayhap I smelt something, Abraham. I couldn't tell for certain. I thought perhaps it was the Coleraine thirty-four in my belly complaining about the Glenmorangie I sipped on top of it. You know, the finest Irish and that pissy-poor stuff the Scots call whiskey, you should pardon my French if you will, Abraham, they don't really get along so well."

"Mayhap," Abraham said, and that was all he said just then.

We had reached the bottom of Rooshian Hill and were navigating the streets of San Francisco. The clouds and misty drizzle of yesterday had blown away and the sun was shining. The streets of this city were crowded with a variety of folk, some men and women in finery such as you'd find in the best cities in the world and some in rough worker's garb or worse. There were rumpots falling down in the gutter and there were ruined souls with the mark of the Chinese hop on their faces.

You could hear every language in the world spoken in those streets, and a kind of street railway pulled by underground cables ran on some thoroughfares while horse cars ran on others and wagons and buggies of every description battled for headroom.

At last we reached a section of the city where new buildings were rising at every turn. On Turk Street Abraham drew up in front of a spanking new building four stories tall. He climbed from his electric buggy, inviting me to do the same, the which I did. He stood looking up at the edifice before us. It was built all of cut stones, as solid and gloomy as a cathedral. There were tall windows of colored glass and patterns that might have meant something if they hadn't been so murky and shifty-looking, like castor oil dropped in a pan of water. There was a weathervane, I think, on the roof. It was hard to tell just what it was meant to represent. Maybe a rooster.

Abraham was wearing what the Frenchies call a sacque suit all of black, a shirt the color of a ripe plum, a four-in-hand cravat and a bowler hat over his biretta thing, which he told me Hebrews call a *yarmee-kee*. He had brought one of those new electric torches with him in his horseless carriage. Oh, he was an electric man, was Abraham ben Zaccheus. He cut a noteworthy figure altogether but I felt comfortable in my new denims and boots with a knitted watch cap to keep my ears warm.

One odd thing about this city, it doesn't have a climate. You can travel a mile in any direction and go from sunshine to fog, warm air to chill wind. The weather had been as pleasant as a bright morn in early springtime up there on Rooshian Hill. Here on Turk Street the sky had turned a dull gray and the wind blew specks of grit in my face.

Abraham placed his hand on my forearm. He had a heavy hand, not the soft thing that you'd expect a bookish fellow to have, no less a gentleman of royal birth, for I was still not settled in my own mind as to who Abraham ben Zaccheus really was. He wore a heavy gold ring that looked as if it had once been a living thing that had somehow crawled onto his finger and liked the climate so much it decided to stay. I couldn't tell whether it had eyes or tiny jewels for eyes, but surely it was looking at me even as I was looking at it, and I will confess that I was the first one to look away.

"What do you feel, John?" Abraham asked me.

"Only your hand on my arm, sir."

He shook his head. "Nothing from—" He tilted his head toward the ground beneath our feet.

"Nothing, sir."

He let out a sigh and shook his head. "All right, John, all right. How about the air? Do you smell anything?"

I took a sniff. Indeed, I smelled a great many things. I could smell the Pacific Ocean with all of the life and all of the death that goes on in its waters, from California to Cathay. I could smell the grass and palm trees in Mr. McLaren's great Golden Gate Park. I'll give him credit for that, Scotsman though he is. I could smell the shishkee-bobs that street vendors were making over little charcoal fires. And I could smell the droppings of the horses that pulled carriages and drays through the city's streets.

But when I told Abraham what I could smell, he was clearly disappointed. "Don't you smell something else, John O'Leary? Don't you smell something evil?"

"No," I shook my head.

Abraham muttered into his beard, then he looked up into my face and fixed me with his great dark eyes. "We're going into that building," he said, "and you must be on your guard. I may need your help. My life will be in your hands, John O'Leary."

He took his hand off my arm and grasped me by the wrists. "In your hands," he said again. There was a serious expression on his face, one I hadn't seen before. "When we are in the building I want you to hold your tongue, John. Do not speak to anyone you meet there, no matter who you may think they are, nor what they may say to you. Listen only to me. If you hear me say the word *ayin,* you are to act as if you remembered something very urgent and important and insist that we leave at once."

I didn't know what to make of that, and I suppose I looked a bit puzzled, but then Abraham did something that surprised me. He reached up and grabbed me by the ears, and brought my face down so close to his that I could count the hairs in his dark beard, and he said, "John, our hosts may try to keep us there. I may try to stay, myself. I may tell you that I've changed my mind, that you can leave but that I need to stay behind. You are to ignore everything that happens, everything that I say, everything that anyone says. If you hear the word I've given you, you must get me out of there. Do you understand me, John?"

I said I did.

"And what is the word?" he asked.

I said, "Ayin."

He let go of my head and I straightened up. "Good. Very good. You are a fine fellow, John O'Leary, a very fine fellow. Now remember what I told you. And repeat the word to me once more."

I said, "Ayin."

"Good."

"Abraham," I said, "what does it mean? Ayin, what does it mean?"

He said, "Nothing. Just remember it, and remember what you are to do if you hear me speak it."

We made our way to the house, Abraham taking short strides as befits a man of his height and build, and I taking longer ones as befits a man such as myself. We climbed a stoop and Abraham nodded to me, indicating that I should knock on the door, which I would have done with my knuckles had there not been a splendid brass knocker attached to the wood. It looked something like a sea creature, and I wondered if the house was not the new home of a seagoing trader.

The door let into a darkened anteroom, the likes of which I believe the Frenchies call a *four-yea,* and we stepped inside.

I will confess that my jaw dropped, for where should I find myself but the vestibule of St. Padraic's Church. The doors to the nave were wide open, and there was Father Phinean himself, a greasy, frayed dog collar visible over his chasuble. He smiled at me and reached his hand to me. I thought he was going to give me another clout and I think I raised my own paw to protect my cauliflower ear, but he took my other hand in his and shook it.

His skin was cold.

He said something to me. At first I couldn't tell what he was saying, it was in some language I'd never encountered before, but then I could understand. He was saying, *Welcome, my son, welcome, we haven't seen you at St. Padraic's in a long time, young John. You've come to make Confession, I hope. I know you've sinned, young John.*

Past him I could see the chancel, and above it a clerestory where, glory be, the choir was practicing their parts of the Mass. At least, I thought that was what they were practicing. They weren't singing in Latin and the tune was not what I thought they should be singing.

Come along, Father Phinean said. He put his arm around my shoulders and it felt strange to me, strong as an ox and yet I couldn't tell where his elbow or his wrist were, his arm was all like a single giant muscle inside his skin. *Come along.*

He drew me toward the chancel. He came to the altar and knelt, acting like a proper priest, and made some gesture that I couldn't see but it should have been the Sign of the Cross. I knelt, too, and when Father Phinean stood up again I did the same and then I turned around to see if Abraham ben Zaccheus was still with us but he was nowhere to be seen.

Instead I beheld none other than his high and mighty lordship Bishop Quigley himself, as splendid as he could be in his stole and alb and all the rest of his royal robes, wearing a miter on his head like a crown and holding a crozier in his hand like a royal scepter. The baby priest who had attended him so long ago in Kilkee stood at his side to render help should he be needed.

For all that I was fallen away from the Church I went to my knees and bowed my head before the mighty Bishop and he held out his hand to me. I saw he was wearing a ring. I thought none less than the Holy Father Himself would wear such a ring but Bishop Quigley was wearing one. It was gold and had a sigil all worked into it. I raised it to my lips and felt a jolt go through me like the Holy Spirit Himself, or maybe a wallop of the electricity Abraham ben Zaccheus seemed so fond of.

The Bishop made me stand up.

The choir were singing.

Father Phinean said, *Come along, then, young John O'Leary.*

There was a trap door behind the altar. The Lord Bishop's baby priest opened it and we proceeded down stone steps into the Earth beneath St. Padraic's, first portly Bishop Quigley then tall Father Phinean and then myself, wondering and wide-eyed, smelling the incense of my youth and dreaming up the image of dear Maeve Corrigan with her red hair and green eyes and pale, soft skin.

We tramped down and down. The Bishop was huffing and puffing as he went along, leaning on his crozier. I could feel a hand on my shoulder, and thought that it was the baby priest, Bishop Quigley's driver and man-of-all-tasks. There were walls around us, roughly hewn from bedrock, with carvings lit by cressets that must burn oil, and there was the smell of incense, and there was a rumbling from below as if some great machinery was working away in the bowels of the Earth.

The bowels of the Earth beneath Kilkee.

And singing. Singing. The choir was far above us, practicing away in the clerestory, but there was new singing from below us, from wherever the stone stairs led.

At last we found ourselves in an open area like none I had seen in all my days. I blinked and blinked and tried to tell what it was I beheld, but I could not. Mayhap we were in a natural cavern deep in Mother Earth's dear womb, or mayhap we were out-of-doors in the night, for I thought I beheld stars and planets, swooping comets and distant galaxies, our own Milky Way as I'd seen on many nights looking at the sky above Kilkee and other bodies of stars, great swirling masses and whole universes twisting and writhing like starfish fresh drawn from the briny ocean. There was every color I knew and there were colors I had never imagined could exist.

We walked and there was a pit, and in it great beasts that slithered and wove like worms in a fisherman's bucket only a thousand, a million times the size. It was their pounding and squirming that had made the great thumping and grinding sounds.

But there rose up from the pit a crowd of boys and girls. The great beasts had disappeared and there was a green field and there was a picnic going on. There was Malachy Teague and there was Seamus McCarthy, there was Rogan Doherty and Shane Galloway, and Glenna Lynch, little Glenna Lynch, her hair done up in pigtails.

And there was Maeve Corrigan, Maeve Corrigan alive and flaunting her flaming locks at me, giving me a come-on glance from her green eyes, innocent and eager all at once, and she raised her white as snow hand and gestured to me. It felt as though she touched me. I started forward, started toward my friends Shane and Rogan, Seamus and Malachy, little Glenna and beautiful my love my Maeve.

But up steps Bishop Quigley, shouting at me in some language I've never heard before, saying words I dast not repeat save I heard among them *Ayin, Ayin, Ayin,* meaning, Abraham ben Zaccheus had told me, means nothing. He had his miter on his poll and crozier raised in two hands like a jousting pole and he swings the crozier and smites me in the belly and I blink and Maeve is gone, little Glenna and my Shane and Rogan and Seamus and Malachy are gone and the great beasts are back, with their many heads and their ropy arms and their stench, O God, their stench.

And Father Phinean isn't Father Phinean either, he's one of the beasts only smaller, and the baby priest, Bishop Quigley's man, is another.

And Bishop Quigley, his crozier is the new electric torch that Abraham ben Zaccheus carried with him this day, and his miter is King Abraham's *yarmee kee* hat, and his vestments are King Abraham's black sacque suit. And Bishop Quigley is none other than King Abraham ben Zaccheus.

The not-Father Phinean and the not-baby priest come roaring at King Abraham and at me, shouting words of their own in some language I didn't know, and I rear up, I feel the rage in me, the fury I never knew was even in me, and I take them one in each hand by the neck and I squeeze. They are covered with slime and filth that burns my hands and stinks in my nostrils and makes me gag like rotten food only ten times ten times worse.

With one beast in each hand I lift them from the ground and raise them into the air, into the air that stinks of incense gone to evil, and I toss them like two rotting, stinking dead conies that have lain in the field for a month into the pit where the great horrid beasts open mouths on red horrid throats and close those mouths midst gnashing of teeth and screaming, and swallow them like two delicious morsels.

Abraham ben Zaccheus and I started up the stone steps that had led us down to that evil place. We climbed and climbed. Soon Abraham was huffing and puffing but I kept him going, up and up until we were back in the chancel. We stumbled past the altar and up the nave. Abraham stopped and leaned on me, gasping until he regained some breath and some composure.

The stained glass windows above us showed scenes like the galaxies in the Kilkee sky.

We made our way to the great wooden doors.

Beneath us the rumbling grew louder and the very church began to shake. We stumbled out and paused to slam the doors shut behind us. Would we find ourselves in Kilkee, I wondered, or back on Turk Street in the City of San Francisco?

St. Padraic's church shook visibly on its foundation.

The weathervane rising from its roof toppled and fell with a crash. I saw that it was a starfish kind of thing that seemed almost to be alive, as big across as a calf, lying writhing at our feet.

The stained glass windows shattered with a sound like an explosion and flames and smoke rose from the building. The very Earth shook. There was a stench like the stench I had smelled inside the church, but so powerful that it nearly stole my consciousness from me.

A host of rats came pouring from the building, and I could have sworn that among them were some forms more human than rat. Did I see my acquaintances of the alley, the beautiful Zanna and the nasty Veleno? I couldn't tell, for in a moment they were gone, the rats were gone, and there was nothing to show that they had been there.

Men and women came running to see what was happening, and in a bit I heard the clatter of hoofs and the gongs and horns of a fire company.

Abraham ben Zaccheus grabbed my arm and hustled me into his electric carriage. He moved the lever and we glided silently along Turk Street, passing men and women running to see what was taking place.

An hour later we were in Abraham's house on Rooshian Hill. Abraham had washed himself clean of the filth and the stink of the house on Turk Street, and donned a fresh outfit. I had done the same.

We sat in Abraham's parlor. Xiang Xi-Mei, the fragrant beautiful plum, had brought us both warm broth and biscuits and I found that I had a goodly appetite, as had Abraham.

"That evil place is gone," Abraham said, lowering his spoon and wiping his lips on a square of linen.

"Is there no more menace, then?" I asked him.

He ignored my question and instead placed one of his own. "John O'Leary, what did you see?"

"I saw Bishop Quigley and his baby priest helper, and Father Phinean," I told him. "I saw my old church in Kilkee." I stopped, a bit of biscuit caught in throat, or something, for I could not speak,

"It's all right, John." Abraham nodded kindly to me. The

pictures of his ancestors and his Emperor gazed down upon us from the walls of his parlor. "Speak when you can. Is that all you saw?"

"No," I said. "I saw my friends, Your Majesty. I saw Rogan and Malachy and little Glenna." Another bit of biscuit caught in my throat and brought tears to my eyes. "And my dear Maeve, Abraham, my Maeve was there."

"She was not," he said. "I'm sorry. What you saw was not what was there."

I fixed him with a glare. "Then you did not see Rogan or Malachy or Maeve? You did not see Bishop Quigley or Father Phinean?"

"No." He shook his head.

"What did you see? What did you see, Your Majesty?" I asked.

"No." He shook his head. He was wearing his little biretta thing, his *yarmee kee* hat and a fresh sacque suit and his spade-shaped beard that I thought was all black, I realized, had a few little streaks of gray in it.

"Ayin," he said. "Ayin."

There Are Kings

Indeed, indeed there are kings. There are kings all over the world, you know. Some of them wear crowns and ermine robes, they sit on thrones and hold scepters when they're at home in their palaces and when they travel about they ride in golden coaches.

I've seen pictures, indeed.

They sit in their palaces in Spain and Prussia and Rome and Rooshia. There's the king of the Ottoman Empire, they call him a Sultan, and in India they call them Rogers and they have an emperor in China and another one in Japan. Oh, yes. I've seen pictures.

And there's Edward Saxe-Coburg-Gotha the German libertine King of England sitting there in London and pretending to be King of Ireland. Let him think what he likes, the villain. Ireland has a king of her own, don't you worry, and his time will come. Mayhap I'll live to see an Irish king ruling from Dublin and mayhap I'll be in my grave when he comes, but I have no doubt that he lives somewhere, and when the stars are right he will claim his throne and the Germans will haul their fat selves back to England where they belong.

I don't know why the English want a German king anyway, but that's their business. It is the Irish whose wants I care for, and the Irish want an Irish king!

Now Mr. Abraham ben Zaccheus, he's another tale altogether. I give him the courtesy of calling him Mister because that's his preference, but in my heart I know he's a king. Mayhap he's His Imperial and Apostolic Majesty, by the Grace of God, Emperor of Austria, King of Hungary and Bohemia, and a lot of other things, too, that he denies he is. I know that he is a Hebrew, and I know that Our Lord and Savior was the King of the Jews, by which I know is meant the Hebrews, and this gives me to wonder if King Abraham is not the King of the Jews in this, the blessed Twentieth Century, and he chooses to humble himself by pretending to be a plain Mister instead of an Imperial and Apostolic Majesty.

I would really not know.

But he says to me the other night not long after dinner, "John O'Leary," he says, "John O'Leary, are you ready to take a little trip on the morrow?"

This is his way, is Abraham ben Zaccheus's way. If he is a king he would simply command, would he not, and even if he is the plain citizen that he pretends to be, he is still my employer. He gives me room and board in his fine little house upon Rooshian Hill and he pays me a handsome salary each week in silver and gold. He could simply say, "John, get yourself ready to leave in the morning," but that is not his way.

So I says, "At your service, Your Majesty," and he says, "Stop that, please, just call me Abraham," and I says, "Whatever Your Majesty commands, Abraham."

And I wink at my employer and he winks at me.

We're sitting in his comfortable parlor. Abraham, a wider man than I and sporting as he does a spade-shaped beard and a comfortable corporation beneath his vest, is settled upon the horsehair couch. I, a taller man than he and somewhat narrower in the fundament, am at home in the easy chair. Between us on the polished low table is a bottle of fine dry sherry and a plate of sponge-cake, the latter baked by Abraham's housekeeper Xiang Xi-Mei, a plump and pleasant lady of the Chinee persuasion.

For reasons of his own, I am sure good and sufficient reasons, Abraham chose note to speak of where I was to go in the morning, nor of whether I was to proceed on my lonesome or with company. Instead, he delivered himself of a disquisition on the subject of gods and demons, of priests and saints, some of which I understood and some of which I did not, the all punctuated by regular refilling of our glasses from the golden store.

When the great clock which stood against the red-flocked wall of Abraham's sitting room struck one he blinked and said to me, "John, I've talked too long and said too little. We need our rest. Get to your room and I shall get to mine, and we assemble for an early breakfast if you please."

As I got to my feet he added, "Dress warmly in the morning, John O'Leary."

And I said I would, as if one would dress any other way in the first days of January in this fine city of San Francisco.

I retired and slept the sleep of the somewhat innocent, in my dreams returning to Kilkee as I often do, to my friends Shane Galloway and Rogan Doherty and Seamus McCarthy and Malachy Teague, to Glenna Lynch who taught me a thing or two about her gender and to Maeve Corrigan whom I loved dearly until an Englishman's horse kicked her in the head and we buried her behind St. Padraic's Church so long ago.

And in the morning King Abraham's housekeeper the estimable Xiang Xi-Mei was ready for us with coffee and juice and eggs and sourdough bread toasted atop the woodstove. Abraham pulled a timepiece from the belly pocket of his vest and after consulting it said, "We'd best make haste, John, we've a long journey ahead of us this day."

Xiang Xi-Mei had packed a carpetbag for Abraham and a valise for myself. They stood beside the door and as we exited the house Abraham exchanged a few words with the housekeeper in her own tongue, which talent never ceases to amaze me. Many a hint has Abraham dropped into our chats about the places he has visited, be they the steppes of Rooshia or the high town of Lhasa in distant Tibet, but how old he is and how many lands he has seen I cannot tell you.

It was a journey indeed, by Mr. Halliday's wondrous cable car to the pier, by ferry to the fine town of Oak-Land, and thence by the Central Pacific Railroad's comfortable service eastward.

Abraham was not inclined to converse as our train made its way through delta and farmland. I whiled away the time reading one of the fine novels of Mr. William Westall which I had procured at a shop on Taylor Street in San Francisco. It was *The Phantom City, a Volcanic Romance,* and it served well to while away the hours. At the same time Abraham occupied himself with a heavy volume he had brought from his own library. I would tell you its name but it was one of those odd books the writing of which was in some alphabet we never learned in Kilkee. I think Abraham might have brought that book back from one of his adventures, written by some ancient hand long ago in the mountains of Tibet or in some pillared city in Araby.

After passing the city of Sacramento where Governor Henry

Gage reigns in splendor, our train began its climb through the wondrous Sierras, a range of mountains as beautiful as any in the world. As we rose toward the town of Auburn the graceful pines that covered the slopes began to show signs of the winter's snows.

The Central Pacific furnishes its trains with dining cars where they serve as fine a cuisine as any restaurant. I found myself wondering if the estimable Xiang Xi-Mei had packed sandwiches for Abraham and myself, but to my great pleasure Abraham suggested that we hie ourselves to the dining car, where we put away a delightful repast of fresh trout and tiny potatoes, accompanied by an adequate bottle of local origin.

Night was falling when we debarked at the town of Truckee. A porter transferred Abraham's carpet bag and my valise to the care of the Lake Tahoe Railway and Transportation Company, and after a shorter and less comfortable train ride we found ourselves transferring yet again, to a horse-drawn station wagon that carried us to the Tahoe Tavern. Ah, a lovely establishment that was, as if a giant had ordered built a rustic cabin for himself, only to change his mind and command that it be furnished with the luxury of a grand hotel.

Aye, and Abraham and I found ourselves shortly escorted to the great dining room of the establishment. Formally clad waiters took our order, and elegantly gowned ladies and nicely tailored gentlemen sat at tables surrounding ours. Imagine, imagine, a Hebrew and an Irishman dining off white linen and transparent china, surrounded by such aristocracy. This America is a wondrous land! The repast was splendid, a fillet of local piscines accompanied by a good wine, followed by a tasty nightcap in the saloon.

At one point during the meal I had discovered two ladies seated without companions at a nearby table watching Abraham and myself. They were gowned and hatted as would befit persons of quality, and I detected the younger of the two sending an appraising glance my way. I responded with a merry wink, and was rewarded with a charming blush.

Ah, there is no sight more charming than that of a lady in pleased repose, her hair on her pillow, spread about her face like a saint's halo in a stained glass window.

Later I lay abed, the curtains pulled back and the night sky showing an array of splendor such as I could recall never having seen in my life. The stars were brilliant, the Milky Way seemed to flow across the heavens like a river of lights, and the reflected light of the moon as it peered just over the peak of a snow-covered mountain turning the snow-covered surrounding lawns and woods into an artist's dream.

It was a sheer startlement to me when I felt my shoulder grasped by a strong hand. I had not realized that I had fallen asleep, but I looked up and recognized King Abraham leaning over me, his finger pressed to his lips to indicate the need for silence. I blinked and sat up, rubbing the slumber from my eyes. I whispered, "What is it, Abraham? What time is it?"

"Time for us to be about our work, John O'Leary. Climb into your warmest clothing, and be quick, please."

In minutes we were outside the Tahoe Tavern. The moon had risen higher into the sky and the its brilliant light reflecting off a fresh fall of snow made the world as bright as day, but a day to which the white earth and the black sky with its twinkling stars and glaring moon lent a weird unreality.

Once we were out of earshot of the Tavern, Abraham halted and fixed me with an earnest look. His eyes seemed larger and darker than ever I had seen them. "You've been a patient man, John O'Leary. You've surely wondered why we are here."

"Indeed I have, Your Majesty."

A hint of a suggestion of a grin whipped across his face but he made no mention of my addressing him by a title of royalty.

He said, "We've a walk ahead of us. I'll tell you something of our purpose here as we proceed."

He was a man of his word, was Abraham ben Zaccheus. We were both equipped with heavy boots. I wore two layers of warm stocking beneath my own, and I should have thought Abraham was similarly attired in the pedal department. We both wore heavy gloves and warm hats. The air was cold but so clean and dry after the night's snowfall that it provided great stimulation and refreshment.

"There is a Chinee village not far from here," Abraham told me. "The Chinee arrived as laborers, imported to work on the railroads in California. But the workers were all male, and the authorities chose to exclude their women so as to prevent our state from being overwhelmed by a horde of yellow barbarians."

"I did not know that."

"Few do. And a small number of Chinee women have found one way or another to enter California. My housekeeper, Xiang Xi-Mei, is one such. There are now thriving Chinee communities in this state. These people will not die."

We passed beneath a tall tree at this point. A soft breeze swept snow off its branches and needles, and Abraham and I found ourselves beneath a new snowfall. We continued walking. Abraham continued his explanation.

"The village of which I spoke, however, remained entirely male. With the passing years some of its members have left for other communities. Those who stayed behind grew old and one by one went to their rewards. In due course there were only two men left in the village. They were brothers. One was a Buddhist priest. The other had been a chef and he continued to cook for the two of them. One of them was one hundred four years old; the other, one hundred two. Neither knew which was the older. Each insisted that it was he."

We had emerged from beneath a stand of fir trees and halted on a snow-covered slope. Ahead I saw a pitiable collection of wooden shanties. Smoke arose from a stove-pipe that poked through a thin layer of snow atop one of them, a ramshackle structure that looked little more than a shed.

"A few days ago, one of the brothers died. The one who had cooked for them. I was summoned by the surviving brother. I asked you to accompany me, John O'Leary, for I need your support. You are strong, you have courage and your heart is pure."

"Abraham," I confessed, "I'm not above a dalliance now and then, and I've put my fist through the belly of many a rascal."

He ignored my words, so I took my courage in hand and asked, "How were you summoned, Abraham?"

To this he only shook his head. He crooked his finger at me as best he could through the thick glove that covered his hand. We tramped onward through the fresh snow. The great dark lake loomed at the bottom of the slope.

When we reached the hut with the stove-pipe Abraham knocked on the door and spoke briefly in the language I recognized, now, from his conversations with Xiang Xi-Mei. The response from inside was a murmur so low that I was not sure I heard it at all. Abraham lowered his head and mumbled a few more words that I did not understand. He pushed the door open and stepped into the hut.

I followed him.

An iron stove must have warmed the hut somewhat, but I felt no less cold inside than I had outside. I shoved the door to, behind me. Embers glowed in the stove; through openings in its door they case flickering light into the room.

Sitting cross-legged facing the stove was the oldest man I had ever clapped eyes on. His head was bare and his skull was shaved. He wore a long scraggly beard. He was wrapped in a robe that looked like the toga Julius Caesar himself wore in the history book Father Phinean taught us from back in Kilkee.

The old man's eyes were open and bright with life and with the reflected glare of the embers. He smiled ever so slightly at Abraham, then sighed and closed his eyes and his soul was gone. Gone to wherever souls go. Ah, if I'd expressed that doubt back in Kilkee, Father Phinean would have clouted me for it, but here in America one is free to think what he thinks and to ask what he asks, is he not?

King Abraham leaned over the old man and drew his eyelids down over this eyes. Then he leaned farther and pressed his lips to the cold brow of the dead priest. He straightened, then, and nodded solemnly, and said, "This is why we are here, John O'Leary."

"To bury this man?" I asked.

"No. Others will tend to that, and the body matters not in any case, John. You've much to learn."

Oh, I knew that. He was telling me nothing new.

"This is very bad. This is why we are here."

So saying, His Imperial and Apostolic Majesty King Abraham indicated a thing that the old man had held in his two hands. Even in death he held it, nor did Abraham ben Zaccheus touch it at that moment.

It was a statue, some seven or eight inches high. It seemed made of stone, but so cunningly done that it could have been a real, living thing. In the red glow of the embers from the old man's stove, its color might have been purple or blue or gray, I could not tell.

I moved my hand toward it but to my great surprise Abraham struck me aside. He had never struck me before and I stood waiting for him to explain.

"For the good of your soul, John, do not touch that thing. Your thick gloves may offer some small protection, but you would regret for all your days if you touched it."

"But the old man is holding it," I replied.

"The old man studied for a hundred years, John. He could work wonders that even I could only marvel at. He could handle the statue, but you dare not, believe me."

He looked around the inside of the hut until he found an old wooden box that must once have held raw victuals. He placed the box beneath the statue and carefully pried the old man's hands apart. With a dull thud the statue fell into the box. Abraham drew a bandanna from a pocket of his heavy coat and covered the statue. Then he rose to his feet and proceeded toward the door. He held the wooden box in both his arms. I leaped ahead and cleared the way for him.

We walked from the hut, from the Chinee village, now left without a single inhabitant. At length Abraham halted and knelt in the snow. He laid the box on the cold snow. He uncovered the statue. Now, in the glare of the full moon, I could see it properly, and wish I had not. It was the foulest, evilest thing I have ever beheld. It looked a little like a man, but its head was something like that of a squid like they sell on the wharfs in San Francisco. Its face was horrid to behold, a mass of feelers, and its body was all scaly and rubbery looking. It had arms and legs something like a man's but more like a frog's, with prodigious claws on its fingers and toes. Its shoulders sprouted long, narrow wings that it might have used to fly through the air like a bat or through the sea like a devil-ray. It squatted on a rectangular block or pedestal covered with characters in some script that no human mind had ever imagined.

"Now, John O'Leary," Abraham said to me, "now you know. Now you know what evil truly is." He covered the statue once more. He stood then, and told me to take the box but not to touch the statue itself.

We had cast our shadows in the moonlight, so dark against the pale snow that they seemed almost blue. But there was a crack from behind us and the snow around our shadows became suddenly orange. I turned and saw that the old man's hut had burst into flames. As Abraham and I watched, the conflagration spread to the other shacks in the Chinee village, and in the wink of an eye the village was no more.

"As well," Abraham said. "It's as well. Come now, our night's work is just beginning."

He led me through more stands of trees and more snow-covered hillsides until I had no idea where I was, save that the moon remained a bright lantern among the stars and the lake a dark presence. I wondered that it was not frozen in this cold winter, but there was no white on its face except for the reflection of the moon. I was inclined to ask Abraham where we were going but a single look at his face, his great dark eyes and spade-shaped beard streaked with white, told me that I would receive no answer and that it were best to hold my tongue.

At length Abraham halted and laid a thick-gloved hand on my elbow. With his other hand he pointed to still another village. This one was made of Indian tents. I'd seen others on the Great Plains on my way to California, but this was the closest I had ever been to them. The camp looked newer and more prosperous than the dying Chinee village that now smoldered far behind us on the snowy hillside.

"The Washoes."

I asked what he meant.

"The Washoes," he repeated. "They lived here before the white man came. They named the lake, although the white man's name for it, Tahoe, is a corruption of the Washoe name.

He nodded toward the village and said, "Stay with me but do not put down your burden, and do not let the covering come from off the statue."

Ah, I was not so happy to hold onto that statue, but I was more than happy to leave it covered by Abraham's bandanna.

Abraham went to the largest tent in the camp. He motioned me to stay outside while he went inside and conferred. I heard his voice, and others, but the language was a new one to me. Surely it was not Chinee.

After a time Abraham came back out of the tent. A tall fellow followed him, his hair long and black, his face like a hawk's. He ignored me. He went to a couple of other tents and got a man out of each. He had to be a chief, that was clear. You see, there are kings everywhere. On Rooshian Hill, Abraham was king. Here, the chief was king. I know I said that Indian kings are called Rogers, but this was a different kind of Indian. These kings are called chiefs.

The chief spoke to his men in their language, and then Abraham spoke to them some more in their language, and then we set off down the hillside, through the snow, toward the black lake. I carried the box with that statue in it. For a piece of stone seven or eight inches tall and carved to look like a squid-bat-fish-man, it was heavier than it had any right to be and it kept getting heavier and heavier as we walked.

At last we reached the lake. The Washoes had boats there, flat-bottomed, square-prowed wooden things that would hardly draw any water. Nobody spoke, nor was there any need for anybody to speak. Abraham and I climbed into the boat and sat ourselves down. There were no seats in the boat, just the flat wooden floor or hull or whatever they call boat bottoms, and we sat there, Abraham facing front and me sitting behind him. The Washoes climbed in behind us and pushed off from shore and started to paddle.

This was the strangest thing I had ever seen.

I looked over the edge of the boat and the water was so clear I couldn't see it at all. We seemed to be floating in air, propelled by the Washoes' paddles. The moonlight was so bright, the water so pure, I thought we were flying over the lake bottom.

And then I saw fish swimming beneath us. Gray Mackinaw and speckled rainbow trout, Kokanee salmon with their fancy red scales and cutthroats with their scales striped like tigers and spotted like leopards, and other things, great turtles, and less wholesome things, things with tentacles and claws and feelers like the ones that the little statue had on its face.

I felt something strike my face and thought it was burning me like acid until I realized that it was only water. It was water, splashed by one of the Washoes' paddles, so cold that my face didn't know whether it was scalding or freezing.

Nocturnal birds flew overhead casting their shadows on the lake that seemed to crawl along the bed, and then a great bird that shut us from the light of the moon and put us in total darkness for a moment until it passed off into the night. I watched it, a black, soaring shape that disappeared into the snow- and forest-covered mountains.

At last Abraham spoke, a single word in the Washoe language. I cannot repeat it, it was so strange my tongue won't get around it, but the Washoes dug their paddles into the clear water and our flat-bottomed boat glided to a halt.

And now the strangeness of the night became more strange and more strange yet.

Abraham stood up in the boat and signaled me to do likewise. I got carefully to my feet, not wishing to tip the boat and throw us all into the cold lake.

Before I could stop him, Abraham put one foot over the side of the boat and balanced carefully, one foot on the water and the other in the boat. And then he lifted his other foot, carefully but without hesitating, and he put it over the side as well, and stood beside the boat. Yes, he stood on the water.

He smiled at me and he held out one hand and I knew what he wanted me to do. I stood up and held the box in one hand and reached for him with the other, and when he took my hand I stepped over the side of the boat and stood beside Abraham ben Zaccheus the Hebrew King.

The Washoes paddled past us and I watched them swing their little flat-bottomed boat in a circle and head back for the shore.

The moon above looked as bright as the sun. The lake beneath our feet was clear and we could see the fishes and the other creatures going about their business, although one of the things with tentacles seemed to be awaiting a special treat.

The box with the statue in it seemed so heavy, I was not sure how much longer I could hold it. If I put it down would it float? Would it be carried away? Would it come to the shore and be hidden there, like little Moses in the bulrushes where Pharaoh's daughter found him so very long ago?

It grew suddenly dark again, and I looked up and saw that black shape pass across the face of the moon once again. I was not so sure, this time, that it was a bird.

Abraham reached with his free hand and jerked the bandanna from the stone statue in the box. I saw him tuck the bandanna back into his pocket. He released my hand with his, and I stood there on the water, wondering if this was the work of the Holy Spirit.

I looked down at the water and thought that it was invisible, and that the Holy Spirit was invisible, as well. The Holy Ghost. The greatest mystery, I had always believed, in the great mystery of the Holy Trinity.

That was another question that had got me a good clout from Father Phinean. Our priest was teaching us that God could do anything at all. There were no limits to His power. It was called *arm-nippy-tents*.

No limits? No limits at all?

No limits. That's what arm-nippy-tents means, you nasty boy, John O'Leary.

Could he make me invisible, Father?

Now what did I tell you, John? God can do anything. Of course he could make you invisible.

But then he couldn't see me, could he, Father?

He could if He wanted to.

But what if He wanted to make me so invisible even He couldn't see me, Father?

And why would He want to do such a ridiculous thing?

Well, Father, I don't know why, but what if He wanted to, could he make me so invisible He couldn't see me even if He wanted to see me?

Oh, Father Phinean looked flustered. He just about foamed at the mouth, he did. And then, ah, you know what happened then, don't you?

Of course you do.

The water must have been mightily cold, I marveled that it hadn't frozen over. There were flakes of snow whipping through the air, and back on the shore I could see some bits of orange where the Chinee village had burned and farther away the lights of the Tahoe Tavern, but here on the lake itself Abraham ben Zaccheus was standing as calm and steady as a bishop giving Holy Communion and I was standing there with him wondering what was keeping me from plunging straight down into that black, frigid body of water.

King Abraham pulled his thick winter gloves from his hands and shoved the gloves inside his coat. He reached for the stone statue in the box and grasped it with both hands and lifted it above his head.

The giant bird took another pass across the face of the moon and for just a moment we were in darkness there on the face of the lake, the only light the distant tavern and the Chinee village and the shining stars of the galaxy overhead. Then the statue flared with a light all its own. It sizzled there in Abraham's hands, held above Abraham's head, and then as if it had a life of its own it pulled itself forward and tipped head-downward and dived straight down into the water, pulling Abraham and me behind it.

As we hit the face of the lake it began to swirl and churn like the water in a wash-tub when the washer-woman pulls the plug. That glowing statue, I would tell you the color it glowed but it was something I had never in my life seen before and I can't to this day put a name to it, that statue pulled us along behind it, swirling and swooping in a cold whirlpool, round and round, the only light the statue's glow. I looked over my shoulder and saw a tunnel through the water above us and the black sky and dancing stars at its end. I looked down and saw the waters opening before us like the Red Sea opening for the Children of Israel and I let go a prayer that we wouldn't wind up like Pharaoh's army.

There was a roaring in my ears and a great pinwheel of stars ahead of me and then with a thump we landed, Abraham and yours truly, standing there on a rocky plain surrounded by that whirling, roaring, funnel of water. A great fish whipped past and then one of those horrid things with the feelers and claws, distant relatives, I think of the ugly thing that I'd carried from the Chinee village in a wooden box.

The statue had landed with us and stood tilted a bit from the upright on its base. In front of us was something like nothing my eyes had ever before beheld. I could call it a city but it was not like any city I'd ever seen, not Dublin nor London, England, nor Boston nor Chicago nor San Francisco. No, not even like the cities I'd seen only in pictures, not even the pillars and hanging gardens of Babylon or the pyramids and the Sphinx of Aegupt.

It hurt my eyes just to look at the city, and my stomach churned when I tried to understand its angles and its shapes. It wasn't the way a city should be. I couldn't tell what was wrong with it. The closest I can come is to say it was crooked, but it wasn't exactly that either. It was just wrong.

But it was little. It was like a tiny town set up in the window of Gump's Department Store on Post Street in San Francisco. The children would come to see that for a Christmas treat, and their parents would see the joy in their faces and it brought tears to my eyes when I thought that if Maeve Corrigan hadn't been kicked in the head by a cursed Englishman's horse we might have married when she was grown and had kiddies of our own that we could show a miniature city at Christmastime. There would be tiny houses and little trees and a shops and mayhap even a miniature St. Padraic's. There would be tiny horses and sleighs, and a pond made of a mirror surrounded by white cotton snow.

Abraham was tugging at my sleeve. The village was growing before our eyes or we were shrinking, I could not tell. The thing on the statue was as tall as a man now or taller, or mayhap it was that Abraham and I had shriveled down to six inches or so of height so we were not even as tall as it.

The thing climbed down off its pedestal and began flopping and hopping across the black stone like a creature part frog and part fish, part squid and part man. The feelers that were its face were writhing and whipping like living things, and it was making a sound with what had to pass for its mouth that was fit neither for man nor beast nor anything else made by the loving God but only for something that crawled out of the pit of Gehenna to work a mission of damnation on the world.

The thing flopped through thoroughfares between horrid

crooked blocks of spongy material that sagged and dripped like to make me puke back the fine meal I'd last consumed at the Tahoe Tavern. There was a stench in the air, and each step Abraham took or did I sent up a wet, squelching sound. Our footing had been solid black rock but now it, too, was spongy and unpleasant, as if the ground itself had become a greedy, living thing that with each step wanted to take hold on your foot and draw you down to a wet, dark, slimy Hell.

There was not a soul to be seen in the street, if this could be called a street, but there were sounds in the city that I would never wish to hear again if I live as long as Methuselah. There was a distant, watery chanting and the horrid, flopping thing moved faster, as if it couldn't wait to get to its destination.

At length we came to a great building that must have been a temple. It had columns outside and pilasters and a tall, frightening roof. I felt cold at its very sight and wanted to halt, but Abraham tugged me along and I was barely able to lift my boots from the hungry, sucking stuff we were walking upon.

The temple itself was filled with a congregation of thousands. I could scarcely believe my eyes. They were humans of a sort, some of them, but not proper humans. They were misshapen things, some with blank spaces where eyes should have been, some with broad, thin-lipped mouths that showed rows of glittering, triangular teeth when they opened them to hiss. There were some with scaly skins, or skins of a color no proper human had ever sported, or with horrid, flattened heads that would leave little room for a brain, or with eyes in the palms of their hands that they held up and pointed at us as we followed the thing that had been a statue toward the front of their temple.

The thing pulled itself up onto a dais and turned to face the room. The throng assembled sent up a chant, horrid, discordant words in a language that deserved to be blasted from all human recollection, and then the beast before them seemed to swell, its belly like the obscene womb of a monstrous Madonna preparing to give birth to, I swear it, naught less than the anti-Christ itself.

As the thousands chanted, the monstrosity reared back on its clawed legs and spread its scaly wings with a terrible *snap!* That sent a fetid wind that was a stench in my nostrils and that stung my eyes like acid. It began to sing and the sound of its voice, unbearably lovely, yes, lovely, was more than I could tolerate.

I launched myself at it then, prepared to tear that horrid thing to bits with my bare hands, to rip out its throat with my very teeth as some ancestor of mine prowling the woods of ancient Ireland might have torn out the throat of some half-human monstrosity.

And then, suddenly, all was well. I might have seen the thing reach out to me with its slimy feelers but in the instant that it touched my flesh I was all right. It was as if I were a babe once more, and the thing holding me was nestling me like a loving mother. It touched my face. I looked up at it and it looked down at me, and I saw love in its eyes, and peace. I saw that tiny village with its little wooden horses pulling little painted wagons, its mirror lake and cotton snow, and children playing.

There were children playing. They were running and sliding on the ice, throwing snow at one another, and someone had built a snowman beside the lake and stuck a carrot for its nose and an old hat atop its head. A few flakes were falling and we were shouting and joking, Rogan and Seamus and Malachy, Shane Galloway and Glenna Lynch and Maeve, and I ran across the ice to Maeve and took her in my arms and kissed her and she laughed and pushed me away and scolded me for behaving like a masher and a voice was sounding far away only to come closer.

A voice.

It was reciting, and it had a religious tone to it. I wondered if it was Father Phinean come to warn us all that the day was growing late and it was time to head to our homes so our fathers and mothers wouldn't worry to much about us.

But it wasn't Father Phinean's voice, it was another voice, and each word struck me like a hammer blow.

Aa!

Aah!

Aalu!

Ab!

Abaddon!

Abaris!

I knew now what the voice was speaking.

Abdiel!

Abelios!

Abellio!

Abeona!

I knew, and each word was like the blow of a hammer upon my skull. It was a pain inside my mind and inside my soul, a searing fiery pain and yet I knew that someone was struggling to save me.

I heard the chanting that had welcomed our little procession into the temple, and the song of the monster, its voice as dear as a mother's, its song as sweet as a lullaby and I was drawn to it once more, drawn into peace and contentment and darkness.

But the other voice persisted.

Abog!

Abracadabra!

Abraxas!

Abundantia!

Someone was reciting the names of the gods.

Acheloüs!

Acheron!

Achilles!

Achor!

They were gods of good and gods of evil, gods of the Greeks and of the Romans, the Cretans and the Persians. They were pulling me away from the darkness and the foul joy that the monster offered me. I felt the monster's squidlike tentacles draw my face into it, and I was lifted up the tunnel of water and into the black sky a million miles from Earth.

I saw stars and comets. I saw creatures that could travel between the worlds and between the suns. Creatures that looked like insects or like worms, like great whales that swam in the very emptiness of space, like flying cones with star-shaped heads and a million tentacles trailing behind them for millions of miles. I could be one of them, something whispered to me, I could live with them forever. I could give them the Earth and they could come there and feast on Men, not on their flesh but on their minds.

Kalki!

Kalma!

Kama!

Kami!

Kamui!

Kari!

Karttikeya!

Gods of Japan. Gods of India. Gods of Africa. Gods of the island people.

Xilonen!

Xipetotec!

Xochiquetzal!

Yahweh!

The monster-mother-mother-monster-monster-mother shuddered.

Yahweh! the voice repeated. Yahweh! Yahweh!

There was a horrid bubbling and burbling. My face and then my entire body felt as if I were being bathed in boiling, burning mud. I opened my eyes and saw the face of the monster as it flung me from it, flung me at Abraham ben Zaccheus.

Around us the temple was shrinking, the worshippers fleeing for their lives. The monster that had held me in its claws was shriveling, shriveling, diminishing until it was only seven or eight inches tall, and slumped back onto a little square pedestal where it crouched, its wings folded behind its back, its elbows resting wearily on its knees.

There are kings everywhere, God the King of Universe and for all my money this thing, this monstrous lovely terrible little statue was the King of Hell.

The sucking, spongy stuff beneath our feet began to churn and suck the dreadful things down into the blackness and the muck that lay below the lake, but Abraham ben Zaccheus and John O'Leary did not go below with those things.

With a rending sound Abraham and I burst through the roof of the temple. The city lay in ruins around our booted feet, a city no larger than the Christmas scene on display on Post Street for the pleasure of the city's children.

Propelled by some invisible force, Abraham ben Zaccheus and I rushed upward through the swirling whirlpool. Luminous fish stared at us with their great eyes, turtles swam by, the shape of their mouths making them seem to laugh at our plight.

We flew into the air, then fell back, shattering the smooth

surface of the lake. Behind us, the whirlpool slowed and filled in and disappeared. Above us the night had passed, the breeze brought a few stray snowflakes into our faces. The sun was high overhead, and bright and clean.

A flat-bottomed boat stood nearby. Washoe Indians paddled it toward us, helped us carefully over the gunwales so as not to swamp the little boat, then headed back toward shore.

The Tahoe Tavern was bustling with fine visitors from Reno to the East, Sacramento and even distant San Francisco to the West. I hoped the management had saved our room. I hoped that my new friend was still staying at the Tavern. I wondered whether I ought tell her my story, and whether she would believe it if I did.

Steps Leading Downward

They play a splendid game here in America. Base Ball is its name, and if I have the sense to say that the sun will rise tomorrow, you can believe me when I tell you that this is the grandest game ever devised out of human ingenuity. They play it whenever the weather permits, and it being March in this Year of Our Lord One Thousand Nine Hundred and Six, and what with the lovely mild climate of this city and the fact that spring is well upon us, the lads are swarming the diamonds and the sound of wooden shillelaghs whacking leathern spheres is heard at every hand.

I tell you, those spoiled and spavined English with their game named for a harmless insect have lost another one, and well do they deserve it. If you ask me. Or my name is not John Fergus Tiernan O'Leary. And that is indeed my true name, you can take it from me.

Mr. Abraham ben Zaccheus, my generous employer and secretly the King of the Hebrews as well as Apostolic Emperor of Austria and Hungary and a few dozen other fancy titles, did not need me this day, so I took myself to a vacant lot where a group of lads were playing this Base Ball and watched them go at it for a while. At first the game is a bit hard to follow, but the fact of the matter is that I am an unusually bright young fellow, and with the aid of a gaggle of kids who were watching the proceedings and cheering on one team or the other, I soon caught on to how it works.

All to the good, as in the midst of everything a most attractive young lady arrives upon the scene. She stands watching, too, for a little while. Then the players score something called the "third out" and go rushing to exchange places, the fellows who had been standing about waiting to catch the ball instead setting themselves on a wooden bench while another group who had been sitting on another bench leap to their feet and run to take their places on the field.

All except for the fellow who runs to pick up the shillelagh that another player had dropped after making the "third out." This new player waves the shillelagh in the air and yells at the fellow standing in the middle of the field to go ahead and throw the ball at him. Another fellow is squatting on the ground in a most distressing pose, waiting for the fellow in the middle of the field to throw the ball. Should he miss the player with the shillelagh in his hand, as I've seen happen before, the other lad will catch it if he can and throw it back to the first fellow for another try.

The player with the shillelagh in his hand, in the meanwhile, can use the shillelagh to defend himself against the ball if it comes too close to him.

Well, now, as I told you, this young lady having arrived and observed the proceedings for a bit, walks over to the fellow squatting on the ground and grabs him by one ear. She gives it a twist that would have made a banshee howl and drags the poor lad to his feet.

She begins berating him something awful, I dare not even try to repeat some of the words she uses, but the drift of her tirade is this: He was due home an hour ago at least. She expected to find him in a saloon and has visited a dozen or so of such establishments, finding there most of his friends but no sign of her victim himself.

Aha!, she says to herself, I know where that rapscallion must have got himself to. He's playing a game of Base Ball with a bunch of other wastrels, and indeed here you are and you're coming home with me this minute and do your duties around the house.

Those duties she does not specify, nor will I dare to speculate upon them. Use your own imagination and do not rely on me to do your work for you.

The job of "catcher" on a Base Ball team, I quickly learned, was simple. The "pitcher" throws the ball and if he misses the "batter" or the batter defends himself with his shillelagh or "bat," then the other players have to deal with the matter. If the pitcher misses both batter and bat, the catcher retrieves the ball and returns it to the pitcher.

A wee lad could understand that!

But after a while the other team gets three men on the "bases" and the batter wallops the ball between a couple of "outfielders," and next thing I know these fellows are racing around the footpath as if Satan himself was after them with a blowtorch aimed at their fundaments. They come whizzing right past me. An outfielder throws the ball to an "infielder" who throws it to me and when the next fellow comes running I'm supposed to put a touch on him with the ball.

Are you following me?

We never had anything like this in Kilkee, I can tell you.

Well I'm standing there with the ball in my hand and a big bruiser in canvas trousers and mighty brogans is charging down upon me. All of a sudden, instead of running on, he leaps in the air, feet first, and we collide with a mighty whack.

Then we fall to the ground and he's mad as a wet hen and I'm not in the friendliest of moods myself, having been kicked in the middens with this fellow's size twelves. We go rolling around exchanging greetings in the form of knuckles and knees, and the "umpire" starts yelling at us.

Oh, I didn't tell you about the umpire. He's a kind of presiding judge in the game of Base Ball.

Anyway, the umpire starts yelling at the both of us and waving his arms, and pretty soon he's got his face uncomfortably close to mine so I give him a nice taste of my fist and before I know it everybody is piling on and there's the most glorious free-for-all you can imagine.

The fellows on my team must have appreciated everything I did for them, because they gave me one of those shillelaghs that they use to whack the ball as a gift, and I took it away with me and brought it back to King Abraham's house. Oh, if I get another chance I'm going back and join one of those Base Ball "clubs" as they call them. It is a wondrous grand sport, is this Base Ball.

But I get back to King Abraham's house on Rooshian Hill and I'll admit I was looking a wee bit battered and bedraggled so I went and washed up and put on some clean clothing. I came back to the parlor where Abraham was, as usual, studying one of the musty books from his grand personal library. The sun had set and he had the gaslights going.

He looked up as I entered and closed the heavy book he'd been reading.

"John O'Leary, have you dined?"

"I have not," I admitted. "Will the splendid Xiang Xi-Mei be preparing a repast tonight?"

Abraham smiled at my pronunciation of his housekeeper's name. Mayhap my tongue had a bit of trouble with the Chinee words. I did not take issue, however, with my employer. He makes a gesture with one hand toward the telephone machine that he keeps in his parlor.

"I had a call from a gentleman in need of help," he said. "We are invited to dine with him at the Palace."

Ahah! I said to myself, King Abraham has slipped up at last. Clever scholar though he is, he always denies his royal status and lives in this modest house, but now he has given himself away. Thinking that at last I will get to see his royal court, I told him that I was delighted to be included in the invitation.

"Run a comb through your hair and do on your best jacket, then." He pulled his brass turnip from his weskit pocket, studied its face, and announced, "We have barely time to meet him."

Very well, then. A few minutes passed and I found myself seated besides Abraham in his electric buggy, gliding silently down Rooshian Hill toward Market Street. We pulled into the carriage court of the Palace, all right, and a mighty vizier costumed like the tenor in a grand opera greeted us. A lackey drove Abraham's electric buggy away while the mighty vizier escorted us into the Palace.

It was indeed the grandest building I had ever set foot in. The floors were marble and the ceilings were gold. There were tapestries on the walls and Persian carpets underfoot. There were lovely women in gorgeous gowns and elegant gentlemen in fine outfits that made me almost ashamed to be seen in my plain working man's get-up.

But I was in the company of his Apostolic Majesty, Abraham ben Zaccheus I, by the Grace of God, Emperor of Austria, King of Hungary and Bohemia and also King of the Hebrews, and if my outfit was all right with King Abraham then no man would dast say me no, I was certain of that.

We were escorted to our table, a glittering set-up surrounded by others equally as glittering. Stained glass overhead was no less splendid than you'd find in a cathedral. I glanced at the diners at the other tables, expecting them to rise and make obeisance to

King Abraham, but they went on as if nothing out of the ordinary had happened.

A little orchestra was pumping away at the works of some dead Eye-Tallian fellow, and they continued their labors as we were seated. The conductor turned around and winked at King Abraham. He was a real sight, that orchestra conductor, looked like a Goliath up there with a big pompadour of hair and a moustache and a beard, shoulders out to here and a grin befitting the cat that drank the cream. He turned away and went back to his conducting. Winking at the king, what an amazing place this San Francisco is.

And for an Apostolic Emperor, King Abraham was a mighty democratic monarch!

There was a fellow already sitting at our table and he got up and shook hands with Abraham. Abraham told him my name and he told me his. It was Amos bar Kiva. We all sat down and a waiter came over and poured us some wine and we talked a little about the weather and President Rosey Velt and Governor Pardee and Mayor Schmitz, the head man of this splendid city, and what a grand job everybody was doing. But Mr. bar Kiva seemed like a man under a dark cloud. I wondered what was the matter.

After we'd downed a little of our wine Abraham turned toward me and said that Mr. bar Kiva was a member of the Ohabai Shalome Synagogue on Bush Street and that he was a Shepherd, which I know what that is, except King Abraham said that a Shepherd was a special kind of Hebrew from Spain or Italy and Mr. bar Kiva was in fact from the city of Milan in Italy. In his honor we were going to have an Eye-Tallian feast for our dinner.

Upon the which our waiter brought out a little appetizer consisting of some grilled and marinated vegetables, cured salami, olives, roasted nuts, garbanzo beans, olive oil and rosemary soup, a pretty salad of bitter Eye-Tallian greens, some roasted pancetta, walnuts, and Balsamic vinegar.

I thought that was most tasty and it did indeed serve to buck up my appetite.

While the waiter traipsed off to bring us our meal, King Abraham talked Mr. bar Kiva into telling us what was making him such an unhappy fellow.

"Something is happening to our congregation," he said. "People are disappearing from the temple. Now they're becoming afraid, and attendance is falling off."

He didn't say it exactly like that, understand. As an Eye-Tallian fellow he had a peculiar way of talking, not properly the way Father Phinean taught us to speak at St. Padraic's back in Kilkee, but it wasn't Mr. bar Kiva's fault that he was a Hebrew Shepherd and not a good Irishman like myself or a King like Mr. Abraham ben Zaccheus.

It was Mr. bar Kiva, it turned out, who had called Abraham on the telephone machine and talked him into coming to the Palace to meet him for dinner. Imagine, a king needing an invitation to take a meal at his own Palace!

Three members of the congregation of Ohabai Shalome had disappeared. All women, each expecting a child. All of them had disappeared while going down into the basement of the synagogue to bring up some food that the women of the congregation had prepared down there. The cooks were there already. The women went down to get the food. Several members of the synagogue had seen them go downstairs, but the women in the kitchen said they never arrived.

The first woman to disappear was a recent bride, married less than a year. Her name was Joaquina Ha-Nagid. Her husband had lived in San Francisco all his life. He had written to relatives in Barcelona, sending money for a young virgin to travel to this city to be his wife.

"Did they get along well?" Abraham ben Zaccheus asked Amos bar Kiva.

"What do you mean?"

"I mean, was she happy? The young woman—she was young, was she not?"

"Little more than a child. She married at age fifteen. She had celebrated her sixteenth birthday just the week before her disappearance."

"One so young, thousands of miles from her home and family. She might have run away."

"I think not."

Abraham ben Zaccheus raised his heavy, dark eyebrows. "Why

so?"

"She seemed happy with her husband. He is a gentle man, known for his kindness and charity. He is a dry goods merchant. He was twelve years her senior. Joaquina was expecting a child."

"Ah, ah, yes." Abraham nodded. He reached for a loaf of dark bread, tore off a piece and dipped it in olive oil. He chewed on it meditatively, then said, "The prospective parents, they were pleased?"

"Delighted. Her husband, Yeshurun, had married once before and his wife died in a fire. He hardly moved for seven years, except to go to work and to go to *Shul*. When he finally decided to marry again he sent for a bride and Joaquina came. All he could talk about in recent months was the coming baby."

"And the wife, Joaquina, she was happy, also?"

"Thrilled. She spent all her time sewing clothes for the infant. She wanted to name it for her grandfather or her grandmother, both dead and buried in Spain."

Abraham ben Zaccheus rubbed his face with his hand. "What food were they preparing that night, Amos?"

"You expect me to remember that? This was an occasion of tragedy. A young woman, a bride, a mother-to-be disappears, and you ask me what was for dinner that night?"

"Please," Abraham said, "try to remember."

A cloud passed over Amos bar Kiva's face. His eyes peered into the past, seeing that past occasion. His nostrils twitched and I imagined him smelling the food.

"There was *sopa de avikas*, Abraham, made with beef, olive oil, onions, garlic, tomatoes, pepper and lemon wedges. There was a roasted eggplant salad. And the main dish, Abraham, was *sogliole ai limone. . . .*"

Abraham turned toward me and said, "Sole with lemon, John."

"With sea salt," Amos said, "wine and fish stock, olive oil and lemon juice and chopped parsley."

"Good, good." Abraham was tapping on the fine linen tablecloth with his fingers. "Good. And the other time? When the other pregnant women disappeared, Amos—what food was being prepared in the synagogue?"

"Abraham, does it matter?"

"It matters very much!" Abraham ben Zaccheus is a soft-spoken man most of the time, but he had changed suddenly.

"Yes," Amos said. "All right. Let me remember. Yes, all right. On the other occasion it was *papeyada di berenjena*. You know this dish, Abraham? It was brought by a member of our congregation from the town of Edirne, Turkey. Fried eggplant with sugar. Delicious. A wonderful appetizer."

"And then?"

"Then, let me recall. Yes. *Peshkado Avramila,* poached fish with Abraham's fruit. The women used whole salmon for this, with large tart fresh plums and red wine."

"Yes." Abraham stopped him with a gesture. "Fish. Always fish."

"I don't see why that matters."

"Of course not. The fish gods, Amos. So many peoples have fish gods. The Babylonian Dagon, the Greek Poseidon, the Roman Neptune. Think of the tales of mermaid and mermen, of harpies and sea-witches. The goddess Yemoja of the Umbandists, the god Olokun, Nommo, Enki, the Chinese Fu Hsi, the Hindu Vishnu, the Philistines' Atargis, Nereus, Oe of Babylon, Iris and Electra. And that's just the beginning. There is evil, Amos. Evil beneath the sea and evil beneath the earth. Who knows what was summoned, what beings followed the creatures of the sea to Ohabai Shalome."

Now it was Amos who looked troubled.

Abraham asked, "Was there a smell of the sea left behind when the women were stolen? Was there a trail of water?"

Amos bar Kiva was nearly in tears. He put a hand to his brow. He whispered, "There was. There was a trace of water on the stairs. There was an odor. I thought it was from the cooking, but it might have been more of a fresh sea odor."

Ben Zaccheus muttered something I could not make out.

The orchestra was playing a tune now, something I recognized. I'd heard this one in a Barbary Coast melodeon and I was surprised to hear it played by a fine orchestra here in the Palace. Of course there was nobody singing but I knew the tune just the same. It was *A Woman Is Only a Woman but a Good Cigar is a*

Smoke. Ah, it made me smile to hear it but I thought that big orchestra leader with his fancy pompadour must have a mighty nerve on him.

Between bites of truly excellent food and sips of a variety of wines, my employer was continuing to question Mr. bar Kiva. It was a good thing that I had read some of Dr. Doyle's fine stories. I suspected that Abraham ben Zaccheus had, as well, for I could almost hear the great detective's voice as he spoke.

"What time was it, that Mrs. Ha-Nagid disappeared?"

"Why—I'm not certain. It was a social evening at the synagogue, Mr. ben Zaccheus. It wasn't Shabbat or any special day of the calendar."

"Save that every day the Divine One gives us is special," Abraham commented.

"I think the men were upstairs in the great hall, the women were preparing food, Joaquina was carrying dishes up from the kitchen. She had just set some out and went back for more. When she didn't return, her husband worried. He went downstairs, he said he was afraid she was feeling ill, but the other women had never seen her."

Abraham put his hand to his beard, the thumb on one side and fingers on the other, and drew downward, a thoughtful expression on his face.

"It was after dark, then, eh?"

"Yes."

"The synagogue has gaslights."

"We plan to install electricity but had not done so as yet."

"They were lit?"

"Yes. Otherwise the sanctuary would be very dim after sunset, and the basement would be pitch black."

"I've been in Ohabai Shalome many times, of course, but I'll want to retrace Joaquina Ha-Nagid's steps."

"Of course."

At this point the waiter brought our next course, a most delicious Tuscan roasted rack of lamb, served with Bucatini pasta, garlic, red onions, stewed tomatoes, zucchini, hot chilies, mint jelly and freshly baked Tuscan rolls, roasted garlic and olive oil.

Informal though it was, the Palace served a most admirable

dinner. It was fit for a king, and it was my pleasure to be King Abraham's guest.

King Abraham lifted a Tuscan roll, broke it in half and dipped one piece in olive oil. He chewed it thoughtfully. Then he sipped some wine. The orchestra had changed its tune. I recognized its new ditty as another I'd heard in a melodeon along the Barbary Coast. It was *Rufus Rastus Johnson Brown,* a funny tune indeed.

"Now, then" Abraham said, "you tell me there were three disappearances."

"Correct."

"Who were the other two victims?"

"They were two cousins. Two more married women, although not as young as Mrs. Ha-Nagid. There was Liviya Navon ibn Gabirol, wife of Shamir the furniture maker, and there was Nitza Shazar-Suleiman, wife of Tsadek the tailor. In fact the women were cousins, daughters of two sisters. They were both between twenty and twenty-five years of age."

"They disappeared the same night as Joaquina?"

"No. It was some weeks later. Again, they disappeared from the staircase leading from the sanctuary to the basement, to the kitchen."

"Also at night?"

"Yes."

Abraham cut a generous slice of lamb, speared it with his fork, dipped it in mint jelly and conveyed it to his mouth. I watched him chew, his eyes fixed on some invisible chimera. He seemed oblivious to the music of the orchestra and the hundreds of diners surrounding our table.

A party of San Francisco matrons observed us from a nearby table. I thought they must be watching the king, but one of them caught my eye instead. She wore her reddish hair in a stylish upsweep, and a high-collared gown that did little to conceal her most attractive figure. Kilkee would have been scandalized by such a wench, and by the daring look she shot my way, but in this city one was free to act as one wished. I returned her look and we exchanged nods.

The orchestra had commenced to play a tune called *Razzazza*

Mazzazza and I couldn't help myself but to visit the party of ladies and ask one of them to join me for a dance. To my delight she consented, and I led her out to join the other dancers. At the end of a most delightful whirl across the polished floor I escorted her to her table once more. As we parted she managed to slip something into my hand. It turned out to be her calling card, complete with address and telephone number. I slipped it into my breast pocket as I rejoined Abraham ben Zaccheus and Amos bar Kiva at our own table. I was mightily pleased.

My employer and his companion had continued to discuss the mystery of the disappearing women. By now they were up to the dates of the disappearances. Although they spoke in English, there were words of Hebrew now and then which were puzzling to my ear.

"The first disappearance, that of Mrs. Ha-Nagid, took place on *yon shlishi,* the third day after the first *Shabbos* of *Shvat.* The other tragedies, the disappearances of Mrs. ibn Gabirol and Mrs. Shazar-Suleiman, took place on the eve of the third *Shabbos* of *Shvat.*"

"And the circumstances were just the same?" Abraham asked.

Before Amos bar Kiva answered, the waiter appeared to clear our table and bring the next course, a fine dish of swordfish studded with garlic and smothered in a sauce of green olives and oranges. There were more roasted vegetables and rice, and a fresh bottle of local wine.

Amos bar Kiva nodded.

"Yes. The women were preparing food in the basement of the synagogue, in the kitchen there. On the first occasion, Mrs. Ha-Nagid left the sanctuary to go to the kitchen. The women there say that she never arrived, nor had she been seen since. On the second occasion, Mrs. ibn Gabirol and Mrs. Shazar-Suleiman left the sanctuary to bring food from the kitchen."

He paused to lift his wine glass to his lips, then resumed.

"The first incident had of course been the chief topic of conversation ever since Joaquina had disappeared. Tongues wagged, I must admit. But Liviya and Nitza told some of the men that they would go together to the kitchen, so that whatever demon had seized Joaquina would be confused by the presence of two women at once, and they could escape his grasp."

Abraham ben Zaccheus grunted. He held out a hand, interrupting Amos bar Kiva.

"And what demon would that be?"

Amos bar Kiva shrugged, a bemused expression on his face. "I don't believe in demons, Abraham."

"Nor do I," Abraham replied, and then, after a pause, "except when I do. They have a smell, Amos, did you know that? Demons have a smell all their own, and I have detected it in this city in recent times. I detect it coming from beneath the ground, and if the women disappeared underground I would not laugh at the theory that a demon was responsible."

"Nonsense."

"Not nonsense, my friend. There are demons who will deceive men and the children of men. There are demons who try to fool us. They masquerade as gods. That is why the Sublime One has commanded us to have no other god before Him. He has seen what those demons do, and He gives us warning."

Again, Amos indicated his disbelief.

Abraham said, "Listen to me, Amos bar Kiva. Even a simple soul like my dear helper John O'Leary knows enough to beware of demons. Don't you, John?"

"Of a certainty," I replied. I was enjoying the broiled lamb and mint jelly myself, accompanied by small roasted potatoes and morsels of the fine freshly baked sourdough bread, all of it washed down with a very pleasant wine. But I did indeed know that demons were dangerous. That was one of the few lessons of Father Phinean at home in Kilkee that I ever found sensible.

"Every race has its God or its many gods," Abraham asserted. He reached across the table and poked at Amos bar Kiva's shirt to emphasize his point. "You'll notice that even the Almighty One, the King of the Universe, does not tell us that there are no other gods, only that we must have no other god before Him."

Amos, I must say, was looking ashen. As for me, I thought Abraham made good sense, but then I've always been ready to listen to people who sound as if they know what they're talking about, whether they do or not. And Abraham, well, you don't get to be King of the Jews, not to mention Apostolic Emperor of

Austria and Hungary and all those other things that Abraham was, without learning a lesson or two. I'm not saying that I believed him, understand, but I was assuredly willing to listen.

"Kumarbis," he was saying, "Kumarbis was important to the Hittites and the Hurrites, Amos. We don't hear much of him any more, nor of the Hittites and the Hurrites for that matter, do we? Do you know the *Song of Ullikummis*? Do you know the *Royalty in the Skies*? We have our holy *Pentateuch*, Amos. John O'Leary has his *Four Gospels*. The Hittites and the Hurrites had the *Cycle of Kumarbis*."

"You know too much, Abraham." Amos bar Kiva had put down his knife and fork. He held onto the edge of the fine linen tablecloth with his knobby hands. "You know so much that it confuses you."

Abraham shook his head. "Listen to me," he told Amos, "listen to this. I have read as much as is known of the *Cycle of Kumarbis*. Let me see if I can summon up a few snatches from my cobwebby memory."

He closed his eyes and threw back his head, then opened his eyes again so suddenly there was almost an audible *snap*. It was an odd gesture I had seen him make on occasion. It was as if he was looking for some kind of message, something written in invisible letters across the sky. Then he spoke in a voice so different from his usual, I wondered if it was really Abraham speaking or one of those clever ventrilly quists which perform betimes at the melodeons.

Come, Impaluris! Kumarbis, father of the gods, summons you to the house of the gods. The Issirra will take the child and will convey him to the dark Earth.

Then Impaluris took his staff and set forth. He betook himself to the Issirra. He spoke the same words to them that had been spoken to him by Kumarbis. But you are not to know his motive in summoning you. Hasten, come!

When the Issirra heard these words they hastened, they hurried. They set forth and covered ground without stopping once. They presented themselves to Kumarbis and Kumarbis spoke to them.

"Take this child and take it away with you. Bring it down to the dark Earth! Be quick! Place it like an arrow on the right shoulder of Upelluris. In one day it shall increase a cubit. In one month it shall increase an acre."

When the Issirra heard these words they took the child from Kumarbis's lap. They took him and placed him in Enlil's lap. The god raised his eyes and saw the child as it stood in his divine presence.

Enlil said to himself in his soul, "Who is this? Are they really the goddesses of fate who have raised him? Is it he who shall see the fierce battles of the great gods? By none other than Kumarbis is this vileness done. Just as he raised the storm god, so he has now raised this terrible man of pryoxene as his rival!"

Abraham stopped. The orchestra was playing a merry tune. The ladies at the table nearby were staring.

So was Amos bar Kiva.

"What are you saying, Abraham? What do you mean?"

Abraham had a dazed look on his face, like Malachy Teague back in Kilkee when he insulted my darling Maeve Corrigan, she of pleasant memory, and I cold-cocked him and he wound up sitting on the turf with blood running from his nose and me standing above him asking if he wanted some more of the same, which offer, being a sensible fellow and one of my dearest friends, he declined with thanks.

But I was telling you about Abraham ben Zaccheus, His Majesty, and the dinner conversation he was having with his Hebrew friend Amos bar Kiva. And after a sip of cold water Abraham's face regained its normal expression and he resumed his enlightening of Amos, to which I listened as well, as you can see that I must have, lest I not be able to go on with my tale.

"I have studied the religions of the world," Abraham resumed. "They are marvelous in their color and infinite in their variety, Amos. But at the same time they so often have similarities to one another, one is inclined to think they are all memories of the same truth. Faded and distorted by the passage of centuries, to be sure. But at their heart, true."

"The Divine One forbids us," Amos broke in.

"Indeed He does, Amos. I'm sure He will forgive my frail efforts to rescue his children who have been stolen away by His enemies."

Amos bar Kiva looked grim but he said, "Very well, Abraham. Go on. Who are these Impaluris and Upalluris and Kumarbis and Enlil and Issirra?"

Abraham waited while a fellow in a white jacket cleared off our table and carted off the debris of our meal. A waiter brought a pot of coffee and couple of bottles of the management's best whiskey and a platter of little cakes and another of apples and oranges and grapes. Oh, they eat very well in this city of San Francisco, I can tell you that.

"The Hurrites in particular had an interesting pantheon," Abraham said. I make it a point to remember the words he uses that I've never heard before, and *pantheon* was one of them. I always use Abraham's big Webster's Dictionary when I get back to Rooshian Hill and look them up. I am improving myself every day, here in America. They would be amazed in old Kilkee, were I ever to pay a visit to my little home.

"They worshipped in something called a *kuntarra,* not so different from our synagogue or a Muslim mosque. You need not worry about their different gods just now, Amos, although I find the study of all religions rewarding. The point is that the Issirra were their elder gods, who came before Kumarbis and the rest. The Greeks and the Romans had a similar notion, with Titans who gave way to their own gods."

"You are not going to say that the Divine One was the child of an older race, Abraham!" Amos looked scandalized.

"On the contrary. Our Christian friends have their notions about Yehoshua ben Miryam wa Yosef, they call him Jesus the Son of God. Is that not so, John O'Leary?"

"And also King of the Jews," I said, "according to Father Phinean."

"Ah, Father Phinean. I've heard so much from you about that good man that I feel as if I know him, John O'Leary. I think we would have many a fine debate."

"Well, I doubt greatly that Father Phinean will ever come to San Francisco, Abraham."

"But I might find myself in Kilkee sometime, John. We never

know about these things, do we?"

"Indeed we do not, Abraham." I peeled myself a fine fat orange, as round and lovely to look upon as a dear part of a woman, and as delicious to taste as well. I popped a section of the fruit in my mouth and savored its juice, then followed it with a sip of fine Scotch whiskey, not as good as our fine Irish whisky, but still satisfactory, especially considering the price I was paying. The water of life and the juice of the fruit make a fine combination, I promise. Try them some time and if you don't agree with me then my name is not John O'Leary, late of Village Kilkee, of the Kingdom of Ireland, yet to be restored.

"Gods and children of gods, sometimes rivals of gods, sometimes in rebellion against the gods, Amos."

Abraham was pointing his finger at the other fellow. A stubby finger it was, at that, as fits a stubby man such as Abraham ben Zaccheus. But there was a power in that finger as there was in that man. I would not want that finger pointed at me in scorn, nor would I want to come up against Abraham ben Zaccheus in any kind of struggle, for all that I stood over him by the better part of a foot and outweighed him by half again, and all of my pounds solid muscle.

"Most of the world's religions speak of realms beneath the Earth, as well, Amos, or of realms in the sky. The Egyptians sent Pharaoh, cursed be he, to the sun god and the sky goddess in a boat. The dead of the Greeks were carried to Hades on the boat of Charon. And the Hurrites—the Hurrites—what did they say? '*Take this child and take it away with you. Bring it down to the dark Earth! Be quick!*' Did they mean to bring a child of the gods to the world of Man, Amos? Or did they mean to take a child of Man to the world below? I think the gods of the Hurrites are stirring, Amos. I think the gods of the Hurrites, Kumarbis, Impalluris and the rest, are still at war with the Issirra. And those foul gods, those demons, are stealing babies from the very wombs of the daughters of the Sublime One, blessed be His name."

The orchestra had stopped playing lively tunes and gone back to that drab frog music or kraut music, as if any sensible man could tell the difference or would even want to. The big, good-looking leader had left the bandstand and some little dried-up longhaired fellow had taken his place. The big fellow was making his way across the room, stopping to shake hands and slap backs like a politician.

He arrived at our table and shook hands with Abraham and Amos. Abraham introduced me to him, and the big fellow identified himself as Eugene Schmitz, proud leader of the Union Labor Party and Lord Mayor of the City of San Francisco. I stood up and clasped his mitt in my own and he gave a mighty squeeze and I gave a mightier one and we stood there for a bit seeing who could squeeze the other's mitt the harder.

I think the fellow thought he could get the best of me so to teach him a thing or two I reached down with my free hand and picked up a section of juicy orange and popped it in my mouth, grinning away at Eugene there who was turning red and starting to sweat. Well, thought I, it would be unkind to embarrass His Highness the Lord Mayor so I let go his hand and told him I was proud to make his acquaintanceship and would give him all my votes the next time he needed them.

He thanked me politely, then drew up a chair without even being invited and joined our little party. It turned out that His Honor the Lord Mayor was an acquaintance of King Abraham, not a surprising turn of events, and that he also knew Mr. Amos bar Kiva. I felt like the odd man out at this point, so I excused myself and made my way to a nearby table. I asked one of the ladies sitting there if she would care to trip the light fantastic with me, and she agreed to do so.

If the orchestra had been playing some merry tune like *Jim Judson from the Town of Hackensack* or even a sentimental ditty like *Where the River Shannon Flows* I would have been pleased, but they were scratching away at some Eye Tally Anne tune. Even so, the lady and I managed to enjoy ourselves sufficiently that she suggested a repeat, and then invited me to join her and her friends.

Well, not wishing to be impolite to the King and the Lord Mayor, I asked leave to speak briefly with them. The Lord Mayor and Mr. bar Kiva allowed as how they were delighted to have made my acquaintance. King Abraham said that he would need my services on the morrow but suggested that I have myself a good time tonight, and so I made a polite bow (so as not to have to wreck the Lord Mayor's mitt with another handshake) and did indeed join my new lady friend and her party.

My new friend's name was Taryn Jilleen O'Casey. I knew right off, of course, that she had to be a daughter of the sod, for all that she was born right here in San Francisco. She had the midnight hair and lovely dark complexion of the Black Irish, aye, descended, as our tales have it, from the shipwrecked sailors of the mighty Spanish Armada who washed upon the shores of our island and joined their race to ours. Hair as black and shiny as a raven's wing, skin like a baby's and eyes the color of a stormy sea.

Ah, such a girl was this Taryn Jilleen O'Casey!

She might dine and dance with the swells but she was a self-supporting working girl, a typewriter in a lawyer's office. She lived in a lovely flat on Tellygraph Hill, not so far from Abraham ben Zaccheus's digs on Rooshian Hill, and I will say nothing more about the next few hours for I am a man of utter discretion, not given in the least to kissing and telling, any more than I am to fighting or to boasting, as you of course already know.

When I returned to King Abraham's digs on Rooshian Hill, His Majesty's housekeeper, Xiang Xi-Mei, prepared me a delightful repast which I consumed in the parlor, watching the world go by the windows of King Abraham's house. This was a dandy way to earn my living, indeed. I was a trifle weary. Taryn Jilleen O'Casey has worn me out before serving me a splendid breakfast of bacon and eggs, muffins and grapefruit and spicy tea.

Two meals into the day I heard the voice of my employer summoning me to his library. The walls there were covered with books, more I imagine than there were in the entire village of Kilkee. Abraham ben Zaccheus had taken down some of the biggest books, and from the looks of them some of the oldest, in his personal collection. Some of them were in good honest English, some in German or French or Eye Tally Anne. There were some in Latin, and I was delighted to see one in dear old Éireannach.

Some were in writing that hurt my very eyes to look at, that Abraham told me were Hebrew or Arabian or San Scrit or

Japanee.

Abraham had his nose deep in a huge book when I presented myself. He looked up and closed the book with a loud clap, and a cloud of dust went rising up. Abraham looked tired to me, as if he had been studying all the night while I was at Miss Taryn Jilleen O'Casey's digs pleasing Miss O'Casey with tales of the dear old country and suchlike. This made me feel slightly guilty, but I could deal with it, I truly could.

"We face a very difficult foe, John O'Leary."

"Not the first, Your Majesty, and I'm sure not the last."

"Ah, good for you. I enjoy your spirit, John. You would never give up a fight, would you?"

"Of course not."

"Very well, then. I want you to come with me to the Ohabai Shalome Synagogue. We have the chance to perform a supreme act, John. It will involve a supreme risk, as well."

"And I am your man," I told him.

Ah, the smile that I received, it warms my heart to recall it.

"Very well."

He used his arms to raise himself to his feet. He was wearing a black coat and dark woolen trousers, a white shirt and an embroidered vest of gold and red and green. We walked together from the library to the front parlor. He told me to go fetch the shillelagh that my friends in the Base Ball club had given me, and I did as he asked even though I was puzzled as to his reason. Even before I could move he called out something in Chinee and Xiang Xi-Mei came trotting in from her domain.

Abraham said something to her in Chinee and she said something back and he said something else, shaking his fist not at Xiang Xi-Mei but in the air. Xiang Xi-Mei stamped her foot and shouted something back. Abraham was red in the face. Xiang Xi-Mei started to cry.

Finally she disappeared, then returned carrying a fine-looking bowler hat and a walking stick and an odd-looking little pouch with some fringes hanging down from it. I had never seen Abraham ben Zaccheus carry a walking stick before. This was a splendid one, of polished ebony with writing on it in Hebrew. I recognized the letters even though I could not for all the wealth in the world tell you what they meant. The head of the walking stick was shaped almost like a crown, that I swear was finest gold, with more Hebrew writing on the top of it in raised letters. There was even a ferrule, of gold as well.

A pretty penny that stick must have cost His Majesty, unless it was a gift from some of his loyal subjects, all the Hebrews of San Francisco and of the Earth.

Abraham ben Zaccheus gestured and I opened the door and stepped back so he could precede me. We stood outside on the stoop, watching the late afternoon mist creep up Rooshian Hill. We marched to the carriage house and I swung the doors open. Abraham climbed into his electric carriage and in a trice we were heading down Rooshian Hill, bound for the Ohabai Shalome Synagogue.

Father Phinean had told us in St. Padraic's Church in Kilkee that we were never to set foot in any kind of evil temple, be it Buddhist or Hindoo or Mooslim or one dedicated to somebody called something like Zorro Aster. But the two great sins we were to avoid were stepping inside a Protestant Church or a Hebrew Synagogue. One foot planted, one breath drawn in a Protestant Church or a Hebrew Synagogue and Jesus Christ Himself would leap down off His Cross and pierce us through our evil hearts with a foot-long thorn torn from His Holy Crown.

I remember as a lad being terrified of ever going to the city for fear that I might be lured into a Protestant Church or a Hebrew Synagogue and being pierced through the heart with a foot-long thorn wielded by Jesus Christ Himself. Rogan Doherty and me used to scare each other blue by describing the terrible things that would happen to us someday because sure as the river flows, we would one day find ourselves in the city and some wicked Protestant pastor or Hebrew rabbi would tempt us into his Church or his Synagogue and then Jesus Christ Himself would come charging out from the sacristy and stab, stab, stab, and Rogan and me would fall to the floor with our hearts pierced by the sacred thorn, spurting blood all over the carpet and dying while Jesus Christ Himself stands there laughing and pointing at us and jeering, "Father Phinean warned you, you evil boys, Father warned you and you wouldn't listen, and look at you now, bleeding and dying here in a Protestant Church or a Hebrew Synagogue and now you're sorry, aren't you, Rogan Doherty and John O'Leary, aren't you?"

And here I was sitting all fine and spiffed beside His Majesty King Abraham ben Zaccheus of the Hebrews on my way to the Ohabai Shalome Synagogue on Bush Street in San Francisco.

It's a grand building, I can tell you. Two steeples, not just one, and arches and pillars and lovely stained-glass windows, but the windows have no pictures of the Blessed Savior or his Virgin Mother or any of the Saints. Instead they have patterns like one of them kalidie-scopes that the little children like to play with, all pretty colors and patterns and suchlike but not a picture you can see.

Amos bar Kiva met us at the door and waited while Abraham ben Zaccheus opened that little parcel that Xiang Xi-Mei had given him before we left the house. He took off his bowler hat and put on one of those little yarmee kees that Hebrews wear, and he put a white shawl with some blue stripes on it around his shoulders and he muttered something I couldn't understand, almost like Father Phinean at the secret part of the Mass, and the three of us, King Abraham and Mr. bar Kiva and yours truly made our way into the Synagogue.

It wasn't so different from a church at that, save there was no image of our suffering Savior up on the wall and no statue of his blessed Mother to be seen, but we didn't stay in the chancel or whatever the Hebrews call it very long. We headed for a doorway at the other end of the building and Amos bar Kiva said, "The kitchen is downstairs. There's a dinner tonight and the women are preparing the food already."

I could smell the cooking myself, and a delicious odor it was, I can tell you. There's a lot of fish consumed here in San Francisco, not surprisingly for a city with so much water around it and so many fisher-folks making their living off the bounty of the sea. The Hebrews won't touch the tasty bay shrimp or fine Dungeness crabs that other San Francisco folks enjoy, but they are fond of all the finny folk and they make them up in delicious ways with all sorts of fine sauces. Yes, indeed!

Amos bar Kiva ushered Abraham ben Zaccheus and myself

through the doorway and onto a landing. We looked down a flight of stairs. "You see," he said, "this is where the three women disappeared. The stairs lead downward, then there is a landing and a turn, then they continue down to the kitchen."

"How many steps?" Abraham asked.

"Twelve."

"All right." Abraham asked Amos and myself to wait where we were. He made his way down the stairs, out of our sight. I heard the voices of women greeting him and Abraham answering in a language I'd never heard even my employer use before. I learned later that it was Ladino.

After a bit Abraham rejoined Amos and myself. "How many steps did you say?" he asked.

"Twelve."

"So you did, so you did. Wait here, please."

Again Abraham descended. This time he returned immediately. "Twelve, eh?"

"Twelve," said Amos.

"Very well. Amos bar Kiva, please descend the stairway and wait at the bottom. Do not permit any of the women to leave the kitchen. But before you go, I want you to lock the door behind you. No one may enter or leave this section of the temple. Can you do that for me, Amos?"

Amos assented. He pulled a ring of very large keys from his pocket and turned one in the doorway behind us. Then he made his way down the stairs. I heard him go.

Abraham put his hand on my shoulder. "John O'Leary, I am going to rescue those women and their unborn children or die in the attempt. Die, or something far worse. I want you to remain here. Keep your eyes peeled and your ears open. If I call for you, will you come to my aid, even at the risk of your own safety?"

"You mean the risk of my life, Abraham."

"I mean more than that, John. I mean at the risk of your soul."

I was still holding the Base Ball shillelagh in my right hand. I shifted it to the left. Abraham held his ebony-and-gold walking stick in his left hand. We clasped right hands, then Abraham turned and started slowly down the stairway. I listened to his progress. He took six steps, then a seventh. At that point he disappeared from my view.

For all that I'd promised to come to his aid if he needed me, I will confess that I disobeyed my employer and followed him partway down the stairway.

Abraham was standing on the landing beyond which the stairway took its turn. As close as I could tell, he was standing on a single slab of black paving slate, what they call hereabouts flagstone. He held his stick by its head and placed the ferrule against the slate. He drew a pattern and stood in the middle of it.

In a loud voice he called out something in Hebrew, then he repeated it—or something that sounded like it—in another language, and then in another, over and over, coming at length to the dear Éireannach, and finally in English. What he said made me shudder. It was this:

In the name of the Sublime One, I command you, Impelluris, Upalluris, Enlil and all you foul demons and so-called gods, and all you Issirra and all you foul demons, to appear and yield up the woman Joaquina Na-Hagid and her innocent unborn one, and the woman Liviya Navon ibn Gabirol and her innocent unborn one, and the woman Nitza Shazar-Suleiman and her innocent unborn one. Hear me, you evil ones, in the name of the Sublime One, I command you!

Abraham reversed his walking stick and with its golden head he smote the rock he stood upon.

At this point there rose from the Earth beneath the synagogue a roaring and a rumbling. The building shook as if the Earth itself was trembling and preparing to quake mightily and a voice so loud it shook the synagogue shouted:

Begone, Hebrew fool, the women you may have but the children will be mine to use for my great work!

Then in a loud voice Abraham called out something in Hebrew, then he repeated it – or something that sounded like it – in another language, and then in another, over and over, coming at length to the dear Éireannach, and finally to English. What he said made me shudder. It was this:

In the name of the Creator, of I-Am-Who-I-Am, I command you, Impelluris, Upalluris, Enlil and all you foul demons and so-called gods, and all you Issirra and all you foul demons, to appear and yield up the woman Joaquina Na-Hagid and her innocent unborn one, and the woman Liviya Navon ibn Gabirol and her innocent unborn one, and the woman Nitza Shazar-Suleiman and her innocent unborn one. Hear me, you evil ones, in the name of the Creator, of I-Am-Who-I-Am, I command you!

A second time Abraham smote the rock he stood upon with the golden head of his walking stick, and the stick broke in two.

A light flashed up from the rock, bathing Abraham in its glare, and a roaring like the very ocean sea in the fury of a great storm, and a stench that blasted my nostrils even where I stood, and stung my eyes like the whips of a jellyfish, a stink like a dead kraken that has lain on the beach in the summer sun for days, and now a terrible low voice whispered so I had to strain my ears to hear it, and it said:

Begone, Hebrew fool, the women you may have but the children will be mine to use for my great work!

Abraham knelt on the rock and shouted out:

In the name of the King the Universe, He who made even the likes of you, I command you, Impelluris, Upalluris, Enlil and all you foul demons and so-called gods, and all you Issirra and all you foul demons, to appear and yield up the woman Joaquina Ha-Nagid and her innocent unborn one, and the woman Liviya Navon ibn Gabirol and her innocent unborn one, and the woman Nitza Shazar-Suleiman and her innocent unborn one. Hear me, you evil ones, in the name of the Sublime One, the Creator, of I-Am-Who-I-Am, of the King of the Universe, I command you!

This time there was no answering voice. The light shone again and the stench came again and the rock where Abraham knelt turned to fog and with a cry Abraham disappeared into the flickering darkness.

He didn't call for my help but I determined to give it anyway. I leaped into the air and fell through the opening after him. I found myself in green water surrounded by creatures with faces like men and bodies like fish, hands like crabs, some of them with scales like carp and some with smooth skins like the bellies of eels and some with hard shells like the crayfish and the crabs of the seas; some with tentacles like the kraken and the devilfish and the stinging jellyfish.

Abraham was there gesturing with his hands and the creatures backed away from him. From among them there appeared three women with bellies like barns and they formed a square with Abraham, holding hand to hand, and they rose through the water and disappeared above us.

The monstrous creatures were all in a circle, swimming and slithering in the round, and in the middle of the circle I stood with my Base Ball shillelagh in my hand, and from among the circling creatures there emerged a great evil one with a head like a cathedral and a single monstrous eye in the middle of its face. Its mouth was filled with row upon row of glistening teeth and it had as many legs as a centipede, each and every one of them tipped with a claw like a pair of cutting shears. It came at me, its one great eye blazing.

I said, "In the name of the Father and of the Son and of the Holy Ghost, begone!"

The creature did not retreat an inch, did not stop for a moment. It launched itself at me and I swung my Base Ball shillelagh at it and smashed its one great eye like a globe of jelly. The creature drifted away. Mayhap it was dead, mayhap only wounded, blinded, suffering. I cannot tell you. I felt something drawing me upward and in a moment I was standing with Abraham ben Zaccheus and the three Hebrew women with their big bellies.

Abraham said, "You are the hero of the day, John. Together we have saved these three women, these three precious goddesses of fate, these three who will be mothers and the three new souls who will do God's good works."

I said, "But Abraham, your holy stick. It was your scepter, was it not? And it was smashed and lost, its gold head and all."

Abraham said, "John Fergus Tiernan O'Leary, it was just a stick. I've a closet full at home. And now, I think we'll be invited to stay for dinner with our friends."

We were standing at the top of the staircase. I looked down and there were twelve steps and no landing and no turning. The landing would have made thirteen steps but now there were only twelve. The smell of the food from the kitchen was lovely indeed.

"Will Xiang Xi-Mei not expect us at Rooshian Hill?" I asked.

Abraham said, "No, I told her we would be late. But what about your friend on Telegraph Hill?"

"Miss Taryn Jilleen O'Casey? Why, do you think these good people would welcome her as well, for dinner?"

"I'm sure they would, John. I'm very sure. I think you should go now and fetch her."

"I think I'll do just that, Your Majesty," I told King Abraham ben Zaccheus. And I made my way to Telly Graph Hill to Miss O'Casey's apartment, and Miss O'Casey was most pleased to accept my invitation for dinner.

Ankareh Minu

Captain Samson always kept a neat desk. The glass covering was spotless. As Rebekkah stood rigidly facing Samson she could see his neat suit, his perfectly knotted tie, his craggy features and razor-cut steel gray hair reflected in it. She knew that her midnight blue sergeant's uniform was in good order, her gold badge carefully polished, her own jet black hair trimmed and combed to perfection. Even so, she felt shabby compared to the captain.

The commander's chin bobbed a fraction of an inch. "Close the door, Sergeant ben Zaccheus, and sit down." When she had complied he resumed. "You know how political this city can be. You know when the supervisors say jump, we can only ask how high."

Rebekkah didn't respond except with a slight nod of her own.

"Did you watch last night's meeting of the Board of Supervisors?"

"On TV, sir."

"You know that we're taking a beating over this series of fatalities by fire."

"Yes."

"Supervisor Moran really let us have it. And you know why, of course."

"Speak freely, sir?"

Samson smiled. "Taping system's turned off, Sergeant." Rebekkah watched, waiting to see if Captain Samson would allow himself a smile. He almost did. Then he slid the case folder across his desk.

Rebekkah opened it. There were incident reports and gruesome photos.

"What do you see, Sergeant? What makes this case unique?"

Rebekkah pursed her lips. She'd been a San Francisco cop for almost a dozen years, since she was a fresh-faced kid out of SF State. All her pals were eager to get down to Silicon Valley or up to the Financial District and show that women can rise as high and make as much money as men. When Rebekkah announced her intention of becoming a cop she got back a combination of sympathetic, baffled, and slyly knowing looks.

She'd seen enough cold corpses in those years, and in the Tenderloin, enough living corpses, to feel only a little shock. "The bodies are all burned. But none of the incident scenes show any fire damage."

Captain Samson nodded. "I knew you'd spot that. Good. But, Sergeant, what does it mean?"

Rebekkah poked her thin, cleft chin with a fingertip. "First thought, Captain. Somebody's killing people and burning the bodies to disguise their identities or the cause of death, or both. Second thought. File shows each body found in a different location. Identification by dental records, each one found in his own home. All male. Mixed ethnicities."

"Yes, good. You know how to read a file. However . . ." He opened a desk drawer, drew out a manila envelope and handed it to Rebekkah.

"Contra Costa County. We generally have good cooperation from them, but this one must have fallen through the cracks. Somebody over there finally woke up and sent this to us."

Rebekkah studied another crime scene photograph, another blackened corpse. She turned to the Medical Examiner's report. This victim was a female, although you couldn't have told that from the photograph.

Captain Samson asked, "Where does that get us, Sergeant? Do you have any ideas? Are these cases connected?"

"About a week apart. Might be some kind of nut. Somebody who has to kill every Thursday night because his mommy and daddy made him go to church and miss his favorite cowboy show. But I don't think so. This is nasty. And it's going to be tough. And based on last night's performance, Supervisor Vincent Moran is really pounding us over this."

Rebekkah pursed her lips.

"Why? They're not concentrated in his district. They're scattered all around the Bay Area. Mostly here in the city, but here's one in Marin, one in San Mateo, Oakland, Moraga. Why Moran?"

"Good question, Sergeant. Suppose you visit Mr. Moran. Tell

him you're hot on the case. No, that's not the right way to put it. Anyway, flash the badge, show the colors, let him know that the department is putting its full resources into this one and we'll keep him fully informed."

Rebekkah drew a deep breath. "Captain, politics is politics. I need to know, sir, are you really putting me in charge of this case or do I just go hold the Major's hand?

Samson grinned and shook his head. "You're not afraid to ask tough questions, are you, Sergeant? Okay, fair is fair. Yes, you're really in charge of this. You'll get whatever support you need. What do you want?"

"For starters, sir, I just want my partner. Officer O'Leary."

"Irish Liam O'Leary?" The grin widened. "You and he go way back, don't you?"

"Actually, our families do."

"Done. Go."

Hall of Justice to City Hall was a five minute jaunt across downtown San Francisco. In Supervisor Moran's outer office a sharply attired Asian woman looked up from her computer keyboard and smiled at Rebekkah. Her eyes flicked to the metal strip on Rebekkah's blouse. "Sergeant ben Zaccheus, Mr. Moran is eager to chat with you."

Rebekkah returned her best *We're here to protect and serve* smile.

Supervisor Moran's office was filled with memorabilia. A Presidential citation for his service in Iraq and another for time in Afghanistan. A Silver Star, a Bronze Star, a Purple Heart. Photos of a boyish Lieutenant Moran with General Powell, of an older Major Moran with General Petraeus, of Vincent Moran kneeling in front of a primitive structure, surrounded by ragged, admiring Afghani children, of Moran surrounded by his buddies, of Moran lying in a military hospital bed grinning bravely while a worried-looking woman—his wife?—sat by his bedside holding his hand.

And a framed photo that Rebekkah recognized from a recent copy of the San Francisco *Chronicle* of Supervisor Moran shaking hands with the Governor himself in front of sign that read, *Vince Moran for United States Senate—The People's Hero, the People's Fighter!*

Oh, yes. Supervisor Moran had his eye on the prize, all right. Not yet forty, a term in the Senate, an easy re-election, and the sky's the limit.

He stood up and extended his hand. The expression on his face was either that of a seriously concerned man or a man very adept at feigning serious concern.

"Sergeant, ah, ben Zaccheus. Thanks for coming over. I know you must be very busy."

Oh, this guy was good!

Rebekkah nodded. Next he would offer her a seat.

Yep.

"I don't believe in politicians interfering in public safety operations but I also feel a definite responsibility to the voters who put me where I am. And, as you know, this series of incendiary fatalities is threatening to get out of hand."

"I'm aware of that, sir."

"Is the department doing anything? I've already talked with the chief and got back the usual line about available resources, concern for the public, blah, blah, blah. That's why I asked him to have someone who's actually working the case come and talk with me."

"That's why I'm here, Supervisor."

"You're newly assigned to this case?"

"We've had people working on it, Supervisor. I've read the crime scene reports, forensics, medical examiner's documents. Captain Samson feels that he needs an experienced officer to pull everything together."

"And that's you, is it?"

"Yes, sir."

He didn't look happy but at least he didn't say anything about sending a girl to do a man's job. Instead he said, "I want to be kept informed regularly, Sergeant. I know your chain of command goes up through the Detective Bureau to the Chief's office to the Commission. I'm not trying to shortcut them. But if this case gets out of hand—so far, the media have played it down, they've treated each case as a separate incident, but there's no way they won't connect the dots. And pretty soon. We don't want another Zodiac or Night Stalker, Sergeant. This is urgent."

She got away as quickly as she could. She made her way back to the Hall of Justice, downloaded information on the case to her laptop, and headed for home.

She shared an apartment on Dolores Street with Officer O'Leary, Liam Francis Xavier O'Leary. Their families had been together in San Francisco for over a century, since a young immigrant, John O'Leary, had answered a want ad in a cast-aside newspaper and gone to work for the famed Kabbalist and psychic detective Abraham ben Zaccheus. It was Liam's night to deal with dinner and he took Rebekkah to a Spanish restaurant within walking distance of their apartment. They shared *Rioja* and *tapas,* flan and espressos and rich, dark chocolates with golden liquid centers.

Afterwards, at home, Liam built a fire. They settled opposite the dancing flames to drink golden *tsikoudia* brandy from Crete and talked about the case. Liam O'Leary was intrigued by Supervisor Moran's interest in the killings. "You think he wants to ride this into the Senate?"

Rebekkah nodded. "I think that's part of it. He's got to win the primary first, and something like this could get him over the old San Francisco liberal, soft-on-crime, brie-eating business. He's pushing his war record, too. That'll be big in the Central Valley. Wounded veteran. Tough on crime. Social moderate—at least by local standards."

"So we bring in some wacko who gets his jollies burning people to a crisp and Major Moran goes the Washington. As simple as that."

"Not as simple as that." Rebekkah stared into the fire as if hypnotized. "I don't know, Liam. I picked up something else."

"You don't mean a clue."

"No."

"Right. You felt a vibration. A cold breeze, a whispered word, things that go bump in the night."

"Don't start, Liam. You know how I feel about you, but just

don't start."

He reached for her hand. "I'm sorry, Rebekkah. I know you believe in—well, what you believe in. Not for me to say it's all nonsense. What was it that you got, and what do you want to do with it?"

"You don't mind working this case with me? I asked Captain Samson and he okayed it, but if you're uncomfortable you can get off it."

"No, Rebekkah. You're a ben Zaccheus and I'm an O'Leary and we've both a tradition to carry on. Just tell me what you want to do."

"I want you to come with me tomorrow. We're going to visit the crime scenes, some of them anyway."

"Forensics and Crime Scene kiddies not good enough?"

"You know there's no substitute for walking over the ground, Liam."

"That I do. But, Rebekkah, now I'm the one who senses that there's something more to your thoughts."

"What do you think?"

"Ah, sweet sergeant of my heart, you want to hear that ghostly whisper in your ear. *'Twas me wicked nephew what done me in, oo-woo, oo-woo.*"

"Maybe."

"And then?"

"Then I want to go somewhere else for a while. I'd like you to drive with me."

"Of course, me sergeant." He drained the last of his *tsikoudia* and placed the empty snifter carefully on the low table. "Well, unlike you high and mighty sergeants, we patrolmen work for a living. I'm tired and I'm ready to retire for the night."

"You go ahead, Liam. I want to think about this for a while."

She refilled her brandy snifter and sat warming the thin glass between her palms, her feet on a hassock, inhaling the brandy fumes rather than imbibing the fluid, gazing into the fire.

The flames had a hypnotic effect, or maybe it was the *Rioja* she'd had with her dinner and the *tsikoudia* she'd sipped and the fumes she'd inhaled after Liam left the room. The red and orange shapes formed faces, or seemed to do so. There must have been some sap left in the wood, and some pine knots, for the flames danced and the sap sizzled and hissed incomprehensible messages to her. The chimney drew well but a sudden gust of wind must have swept in from the Pacific, driving a small puff of smoke back into the room. Rebekkah breathed in its odor. Here eyelids drooped until the dancing flames filled her vision and the sound of the whispering, bubbling sap filled her mind.

She was jolted awake by the explosion of a pine knot. The empty brandy snifter had fallen from her hands and rolled across the carpet. She drew a deep breath, pushed herself erect and retrieved the snifter. She set it back on the table and stretched out on the sofa and slept.

If she dreamed she did not recall the experience when she was awakened by the sound of Liam O'Leary clattering in the apartment's small kitchen.

"Ah, the sergeant awakens." He carried a tray from the kitchen and lowered it to the table.

Rebekkah rubbed her temples with her fingertips to get her brain into gear. "Coffee! Toast! Breakfast fit for a goddess, Liam. And the *Chronicle* to nourish the intellect. An angel thou art!"

He'd opened the *Chron* to the local section and folded it back to expose the story of another death by burning. The tragedy had taken place in a home on one of the worst streets in Hunter's Point, a crime-ridden ghetto. You would have had to look hard to find the report. Crimes in Hunter's Point didn't garner much attention from the media or from the police.

Rebekkah phoned the Hall of Justice and got the shift commander. Crime Scene investigators had already worked the job and the ME had removed the victim's remains. The commander gave her a rundown on the preliminary report. Rebekkah thanked him. She climbed into her uniform. Five minutes later she and Liam O'Leary were headed for Hunter's Point.

The woman who answered the door to the victim's apartment could have been anywhere from forty to sixty years old. She wore a stained sweatshirt and jeans, her hair covered with a faded kerchief, her skin an unhealthy shade of burnt sienna. Her cheeks were frighteningly sunken.

"I already talked to police. What else you want of me?"

The apartment was tiny. It smelled of overripe cat litter and stale cooking. There were dishes and pots in the sink and full ash trays and empty wine bottles.

"I'm sorry, ma'am. I know this is a terrible time for you. If you would just go over the facts for me again."

Liam O'Leary was standing back, clipboard in hand. Out of the corner of her eye Rebekkah observed him studying the room.

"How am I supposed to live now?" the woman was complaining. "Look at me, woman. I can't work. I can't get no job and I can't work. He was on disability, you know? From the army. He got wounded over there in Afghani. And he got sick. I don't know what that sickness is, a lot of them get it. He couldn't hardly stand up. I had to practically carry him to the VA, he was so sick, and they said it wasn't the army's fault. At least they sent him a check every month. Now what am I supposed to do? I suppose the checks will stop and I can't work and the welfare don't hardly give out money no more."

She sat down on a dirty sofa and started sorting through cigarette butts until she found one that appealed to her. She struck a match and smoked it.

"If you could just tell me what happened, please."

There were sounds of voices from the street and thumps. Somewhere nearby an argument broke out; the voices were those of women. They seemed to be competing in cursing each other.

Rebekkah repeated her request.

"What am I going to live on now?" the woman wailed. "I needed the disability. Now what do I do?"

"Please. Where were you, and where was the victim, please."

"All right, all right." The woman poked her cigarette into the pile of butts in the ashtray. Smoke rose slowly from it. "I was in the bathroom and he was sitting here watching TV. You see that TV there? Don't get nothing worth watching, just a waste of time.

He was watching it and I heard him hollering and somebody else talking."

"Could you understand what they were saying?"

"I understood my man. He was saying, *Get away from me, get away, I don't want you, go back there, I won't do it.* That's what I heard him saying. He was so weak, you wouldn't think he could talk so loud but he was shouting."

"And the other voice?"

"I never heard nothing like it. So low, like you could feel it more than you could hear it."

"A man's voice, a woman's? Could you tell?"

"Too deep for a woman or even a man. Like something from the bowels of hell, that voice. I couldn't understand one word, not a word, but it was nasty, I could tell that."

"How long did this go on?"

"I don't know. I was scared. I wanted to come and help him but I was too scared. I just stayed in the bathroom. I didn't want that thing to know I was there. And then I heard my man give a loud scream and I heard something like a crack, like something catching fire and I heard my man scream and then just moan and I heard the other thing, the voice, make like laughing only ugly, ugly, and then a thump and I come out of the bathroom and there was nobody there but my man lying on the floor all burned up and dead. And what am I gone do with no more check every month?"

The house in the Castro was a gaudily painted Victorian, the kind with elaborate gingerbread and a multicolor paint job that wind up in expensive coffee table books on San Francisco architecture. The man who admitted them wore a spotless turtleneck shirt and sharply creased trousers, a bulky cardigan sweater and Birkenstock sandals.

He led Rebekkah and Liam into a parlor and offered them seats upholstered in *faux* tapestry depicting medieval hunting scenes. Tall windows looked out on a tree-lined, hilly street. On the wall Rebekkah saw a framed marriage certificate and an enlarged photo of two men in tuxedos joining hands before a woman in ecclesiastical robes. Another photo showed a young man in an army dress blue uniform, lieutenant's bars on the shoulder boards. It was draped in black crepe.

"Would you like an espresso? Chamomile with lemon? Is it too early in the day for a glass of wine?"

"Tea, please. You're very kind. It's chilly today."

Rebekkah could see into the kitchen from her seat. It was brightly tiled. There was a large work table and a Wolf stove.

The man brought the tea service on a polished tray. He poured for them all.

"I suppose you want to know about my husband's death."

"Please."

"I'm sorry, there's really very little I can tell you. I was at work when it happened. I work on Montgomery Street. I usually get home by seven but I was working late that night. I phoned to see if he was home yet and he was, he said he was making something special for dinner. I said I'd get away as soon as I could but it might be a while."

He had seemed perfectly composed but he lowered his face suddenly into his hands. When he looked up again his cheeks were wet. He found a handkerchief and wiped his face. "I'm sorry."

"Of course."

"I can deal with it sometimes. I put in a lot of hours at work. My friends come by and try to help. We had a lot of friends, you know. A lot. But every now and then—"

Rebekkah waited for him to resume.

"All right. All right, yes. Go ahead, please. Ask away."

"In your own words, then."

"When I got home I brought a little gift, a Scharffen Berger chocolate bar. They're the very best, you know. Pricey but worth it. It was a token of affection we used to have. When one of us wanted to apologize for some little thing, he'd bring home a chocolate bar and we'd break it in half and share it and make up."

He leaned forward, lifted the tea pot and refilled Rebekkah's cup. Liam had hardly touched his.

"Would you rather have coffee, officer? No? All right."

He took a breath and blew it out. "He didn't come to greet me. I thought he was really angry, I was so late and he'd made us a fancy dinner. But then I came into this room. This very room. And there he was, on the floor. Black and dead. He was still—"

He stopped and shook his head. He was wracked by a sob.

"—smoldering."

There wasn't much more. The neighbors hadn't heard or seen anything untoward. There was no fire alarm or police call. Just a man turned to a blackened corpse.

There were witnesses to the next one. The death took place at two in the morning in the middle of People's Park in Berkeley. Members of the permanent homeless community had built a campfire and were sitting in a circle. The guitars had been broken out, a variety of voices were singing fragments of songs their owners had grooved to three decades before, bongs and joints and bottles were making the rounds.

A bearded man clad in a warm army jacket, jeans, and worn combat boots jumped to his feet screaming. The singing stopped and the guitars fell silent as he danced in a circle around the campfire.

"At first," a visibly pregnant woman with a child in each hand recounted, "at first, I thought he was doing a war dance. You know, like an Indian war dance. He was jumping around, he started going *woo, woo, woo,* like in the movies, you know, and then I thought I saw somebody next to him. I thought he maybe came down out of that tree over there, I don't know, or out of the sky, maybe he was in one of them black CIA helicopters, they come over here all the time, you know?"

"Yes, please."

"Oh, you mean about—well, this other guy, I don't know, he must have had one of them invisibility cloaks that they have now, you know, he looked all furry or weird, I don't know, I think he maybe had wings and he was burning and he grabbed the poor guy, hugged him and they burned up together, they looked like a holy picture or something, you know, only not a halo, real flames, and then he dropped the poor guy and he faded out and the other guy fell on the ground and thrashed around a little, people were trying to help him but he just died. And they came and took him away. Probably was the CIA, I think."

And that was the best witness at People's Park.

It was an unconventional working arrangement to say the least. On the job they were sergeant and patrolman, case officer and subordinate. Rebekkah made the decisions and led the investigation, Liam did the scut-work, took notes, navigated unfamiliar routes. They wore uniforms or plainclothes as the situation indicated.

In the evenings they relaxed. Sometimes they discussed the news of the day, colleagues at work, plans for their future. At the moment, the biggest issue was whether to get one cat or two. The most urgent was what to do about dinner. It was Rebekkah's night to decide and she chose a favorite robata bar that served the freshest sushi in the Mission.

Over kaiten-zushi and unfiltered saki Liam asked if Rebekkah thought they were getting anywhere with the incendiary murders. "I don't see any pattern, myself," he admitted, "but maybe your voices will tell you what's going on."

She shook her head. "Not yet. I'm still looking for a pattern, Liam. And I don't see one. All the victims are male, at least so far. Black and white, rich and poor, gay and straight. Geographically scattered. No business connections I can see."

She lifted a tekka-maki, dipped it in a mixture of wasabi and soy sauce, and popped it in her mouth. She washed it down with a sip of hot herb tea.

"Tomorrow, though, something different."

"And would my leader be so kind as to inform me as to the battle plan?"

"Moraga."

"Ah, the poor folks. And how will that be any different from the survivors we've visited so far?"

"First female victim."

They finished their meal and walked back to the apartment on

Dolores Street. They climbed the old stone stairway from the sidewalk and Rebekkah put the key in the lock. She paused before turning the key. Finally Liam reached and took her hand, assisted her in opening the lock. They went upstairs.

"It's a warm night and your hand was very cold," he remarked.

"I felt something." She was pale.

"It's this place, isn't it?"

"Do you know what was here before—before these buildings went up?"

"It never bothered me, Rebekkah. They're old buildings. Pre-quake." Everything in San Francisco is either pre-quake or post-quake. That's the kind of city it is.

"It was the old Hebrew cemetery. *Gibbath Olom*. The Hills of Eternity."

"A lovely name for a place of rest," he said.

"They moved it to Colma. Land here was getting too valuable. Why leave it for the dead when you could sell it to the living?"

"That must have been a long time ago."

"I heard the story from my mother. They opened it in 1861. There were Civil War dead buried here. Closed it in 1888 and moved all the graves to Colma. All the graves they could find. Nobody knows if they found them all. There may be dead Jews living under our feet."

"You don't mean that."

"What?"

"Living. Dead Jews living under our feet."

"Did I say that? Well, you know what I meant."

"Your ancestors?"

"No. Abraham was the first of my family to come here and he didn't die until 1907. Post-quake." She made a little sound that might have had some laughter in it, but not much.

The conversation lapsed and they turned on the TV and watched an old *Streets of San Francisco* episode in rerun, giggling at the silly plot and the low-budget production. It was great fun. They cracked a couple of Kirin beers just to keep in the spirit of the night, then went to bed.

❦

Moraga was across the bridge and through a tunnel and the house they were seeking was up a series of hilly, winding roads.

The house was modern, attractive, clearly well kept. All on one level, as if designed for occupants whose knees were not as supple as they had once been. There was lush landscaping and a three-car garage. The door was down and none of the vehicles were visible. There was a circular driveway covered with sparkling white pebbles that looked as if each one had been washed and polished that morning.

The occupants were a retired couple and they were expecting the visit. Rebekkah and Liam were ushered into an airy living room. There was a fireplace with a gas log but it was not burning. Family photographs were ranged on the mantle. Mr. and Mrs. in much younger days, he with an Afro and a beard; she in a long dress, wearing granny glasses. Another, looking a few years older, he with shorter hair and a moustache, she in jeans and a Greek sailor's cap. Then the two of them with a baby. He looking proud, clean-shaven, respectable; she, maternal and joyous. Pictures of the girl growing up. Then one with him in business suit, her in flowery dress, their daughter in cap and gown. And finally their daughter posing proudly in army uniform, an airborne patch on her cap.

"That's our story," the mother announced.

"I didn't mean to stare," Rebekkah apologized.

"It's all right. We loved her very much."

The father, now white-haired, wearing casual clothes, added, "We were proud of her. Very proud."

"She was in the army?" Rebekkah asked.

"I don't know why she enlisted," the mother said. "I couldn't understand it. I think—maybe she wanted to follow in her father's footsteps."

"You served?" Rebekkah asked.

"I was in Vietnam."

He did not seem eager to talk about that.

"She may have thought we were disappointed, I was disappointed, that we never had a son. I wasn't. I couldn't have loved her more, I couldn't have been happier. But she may have thought that."

Rebekkah consulted her notebook. "She died more than a year ago. She was the first in this series of deaths. I hope you'll tell me as much about it as you can."

The father made a sound and got to his feet. He said something unintelligible and left.

The mother said, "He's not over it. Neither am I. Do you have any children, Sergeant? No? Then you can't understand. I'm not over it either, but I can put up a better front. See?"

She managed a ghastly smile.

"She had a degree from Berkeley. She could have done anything she wanted. She had a boyfriend, too, a fine boy she met in school. But she wanted to do this thing. She went to Afghanistan and came home without a scratch. She said she liked the army, liked the sense of belonging that it gave her. She made sergeant, then they sent her to OCS. You understand OCS? Officer Candidate School? She passed with flying colors. She was a lieutenant. But she always had to challenge herself. She volunteered to be a paratrooper. She was on a training jump. They take them up in helicopters now. She jumped out and something happened. Nobody knows what. She seemed to burst into flames halfway to the ground. It took less than a minute. She was fine when she jumped and she was—she was dead before she reached the ground."

"They got to you, didn't they? The mom and dad?"

Rebekkah and Liam were in the Dolores Street apartment.

"They got to me."

"You want to stay home tonight? I'll make a sandwich, maybe nuke some broth."

"You're too good."

He put on some quiet music. He knew her favorite album, Fairport Convention, *Liege and Leaf.* She listened to the voice of the dead Sandy Denny. Liam didn't say anything. She put her head on his shoulder and cried softly for the old couple with the dead daughter.

In the morning she said, "I'm ready now. I need you to go to

Colma with me, Liam."

"At your command, *mon sergeant.*"

At the relocated Hills of Eternity he waited at a respectful distance while she visited her ancestors. There were many graves in the plot, but she walked from grave to grave, touching the stones, tracing her own direct ancestry, from her father to her father's father to her father's father's father, leaving a pebble atop each to show that a loving visitor had been there.

Each stone had only a name and dates of birth and death, the years given since the Almighty had created the world.

Moses ben Zaccheus, 5710-5768.

Jacob ben Zaccheus, 5684-5764.

Isaac ben Zaccheus, 5666-5727.

Abraham ben Zaccheus, 5615-5667.

They rose from their tombs, their voice spoke to her.

"I am your daughter," she told them. "To each of you was born a son, through the generations, but now I alone am here. Do not turn from me. Help me, Abraham, Isaac, Jacob, Moses. Help your daughter."

They gathered around her and spoke ancient words in a language she did not even understand. But one phrase was whispered in her ears, one name. *Ankareh Minu. Ankarah Minu.*

The sky was clear and the air was warm, but she was taken by darkness and cold. When she could move again she went as quickly as she could to Liam O'Leary and he took her back to their apartment.

At the Hebrew Institute she found what she was looking for. *Ankareh Minu.* The concept was Zoroastrian. In that ancient and noble religion Ankareh Minu wasn't the devil. The followers of Zoroaster recognized an evil deity, Ahriman, the foe of the good god. No, Ankareh Minu was something else. Not even a demon. It was pure evil, more evil than Ahriman, it was the evil side of human nature.

But why had her ancestors whispered those words to her in the

Hills of Eternity? Zoroaster had lived and died thousands of years ago. And Zoroastrianism was a nearly extinct religion, its few remaining adherents concentrated in Iran. What connection was there to the dead in California?

She studied the incendiary deaths. Rich and poor, black and white, gay and straight. Now add female and male. Educated and ignorant, add that, too.

But one had been on disability after being wounded in the army, and died.

One had served proudly, *don't ask, don't tell,* and returned to San Francisco, and died.

One had worn an army jacket, probably his own, kept as a souvenir after serving, and died.

One had served proudly and volunteered for airborne service, and died.

And at the heart of the investigation, the man who had brought pressure on the department, who had prodded Captain Samson into assigning Sergeant Rebekkah ben Zaccheus her tour of the dead, was Supervisor Vincent Moran. Supervisor Moran who soon would be Senator Moran, who might someday be President Moran.

It was not easy to get hold of Moran's service record. He was happy to remind the voters that he was Major Moran, that he had served in Iraq and in Afghanistan. He had the medals to show for it, and show them he did at every opportunity. But as for the full service record—it was not easy to get hold of that but Sergeant ben Zaccheus got it.

Moran had been a lieutenant during the 1991 Gulf War, had served with distinction, won his decorations, and stayed in the National Guard after the war. A decade later, a captain now, he volunteered for active duty again. He led troops in the battle of Kunduz in October, 2001. He helped put down the prison revolt at Qala-I-Janghi, supervised soldiers as they routed Taliban at Mazar-I-Sharif.

But what had any of this to do with Ankareh Minu?

Then came the break, the wild break that gave Rebekkah what she needed. It was her day off. Yes, even cops get a day off. Liam O'Leary was on duty at the Hall of Justice, and Rebekkah drove across the Golden Gate Bridge, bypassed the tourist attractions of Sausalito, made her way to a classmate's home in the hills above Mill Valley.

They went for lunch in the community's miniature downtown. They were sitting in a café, eating salads, when an uproar brought the establishment to its feet. A man stood screaming in the middle of the street. Traffic had come to a halt. Rebekkah ran from the café. The man was punching and kicking at an invisible assailant. Passers-by halted to stare and point.

No, not invisible. As Rebekkah approached she saw a cloud of black smoke as tall as a man, swirling like a miniature tornado, sparks and tongues of flame spurting from it.

The victim was caught in the vortex, spinning in opposition to the black and orange whirlwind, both the whirlwind and its victim gaining in speed, smoke rising now from the man.

Rebekkah ran toward the mad duo, her arms spread to encompass them both. She heard herself chanting, not in her own voice, not in one voice, but in chorus, in a language she recognized but did not understand. The chant became an exorcism, a command thundered in the name of the Almighty.

The black and orange whirlwind stretched skyward. Its peak took human form, the form of a naked, aroused male. It dipped and dived at Rebekkah. She faced it, shouting in voices, shouting the Sacred Name of the Almighty.

The whirlwind dived at her. She did not flinch. Closer. She did not cower. She made a sign, the Faravahar Symbol, a sign she had never made, never seen, nor knew, but nevertheless made.

The black whirlwind rushed past her, so close her hair was singed, her skin pained, her clothing blackened. The black whirlwind plunged through the surface of the street, poured into the very earth, and was gone.

Its victim had fallen to the ground. Smoke rose from his clothing and his flesh. His hair was gone, his skin blackened, but he moved and groaned.

When the ambulance arrived Rebekkah showed her badge and rode with the man to the hospital. Rebekkah talked with the man's doctor, learned that he was pumped full of morphine, was being hydrated and treated for his burns. He would probably survive. He could talk, if Rebekkah would be brief. And he might be incoherent from his injuries and the drug.

"Ankareh Minu."

That was all he would say at first, but he could see and hear and he told his story.

He had been in Afghanistan, had been under command of Captain Moran. From Kunduz they had fought the prison revolt at Qala-I-Janghi, on to Mazar-I-Sharif, and found themselves in an ancient village called Balkh.

Balkh, where a squad of Captain Moran's soldiers, men and women, hormones pumping from the challenge of battle, the fear of death and the ecstasy of killing, had found a tiny Zoroastrian community, an island surviving in a Muslim sea. The captain himself had led the rapine and slaughter. When it was over the captain and his soldiers had sworn a solemn pact of silence.

But there was no escaping justice. The Ankareh Minu, the evil of the world, had found personification, had found a brother soul in Vincent Moran, and was destroying the soldiers who had destroyed the Zoroastrians of Balkh.

"What happened to you, Sergeant?" Vincent Moran pushed himself back from his desk and rose to his feet. "I heard from Captain Samson that you'd been injured. You—your face. Are you all right?"

"I'm all right, Supervisor Moran."

"Well, sit down, let me get you something to drink. You've been burned. What happened?"

"No thank you. I would place you under arrest for murder, Supervisor, if I thought I could make the case stick. But I know what's been going on. I know how those people died. I was lucky to save one victim, he's in a burn ward now."

Moran frowned. "I don't know what you're talking about. You must be delirious, Sergeant. I can't blame you. I'll see to it that you're put on medical leave. I—"

"No you won't. I know all about Balkh. How many people did you murder? How many women did you rape? How long did it take you to come to your senses?"

"You're the one who needs to come to her senses, Sergeant."

"No, Supervisor. No. You made a deal with the devil. We're modern people, we don't believe in such superstitious nonsense any more. But Afghanistan isn't a Twenty-first Century country, is it? The past lived there. Ancient gods and demons live there. Zoroaster lived there. Ankareh Minu lives there."

"Bosh."

"No. No, Supervisor. You swore your troops to secrecy, and they kept their pledge, every one. Every one until today. You trusted them, you relied on them, but your sights are set high now. You know about opposition research. You've used it against your opponents, you know they would use it against you. And you called on Ankareh Minu and he came. He came when you called and he killed when you commanded."

The Supervisor stood facing her. He raised his hands, he made a sign with them, a sign like the Faravahar Symbol, but with his hands reversed. He called out in a language Rebekkah did not know, and she called out in the language of her ancestors and in the voices of her ancestors.

A cloud formed outside the office windows and smashed through them, glass shards scattering across the room. One pierced Rebekkah's cheek and she felt blood spurt.

The being she had seen in the street in Mill Valley stood between her and Vincent Moran.

Moran shouted at the whirling cloud.

Rebekkah opened her mouth to speak and heard only whispers, but the whispers of a congregation of the dead.

Fear spread across Moran's features. Then he was enveloped by the cloud, merged with it, and the cloud rose through the smashed window. Rebekkah stumbled to the window in time to see the black whirlwind plunge into the courtyard, into the earth.

As far as I can recall, "Petroglyphs" is the only Western I've ever written. It's an example of the story written more-or-less to order, that misses its original target but ends up elsewhere and becomes successful. Darrell Schweitzer had asked me for a Cthulhuvian piece for a one-shot horror-western magazine, *Weird Trails.* Turned out that "Petroglyphs" wasn't exactly what Darrell wanted, but it has been popular with a lot of others. I've even used it as a one-man performance piece with great success.

Some readers may note the recurrence of certain names in the stories in this and other books of mine. There are Delberts, Marstons, and Van Hopkinses. And, in the preceding section of this book, the ben Zaccheuses and the O'Learys. Some book collectors have even discovered a little paperback novel called *Death in the Ditch*, by Del Marston, its protagonist also named Del Marston, just as Ellery Queen was known for his (actually, their) fictitious amateur sleuth, also named Ellery Queen.

If you are inclined to trace out the genealogy of my fictitious families, feel free to do so, and with my blessing. On the other hand, if you'd rather just take the stories as they come, that's also fine.

"You gotta make up your mind, Delbert. Do you want to be an office boy and printer's devil all your life and make coffee fer other men, or do you want to make something of yerself?"

The paper was put to bed. She'd be coming off the press in a little while. Edgardo Carrero, our pressman, was giving the press its third or fourth check-up. Nothing escaped his eye and I guess it was all that checking and rechecking that kept the *Sentinel* on her schedule. Every Friday morning, regular as clockwork, there was the *Sentinel* on the street, getting people upset.

Bill van Hopkins, founder, editor, and publisher of the Sour Creek *Sentinel* had his feet up on his desk and a coffee cup full of bourbon in his hand.

"You know I want to be a newsman, Bill."

"Mr. van Hopkins."

"Sorry. Mr. van Hopkins."

Bill took a deep swig of his bourbon. I figured, another refill or so and he wouldn't mind my calling him by his first name. It was a ritual, every Thursday night.

"How old are you, son?"

"Fifteen," I told him.

He squinted at me over the edge of his coffee cup. His cheeks were bright red and his hair was falling over his forehead. He needed a haircut.

"Fifteen, eh? You don't look it to me. You sure you're that old?"

"Yes, sir."

"Where you from, son? Your name's Delbert, ain't it? Delbert Marston?"

"Yes, sir. You know me, Mr. van Hopkins, sir. I was born right here in Sour Creek."

"Call me Bill, son. No need to be formal around here."

"Yes, sir."

"You want a sip of this here coffee, Delbert?" He didn't wait for me to answer. He picked up another coffee cup and poured a couple of fingers of bourbon. He handed me the cup and I took a very small sip.

I really am fifteen, or pretty close to it anyhow, but I'm short for my age and kind of skinny, and I don't like liquor much. I know who my mother is and I see her around town once in a while and I'm always polite to her. I don't know for sure who my father was. My ma'am says he got murdered before I was born. She calls herself Mrs. Marston, so I guess my pap was Mr. Marston. Ma'am says he was a Major in the Confederate Army and he come home from the war and married her and got me started in her and then he went out one night and got hisself murdered.

That's a good enough story for me.

"Well, son, you falling asleep or which?" Bill van Hopkins asked. He reached over and kicked me, but not hard.

I said, "No, I ain't asleep. Did you ask me something?"

"I was going to but you fell asleep, you damned lazy wretch."

I know he didn't mean that, it's just his way of showing affection. "What were you gonna ask me, Bill?"

"Do you feel like covering a story, Delbert, that's what I was gonna ask you. You don't do nothing useful here in the office except get in the way. So how's about you going out and doing some reporting and earn your salary for once in your good for nothing life."

I put my coffee cup down and got to my feet and stood to attention the way my pap must of done in the war. I said, "Here am I, Lord, send me."

Edgardo Carrero must have been satisfied with the condition of the press because he started her up and he was working her slow and steady, the way he done every week, every Thursday night. *Ker-whumpa-ker-whumpa-ker-whumpa.*

"What's the story?" I asked Bill. "Ain't heard of no hangings coming up, no gunfights, no buildings burning down."

"Delbert, there's a big opening of that new Gilbert and Sullivan show over to the Superba Opera House this weekend. Miss Billie Benton herself is goin' to be in it, playing some kinda Japanee geechee girl or something."

I must have drooped a little but I figured, this was my first break from being an office boy and printer's devil, if I did a good job I'd get more reporting work and less making coffee for the boss.

So I said, "I'll do a great job, Bill, you can count on me. I'll get over to the Superba and interview Miss Benton and write up the show, too."

"No you won't."

"I won't?"

"Jabber's handling the opera show."

Jabber is Walter Jabbert. He's the *Sentinel's* ace reporter. He has a notorious eye for female flesh and I could have guessed that he'd nab off the assignment of meeting Miss Billie Benton. He'll probably offer to buy her dinner and a drink while he's at it. I know he was after my ma'am at one time, but I put the kibosh on that scheme of his. He's got me by sixty pounds and half a foot, but he's slow on his feet and he don't take a wallop on the chin too good.

We're friends, now that he knows what's what.

"Okay, Bill. Jabber goes to the opera. Where do I go? Courthouse open tomorrow? Got some good case to handle?"

"Nothing like that. We got a professor about to descend upon our humble little town. One Professor F. L. Grey, of the great University of Springfield. Imagine, traveling thousands of miles just to come to Sour Creek."

"What's he coming here for? Hardly no books in this town, and not a single statue."

"Nope."

The press was going faster now. *Ker-whumpa-ker-whumpa*. Once he gets going, Mr. Carrero gets a look in his eyes and nobody better go anywhere near him.

"Couple of paintings in the saloon, though," I said. "Think he wants to look at them?"

Bill laughed. "You're gettin' warm, Delbert. Gettin' warm. Professor Grey wants to look at the rock pitchers out near the butte."

"What's he need me for, then?"

"Needs a guide, mainly. He's coming on the stage tomorrow morning. He'll check into the Lee's Arms and then you help him rent a horse from Shipley's and you ride out to the butte with him and show him the pitchers."

"That's all?"

"Make a story out of it, son. You do a good job, you might could get a real nice story out of it. Do that, you get more. You foul this up, it's back to making coffee for you."

"What if he wants to know about the pitchers?"

"Know what?"

I shrugged. Bill was refilling his coffee cup. He held the bottle of bourbon toward me until he saw that my cup was nowhere near empty. "Call yourself a writer?" he grumbled.

Then, "What if Professor Grey wants to know something about the pitchers? I don't know nothing about 'em. Nobody much does."

"Ah," Bill said, letting the word out slow and satisfied sounding. "You tell him anything you feel like. That way you'll get to be a famous scholar and Professor Grey will sit you in his book. Make you an important figger, getting sitted in a book by a professor."

"But I don't know nothing about the rock pitchers," I insisted.

Bill shook his head from side to side, a sad expression on his face like when you try real hard to explain something to some poor simple soul, and the simpleton just don't understand what you told him.

"Delbert," Bill said, "don't nobody hereabouts know nothing about them pitchers 'cept Crippled John Smith the Navajo. And he ain't no newspaper reporter, so you'll just have to make it all up. That's all. This professor don't know no better or he wouldn't have to ask. So you just make up a good story for the professor and he'll be happy and go back to Springfield and write his book, and you'll be happy and you'll come back here to the *Sentinel* and write your own story and I'll be happy. And you want me to be happy, don't you?"

I said, "I sure do, Bill." I kept my thoughts to myself, but I was thinking that Crippled John Smith was no more no Navajo than the man in the moon, he just claimed he was Navajo and got people to buy him drinks by telling 'em wild stories about the old days.

Ker-whumpa-ker-whumpa-ker-whumpa.

Mr. Carrero was working away at it at the printing press like a love-crazed stallion going at it with a willing and eager mare. I was pretty tired but Bill van Hopkins was pretty obvious getting into one of his philosophical moods and in no hurry to go home to Mrs. van Hopkins. And even if he did, there was no point in my crawling into my sleeping bag in the back of the office and trying to get any shut-eye, not until Mr. Carrero finished his work and locked up and went home.

Ker-whumpa-ker-whumpa-ker-whumpa.

I went over and picked up a copy of the *Sentinel* for Bill van Hopkins and one for myself and we sat in neighborly silence (except for the continuous thumping of the press) sipping our bourbon and reading the *Sentinel*. We always print the paper on Thursday night but it's dated the next day and it always gives me the creeps to think that I'm reading a newspaper out of the future.

Finally Mr. Carrero finished. A weird kind of silence fell over the *Sentinel* office. It was one of those moments. Some folks say that an angel must have just flew over. Some folks say it means that somebody just walked on your grave. Anyway, it was real, real quiet in the *Sentinel* office.

Then Bill van Hopkins said, "Ladies and gentlemen, it is time for all good souls to seek their nightly repose. And so, I bid you, *bon jewels*." He downed the last of his bourbon, pushed himself to his feet, and clamped his hat on his head.

Mr. Carrero took the hint. He took off his apron, hung it on its hook, and headed for the door. Mr. van Hopkins waited for him to step outside, then he followed him. He turned around and stuck his head back inside the office.

"Bright and early, Delbert," you have work to do in the morning." He meant, delivering *Sentinels*. My favorite part of my job.

Just joshing.

It was getting dark so I lit a kerosene lantern and climbed into my sleeping bag with a dime novel. Reading about detectives in the big cities back east always helps me to sleep and gives me good dreams. I need that. Otherwise I have other dreams that I don't like, and I wake up shaking and crying. Nobody gets to see me like that. Nobody. That would never do.

In the morning I went over to the saloon for breakfast. I figured there would be a few customers who'd stayed over sleeping in with the girls—they charge extra for that but if the customer is willing to pay they're happy to take his money.

A couple of cowboys were drinking at a table. I couldn't tell whether they were getting an early start on the day or had simply forgot to quit last night. I recognized 'em and we said good morning to each other.

Then I went up to the bar to get some breakfast and would you guess who was there to serve booze and fry food. No, don't guess, I might as well just tell you. It was my mother.

She smiled at me and said, "Good morning, Delbert. How are you today?"

I said, "Hungry, ma'am."

She said, "Well, how about some nice bacon and eggs? I can fry some up for you in a jiffy. How about a piece of hard roll and a cup of coffee while you wait?"

I couldn't believe it. Butter wouldn't melt in that woman's mouth. I think the only reason I don't quit this town and start over is I'm too stubborn to let her know she's beat me, and the only reason she won't leave town is cause she don't want me to have the satisfaction of seeing the hind of her.

But the coffee was hot and the breakfast was good and I was still the first one at the *Sentinel* office to start distributing newspapers. After we finished that chore it was back to the office and sit down and address the out-of-town subscriber copies. You'd be amazed at how many people want to get the Sour Creek *Sentinel*. We have subscribers in Mexico, China, and Jerusalem. Can you imagine what some bearded old Hebrew in Jerusalem thinks about weddings and funerals and hangings in Sour Creek, Arizona Territory, You Ess of Ay? And why is he interested?

The stage arrived at noon and I met it and introduced myself to Professor Grey. The Professor was a woman—no joke! It took me a while to figure that out. She was taller than I was by four-five inches easy, and she dressed like a man and she had her hair pushed up under a broad-brimmed Stetson. Had a mighty handshake, too, and she didn't act or talk girly-girly, but she was still a woman. I guess anybody can be a professor nowadays.

Her name was Professor Frances Loretta Grey and she said she answered to Frances or Frankie but she preferred Frankie and got deef whenever anybody tried to call her Lottie.

I told her my name was Delbert and I didn't have no other preferences so she might as well just call me that and she said okay she would.

She didn't have near as much luggage as I'd have expected of a woman, neither. Just a couple of carpetbags and a box that she said had her *ee*-quipment in it. I asked her what *ee*-quipment that was and she said it was her scientific *ee*-quipment and it was fragile and had chemicals in it so would I *please* be very careful with it and I said, Well, of course, what do think I'd do, roll it like a hoop? And she got annoyed and said she just wanted to make sure it was properly cared for and I said, But of course, Your Professorship, Madame, thou needst not fear that thy *ee*-quipment will be properly cared for.

I took her over to Shipley's Hotel and Livery and saw to it that she had a nice room and asked her when she wanted to go look at the rock pitchers and she said right away if she could just get "a bite to eat" first.

So I took her over to the saloon, which was starting to fill up mainly with cowboys in for a drink or a quick nooner with the ladies. My ma'am was still on duty so I introduced Professor Frances Loretta Grey to her and my ma'am extended her hand and said, "Pleased to meetcha, Lottie," which I knew at once did not bode well for their forming no intimate bosomhood together.

Frankie and me each had a sandwich and then we walked back to Shipley's and rented her a horse and I got on my horse and we headed out to look at the rock pitchers. All Frankie took with her was a pad of some kind of thin paper, about a quarter as thick as newsprint, and some soft pencils. She said she'd have to rent a wagon and bring her *ee*-quipment out with her some other time.

We rode for a couple of hours to the rock caves and went in and Frankie stopped and stared at the pitchers for about three weeks time, it seemed like, maybe ten minutes actual, without saying nothing. Then she said, "These are wonderful, they're just wonderful."

She took out her paper and pencils and leaned against the pitchers and started scrabbling a soft pencil back and forth on the pitcher. It might of looked strange to me, what she was doing, except we used to do it when I was a kid. If anybody had a penny we'd put a piece of paper on top of it and scrabble a pencil back and forth and you could make a nice copy of the penny that way.

Frankie Professor Frances Loretta Don't Call Me Lottie Grey was doin' exactly that making copies of the rock pitchers.

After a little I got bored watching her and went for a walk, saw a couple of interesting snakes and some nice lizards and a couple of eagles out hunting for rabbits but I didn't see no rabbits so good luck to them eagles.

We went back to Sour Creek and Frankie went upstairs at Shipley's to freshen up and invited me to have dinner with her on her *expense account*. I asked her what that was and she explained it to me. I thought that was the best idea I'd heard of in a long time and decided I'd ask Mr. Bill van Hopkins to let me have one of them things, too. Frankie said she wished me luck and I thought about them eagles looking for rabbits where there wasn't no rabbits around.

Fat chance.

But I could always try.

I had a little notebook with me and a pencil and I asked Frankie about what it was like being a professor and why she was interested in the rock pitchers and what she was going to do when she got back to the University of Springfield and made copious notes about her answers.

The next morning we started off bright and early. Frankie had returned Shipley's horse all safe and sound and rented a wagon and a horse to pull it. I carried her box down from her room and loaded it onto the wagon and we headed for the caves again.

Frankie said we had a lot of work to do so we took a couple of jugs of water and some sandwiches with us. She was wearing her big Stetson, which was smart even for a professor from the University of Springfield. Not as smart as me, of course. I wore a straw hat. Just as good for protecting from the sun and a lot lighter, but even so, she didn't do so bad. She wore canvas britches and a plaid shirt and she didn't look too bad at that. Certainly a hell of a lot different from my ma'am or any of the girls that work at the saloon.

We got to the caves and I tethered the horse and lifted the box down off the wagon. I was doing a lot of work for Professor Frances Loretta Grey and not getting paid for it, just my salary from the *Sentinel* plus I figured I was getting some meals paid for off Professor Grey's *expense account.*

I guess by now those cave pitchers are pretty famous and everybody knows what they look like, but then hardly nobody knew about them except the kids from Sour Creek. We used to go out to the caves when we weren't working or at school and look at the cave pitchers. When I was a little kid we used to go out there and make up stories about the cave pitchers, we decided they was made by old people a long time ago, not the Navajos or anybody like that but people who lived here longer ago than the Navajos and made those pitchers before they left or when they knew they was going to die or something. We made up scary stories.

Once we decided to have a contest. Everybody put in a penny and anybody who was brave enough to stay in the cave with the pitchers overnight would win the prize. My friend Danny Wilson said he was the bravest kid in Sour Creek and he'd be the first to stay in the cave overnight and win the prize.

We all went out there and had a meeting and swapped stories and we left Danny with a bag of sandwiches and a canteen and everybody went home. We went back out there the next morning and Danny was gone and so was the bag of sandwiches and the canteen and we never saw him again so everybody took back his penny except we didn't know what to do with the extra penny so we went to Danny's ma'am and gave it to her to keep for him.

The Professor's *ee*-quipment was a photograph camera and photograph plates and chemicals for developing the photographs. She set up her camera and said she was going to take photographs of the rock pitchers. To take each photograph she would put a plate in her photograph camera and pull out a slide and then we would just wait and wait for the photograph to get took.

She said she could work faster if she had more light but it wasn't very light in the caves so she had to make a longer exposure. I said, Oh, sure, ever'body knows about longer exposures and shorter exposures. I don't think the Professor believed me because she laughed but she didn't say nothing to challenge me.

While she was taking her photographs of the rock pitchers she asked me questions about the pitchers but I couldn't tell her much because nobody really knew who made them or when or why. I told her about our meetings when I was a kid and when I told her about Danny Wilson she got excited and wanted to know more about him but all I could tell her was that he disappeared and his ma'am was really upset when we told her about it and after a while she left town.

I wish my ma'am would do the same.

We was taking a break for lunch when Crippled John Smith the Navajo come upon us. I won't say he was no sneak but he was leading his horse and walking, not riding, which he was able to do quieter that way so he arrived and we didn't know he was there until the cave got darker than it was already. We was eating our lunch in the cave, Frankie and me, because it was cool in there out of the sunlight, and without no warning the light got mostly cut off and we looked and there was Crippled John Smith standing in the mouth of the cave looking at us.

Frankie Grey took me by the elbow and leaned over and hissed into my ear, "Who is that man?"

I said, "That's just Crippled John Smith."

"Is he dangerous?" Frankie asked me.

I said, "No. He's a little bit crazy but he don't do nobody no harm."

Crippled John Smith took a couple of steps inside the cave so he wasn't blocking the mouth no more and the light got a little better. Professor Grey's photograph camera was standing there pointed at one of the rock pitchers. She stood between the photograph camera and Crippled John Smith. I thought she was going to say something to him but he spoke first.

"What are you doing?"

Professor Grey said, "I'm investigating these petroglyphs."

That was a new word to me but I figured Professor Grey was talking about the rock pitchers and either Crippled John Smith knew what it meant or else he just didn't care to stop and ask.

What he did, though, was talk the way he did in Sour Creek, that made everybody know he was crazy. He started his crazy talk, which sounded to me like a combination of regular words mixed up with some Chinee or Japanee words and some Hebrew and some Latin that I once heard a Jewish rabbi and a Popish priest talk when they came through Sour Creek on the stage on their way to Seattle or someplace.

Crippled John Smith can talk regular, and when you ask him about the crazy talk he says he's talking Navajo, but a couple real Navajos came through Sour Creek one time and I remember Crippled John Smith tried talking his crazy talk to them and they didn't understand him at all. They just shook their heads. They could talk a little regular and they said he wasn't no Navajo, he was just a crazy man.

Which I believe is the truth.

The rock pitchers, well, I ain't going to describe 'em much because Professor Grey's photographs been all over the world by now, including in a special roady graver supplement to the Sour Creek *Sentinel*. We even got extra copies down to the *Sentinel* office. If you want one just come by and lay out your scratch and your wish shall be our command. If I ain't there Mr. Bill van Hopkins or Mr. Walter Jabbert or even Mr. Edgardo Carrero will sell you one. Or if you don't live hereabouts you can even send in the price by mail and I will personally address a copy of the supplement myself and make certain that it goes out to you safe and sound.

But for the moment, the rock pitchers showed some really strange galoots in what look like deep sea divers' outfits like in those stories Mr. Verne writes over in France, Europe. You know, they're wearing heavy boots and baggy suits and what look like helmets on their heads with little winders in front to look out of. And if you can make 'em out, you can look *in* the winders and see their faces a little.

But I think the artist wasn't very good at his work. Heck, I can draw better-looking people than them and I ain't never been to artist school. Or maybe he was just cock-eyed. I mean, those folks look so tall and skinny, they must be 'leven feet tall. You can tell because the artist he put a couple regular size people in the pitchers too, so you can tell.

And their faces ain't no Money Listers neither. He got their eyes all messed up, weird and slanty like a Chineeman only lots bigger and black and shiny.

Also the artist he put some kind of crazy boats in the pitchers, too. You know what they look like? You read that crazy book by Mr. Verne about some Captain name of Nemo? You remember that boat he had that went under the ocean? Well, these boats in the rock pitchers look like that.

Submarines, they're called. You could look it up in Mr. Webster's dictionary.

Crippled John Smith says they ain't no submarines, and for once he made sense to me cause there ain't no ocean for a submarine to *go* under in Arizona Territory.

Crazy.

You know Sergeant McWhorter?

Town like Sour Creek has plenty of strange characters in it. Sergeant McWhorter, he's an old-timer. Says he was just a boy back in 1860, wound up in the army during the late unpleasantness of that time.

One time I was eating breakfast down to the saloon and Sergeant McWhorter must have been lonely cause he came over and started up a conversation. He wanted to talk about the late unpleasantness and I figgered just to be polite I'd let him rare back and have at it. I even encouraged him by asking him which side he fit on and he said, both sides.

I said, How was that, wasn't you either a Union or a Reb? And you know what he said? I'll tell you what he said.

He said, and I remember his exact words, swear it on a Bible, his exact words, he said, "I useta be twins. Always fit with my brother. Couldn't agree with him about nothing. I said a apple was green, he'd say it was yaller. I said a dog was yaller, he'd say it was off-white. Now I ask you, what in the world is a off-white dog? A dog is white or it ain't white, it ain't off-white, no more'n an apple is a off-apple or a horse is a off-horse."

See, George McWhorter, he rambles.

So I got him back on the track and he says, "The war broke out and my brother says, 'I'm going out and enlist,' and I said, 'Which side you figger to enlist *on*?' and he told me, so of course I had to go out and enlist on t'other side."

George looks at my plate, I got half a sandwich left of what I was eating, he says, "You gonna finish that?" and I says, "Dunno, ain't decided yet," and he says, "Here, son, I'll save you the trouble," and he reaches and takes my half a sandwich and eats it up every bit before I have a chance to stop him.

Anyhow, I showed him one of Professor Grey's photographs of the rock pitchers and asked him what he thought of them and he looked at the submarine and he said, yep, it surely was a submarine, they had 'em in the late unpleasantness, the Rebs they had one called the *Hunley* and Union side had one called the *Intelligent Whale* and another one that they bought from France, Europe, called the *Alligator*.

I asked him once again which side he fit on and he said, real sad, real real sad, that his brother fit on one side and he fit on t'other and he got kilt dead so his brother had to take over and be both twins, and that was him, now. It wasn't him sitting there in the saloon, my own ma'am watching us disapproving, it was his brother.

But meanwhile I guess I got away from my story because there was Professor Grey and Crippled John Smith and me standing there in the cave looking at the rock pitchers and Professor Grey taking her photographs and all of a sudden Crippled John Smith says, "They're a-coming back. They're a-coming back. The old people went away and they forgot me, the sonsabitches, they forgot to take me with them, so they're coming back and they'd better take me with them this time."

He was talking regular, see? None of that crazy German-Russian-Greek stuff that he called Navajo. He said, "You two git on back to town because you ain't from the old people and they'll kill you dead they find you here but they'll take me with 'em this time or I'll know the reason why!"

He was really, really, angry. I'd use a different term to tell you how angry he was, but that wouldn't be polite. So I'll just say, he was really, really, *really* angry.

So Professor Grey and me, we figured we'd pack up and head back into Sour Creek for the night, and we did. She went to her room at Shipley's to "powder her nose and freshen up a bit," as she said it, and we met later and had a good drink together and dinner. And Cripple John Smith stayed out there at the caves.

Professor Grey and me went back out there the next morning and there was no sign of Cripple John Smith, we figgered he'd got cold in the night and headed back into Sour Creek, but when we got back to Sour Creek nobody said they'd seen him. And nobody ever did see him again.

Maybe the old people came back for him in their submarine.

I wrote up the whole thing for the Sour Creek *Sentinel* and Mr. Bill van Hopkins liked it so much he gave me a fifteen cent bonus.

Written at the request of anthologist Mike Ashley, "Brackish Waters" is based on an actual incident, the destruction of a munitions ship being loaded for movement to the Pacific Theater of Operations in the Second World War. The devastation was great, there were hundreds of casualties, and the entire town of Port Chicago, California, was destroyed. Rumors that the ship was sabotaged by Axis agents, or that the explosion was of a nuclear bomb, have persisted for sixty-five years, but in all likelihood the disaster was caused by arrogant young naval officers "racing" their stevedore gangs to see who could finish their work the fastest.

Brackish Waters

Delbert Marston, Jr., Ph.D., D.Sc., was the youngest tenured professor on the faculty of the University of California. He was widely regarded as a rising academic star, not only on the University's premiere campus at Berkeley but throughout the huge multi-campus system and, if the truth be known, throughout the national and international community of scholars.

Tall and dark-haired with a touch of premature gray at the temples, he was regarded as a catch by female faculty members who competed vigorously for his attention. He dressed conservatively, held his tongue in matters of both public and campus politics, drank single-malt scotch whiskey exclusively, and drove an onyx-black supercharged 1937 Cord Phaeton. Perhaps it was Marston's otherwise thoroughly conventional lifestyle that caused his vehicular preference to be regarded as a sign of high taste and acceptable self-indulgence rather than one of eccentricity.

He had the Cord serviced regularly at an exclusive garage on the island of Alameda, the owner of which establishment catered to fanciers of the three marques formerly built in Auburn, Indiana—the Auburn, the stately Duesenberg, and the tragically short-lived Cord. The Auburn Motor Car Company, or what was left of it, was now producing Lycoming aircraft engines and B-24 Liberator bombers for the Army Air Forces. Once the war was over there was no predicting the future of the discontinued automobiles but in Marston's estimation their prospects were poor.

On the night in question—the night, at any rate, that would initiate the series of events destined to lead to Delbert Marston's apotheosis—the sky above the San Francisco Bay Area was black with a cold storm that had swept down from the Gulf of Alaska and attacked the Pacific Coast with fierce winds and a series of hammering downpours of pelting rain laced with occasional hints of sleet. Such weather was not uncommon in Northern California during the winter months, and the winter of 1943-44 was no exception; the onslaught of wind and water was regarded as anything but freakish. The Bay Bridge was swept by an icy gale but the Cord held the roadway with a steadiness unmatched by vehicles of lesser quality.

Professor Marston was accompanied by an older colleague, one Aurelia Blenheim, Ph.D. Gray-haired and dignified, Professor Blenheim had served for some years as Marston's mentor and sponsor. It was her spirited championing of his cause that had persuaded the Tenure Committee to grant him its seal of approval despite what was regarded as his almost scandalous youth. Marston's intellectual equal, Aurelia Blenheim had found in the younger academic the friendship and platonic camaraderie that her lifelong celibacy had otherwise denied her.

"I don't know why I let you talk me into spending an evening with this squad of eccentrics, Aurelia." Marston braked to keep his distance behind a superannuated Model A Ford that looked ready to topple over in the gale.

"Why, for the sheer pleasure and mental stimulation of bouncing off some people with unconventional ideas. Besides, the semester's over, most of the kiddies who have managed to stay out of the service have gone home to Bakersfield or Beloit or wherever they came from. What else did you have to do?"

"You've got to be kidding. The Oakland Symphony is doing an all-Mahler program, the San Francisco Ballet has a Berlioz show, and the opera is offering *The Marriage of Figaro*. And we're going to meet a bunch of wackos who think—if you can call it thinking—as a matter of fact, Aurelia, what in the world is it that they think?"

Aurelia Blenheim shook her head. "Come now, Delbert. They have a lot of different ideas. That's the fun of it. They don't have a body of fixed beliefs. Attending one of their meetings is like sitting in on a First Century council of bishops and listening to them debate the nature of the mystical body of Christ."

"I can't think of anything less interesting."

They had reached the San Francisco end of the bridge now and Marston maneuvered the Cord through merging traffic and headed south. A rattletrap Nash sedan full of high school kids pulled alongside the Cord. The driver lowered his window and yelled at Aurelia, "Why don't you put that submarine back in the water where it belongs, grandma?"

Aurelia Blenheim turned to face the heckler and mouthed some words that remained unheard and unknown to Delbert Marston. The expression on the face of the heckler changed suddenly. He raised his window and floored his gas pedal. The Nash sped away. Three kids in the backseat stared openmouthed at the gray-haired professor.

"Aurelia," Marston asked, "what did you say to them?"

"I just gave them a little warning, Delbert. Best keep your eyes on the road. I'll get us a little music." She reached for the radio controls on the Cord's dashboard. Although the radio had added to the price of Marston's Cord he had ordered it installed when he purchased the phaeton.

The sounds of Franz Liszt's *Mephisto Waltz* filled the Cord's tonneau.

A particularly dense sheet of rain mixed with a seeming bucketful of hailstones crashed against the Cord's roof and engine hood, adding the sound of an insane kettle drum concerto to the music.

"There's our exit sign," Aurelia Blenheim shouted above the din.

Delbert Marston edged into the exit lane and guided the Cord off the highway and onto a local thoroughfare. Aurelia Blenheim navigated for him, giving instructions until she finally said, "There it is. You can park in the driveway."

The house stood out like an anomaly. Curwen Street and its environs—still known as Curwen Heights—had once been among San Francisco's more fashionable neighborhoods. Victorian homes had reared their turrets and cupolas against the chilly air and damply cloying fog. Families who claimed the status of municipal pioneers, direct descendants of the leaders of the Gold Rush and survivors of the earthquake and fire of 1906, had erected gingerbread-encrusted mansions and filled them with children and servants. Carriage-houses and stables were discreetly placed behind the family establishments.

But the passing decades had brought changes to Curwen Street and Curwen Heights. Urban crowding had driven the wealthiest families to Palo Alto, Burlingame and other lush, roomy suburbs. The construction of the Golden Gate Bridge and Bay Bridge in the 1930's had opened the unspoiled territories and sleepy villages of Marin and Alameda Counties for the use of daily commuters. Key Route trains brought workers from Oakland and Berkeley into the city each day.

Marston switched off the engine and half-blackened headlights, and climbed from behind the steering wheel. He exited the car and helped Aurelia Blenheim to do the same. He carefully locked the vehicle's doors and escorted her to the front entrance of the house. In the darkened street and with storm clouds blackening the sky it was difficult to see anything. Even so, the house had the appearance of a onetime showplace, long since fallen into disrepair. Blackout curtains made the windows look like shrouded paintings. Marston searched for a doorbell and found none. Instead, a heavy cast-iron knocker shaped like a gargoyle signaled their arrival.

The door swung open and they were greeted by a rotund individual wearing thick, horn-rimmed glasses. He peered owlishly at Marston, then dropped his gaze to Aurelia Blenheim.

"Dr. Blenheim!" He took her hand in both of his and pumped it enthusiastically. After he released her she introduced Marston. The rotund youth identified himself as Charlie Einstein, "No relation," subjected Marston's hand to the same treatment Aurelia Blenheim's had received, and ushered them into the house.

Voices were emerging from another room, as was the odor of fried food. In the background a radio added to the din.

Charlie Einstein led Marston and Aurelia Blenheim to a high-ceilinged parlor. Men and women sat on worn furniture, each of them holding a plate of snack food or a beverage or both.

Einstein clapped his hands for attention and conversations wound down. The radio continued to play. Einstein said, "Ben, would you mind?" He gestured toward a Philco console. "You're the closest."

A painfully thin and painfully young-looking man in a navy uniform reached for the Philco and switched it off. "Nobody was paying attention anyhow," he said. He turned toward Marston and Aurelia Blenheim. "Aurelia, hello. And you must be Professor Marston."

Del Marston nodded.

"Ben Keeler," the sailor said. His spotless winter blues bore the eagle-and-chevron insignia of a petty officer. He shook Marston's hand. "We've been hearing about you for weeks now, sir. I'm so pleased that you could finally make it to a meeting."

Charlie Einstein set out to fetch beverages for Marston and Aurelia Blenheim. Keeler pointed out the others in the room, giving their names. Marston nodded to each.

One of them was a thirtyish woman whose mouse-brown sweater was a perfect match for her stringy hair. She was sitting next to the fireplace, where a log smoldered fitfully. "This is Bernice," Keeler announced. "Bernice Sanderson."

The woman looked up at Marston and Aurelia Blenheim. It was obvious that she knew Blenheim; they exchanged silent nods. "So you're the famous professor." She glared at Marston. "The skeptic who doesn't believe in anything he can't see for himself. You've got a lot to learn, professor."

She turned away.

Keeler took Marston by the elbow and steered him away. "Sorry about that, sir."

Marston interrupted. "Please, just call me Del."

"Fine." The sailor grinned. You know, I was an undergrad at Cal until we got into this war. I'm accustomed to calling professors, *Sir.*" He reddened. "Or, *Ma'am,*" Professor Bleinheim."

"Aurie."

"Yes." Keeler turned a brighter shade of red. "Anyway, once the war is over I plan to go back and finish up my degree."

Marston nodded. He saw that Keeler wore an engineer's rating on his uniform sleeve. "Good for you," he said. "There will be plenty of need for good engineers in the postwar world."

Keeler said, "Yes, sir. In fact—" He was interrupted by Charlie Einstein carrying a tray with two steaming cups on it. "I know Aurie likes these things and she told me that you did, too, Professor."

"Del."

"Right. Hot rum toddies. Good for a night like this."

When Einstein went on his way, Ben Keeler resumed. "I'd hoped to have you as my faculty adviser when I get to grad school. If I'm not being too pushy, that is."

Marston shook his head. "I'm flattered. Sure, come and see me when the war's over. I envy you, Ben, serving in the Navy. You just went down and enlisted when Pearl Harbor was attacked?"

"I thought it was the right thing to do. In fact, I'd have thought that a man with your credentials would have a commission. If you don't mind my saying so, Professor. Del."

Marston sipped at his rum toddy. "They turned me down. Said I couldn't march right, and besides, they wanted me to hang around and lend my expertise when they had problems for me to play with. Said I was more valuable as a civilian than I would be in the Navy."

Keeler nodded sympathetically.

Marston breathed a sigh of relief. The rum couldn't be that strong and fast-acting, it was just careless of him to mention not being able to march right. He'd been born with minor deformities of both feet. They'd never kept him from normal activities, in fact he felt that they helped him as a swimmer. But the navy doctors had taken one look at his feet and told him to go home and find a way to contribute to the war effort as a civilian.

Still, the Navy had accepted him as a consultant, calling upon his expertise as a marine geologist and hydrologist. He'd received a high security clearance and worked with naval personnel whenever he wasn't busy teaching. He looked around, observing that nearly everyone in the room was young. Aurelia Blenheim had persuaded Marston to attend a meeting, but this looked more like a party. There were plates of snack foot scattered around the room and bottles of soft drinks. There was a low, steady hum of conversation. Marston spotted only two girls among the crowd, discounting the acerbic Miss Sanderson. Outnumbered as they were by males, they were twin centers of constant attention and maneuvering.

A fireplace dominated one end of the room. A young man of neurasthenic appearance wearing a baggy suit and hand-painted necktie had stationed himself in front of it. He held a brass bell and miniature hammer above his head and sounded the bell.

"The twelfth regular meeting of the New Deep Ones Society of the Pacific will come to order." He looked around, clearly pleased with himself. Conversation had ceased and he was the target of all eyes. "We have a distinguished guest with us tonight, Professor Marston of the University of California. If anyone can shed light on the problem of the Deep Ones, I'm sure Professor Marston can."

Now attention shifted from the young man to Del Marston. What a farce this was turning into. Marston mulled over suitable forms of revenge against Aurelia Blenheim.

"Professor Marston," the young man was babbling on, "perhaps you'll be willing to address our little group."

Marston was holding a thick sandwich in one hand and a soft drink in the other. He put them on a table and said, "I'm afraid I'm not quite prepared for that. Maybe you'll tell me a little bit about your group, starting with your name."

"Albert Hartley, Dr. Marston. I'm the President of the New Deep Ones Society of the Pacific. Our members are dedicated to unraveling the mystery of the Deep Ones. Hence our name." He giggled nervously, then resumed.

"And Dr. Blenheim says that you're the leading marine geologist in the region."

"Dr. Blenheim flatters me. But tell me about your New Deep Ones Society. Does the name refer to the fact that you're all deep thinkers?"

"Now you flatter us," Hartley replied. They had settled onto chairs and sofas by now, the boys clustering around the girls while Albert Hartley tried to hold their attention. "The Deep Ones," (Marston could almost hear the capital letters) "are strange creatures who live on the sea-bottoms of the world. People have known about them for thousands of years. They're in Greek mythology, Sumerian mythology, African mythology. And in modern times authors keep writing about them. But nowadays they have to disguise their books as fiction."

"Why?"

Hartley looked startled. The room was silent.

Then somebody else made an ostentatious demand for the floor. Del Marston recognized the new speaker as Charlie Einstein. The ponderous Einstein blew out a breath. "There are people in the government who don't want us to know about the Deep Ones. People in every government. You wouldn't think that the Nazis in

Germany and the Reds in Russia and the Democrats in Washington could agree on anything while they're fighting this huge war and all, but they have secret meetings in Switzerland, you know. The Japs are there, too."

"You mean the war is a front for something else?" Marston asked. "Cities getting blown up, soldiers dying in foxholes, aerial and naval battles, people suffering all over the world—it's all a put -up job?"

Einstein shook his head, his too-long, dirty-blonde hair falling across his face. "Oh, the war is real enough, okay. My brother is in the Army, he was at Tobruk in North Africa and was wounded and he's back in England now, in the hospital. The war is real, you bet, Dr. Marston. But the big shots who are running things still have their secret agreements. You'll see, when it ends, nothing much will change. And they really don't want us to know about the Deep Ones. Lovecraft wrote about them, too. In fact, he was writing about them even before that Czech guy, Karel Capek, wrote his book *War with the Newts*. They're everywhere. Lovecraft was a New Englander and he knew about them, they have a big base at Innsmouth, in Massachusetts."

"But that was just fiction." Marston tried to calm the excited youngsters. "Foolish stories about monsters. As silly as Orson Welles' radio play about Martians. There are problems enough in this world without having to invent more."

"Oh, no. Oh, no." Einstein shook his head. His fleshy jowls shook with emotion. "And another thing. There's the 1890 Paradox."

"The what?" Marston could barely keep from laughing.

"The 1890 Paradox," Einstein repeated. "Karel Capek was born in 1890 in Bohemia, in what is now Czechoslovakia. Howard Phillips Lovecraft was born in Rhode Island. And Adolf Hitler was born in Linz, Austria. You can't call that a coincidence, can you?"

"Of course I can." Marston frowned. "Millions of people are born every year. You can pick any year out of history and find musicians, authors, politicians, scientists, generals, philosophers, all born that year. Of course it's a coincidence."

After a moment he added, "Besides, I'm pretty sure that Hitler was born in 1889, not 1890. Do you have an encyclopedia here? Let's look it up."

Einstein looked pained. "Well, 1890, 1889, those records aren't exactly reliable. It's close enough, Dr. Marston."

Marston smiled and waited for Einstein to go on.

"Then what about their deaths? Lovecraft and Capek both wrote about the Deep Ones, both exposed their intentions, and both died within a matter of months! Explain that for me, if you can, Dr. Marston."

"I can't explain it. There's no explaining to do. Out of all the millions of people born in 1890, I imagine that tens or hundreds of thousands would have died in—what year was it that your two writers passed on?"

"Lovecraft died in 1937, Capek in 1938."

"And Hitler?"

"You know he's still alive. That's because the stars were right for those births in 1889 and 1890, and they were right for the two deaths in 1937 and '38. As for Hitler—he's no menace to the Deep Ones. It wouldn't surprise me if he's in league with them. Malignant beings have a long history of making alliances with humans willing to sell out their species for personal gain, like vampires offering their sort of undead immortality to their human servants. And the Deep Ones have a lot to offer their allies. Long, long life for one thing. And incredible pleasures obtained through their unspeakable rites. That's what the Deep Ones have to offer."

"And we believe they're here, Dr. Marston." This from Albert Hartley, taking back the center of attention. He was interrupted by a middle aged woman who entered the room wearing a housedress and apron. "There's coffee and cocoa on the stove for anybody who wants them," she announced.

Hartley looked exasperated. "Thanks, Mom. Not right now, please."

The woman withdrew.

"They're out in the Bay, even as we speak," Hartley resumed. "They have a whole city down there. When people disappear, when you hear about people jumping off the new bridge to Marin, the Deep Ones are involved in that."

Marston frowned. It was hard to take these kids seriously but he had promised Aurelia Blenheim and he was going to do his best. "I think the jumpers are suicides."

"That's what you're supposed to think. The Deep Ones, they're amphibians. Lovecraft said so in his writings. They look like regular people at first. They grow up among us, they could be anybody. Then as they get older they start to show their true nature. It's called the Innsmouth Look. They start to resemble frogs or toads. Eventually they have to go back to the sea, to live with their own people."

Marston picked up his abandoned sandwich and took a bite. Mom Hartley made good snacks, anyway. The sandwich was spiced salami and crisp lettuce with a really sharp mustard, served on hard-crusted sourdough. Marston had a good appetite, and besides, chewing earnestly away at Mom Hartley's salami sandwich gave him an excuse not to answer young Albert Hartley's wild assertions.

Now a girl sitting surrounded by boys spoke up. "My name is Narda Long, Dr. Marston."

Del Marston nodded.

"We don't think that there has to be war with the Deep Ones." Narda wore her medium brown hair in curls. Her face would be pretty, Marston decided, in a few years when she shed her baby fat. It would help her figure, too. For now, she filled her pink blouse and plaid skirt a bit more amply than she might, but in this crowd anyone young and female would get all the attention she wanted.

The room was filled with a buzz. Apparently the New Deep Ones Society was divided between those who thought they could make league with the wet folk and those who considered the amphibians the implacable enemies of land-dwellers.

"If we'd just make friends with them, I'm sure they'd leave us alone. Or even help us. Who knows what treasures there are in the sea, on the sea bottom, and we probably have things here on land that would help them."

"That's right." The boy sitting next to Narda Long agreed. "We have these battles and we go shooting torpedoes around and we set off depth charges, we're probably ruining their cities. No wonder they're mad at us."

"What can you tell us about the Deep Ones, Dr. Marston?" The only other non-hostile girl in the room, a freckled redhead, asked.

Marston shook his head. "I think you invited the wrong person to your meeting. You need a folklorist or maybe a mystic. Somebody from the Classics Department might be good. I'm just a marine geologist. I study things like underwater volcanism and seismology, and their effect on shore structures and the way bodies of water behave. It's all pretty dry stuff."

Nobody got the joke.

The debate went on, the let's-be-friends-with-the-frogs group versus the it's-a-fight-to-the-finish group. Finally Del Marston looked at his watch and exchanged a signal with Aurelia Blenheim.

"I'm sorry but I have to teach an early class tomorrow," she announced. "You know, we old folks can't stay up as late as we used to, not if we're going to go to work in the morning."

"Thanks for getting us out of there," Marston addressed Aurelia Blenheim. "Another five minutes and I was about ready to take a couple of those young blockheads and knock their skulls together."

Aurelia Blenheim laughed. "They weren't that bad, Delbert. They're young, they can't help that, and a certain amount of foolish passion goes with the territory."

"I suppose so," Marston grumbled. "And a couple of them even seemed moderately intelligent. The only one who seemed sensible was the young sailor—what was his name?"

"Ben Keeler. You weren't just impressed by his hero-worshipping attitude, by any chance."

"Not in the least. Sincere and merited admiration is never misplaced and is always appreciated."

"What a lovely aphorism." Aurelia Blenheim leaned forward and switched on the Cord's radio. The phaeton had cleared the Bay Bridge, the structural steel and giant cables of which would have interfered with reception. A late-night broadcaster was rhapsodizing about the progress of General Clark's forces in Italy and the successes of Admiral Nimitz's fleet against the Japanese. The announcer must have been local because he went on to talk about Nimitz's pre-war connection with the University of California in Berkeley.

When the news broadcast ended Marston switched to a station playing a Mozart clarinet piece. "You don't really think those kids have something, do you?" he asked his companion.

"I try to keep an open mind."

Marston asked, not for the first time, how his friend had first encountered the New Deep Ones. As usual she referred to a vague relationship between herself and Mrs. Hartley. "We went to school together a million years ago. I was in her wedding. Poor Walter, her husband, was on a sub that went down in the Pacific. She carries on and I try to keep her spirits up."

"And you really do have a class in the morning," Marston commented. He drove through Berkeley, dropped her at her home on Garber Street and returned to his home on Brookside Drive.

He refused further invitations to attend meetings of the New Deep Ones. His feet were bothering him and walking had become difficult and uncomfortable if not downright painful. And he was having problems with his jaw and teeth. He consulted his dentist and his medical doctor alternately. Each reported that he could find no source for Marston's difficulties and referred him to the other.

Marston worked at his office on campus, solving problems brought to him from local naval installations. He reduced his social schedule until he was a near recluse, moving between his bachelor's bungalow and his office on the university campus. He met requests for his company with increasingly abrasive refusals until the day he realized he was excluded from faculty cocktail parties and all but the most compulsory of campus events.

The conversation he had in part overheard, in part contributed to, at the meeting of the New Deep Ones preyed on his mind. Several times he sought out Aurelia Blenheim, by now not only his longest-enduring acquaintance but virtually his only friend. Over a cup of coffee or a glass of wine he queried her about Selena

Hartley, young Albert's mother. At least Aurelia Blenheim had revealed her friend's first name.

Her maiden name had been Curwen. She was a native San Franciscan, descended from the founder of Curwen Heights. She had married Walter at the height of the tumultuous Roaring Twenties and had struggled at his side through the years of the Depression to preserve their relationship and to keep the old house, built by the original Eben Curwen in the previous century, in the family.

Beyond that, Aurelia Blenheim had no information to share with Delbert Marston.

Naval Intelligence had ferreted out Japanese plans to send submarines against the West Coast of the United States. To Marston this made no sense. Earlier in the war, after the Japanese had decimated the US Pacific Fleet at Pearl Harbor and had conquered the Philippines and Wake Island, it would have made sense. But the Japanese were being forced back by General MacArthur's island hopping campaign and General LeMay's firebombing of the home islands.

An antisubmarine net had been strung across the Golden Gate in 1942, when a direct attack by Admiral Yamamoto's forces seemed imminent. The attack had never come, but the Navy had been spooked by their intelligence and Marston was called on to help design a new and improved underwater defense line. Knowing the Navy, the war would be over before the new defenses were built and the defenses would be outdated before another war could make them useful, but Marston was not one to shirk his duty.

He spent his days touring the Bay and the Golden Gate in naval motor launches, alternating the excursions with long days at the desk calculator and the drawing board. His nights he spent in his living room, looking out over Brookside Drive, listening to music, and drinking scotch whiskey. It was almost impossible to find good single malt nowadays, far more difficult than it had been during the laughably ineffective Prohibition of Marston's youth. He shuddered at the thought of having to switch to blended swill.

As walking became increasingly painful he spent more hours in the University pool. Even sitting in an easy chair or lying in bed he had to deal with discomfort, and the ongoing changes in his jaw and teeth made eating a nasty chore. He was losing his teeth one by one, and new ones were emerging in their place. He'd heard of people getting a third set of teeth, it was a rare but not-unknown phenomenon. His own new teeth were triangular in shape and razor-sharp. Only when he had slipped into the waters of the pool did the pain in his extremities ease, and even his mouth felt less discomfort.

Yet he was drawing unwelcome glances in the changing area at the pool. He altered his routine, suiting up at home and wearing baggy clothing over his trunks until he reached the locker room. There he would doff his outer costume and plunge into the water, staying beneath the surface as long as he could before rising for air. As time passed he found himself able to stay under for longer periods. He ascribed this to the practice of almost daily swims.

One day he stayed under for a period that must have set his personal record. When he surfaced he was the center of attention. One of the other swimmers muttered, "Say, you must have been down there for five or six minutes. How do you do that?"

Marston growled an answer, then hastened to his locker, pulled his baggy clothing on over his wet body and dripping suit, and headed for home.

That night he drove to the Berkeley Marina. He parked his Cord, looked around and ascertained that he was alone. He walked to the water's edge, disrobed, and slipped into the Bay. The water was icy but somehow it eased the now-constant ache in his legs and feet. His hands, too, seemed to be changing their shape in some small, subtle way. They were uncomfortable, as well. He wondered if he was developing arthritis.

He swam out toward Angel Island. He had no way of knowing just how far he had gone or how long he had remained submerged, but he felt that it must have been fifteen or twenty minutes. He broke surface and realized that he was not out of breath. In fact, he had to force himself to inhale the fog-drenched night air. His neck itched and he rubbed it with his hands, feeling horizontal ridges of muscle that he had never noticed before.

He looked around, searching for landmarks, but the enforced wartime blackout precluded the use of bright lights in the cities that lined San Francisco Bay. He made out the silhouette of the Bay Bridge against the sky, then that of the Golden Gate Bridge. He turned in the water, recognizing the forbidding fortifications of Alcatraz. Without inhaling again he ducked beneath the surface and swam back toward the Berkeley shoreline. In time he waded from the cold, brackish waters of the Bay. By contrast, the night air felt warm against his body. He shook like a dog to rid himself of water, pulled on his clothing, and drove home.

In the Brookside Drive cottage he drew a polished captain's chair to an open window. Through the window he could hear the soft gurgle of the nearby stream that gave the thoroughfare its name. Odd, Marston thought, that he had never noticed this before. The sound brought with it a melancholy, pleasant feeling. He thought of putting a record on the turntable, had even selected Handel's *Music for the Royal Fireworks,* and pouring himself a scotch while he listened to the recording, but instead brought a pillow from his bedroom and placed it on the living room carpet.

He lay down in darkness and closed his eyes, letting the sound of the stream fill his consciousness. He fell asleep and dreamed of dark waters, strange creatures and ancient cities beneath the sea. He awoke the following morning and staggered to the mirror in his bedroom. He brushed water from his hair.

By the end of May, in normal times, the university's spring semester would have ended and the students departed, leaving Berkeley a quiet suburb of Oakland instead of the bustling community of scholars it became during the academic year. But in wartime the military had set up accelerated programs for the education of junior officers, and the University of California was on a year-round schedule.

Delbert Marston's assignments from his naval superiors had changed as well. The computations and design of the antisubmarine defenses were completed and construction was well under way. The data provided to Marston now was peculiar and the requested analytical reports were more peculiar than ever. In Europe the long-anticipated cross-channel invasion had taken place and Allied forces were pushing the Wehrmacht back toward Germany. In the Pacific Japanese troops were resisting with fanatical dedication, whole units dying to the last soldier rather than raise the flag of surrender.

But as the Office of War Information reminded the American public, the conflict was far from over. The Germans had developed flying bombs and rocket weapons and were using them against Allied forces in France and Belgium, and sending them to wreak havoc in England. If they could develop longer-range models, even the US would be in danger. A Nazi super-scientist named Heisenberg was rumored to be developing a weapon of unprecedented power that could be delivered to New York by a jet -propelled flying wing bomber. The whole thing seemed like a scenario from a Fritz Lang movie.

Still, Marston made his way to his office each morning, laboring on feet that sent agony lancing up his increasingly deformed legs. Once at work he found it hard even to hold a pencil, relying on an assistant to take dictation rather than try to write up his own notes. He seldom spoke with anyone save his naval superiors and assistants.

His only pleasures were his solitary, nocturnal excursions beneath the surface of the Bay. He no longer bothered with the fiction of breathing air once he entered the Bay, relying on water inhaled through his now wide mouth and expelled through the gill slits in his neck once his body had extracted its oxygen content.

He saw shapes beneath the water now, sometimes dark, sometimes sickly luminescent. At first he avoided them, then he began to pursue them. He couldn't make out their shapes well, either, although as time passed he began to develop more acute vision in the dark medium. From time to time one of the shapes would swim toward him, then flash aside when he reached out to touch it.

One night he found one of the creatures drifting aimlessly a few feet beneath the surface. He swam to it and saw that it was more or less human in shape but clearly not human. He reached for it and it did not flash away. Once he grasped it he realized that it was dead, its flesh horribly torn as if it had been caught in the propeller of a passing ship. Even as he studied the strange cadaver two more shapes flashed into sight and snatched it from his grasp, moving first out of his reach and then out of his sight.

But he had touched the remains. The flesh was white and stringy, the skin as smooth and slick as that of a giant frog.

Despite the changes he was undergoing he managed to maintain the pretense of normality, taking his meals, filling his Cord Phaeton with precious, rationed gasoline, sending his laundry out to be done, keeping his modest lodgings in order.

Late one Saturday afternoon he nearly collided with Aurelia Blenheim while pushing a shopping cart in the aisle of the grocery store nearest his home. He was shocked at her haggard appearance. How long had it been since their last meeting? How could she have aged so badly? He thought of his own changed appearance and wondered if he looked as worrisome to Aurelia as she to him.

The expression on Aurelia Blenheim's face showed shock and deep concern. "Delbert," the elderly woman exclaimed, "are you all right?"

"Of course I am."

"But you look so—are you certain?"

"Yes," he growled. He should have turned and left the store the instant he spotted Blenheim, but he had failed to act and now he was caught. "I'm just a little tired," he explained. "Very tired, in fact. The war. So much work."

"I'm coming to your house," Blenheim asserted. "I'm going to make dinner for you. You're not taking care of yourself. You're headed for the hospital if you don't get yourself together. You should be ashamed!"

When they reached Marston's cottage he turned his key in the door lock and stood aside to let Aurelia Blenheim enter first. Marston carried the bag of groceries Blenheim had helped him select. She had even loaned him a few ration stamps and tokens to complete his purchase.

The selection of foodstuffs was far more extensive than the Spartan diet Marston had been living on in recent months. In fact he occasionally supplemented his nourishment during his nocturnal swims in the Bay. That body was densely populated with marine species that throve in its cold, brackish waters. Marston became ravenous when he came upon the abalone, eels, crabs, clams and small octopods that lurked in the silted seabed.

When he came upon one he would devour it raw, fresh, and sometimes living. His new teeth could pierce the shell of a living crab as if it were paper.

Just inside the doorway Aurelia Blenheim bent over and picked up a buff-colored envelope. "Here's a telegram for you, Delbert."

He took the envelope from her and opened it. The message was typed in capital letters on strips of buff paper and glued to the message form. The telegram came from a Captain Kinne, commanding officer of the Naval Weapons Station at Port Chicago, a village on the shore of Suisun Bay, an extension of San Francisco Bay fed by the Sacramento River.

The message itself was terse. It directed Marston to report to the commanding officer's headquarters first thing Monday morning. In traditional naval fashion Marston was told to show up at or about 0600 hours, on or about 3 July 1944. Marston had never heard of anyone in the Navy arriving after the designated time and date with the excuse that he had arrived "about" the indicated time.

Aurelia Blenheim steered Marston into an easy chair and carried the bag of groceries into his kitchen. She had visited the Brookside Drive cottage before, although months had passed since her last visit. Marston put some light music on the turntable, an RCA Red Seal 12-inch recording of *Vltava* by the tragic Bohemian madman Bedrich Smetana.

With astonishing speed Blenheim produced a tempting bouillabaisse. The odor coming from the kitchen was mouthwatering and the flavor of the marine stew proved delicious. The only problem, for Marston, was that everything seemed overdone. He would have preferred to consume the aquatic creatures uncooked.

After dinner they relaxed in Marston's living room with glasses of prewar brandy. Jokingly, Aurelia Blenheim asked why Marston's mother hadn't taught him to take better care of himself. When he reacted to the question with frowning silence the older woman set down her glass and took his free hand between both of hers. "I'm sorry. I didn't mean to upset you."

Marston drew away. Of late his arthritis had become worse. The last joints of his fingers and toes had curled downwards and his finger- and toenails seemed to be turning into claws. He worked to keep them trimmed but they grew back rapidly. The small triangles of flesh between the bases of his digits were growing, also, a change that proved helpful in water but embarrassing in public.

Desperate to draw attention away from his increasing physical abnormalities, Marston said, "No, I'm afraid she didn't."

Blenheim frowned, "Who didn't what?"

"My mother. She never taught me to take care of myself. She never taught me anything. I never knew her. My father told me that she loved to swim. They lived in Chicago and she would swim in Lake Michigan all year round. She joined a group, they called themselves the Polar Bear Club, and they would plunge into the lake every New Year's Day, no matter how cold it was, even if it was snowing. But that was just a stunt. They used to get their picture in the Chicago *Times* and the *Tribune* and the *Sun*. But Mother took it all very seriously. The photographers loved her, she was the only female Polar Bear."

He took a deep draught of golden liqueur.

"She was an immigrant," he resumed. "I never knew where she was born. Father just said it was a cold country. I was born on December 25, you know," he changed the subject. "I was a Christmas baby." He said it with bitterness. "Father brought Mother and me home from the hospital on New Years Eve. The next day Mother insisted on her annual plunge with the other Polar Bears. They used to run out into the lake, throw themselves into the surf, frisk for a few minutes and then come running back out of the water. But Mother swam out. Snow was falling, Father told me, and visibility was poor. Mother just swam out into the lake. They sent search parties after her but they never found her."

"I'm so sorry," Aurelia Blenheim said. She started again to reach for his hand, then drew back, avoiding a repetition of his previous withdrawal. After a moment she said, "Did your father ever remarry?"

Marston shook his head. "He raised me alone, as best he could, until he was gunned down when I was six. I had no other relatives and I wound up bouncing from one orphanage to another until I went out on my own."

"But you've made such a success of yourself, Delbert. I never know about your childhood. How sad. But look at you now, a tenured professor, a respected member of the community. I'm so proud of you, and you should be proud of yourself."

She insisted on clearing the dishes and cleaning up Marston's kitchen. She returned to the living room and said, "You know I live nearby. I'll just walk home, it's such a warm evening. Please promise me you'll take better care of yourself. And let me know how things work out at Port Chicago. As much as the Navy lets you tell me, of course."

He stood on his lawn and watched until she disappeared. He returned to his house and filled another snifter of brandy, then sipped until it was gone. The summer evening was long and he was in agony by the time full darkness descended. Then he left the house and drove to the marina. He parked, disrobed at the water's edge and slipped into the Bay.

Monday morning he rose early and drove to Port Chicago. The naval base consisted mainly of warehouses and barracks. A railroad spur ran onto a pier that extended into the Bay. Even at this early hour he could see crews of colored stevedores in navy fatigues working to move munitions from railroad cars to the hold of a ship moored to the side of the pier. The stevedores were supervised by white men in officers' uniforms.

A guard had demanded to see Marston's identification and the telegram summoning him to the base. Once satisfied, the guard directed Marston to the headquarters building, a wood-frame structure badly in need of fresh paint. Once inside he was escorted by a smartly-uniformed WAVE into the commander's office.

Captain Kinne looked as if he had stepped out of a bandbox. Every crease in his uniform was knife-sharp, every button glistened.

Marston of course wore civilian garb, the academic uniform of tweed jacket, flannel slacks and button-down shirt. He had replaced his customary striped necktie with a scarf that concealed his gill-slits and added a pair of oversized dark glasses. He stood in front of Captain Kinne's desk wondering whether he was expected to salute or shake hands. The WAVE introduced him and Kinne looked up at him. "You're Marston, eh?"

He said, "I am."

"All right, I just wanted to get a look at you. Tell a lot about a man with one look. You'll do. What happened to your hands, Marston? Some kind of tropical disease? Jungle rot?"

Marston started to answer but Kinne went on.

"Jaspers," he addressed the WAVE, "take Mr. Marston down the hall. Give him to Keeler." He turned back to Marston and nodded curtly. "Go with Jaspers. Keeler will tell you what to do. Thanks for coming."

The WAVE, obviously Jaspers, led Marston to another office. She halted and knocked at the door, then turned the knob and opened the door a few inches. "Mr. Marston is here, sir."

She gestured and Marston stepped past her into the office. He heard Jaspers close the door behind him. He found himself in a smaller office now, surrounded by charts and manuals. The man who stood up to greet him wore a set of summer khakis with the twin tracks of a Navy lieutenant on the collar.

"A real pleasure to see you again, Dr. Marston. After that little party in Curwen Heights I was afraid you wouldn't want anything to do with us."

"Ben Keeler?" Marston said. "You've certainly risen fast. You were a junior petty officer the last time I saw you."

Keeler grinned. "Petty Officer Third Ben Keeler, Lieutenant Benjamin Keeler, same fellow. ONI put me in that EM's uniform to check out the New Deep Ones Society. They were pretty worried at one point, those kids were getting too close to the truth and Naval Intelligence wanted them steered off. That was my job. I still attend their meetings, by the way. If you ever want to come by again, I'd love some moral support. Just don't blow my cover."

"All right," Marston smiled. "I wouldn't want to get you in trouble with Naval Intelligence."

"And they're just a bunch of harmless eccentrics, you know," Keeler added. He walked around the desk and put his arm on Marston's shoulders. "Take a walk with me, Dr. Marston. There are some things you need to see, and then some questions I'll want to ask you."

Marston acceded, determined not to show the pain that he knew he was in for. At Keeler's side he made his way along the pier. A freighter stood in the middle of Suisun Bay, black smoke pouring from its stacks. It would clear the Golden Gate before noon, Marston knew, *en route* to the soldiers and marines fighting the Japanese in the Pacific. An empty ship had already taken the place of the freighter on one side of the pier, while another, opposite it, received pallets and crates of munitions.

As they moved past work gangs Keeler took salutes from ensigns and petty officers supervising the stevedores. The latter continued to work as Marston and Keeler passed.

At the end of the pier they halted. A breeze had kicked up and the surface of Suisun Bay had turned choppy.

Marston gestured back toward the work gangs they had passed. "All of the stevedores are Negroes, all of the officers are white," he commented. The question was implicit.

"That's Navy policy," Keeler said. "Not very long ago the Navy was trying to get rid of all its Negroes, even though they were just mess-men and laundry workers. Filipinos make better workers. But there's too much pressure from Washington, finally the service gave in. And these colored stevedores are pretty good, as long as you keep a close eye on them."

They turned to face the buildings of Port Chicago. "What we're concerned about, Del, is a very special cargo that we're going to ship out this month."

Marston nodded, then waited for Keeler to continue.

"It's a very special bomb. It's coming in by train next week, and Captain Kinne wanted to get your help in handling it."

Marston shook his head. "What do I know about bombs?"

"Oh, we have plenty of people who know about bombs," Keeler grinned. "We need somebody who knows hydrology and submarine geology to keep this baby safe."

"What is it, something bigger than the ones LeMay is dropping on Japan? The closer we get to the home islands, the easier it's going to be to hit 'em."

"No," Keeler shook his head. "This is something different. Look, everybody knows that we're close to finishing off the European war. Ike took a big risk with the Normandy landings but that was a big success and Patton and Montgomery are rolling through

France. Italy's out of the game. And the Russians are closing in on the Nazis from the East. It's just a matter of time now."

"And in the Pacific, too, don't you agree, Benjamin?"

"But we're taking terrible losses. The President is up for reelection this November and those casualties are going to hurt him. He's put pressure on the War Department and the Navy Department to give him this bigger, better bomb. We figure once we drop a couple of these babies on Japan, maybe one on Tokyo and one on Kobe, even the fanatical Nips will cave in. Washington doesn't want to have to invade the home islands, don't you see. That's what this is all about, Del."

There was a moment of silence as a zephyr swept in from the Bay, bringing the smell of brine and brackish waters with it. Then the wind shifted and the clatter of tools, the sound of voices, the roar of donkey engines came to them from the ships and the railroad cars.

"And there's another thing," Keeler added. "You know Uncle Sam didn't much care for the Bolshies when they first took over Russia twenty-five years ago. President Wilson even sent some troops over there. The government doesn't like to talk about that any more now that Joe Stalin is our buddy but you know we took sides in their civil war and we picked a loser."

"That was a long time ago," Marston put in.

The combination of the choppy Bay and the increasingly brisk breeze whipped up a spray of salt-flavored water that pelted onto the pier and onto Keeler and Marston. Keeler pulled a bandanna from his uniform trousers pocket and wiped his face, frowning. Marston licked his lips. He felt hugely refreshed.

"The US wouldn't even recognize the new government in Russia until Roosevelt came in, and there are still a lot of powerful men in Washington who don't trust Stalin and his gang. They want to get this new bomb and use it before the war is over as a warning to the Reds not to get too big for their britches."

He hooked his arm through Marston's and the two men strolled back along the pier, returning finally to Keeler's office. Keeler said, "Will you get to work on this, Del? Captain Kinne has already worked it out with his counterparts, you'll be excused from your other duties until the special bomb is safely out on the ocean, on its way to a bomber base in the islands. We need your analysis and your recommendations about the seabed and waters from here to the Farralons. And we need your report before that ship moves. The bomb is coming in next week, and we need to get it out of here on the *Quinalt Victory*. Our Negroes will be working on the *Bryan* most of the time, that will serve as cover for the bomb going out on the *Quinalt*."

Keeler opened a safe and extracted a pass for Marston. "This will get you anywhere on the base," he said. "Guard it, Del, it could be dangerous if it got away from you."

Marston accepted the pass, slipped it into his pocket and left.

He spent the next few days alternating between Port Chicago and the University campus in Berkeley, studying the physical layout at Suisun Bay and existing charts and studies of the area. He could hardly hold himself back from examining the seabed in person, but he resisted the temptation until he felt ready.

Then he drove from Berkeley to Port Chicago after dark, parked the Cord, and walked out to the pier. The work here went on around the clock, seven days a week. There was no way he could use the pier without being observed, so he informed the young officer supervising the loading work of his intentions.

At the end of the pier he left his clothing, climbed down a ladder, and slipped into the water.

The Bay water was cold and dark and as it welcomed him he felt the aches leave his body and limbs. He had always been a strong swimmer; now, the webbing between his fingers and between his toes turned him into a virtual amphibian. His eyes, too, had developed a sensitivity that permitted him to maneuver in the dark, brackish water.

He spotted a huge dark-green crab scuttling toward a large rock on the seabed. The creature didn't have a chance. Marston's new, powerful jaw and strong, triangular teeth crunched through its shell. The living meat was sweet and the juices of the crab were more delicious than the finest liquor.

Marston saw human-like forms swimming nearby and pursued them. Ever since his encounter with the dead creature he had wondered about these beings. They might be a species of giant batrachian hitherto unknown to science, far larger than any recorded frog or toad; perhaps they were survivors of a species of amphibian that had evolved eons ago only to disappear from most of the world.

He swam after them and they permitted him to approach them but not to establish direct contact. They swam with the current created by the waters of the Sacramento River as it emptied into Suisun Bay. They looked back from time to time as if to encourage Marston to follow them, but the speed and stamina with which they swam far exceeded even his enhanced abilities.

Finally he gave up and swam back toward the loading pier and the two ships at Port Chicago.

He climbed the ladder, then drew himself onto the pier. The young ensign he had spoken with earlier greeted him with a shake of his head. "I was getting pretty worried," the ensign said. "Do you know how long you were gone, sir? And do you realize how cold the Bay is, and how tricky the currents can be?"

Marston didn't feel like talking with this youngster but he managed a few polite words. Yes, he knew exactly what he was doing, he had never been in danger, there was nothing to worry about but he appreciated the ensign's concern.

During the brief conversation he had been pulling his clothing back on. He had purchased new shoes, as wide as he could find, to accommodate his newly altered feet. Even so, it was fiercely painful to force his feet into them.

He repeated his activities each night. The underwater creatures gradually grew accustomed to him, permitting him to approach ever more closely, permitting him to accompany them farther and farther from Port Chicago. It was clear to Marston that they communicated with one another, mainly by means of subtle gestures made with their broad, webbed, clawed hands. Marston inferred that they had a language as sophisticated and complex as any spoken by land-dwellers.

Now that he was affiliated with the Port Chicago base Marston had discontinued all contacts with his former associates in Berkeley. He did not worry about running into Aurelia Blenheim at the grocery as he now relied entirely on a diet of creatures he encountered during his nocturnal explorations of the Bay's waters.

He maintained a relationship with Lieutenant Keeler and though him with Captain Kinne, furnishing reports and recommendations as required of him. He resented every meeting he had to attend, every conversation he had to conduct; in fact, he found himself living for his submarine excursions and suffering through each hour he spent walking on land, breathing with his gradually atrophying lungs instead of his gills.

On Friday, July 14, Keeler demanded that Marston attend a meeting with Captain Kinne. Also present were two high-ranking officers, one from the Navy and the other from the Army, the latter with Army Air Force insignia on his uniform blouse, and the commanders of the Negro stevedoring gangs.

Captain Kinne's WAVE secretary, Jaspers, ushered Marston into the commanding officer's area. When the meeting participants were assembled they were joined by a pair of armed shore patrolmen and the doors securely locked.

"The bomb will arrive in forty-eight hours," the army officer announced. A major general's paired silver stars glittered on his uniform shoulders. "We will deliver it to the loading pier, then we need a sign-off from the Navy and our job is finished."

"And ours begins," the naval officer took over. His uniform sleeves bore the broad gold stripes of a rear admiral. "Captain Kinne, are your men ready to get the bomb stowed in *Quinalt Victory* Monday evening? ONI insists that we do the loading at night, but it must be finished in time to catch the late tide out of the Golden Gate." The admiral cast a sharp look at Marston. "Dr. Marston has provided all the information we'll need to get *Quinalt Victory* safely out of the Bay and on her way by midnight?"

The utterance was worded as a statement but spoken as a question.

"We have everything, sir," Keeler furnished.

"All right. Let's go over the complete plan again," The admiral growled. "There must be no slip-ups, I can't emphasize that too much."

They spent the rest of the day going over the details of unloading the special bomb from its railroad car and loading it into the hold of the *Quinalt Victory* without a hitch. A squad of white-jacketed mess-men served coffee and rolls at midmorning and a full meal at noon. No one left the meeting for any reason. Marston was able to pass up the coffee and rolls but by lunch time he was forced to consume a few sips of beverage and half a sandwich. This disgusted him.

When the meeting ended he drove into Port Chicago. He had seen the town fleetingly each day but today for the first time he parked his Cord and walked through the town. He found a motion picture theater and purchased a ticket. They were running a long program, the dramatic film *Lifeboat* with Tallulah Bankhead and Canada Lee, the lightweight *Bathing Beauty* with Esther Williams, a newsreel and a chapter of "Crash" Corrigan's old serial, *Undersea Kingdom.*

Once inside he settled into a seat and unlaced his shoes, finding a modicum of relief for his aching feet. He leaned back and studied the neon-ringed clock mounted high on one wall of the auditorium. Most of the patrons were servicemen in uniform, whiling away their off-duty hours. None of them were colored, of course. Negroes were excluded from the theater and from the town's plain restaurants. They had to find their own entertainment, or make it.

Marston ignored the images on the screen and closed his eyes. Images of undersea life swam through his mind, the peace and serenity of the submarine world contrasting with the pain and violence that dominated the world of the land-dwellers.

After a while he opened his eyes and glanced at the illuminated clock-face. Even in the long July evening, darkness would have fallen by now.

He drove back to the naval base, showed his pass to the gate-guard, and parked as near to the water's edge as he could. He carefully locked the Cord and walked to the base of the pier. A special guard had been placed there, and even Marston's special pass could not gain him access to the pier.

Instead he walked back to his car, unlocked the door and climbed inside. He disrobed, left the car again, and walked undiscovered to the edge of the Bay. He slipped into the Bay and swam away from the shore.

He made his way to the cold, flowing water that he knew came from the Sacramento River. The river water had less flavor than the Bay water. With a start Marston realized that he had never experienced the richness of the Pacific. He turned to swim with the current. His anticipation of the new experience filled him with an almost sexual excitement.

When he reached the submarine net at the mouth of San Francisco Bay he paused briefly, then pulled himself through it into the ocean. He was terrified but soon calmed himself. He had undergone a rite of passage, he felt, had experienced a sea change. He would explore farther in later days, he decided, but for now he felt emotionally drained and physically exhausted.

He turned and began the long swim back to Suisun Bay.

He had seen fewer of the human-like creatures than usual on this night, but as he approached Port Chicago they became more numerous. He was beginning to learn their language and felt eager to converse with them, find out who or what they were, but they kept their distance from him this night, and instead of joining them he continued on his solitary way.

In time he recognized the submerged landmarks that told him he was at his destination. He had been swimming along the sea bottom, insulated by fathoms of brackish water from the world of men, immune from the noisome companionship of air breathers and land dwellers. He rose slowly toward the top of the water. He was shocked as he breached to realize that he had spent the entire night under water. The brilliant sun now blasted down from a bright blue sky.

He made his way to his Cord, drove home and slept around the clock. He awoke Sunday morning and spent the day in seclusion, sustaining himself with alcohol and music. After dark he made his way to the nearby stream and stood in it, letting its waters soothe his feet. He went home and slept, dreaming once more of an undersea city, and rose late on Monday. He hadn't realized how far he had swum on Friday night, or how exhausted the effort had left him. Still, the experience had been an exhilarating one and he looked forward to spending even more time beneath the surface, to travelling farther into the ocean.

When he reached Port Chicago on Monday the transfer of the bomb from railroad freight car to the hold of *Quinalt Victory* was well under way. Marston's expertise had been of immense value, he would be told. He encountered Captain Kinne himself on the pier and the usually stern Kinne recognized him and thanked him for his assistance.

Powerful electric vapor-lights had been rigged to illuminate the operation once the sun had set and their peculiar glare gave the faces of the men on the pier, both white and colored, a ghostly look.

Marston walked to the end of the pier. When he turned back toward the center of activity he saw that all eyes were fixed on the delicate work at the *Quinalt Victory*. He checked his wristwatch and saw that it was ten o'clock. Bright moonlight was reflected off the surface of the Bay.

Instead of climbing down the ladder to the water's surface, Marston left his clothing in its usual neat pile, stood on the edge of the pier, and dived into the Bay. He swam to the seabed, taking delicious water in and passing it through his gills, letting his eyes grow accustomed to the faint phosphorescence that provided illumination in this world.

He turned to observe the hull of the *Quinalt Victory*. He was astonished at the number of human-like forms moving around the ship, gesturing meaningfully to one another, attaching something, something, to the metal hull of the *Quinalt Victory*.

Marston swam toward the ship, curious as to what the creatures were doing. This was the first time he had seen them using anything that looked like machinery. As he drew closer several of the creatures turned and swam toward him. As they approached he realized that they were like him in every way. The wide mouth and triangular teeth, the splayed limbs, the webbed hands and feet, the hooked claws, the oversized eyes and flattened noses.

How had he managed to pass among men until now? How had his alienness gone undetected? The scarf and dark glasses had helped but surely he would be caught out soon if he tried to continue his masquerade as human. He raised a hand and gestured, showing these aquatic beings that he was one of them, telling them in their own language, a language which he was just beginning to comprehend, that he was not a human, not a land-dweller.

He was not the enemy.

He was shocked by a brilliant flash from the *Quinalt Victory*, a glare that seemed as bright as the sun. Marston felt a shock wave, felt its unimaginable, crushing pressure as it reached him. Then, even before he could react, there was a second flash, this one brighter than a thousand suns, and a second shock wave infinitely greater than the first. But he felt it for only the most fleeting of moments, and then he felt nothing more.

Historic Note

At 10:20 PM, Monday, July 17, 1944, a huge explosion occurred at Port Chicago, California. Two ships were moored at the loading pier of the naval station there. The *E.A.Bryan* was fully loaded and ready to leave for the Pacific theater of operations with a huge cargo of high explosives and military equipment. The *Quinalt Victory*, a brand new vessel built at the Kaiser Shipyard in nearby Richmond, California, was preparing to take on its own cargo.

Some 320 individuals were killed in the explosion, most of them African-American stevedores. An additional 400 persons were injured. A common form of injury was blindness caused by flying splinters of window-glass in naval barracks. The main explosion was preceded by a rumble or smaller explosion, reports differing, which drew many off-duty stevedores to the windows to see what had caused the sound.

The brilliant flash, the roar of the explosion, and the shaking of the earth that resulted, were seen, heard, and felt as far away as the cities of Berkeley, Oakland, and San Francisco.

The *Bryan*, the *Quinalt Victory*, the loading pier, the railroad spur running along the pier, and the ammunition train that was parked on the pier at the time, were all totally destroyed. The town of Port Chicago was obliterated and a visitor to its site today will find only a few forlorn street markers to show where once a community thrived.

While official statements about the disaster aver only to the high explosives which had been loaded in the *E.A.Bryan*, critics in later years suggested that the explosion was nuclear in nature. In the summer of 1944 the atomic bomb was top secret and the very existence of the Manhattan Project was shrouded in layers of security. But once the bomb was dropped on Hiroshima and Nagasaki, speculation began that more than dynamite had been involved in the Port Chicago disaster.

If the Port Chicago explosion was indeed nuclear in nature, further speculation is divided between those who believe the explosion was accidental in origin, or was in fact a test by the United States government to measure the effects of a nuclear bomb. Certainly the weapons base at Port Chicago would have made a fine test subject, with ships, a railroad spur, temporary and permanent buildings, and many hundreds of expendable human subjects.

Perhaps the Port Chicago explosion was a nuclear accident. If so, it represented a major setback to the American nuclear weapons project. The successful Alamogordo test did not take place until July 16, 1945, one day short of a year after the Port Chicago explosion. Nuclear weapons were exploded in the air over Hiroshima and Nagasaki the following month, bringing about the end of the Second World War and providing an object lesson for Josef Stalin.

Where the Port Chicago naval weapons depot once stood, there is now the Concord Naval Weapons Station, a major loading area for the United States Pacific Fleet. The storage of nuclear weapons in barrow-like bunkers at the naval weapons station, while not officially acknowledged by the US government, is one of the most ill-kept secrets of our era.

This is the oldest story in the present collection, written in the late 1960s when I was employed by the International Business Machines Corporation and living in a classic "company town" some miles north of New York City. It was a time of great turmoil in this country, a period that tried the consciences of millions of citizens even though they lived comfortable lives far from the war zone and even though they were not themselves the victims of political oppression. I was one of those citizens. For the title of the story I am indebted to my son Thomas Daniel Lupoff.

A Freeway for Draculas

How it started David Starke never knew. He rose and shaved, Bertha brought him coffee, balancing the delicate china cup and saucer in her plump hands, and he drank it. He pulled on his white broadcloth shirt, knotted his maroon J. Press tie, tugged once at the bottom of his gray suit jacket and left the house.

It was no different from any other morning, five mornings each week, forty-nine weeks each year.

He bent his stocky body and picked up the newspaper from his lawn. Without removing the rubber band that held it furled, he glanced at a few headlines: war, scandal, repression. He tossed the paper over his shoulder so it landed at the front door for Bertha to read later.

No different from other mornings.

At the end of the driveway he stopped, glanced at his watch to see how long before Rolly Poletsky's little electric Fiat would roll up for him. It was Rolly's turn to drive. Starke's watch said 8:24—Rolly would arrived in two minutes as he did every alternate morning, regular as clockwork.

As Starke dropped his hand the crystal of his watch caught the sun at an odd angle, reflecting the light into Starke's eyes. For a moment he staggered at the brightness, then stood blinking at the oddly colored afterimage that quivered momentarily on his retinas, expanding and contracting as it slowly faded.

He steadied himself against the mailbox, rubbed one hand against his eyes, then ran it through his thick, wavy hair and laughed. He glanced up the street, saw the light green of the Fiat and began to step forward.

Then he blinked. The Fiat was gone.

No explosion, no blinding flash—the pulsing afterimage of the glare in Starke's eyes did not recur. He stepped out into the little-used residential street to see if Poletsky had made a sudden and unexpected turn into one of the driveways feeding from the street, and as he did so the green Fiat drove into view, rounding the gentle curve a few hundred yards from Starke's house.

Starke shook his head and studied the little car as it purred smoothly to a stop a few feet from him. He leaned over as Poletsky reached across the cockpit and unlatched the passenger's door from the inside.

"Strangest thing," Starke said as he eased himself into the black leather bucket. He slammed the door shut.

"What's that?" Poletsky asked.

Starke laughed uneasily. "Strangest thing," he repeated. "I was standing next to the mailbox waiting for you the way I always do and I could have sworn I saw your car driving up."

Poletsky snorted. "I don't see what's strange about that. I *was* arriving. No?"

"Well, that's not quite it, Rolly. I'd looked at my watch and you weren't due for a couple of minutes. Then I saw your car, and then it was gone."

"Disappeared?"

"No. I mean, not in a puff of smoke or anything, it just wasn't there any more. And then—a couple of seconds later it was back again, coming around the curve." Starke felt himself pressed back into the bucket seat as Poletsky pressed down on the accelerator and the little car moved quickly forward.

"Upset about it?" Poletsky asked. He shot a concerned glance sideways at Starke, lines appearing in his slim, pale face.

Starke said, "I guess not." For a moment there was only the gentle hum of the little car, the crunch of its tires rolling along on the cold gravel of the bare winter street. "I just don't understand it," Starke said. "It was so odd. But I feel all right now." He stared through the windshield, took off his thick-framed glasses and studied them as if they might contain an explanation, put them back on and gazed, distracted, at the gray overcast sky.

They rolled through the little shopping center and Poletsky swung the Fiat onto the service road, ready to head for 909 and the run toward the computer works.

"Come on, David," Poletsky said, "don't let it get you down. Here—" he reached past David's knee and punched the ON button of the sports car's Blaupunkt FM receiver. As the radio snapped to instant life he said, "See what you can get, will you? It's been as bad as AM lately. I think going to throw it out altogether and get a tape rig for the car."

"Oh, sure, Rolly," Starke said, called back to the reality of the Fiat. The car's quad speakers were blaring the strains of Bach's Seventh Brandenburg Concerto as performed on an ARP synthesizer. Starke punched a news button and the synthesizer gave way to a low-interest loan commercial. He punched again and a network news broadcast replaced the ad.

"Okay," Poletsky said.

They were stopped at the freeway entrance, waiting for a break in the morning rush-hour traffic. Starke used the momentary halt of the car to fine-up the tuning of the FM set. The news was a standard Pentagon spokesman tape: so many missions by American aircraft against aggressive guerrilla forces designed to assure the survival of a peace-loving democratic regime, etc., etc.

"I'll be pleased when they get that automatic traffic channel on the air," David said. "Morning news it too much for me to take some days."

"You take it seriously," Poletsky said. "There's nothing you can do about it, is there? So why let it get you down?"

The announcer had finished the war bulletins and was turning to other topics, mostly more government handouts on improvements in environmental regulations. A high administration spokesman, the smooth voice was assuring its listeners, had told the industrial leaders that the President would not let idealistic concerns for a few bugs and weeds interfere with the economic well-being of the nation.

"Take it seriously?" Starke reacted. "We both work for the same outfit, Rolly. Don't you think that all the talent that goes into our products could do something to help the situation? Don't we have a responsibility for what we create? Couldn't you grow these integrated circuit crystals for something better than weapons-control systems? Couldn't I design programs for something more constructive than government surveillance files? I mean—" He let his sentence fade out as the highway condition report finally began.

Freeways all the way from their present location to the computer works were crowded but flowing smoothly. Starke let the droning, surrounding voice fill the car while his eyes, bored with the sight of freeway traffic through the Fiat's windscreen, slowly rose to gaze, distracted, at the dully glowing sky.

Far ahead, over the downtown area, formations of long silvery shapes with huge tailfins swept silently across the sky. They came in herringbone rows, bright swept-back wings defining the relationship of one to another. High, high they were, barely distinguishable against the silver overcast.

The radio voice droned in the Fiat's cockpit; the hum of its mechanism and the gentle shushing of its tires against the freeway surface made a hypnotic wall of background noise. The aerial titans seemed almost to be standing stationary over the city, their arrangement in swept-back triangles led Starke's eyes through a dull iteration of their geometry: three aircraft placed at the apexes of an equilateral formation, and three groups of aircraft arranged to state the angles of a meta-formation. Three threes of three forming a meta-meta-formation.

The Fiat sped ahead, Poletsky intent on the freeway and the cars around his own, Starke staring distracted at the aircraft. Tiny specks of black seemed to fall from their bellies.

"Rolly," Starke heard himself saying, "they don't use those old B-52s any more, do they?"

"Huh?" Poletsky responded. "No, I think they junked the last few a couple of years ago. Why?"

Starke turned to face Poletsky. "Because there are some—" He looked back, trying to get a fix on the formation above the city.

"I thought—I could have sworn—" He leaned forward, bracing both his hands against the dashboard above the FM radio dial.

Poletsky's voice broke into his examination of the sky. "Are you sure you're all right, David?"

"Yes. I mean—" He stared at the sky, trying to see anything besides the gray wintry overcast. His neck felt very stiff and he leaned back in his seat; rubbed his neck with one hand.

"I could have sworn I saw a formation of B-52s over the city."

"Were they doing anything?"

Starke took off his glasses again, rubbed the bridge of his nose between thumb and forefinger. With his eyes still shut, the pressure of his fingers making vague red patterns swirl inside his eyelids, he answered. "It looked as if—as if they were dropping bombs on the city," he whispered.

Poletsky was silent. He reached across Starke and punched the music button on the FM receiver. The sounds of a Vaughan Williams symphony, its tones a tapestry of restraint, came from the speakers.

"Sounds like the *Antarctica,*" Poletsky said. "Only two channels, they must have an ancient recording."

They drove along unspeaking, the notes of the orchestra filling the Fiat. "Yeah," Poletsky resumed, "that's the Seventh okay. Bet it's the old Adrian Boult recording."

"They wouldn't be bombing the city, would they?" Starke said. "I mean, there are no more B-52s anyway, and if there were they wouldn't be bombing *us.*"

Poletsky said, "It's worth having only two channels to hear real instruments instead of synthesizers, don't you think?"

"Besides, they'd have a bulletin on the radio."

"Some of those old performances have never been equaled. We're lucky they still exist, even in simple stereo."

Poletlsky hit the turn signal and edged the Fiat into the freeway's exit lane.

Starke took a last look ahead of the car, toward the city, just before the Fiat rolled onto the exit ramp and down toward the service road. There was a moment of dazzling brilliance ahead, then a series of secondary flashes, and a huge glowing cloud began to rise over the city.

The Fiat dived onto the service road, Poletsky pulling it skillfully into an opening between a huge Ford station wagon and a snappy Volvo 1800. Starke gripped the little courtesy handhold over the Blaupunkt. The afterimage of the flashes pulsed and faded in double exposure with the square tailgate of the Ford wagon. His ears rang, a muffled roar rising from somewhere inside his chest. Steadying himself on the handhold he twisted in his seat to look at Poletsky.

The Ford wagon pulled up at a stop sign where the freeway service road fed back into a commercial street; Poletsky braked the Fiat to a halt behind the Ford. Poletsky turned toward Starke. "What's the matter, David?"

Starke said, "Didn't you see it—see the sky?"

"I've been concentrating on the road. What was it?" He leaned forward, craned his neck to look straight up. "I don't see anything."

The Ford pulled away, turning into heavy street traffic. Poletsky followed, heading toward the computer works.

Starke punched the news button on the radio. A woman's voice was describing an international conference on abortion. He punched another button, got a commercial for an air filtration system, tried the news again, then gave up and turned back to the Williams symphony.

"Why—you didn't," he stammered, "you didn't see anything. And there's no bulletin on the radio."

"David, what is it?"

"I must be—there must really be something the matter with me. If I see things that nobody else can see, I mean,"

"Oh, come on. This isn't a horror movie."

Starke removed his grip from the handhold in the Fiat, forced himself to lean back in his seat. Poletsky said nothing more. Starke closed his eyes and let the flowing texture of the Williams symphony fill his mind. A horror movie, he was acting foolish. Next thing he'd be seeing monsters.

He felt himself sway sideways as Poletsky pulled the Fiat out of the last traffic lane and up to the gate of the computer works. Starke watched him as he braked the little car at the guard station, reached into his jacket pocket and pulled out his identification badge. Starke did the same and leaned across the car to show the badge to the security guard.

The face of the guard, leaning down to peer at the badges through the car window, was a pale, cold white tinged slightly with a fungus-like green. Black shaggy hair was chopped off in a crude bang over his forehead, partially covering the terrible scar that ran from scalp to eyebrow. The guard's eyes glimmered with a terrible animal redness; a thin line of spittle hung from his narrow lips.

Pulling away from the car to stand upright again, the guard waved with one hand and said, "Pass right in, sir."

As the Fiat pulled away from the guard station Starke glanced back at the guard. Two small electrodes, their metallic finish shimmering in the brightly overcast morning, protruded from his neck.

In the reserved parking lot Poletsky pulled the little Fiat into a narrow space between two Detroit sedans and climbed out. Starke followed suit, slamming the door shut behind him. He stood still for a moment, the bright electrodes pulsing in afterimage. He stayed himself with a hand on the car's roof.

"David?" Poletsky said.

"Oh, uh, thanks for the tide, Rolly. I'll see you back here after closing, okay?"

"Are you sure you're okay?"

David shook his head, "Something odd but I'll be all right. Thanks."

He watched Poletsky stride across the parking lot and disappear into the engineering development wing of the building. Starke took a deep breath and walked toward the entrance of the programming center. Just outside the building he checked his wristwatch against the clock in the commercial tower across the street. There was no peculiar reflection this time and he pushed the twin glass doors open and walked in.

On the second floor of the programming center he stopped at the automatic vending machine, bought a cup of coffee, nodded a good morning to Angie Turner at her central secretarial station and walked into his own two-man office. He closed the door behind him, put his cardboard cup carefully on his desk blotter and hung his coat on the corner rack.

He looked at the worker at the other desk, already immersed in stacks of computer printouts, felt-marker-scrawl-covered manuals, typewritten sheets and electrostatic copies. The other man looked slowly at Starke, pulled at his beard with his dirty fingernails, and drawled, "Hi there, Starke. How goes it?"

At least Marston looked normal! But then so had Rolly and so had Angie, hugely overweight, stuffed into clothes that might have looked chic on a woman sixty pounds lighter and fifteen years younger. And Marston—slovenly, unkempt, the only employee Starke knew who didn't at least come near to the image of the bright professionals climbing through the hierarchy of the computer works—Marston looked no different than usual. Why had the security guard looked like a—Starke almost let go an incoherent exclamation—like a Hollywood film monster?

"Oh, it's, uh, okay I guess," David managed to blurt out.

"What's that?" Marston asked.

"Didn't you ask me how I was?" Starke replied.

Marston looked at him puzzledly. "That was five minutes ago, pal. When it looked like you weren't going to answer me I went back to work."

Starke held onto his desk with both hands. "Sorry," he said. "I guess I was distracted. I feel a little odd today."

"'s okay," said Marston. He turned back to his papers, reached into a lower desk drawer and pulled out a battered pipe.

Starke pulled a computer printout from his own *in* tray, flipped past the heading information and began to study the overnight machine printout on his new sort-and-retrieve model, series 10, Sarm-X. At last there had been a good machine run, he should be able to able to complete his development level study and begin a project report, with Marston doing the tech writing and documentation half of the job.

Funny, thought Starke, his forehead on one hand as he scanned the columns of machine print. Funny that a man like Mel Marston should reach his place in the world, a documentation specialist in the computer works where all the others followed the corporate model by keeping their personal grooming neat as a pin, their manners sober as a judge, their dress conservative as a Nixon.

Marston looked a mess, showed more interest in poetry than in technical writing, was known as an off-hours drinker and didn't even put much vehemence into his denial when someone suggested that he was a pot-smoker. Yet, somehow, he had advanced to a responsible and well-paid position. Probably on the basis of sheer talent and competence, but it never ceased to leave Starke wondering.

He turned his attention back to the computer printout before him. The sort-and-retrieve program seemed to be working fairly well on the test information provided. An old company telephone directory sequenced by extension numbers. The calling sequence of the test specified abstracting all employees with six-, eight-, or eleven-digit last names beginning in consonants from L to Z, then alphabetizing the names and printing them out.

Starke began to check the names: LANDOR L E / LAPTIPPE F T / LAZZARRA A J / LEACHPIT R P / LEACHPIT J F / LUTHER F X . . . wait a minute! LEACHPIT R P before LEACHPIT J F? The alphabetizing routine seemed to be shutting off after the surname, not continuing through the initials, else how could LEACHPIT R P come before LEACHPIT J F?

Starke reached for the telephone to check out the discrepancy with the linkage generator group in the next corridor, then decided to talk it over first with Mel Marston. He dropped the phone receiver back onto its cradle and said, "Mel?"

The only reply was a muffled, "Mph."

Starke turned to look at Marston. Marston's collar-length hair had grown the better part of a foot, flowing wildly over his shoulders. It was held away from his face by a woven, bead-decorated headband, a huge turquoise peacock feather rising from the middle of Marston's forehead.

His small moustache and Vandyke had sprouted into a bushy, patriarchal beard.

His rumpled button-down shirt and tie had disappeared, replaced by a multicolored billowing blouse of some gossamer material over which hung a rawhide vest decorated with silver and blue jewels and leather fringes.

The blackened pipe that Marston habitually smoked at his desk had been transformed into a Persian hookah, its bottom a bubbling globe of water, its top an elaborate hammered brass bowl filled with slowly charring shreds of something that Starke *knew* was not tobacco.

Marston turned to face Starke. He held a flexible tube toward him, one end connected to the hookah, the other ending in an ivory mouthpiece. As he leaned toward Starke he said, "Om."

Starke gasped, shut his eyes as tightly as he could, pressed the heels of both hands to his temples and ground his teeth together. He held the posture for seconds while the syllable faded from his ears.

Then it came again, only instead of "Om" it sounded more like "Hum," in Marston's voice, delivered with the usual drawl, but with a questioning inflection on its end.

Starke opened his eyes, turned toward Marston, prepared for the sight of the bizarrely arrayed apparition he had just seen. Marston was back at his desk, his hair back to its usual length, his costume back to its rumpled but relatively conventional composition, the pipe in his hand its old self, the odor of tobacco permeating the air of the small office.

"Mel?" Starke said.

"What is it, Davey?"

"Why, I was going to show you these test run results but for a moment you . . ."

Marston waited, then when Starke didn't resume, said, "For a moment I what?"

"You just looked a little odd, that's all."

"Come on, Starke, you're always after me about the old company tie and the old company white shirt. You know I'm not interested in that stuff."

"Not what I meant, Mel. I mean you . . ." Again, Starke was unable to complete the sentence.

"Here, old chum, you'd better get it together a little more. Relax." Marston pulled out his bottom desk drawer, drew a brown bag from it, pulled out a Thermos bottle.

He trundled his chair toward Starke's desk, unscrewed the stopper from the bottle and reached to refill Starke's coffee cup. "Don't see how you can drink that machine stuff anyhow," he drawled. "But then I never did understand you computer people no way." Marston laughed.

"Thanks," Starke said. He lifted his cup, sniffed the steam rising from it, and shot an odd glance at Marston. "There isn't brandy in this stuff, is there?" he asked.

Marston shot back a look of mock surprise. "My innocence is deeply offended, sir. We are all thoroughly familiar with the company drinking policy."

Starke sipped at the coffee. "If this isn't spiked then I've never tasted alcohol."

"Even the walls have ears," Marston said, turning slowly to study the perimeter of the room.

Starke shut his eyes until the thought went away.

"But look, Davey, you really seem upset. Is it that dumb Sarm-X program? You really shouldn't let a little thing like a program bug get to you, you know."

"No, it's—something else. All morning I've been having—ah—odd things have been happening," Starke finished weakly.

"I don't know what you mean."

Starke pulled a fresh linen handkerchief from his pocket and wiped his brow. He removed his glasses and began painstakingly to clean them, first the left lens, then the right, then the left again and the right again.

"Om," said Marston; Starke looked quickly at him, saw the peacock-feather headband, the decorated vest. Or thought that he did, only fuzzily, with his spectacles in his hands. He slipped them back on, looked directly at Marston.

"Hm," said Marston, his tie slightly askew and his pastel, button -down-collar shirt rumpled as usual. "Hm, I don't think I quite understand what you mean, ah, by odd things happening. Sweet Angela didn't jump up and buss you on the way in this morning, did she?"

Starke felt his hands beginning to shake. A drop of cold sweat ran down the side of his neck. "I—I—"

"Say," Marston drawled, "do you want me to take you to the dispensary? Is it—are you sick?"

"I don't know. Maybe if I could—"

"How about Wally? You want me to talk to the boss? Maybe you ought to check out for the day, go home and rest."

"No, it's—no, I have to work on Sarm-X, the deadline is almost here, we have to have the model running before the quarterly budget conference. I—Marston, tell me the truth."

"Of course."

"Latch the door first, will you?"

"Sure, David." Marston took the few steps to the door and flicked the security switch. "This is all mighty mysterious."

"You're a good deal younger than I am, Mel, and I think you're from a different school. More adventurous, less bound by tradition, willing to try anything."

"Not quite anything, but—"

"What I mean is, ah—" He stopped. Took off his glasses and wiped his forehead with a handkerchief again, then put his glasses back on. "I mean, with all the talk about drugs these past few years, I've never asked you if you've used them because it really isn't my business, but, ah—"

"Yes?"

"Mel, what do you know about things like, ah, LSD?"

"Oh, why lysergic acid diethylamide, discovered April 19, 1943, by a chemist named Albert Hoffman—"

"That's not what I mean."

"Oh. Sorry, Dave, that's the only LSD that I've ever heard of. Maybe there's another."

"No, that's the one I mean, the drug. I mean—I mean, ah, Mel, have you ever, ah, taken, ah—"

"The term is *dropped,* Dave, and I'm afraid when you ask me that, you're asking me if I've ever committed a felony, and I can hardly say yes to that, so suppose you ask me something else."

"What I mean is, ah, LSD is supposed to cause hallucinations."

"I've read the literature. It does say that, yes."

"Well, don't be angry, Mel, but that coffee—you poured some for me yesterday and I thought it had a little funny taste."

"The literature says LSD has no flavor. Or so I've read."

"Don't play games, Mel. This is a serious matter!" Starke was sweating heavily now. His glasses had been steamed by the coffee Marston poured for him. He whipped them off and used them to point directly at the younger man. "I want to know if you put any of that stuff in the coffee you gave me. I don't care what you want to smoke or drink or stick in your veins, but I don't want anybody, ah, anybody—"

"I think the term you're looking for is dosing you, Dave. It has been known to happen, but most folks consider it unethical." He drew out the last word, giving each syllable separate emphasis. "I would never do such a thing. Assuming that I had any of that stuff to start with, of course, which I haven't said I do."

"Well, I, ah—"

Marston said, "I give you my word, David. I've never dosed anyone in my life. Maybe I do put a tiny drop of brandy in the java some mornings, but that's the utter limit of it! Look!" And he put the Thermos to his lips and drank.

"That doesn't prove anything," Starke said, "but I'll take your word. All right, then I wasn't drugged. Then what's going on?"

Marston re-stoppered the Thermos, slipped it into his bag and put it in his desk. "You tell me, David. Is it all right if I unlock the door now?"

"I'm not sure. Oh, unlock it, certainly. I mean, I'm not sure what's going on. I was—this morning I thought I saw Rolly Poletsky's car before it arrived at my house."

"Trivial."

"And there were B-52s over the city."

"Oh?"

"And then the security man at the main gate—"

"What about him?"

"He was—he was—" Starke gulped once, "I could have sworn that he was Boris Karloff."

"Dead for years."

"In his Frankenstein make-up."

"Come off it, Davey."

"And then when I looked at you before I could have sworn you were dressed like some kind of hippie."

"I don't go for the white shirt dark suit thing but I'd hardly call these clothes hippie," Marston said, holding his fingertips to his shirtfront.

"No, I know you're not dressed any different from usual," Starke said. He looked at Marston. "You're dressed the way you always dress. But you *looked* different."

"Man, you're seeing things."

"That's what I'm trying to tell you. I can't figure out why. I thought maybe you had, ah, *dosed* me with LSD," he said. He felt uncomfortable using the unfamiliar term.

"Nope."

"Then I guess I'm just cracking up!" Starke put his head into his hands. "I'm just cracking up. I don't know why, I haven't been under any unusual strain, I *feel* normal. At least I felt normal until this morning. Now, all of a sudden, hallucinations. Why?"

"Not Sarm-X? Problems at home? Getting along okay with Wally Cheng?"

"None of these things. At least, I don't think it's any of them.

I—I just don't know."

"Well, I'm afraid I can't do much for you right now, old friend." Marston, standing, gave Starke's should a friendly squeeze. "I've got one of those ridiculous meetings of all the documentation people. Wally asked me to give 'em a pep talk on the use of the subjunctive in discussing possible program errors, exciting stuff like that. Look, that's scheduled to break up by noon. You want to have lunch together? We can eat in the cafeteria or go out into the real world and grab something at Enzo's or at the Golden Garter."

Starke stared straight ahead, silently.

"How about it, David?"

He shook himself back from the moment of fugue. "Uh, yes, thanks a lot. I mean, uh, sure, I think it would be a good idea. To get away for a little while, that is."

Marston picked up a clipboard from which flapped a mass of yellow-lined notepaper and left the room.

Starke worked over the Sarm-X test results the rest of the morning, receiving a few phone calls, making a couple. He looked at his wristwatch every few minutes. He felt jumpy and worried, but managed to keep his mind on the programming project and experienced no further hallucinations.

At twelve o'clock Marston walked back into the office, dropping his clipboard on top of the cluttered desk. The clatter jolted Starke alert. "Aargh!" said Marston. "Maybe those people know something about data processing, but how they ever got past junior high school without learning to write a simple sentence is beyond me."

He slumped into his chair, then sprang upright. "Come on, Dave, let's go scarf down some grub."

They made it outside and into the chill winter noontime. The sky was gray and a light sprinkling of snowflakes was falling. Starke wished he had worn his topcoat that morning. He and Marston broke into a trot as they crossed the company parking lot. When they crossed the security guard's booth Starke steeled himself and cast a look at the guard: he was an ordinary man, middle-aged, black, with a neatly trimmed moustache and a neatly pressed olive uniform.

Across the street from the computer works the red and blue

electric sign in Enzo's front window flashed on and off, throwing long, rippled reflections across the blacktop roadway wet with melting snow. Inside the restaurant Starke blew out the cold, wet air of the short walk from the programming center and drew in the warm, organic odors of wood and leather, hot food and human bodies.

They took the only empty booth in the room, nodding to other workers taking their lunch away from the computer works, ordered sandwiches for their meal. Starke called for coffee to go with his. Marston ordered beer.

"You just love to flaunt your independence, don't you, Mel?" Starke said to him.

Marston grinned a self-satisfied grin. "I figure, they pay me to edit a bunch of stuff and to write a little of my own. I figure, as long as I do a good job, they have no gripe with me, and any time I do a bad job, they can squawk."

Starke shook his head and sipped black, steaming coffee.

For ten minutes they munched silently on their sandwiches; Starke deliberately let his vision fall into a steady, almost hypnotic pulsation along with the neon flashes: red, blue, red, blue. The room was cozy and familiar. For the first time since leaving home that morning he began to feel comfortable and relaxed.

Again his mood was broken by Marston. "Figuring out your little puzzles, David?"

"Huh? Oh, no, I wasn't really thinking about anything."

"You really surprise me, you know? There are brigades of weirdos in this business, God knows, but you've always struck me as totally stable—the last guy I'd expect to flip out."

Starke did not answer.

"Not that you're exactly running berserk, pal."

Starke laughed bitterly. "You're right about that. I always thought I'd come to work one morning and hear that you'd been carted away. Never thought *I* would! But I—" He made a helpless, appealing gesture with both his hands "—I *feel* perfectly normal. A little nervous about the whole thing, but I'm in control of myself, my thought processes seem normal, I'm not in a state of schizophrenic confusion or anything, I'm not frothing or screaming or attacking anybody with a knife."

He picked up the sharp, wooden-handled knife beside his plate, held it for a moment, then dropped it handle first to the wooden table top.

"I mean, can you be crazy," he paused, "in just one very particular way, like seeing hallucinations, and be perfectly normal in every other regard? Maybe I had a stroke. Maybe I ought to go to the doctor."

Marston replied, "If you think so. You don't seem crazy to me, though." He reached inside his jacket and pulled out a packet of cigarettes. "You still off tobacco?"

Starke nodded.

Marston lit a cigarette. "Look, maybe if you try and think back to each, ah, anomaly, you'll be able to see a pattern in them. Do you think so?"

Starke considered. "Well, I was standing in the street waiting for Rolly and I saw him driving up. Or I thought I saw him. Then his car disappeared and actually arrived a minute later."

"So you just anticipated what actually happened, right?"

Starke nodded. "The second thing," he said, "was in the car. I looked up in the sky and I thought I saw bombers over the city, then I thought I saw the city being destroyed."

Marston held a cigarette before himself and concentrated on its glowing tip. "Hmm. That sounds completely different. We know the city wasn't destroyed, we'd certainly have found that out by now. And there probably weren't even any bombers. Back at the office you said they were B-52s and there aren't any more B-52s."

Starke nodded. "Okay, I'll buy that. Then what happened?"

Marston grinned. "I-da-know," he drawled, "maybe if you try and remember what you were doing or thinking just before you saw them."

Starke rubbed his face, reconstructing the moment in Poletsky's Fiat. "Rolly was driving," he said, "we had the radio on. There was a Vaughan Williams symphony, I think, then we got some news. They were talking about the war, about bombing the enemy, and then—" he looked at Marston, startled. "Is that it? Did I see the war? Or—what?"

Marston shrugged.

"All right. The third thing. We pulled into the company parking lot. I looked at the guard and he was Frankenstein."

Marston laughed again. "I'm sorry, no connection with anything?"

Starke considered. "It's really hard to remember." He picked up his coffee cup. It was empty except for a small, cold residue in the bottom. He drank even the dregs. "Just before we arrived at the gate I was talking to Rolly about seeing the bombing. He thought I was silly. He said that—" Starke brought his empty cup down on the saucer hard, sending a spoon clanking and clattering onto the floor. Two or three customers at Enzo's bar turned around to stare.

"Mel," Starke said, "Rolly thought I was just foolish. He accused me of seeing horror movies."

"Ahah! And then you did see one." He rubbed his hands together. "Now we're getting somewhere! And was there anything else?"

Starke put both hands to his face. "One more," he said. "In the office, I didn't tell you this. I had just arrived. I was looking at the Sarm-X test and I was going to show it to you. Before I did I thought about you for a second, wondered how a hippie like you could make it in the computer works, and when I looked at you, you *were* a hippie. You were dressed weirdly, you had long hair, and your pipe had turned into a hookah and you were smoking pot."

Marston slapped the table with both hands and roared with amusement. "Old hippie Mel! Not quite, friend. But that's all right, in fact that's just fine, that caps it. Don't you see the pattern?"

"No. I—what?"

"Why, you're up so close to it, you can't see the forest for the trees. Listen. First you were waiting for Rolly, thinking he was about due, then you saw him right?"

"Then you heard about the war on the radio, you were thinking about bombing, and you I *saw* bombing.

"Then Poletsky said you were seeing horror movies, and you thought about that, and then you saw Frankenstein.

"Finally, you thought I was a hippie, you looked at me, and you saw—what, beads and feathers, that stuff, right?"

Starke nodded, yes, yes, yes.

"Well then, first you *think* about a thing. Then you *see* it. It's that simple."

Starke inhaled with a hiss, suddenly aware that he had been holding his breath while Marston spoke. "So I'm just thinking about a thing, then I see it? But why? What's the trigger? And why is it happening to me?"

Marston shrugged. "Search me. Everybody must have a bunch of images in his head—stray thoughts, fragments of recollections, notions conjured by all sorts of external stimuli, full-fledged fantasies."

"Sure, of course. But these are externalized. Look, Mel, you can tell the difference between thinking about, oh, having the Chairman of the Board pull up a chair and join us for lunch . . . and *actually* having him walk in that door, come over to our booth here, and sit down. No matter how vivid your thought was, you could still distinguish it from a real *occurrence*. You see? But if your theory is right, I *can't* tell the difference. That's what's happening to me."

"It isn't happening now, is it?"

Starke thought for a few seconds. "No. Everything is normal." He picked up his empty coffee cup, peered sadly at its dry bottom, and put it back down. "What I mean is, everything *seems* normal. You know, once you start to have your doubts . . ."

"No. What?"

"Mel—how do I know that I'm not still sitting upstairs waiting for you to get back from that editorial lecture? For that matter, how do I know that I'm not still at home and the whole day's been a dream?"

Marston stood up and began wrapping a striped scarf around his throat. "Sure, David, that's the classic dilemma. There's no logic to counter it any more than there is to knock down the old solipsist paradox. In fact, it's really just solipsism turned around. All the reality you know is what you can see. Or feel, taste, whatever. You don't know that I'm really real, I don't know that you're really real.

We all just have to take one another on faith and keep on truckin' if you know what I mean. Right?"

Starke assented dubiously.

"Come on, Dave. We'd better get back across the street."

Outside Enzo's the snow was still falling. The sky was darker now, the snowflakes heavier and thicker. A coating was beginning to accumulate on the sidewalks and the street. The automobiles in the computer works's parking lot were crusted over with white.

But the security man at the gate was still human, Starke noted gratefully, and inside the programming center everything seemed as usual.

He spent the afternoon conferring with the development programmers assigned to Sarm-X, going over the test data from the previous night's run. Marston sat in on the meeting, representing the documentation area.

The sort turn-off problem, it appeared, could be easily corrected in the next version of the program. Once the system was performing all functions according to specs they could bring their attention to improving performance time and trying to cut down on memory utilization.

It was a good meeting and actually ended before the scheduled quitting time for the day, a rare happening at the computer works.

On his way to the exit Starke passed the office of his boss, Wally Cheng, and stopped to mention the results of the Sarm-X meeting. Angie Turner wasn't at her desk outside Cheng's office. Thinking of Cheng's Oriental coolness and the amusing contrast of Angie's overweight attempts at glamour, Starke knocked once on Cheng's door, heard a calm, "Come in," and opened the door.

For only an instant he saw Cheng garbed as a mandarin in silken cap and robe, Angie beside him wearing a high-slit *cheongsam,* Chinese writing brush poised over a sheet of parchment.

Starke leaned heavily against the doorjamb and shut his eyes. There was a rushing sound in his ears and he felt weak.

"Dave?" said Wally Cheng.

Starke opened his eyes. Cheng was seated at his desk in his usual herringbone suit and white shirt. Angie Turner, in the same outfit she'd worn that morning, was holding a brown wooden pencil and a stenographer's pad half covered with shorthand notes.

"Uh—just felt odd for a minute," Starke said. "I was going to bring you up to date on the Sarm-X thing."

Fifteen minutes later he was back in the passenger seat of Rolly Poletsky's green Fiat. On the way back home on 909 they made some small talk, then David turned on the Blaupunkt and found a station carrying the soothing melodies of Schubert's Fourth, the pleasantly ill-named *Tragic.*

In front of Starke's house Poletsky stopped the Fiat. "I won't try the driveway tonight, Dave. The snow looks too slippery for me to get back up. You be able to get your car out tomorrow?"

Starke already had his hand on the door switch. "Nothing to worry about," he said, "local guy runs a private plowing service, solid as a rock. I'll pick you up in the morning."

He stood and watched the little car round the corner, then made his way back to his house and Bertha.

That night, lying in the big double bed, he moaned and dreamed, reaching that half-awake state of knowing he was dreaming, being able to assess his own visions, yet not breaking from them into full wakefulness.

His strange malady did not disappear with the night's rest. Instead it spread, like a virulent plague, striking first his wife, his closest friends and coworkers at the programming center. Then it moved onward into successive waves as circles of acquaintances passed the infection on to their own companions.

Everywhere the mental fantasies of the stricken appeared, externalized. Daily the number, the concentration, the variety of images grew greater.

Public places became filled with wild beasts of all eras; wolves and snakes, condors and tyrannosaurs; and imaginary creatures: gryphons, unicorns, chimerae, basilisks, monstrous sandworms. Marilyn Monroe walked the streets, jostling a group of Beatles, a brigade of John F. Kennedys, an army of Jesuses.

Not only did any figure appear when summoned by the fleeting thought of a mind: the same figure could be conjured up in endlessly replicated images by a single thinker or by any number independently. For not only did each person conjure his own fantasies, now the fantasies of all coexisted, intermixing in a common conjoined reality.

Before long the thronging figures began to overcrowd all available space. A whole section of the municipal airport was filled with invoked images of the *Spirit of St. Louis,* of the infamous *Air Force One,* of the tragically remembered *Enola Gay.* Sports fans filled the giant stadium with Joe DiMaggios, Jim Thorpes, Jack Dempseys.

An entire jungle sprang up, populated by endless varied versions of Tarzan.

The sky was filled for an entire afternoon with muscular figures in variously colored costumes as a group of comic-book enthusiasts exchanged recollections of their respective favorites.

When an old Bela Lugosi film turned up at a revival showing, the theater was miraculously transformed into a huge, shadowy castle; a freeway leading to its creaking gate was filled with hundreds of caped and fanged images crowding to join the audience.

With a start David awoke.

He reached out and placed his hand on the figure of Bertha lying beside him in the bed. Somehow the familiar sensation of her skin beneath his hand seemed altered.

He switched on the bedside lamp and the room was flooded with a startling, pulsing, emerald hue.

He jumped from the bed, flung open the bathroom door, and stared into the mirror.

He screamed and screamed and screamed until they came and took him away.

Even then the ride to the hospital was delayed because of the crowd of Draculas jamming the freeway.

My friend Jim Harmon asked me to write a story for an anthology of stories based on classic-era radio drama. These would not be in the form of scripts. Rather, they would be formatted as conventional short stories—but would be designed to recapture the spirit of those glorious long-ago evenings when families would gather in the living room after dinner and actually *listen to the radio*. I hope that you have as much fun reading "The Peltonville Horror" as I had writing it.

A Witch's Tale

The Hudson-Terraplane roadster's electric headlights cut twin channels of brilliance through the swirling fog of the Peltonville Turnpike. The hour was late and traffic was almost nonexistent, save for the sporty little car's sleek, bright blue form.

The shrieking voice that had come from the automobile's custom-fitted Stromberg-Carlson radio gave way to the less disturbing and more polished tones of a staff announcer. "Tune in again next week for another Witch's Tale," he urged listeners. "But for now, sit back and relax, put your feet up and enjoy the melodic musical stylings of the Stan Sawyer Orchestra."

"What a relief!" Delia Davis managed a quiet little laugh, tinged with a suggestion of nervousness. "I never did like those spooky programs, Paul darling. If I didn't love you so much I don't think I could ever put up with them."

"But, Delia," Paul Carter reached across the seat to pat his sweetheart's hand, "it's all just make-believe. You don't think there's really an old witch named Nancy who's more than a hundred years old, and lives with a wise black cat named Satan, do you?"

"No." Delia hesitated. Then she repeated, "No. I guess not." Paul released her hand and she tightened the scarf over her head. Her hair was jet black; by candlelight Paul Carter said that it showed bits of midnight blue that matched the color of her eyes. Delia had let her hair grow longer now that the boyish look and the bobbed hair of the previous decade had been abandoned for a more feminine look. "I do so love the feel of the wind and the smell of the fresh air out here in the country. But it's getting awfully cold now that the sun is down. Feels more like winter than spring."

Paul laughed. "Changing the subject, are you?"

"I guess so. When we crossed that bridge over the Beeton River a while ago, I could just imagine we were flying through the stratosphere." Delia reached for the tuning knob on the dashboard. The signal had drifted and she brought it back so the sound of saxophones and trumpets filled the convertible's tonneau. "I guess I just don't enjoy being scared. Well, maybe just a little, like at those frightening movies. But then I know you'll put your arm around me and I feel all safe. I wish we were married, Paul. Then you could put your arm around me all the time and I'd never be frightened again. Oh, Paul, will we ever be married? Can't we even set a date?"

"As soon as this depression is over and the economy picks up again," Paul replied. "You know, I'm lucky to still have a job at all, but since they've been cutting salaries every few months, I can barely pay the rent on a furnished room. There's no way I could afford an apartment and support a wife."

Delia lowered her eyes to the engagement ring on her left hand. "We could sell my ring." She toyed with the narrow band and its tiny, glittering stone. "And we don't really need a car. As much fun as it is, Paul, you could take the streetcar to work at the plant."

Paul shook his head. "I bought the car before the crash. Some timing, wasn't it? I couldn't get a quarter of what it's worth, now. And you'll never sell your ring, Delia, not as long as I can draw breath and do a day's work. Listen—"

Delia interrupted him with a gasp. "Paul—what was that?"

"What, Delia? I didn't see anything."

"Right over there, Paul. I thought I saw something moving in the woods, and then—then there was a flash. I don't know what it was. Something bright, a point of light, two points of light. No, there were more. They kept blinking on and off. I think there were eight of them. I—they were some color I've never seen before. Something like red, I think, but so deep, so powerful—so frightening, oh, Paul, what could it be?"

Paul eased up on the roadster's accelerator and the little car slowed. "I don't see anything, Delia. Through this fog, I don't know how you did. But maybe there was a momentary break. It might have been an electric power line or a radio tower. Or maybe you just caught sight of a couple of stars."

"No, Paul. It was nothing like that. It was—oh, never mind. It's gone now, whatever it was. Let's go on."

A distant flash lit the night sky above the woods to the west. Paul pushed the car to a higher speed. As he did so a low, distant rumble followed the lightning. "Uh-oh. I hope we're not going to get rained on."

"Maybe we should stop and put the top up." Delia looked around them. The fog had largely lifted but the night had actually grown darker than ever. A bright moon struggled to send its light through thick storm clouds, but only an occasional break in the clouds permitted a brief moment of illumination.

Lightning flashed, closer and brighter, a sinister greenish sheet silhouetting dark deciduous vegetation. "Look!" Delia exclaimed, "there it is again!" She pointed toward the east. "Those lights, blinking like terrible, hungry eyes!"

This time Paul pulled the little car onto the shoulder of the road. He turned off the engine, followed Delia's pointing finger with his eyes. "I don't see anything."

"No," Delia shook her head. "They're gone. But wait, Paul, listen." The radio had of course lapsed into silence when the roadster's ignition was cut, and the whisper of the gathering storm sounded through pines and oaks.

There was another flash of lightning. This time Paul counted the seconds until thunder boomed. "What's the saying," he muttered, "a mile a second? That storm is only a few miles away now. In fact, I think I just felt the first raindrops on my face. Help me, Delia, let's get the top up!"

Delia cocked her head, "Listen to that, dear."

Paul frowned. "I hear the wind and rain."

"No, there's another sound. A sort of piping and hissing and scratching. Like some incredibly gigantic—oh, Paul, I don't know. Something horrible. Could there be a spider so huge that it towers above the trees? Is it possible?"

Paul put his arms around her. "No, Delia. It's just the storm. The thunder and lightning and wind. Really, dear, it's just the storm."

Paul fumbled for the three-cell flashlight that he kept in the Hudson-Terraplane. It blazed into light and he used it now as a work-lamp.

It took the effort of a few minutes to raise the canvas top on the little roadster and button it in place. Even so, Paul and Delia were halfway to a good drenching by the time they scrambled back into the car and slammed the side doors that turned it into a snug refuge from the storm. With the optimism of youth they laughed off their wet condition. Delia undid her scarf and primped her raven curls with a brush she'd carried in her purse.

Paul ran his fingers through his own rust-colored hair. He was overdue for a trim; the hair was beginning to curl over his collar. He turned the ignition key and mashed down on the self-starter switch with his heavy brogan. The Hudson-Terraplane's six-cylinder engine coughed once as if clearing its throat of the falling rain, then purred happily. Paul switched on the headlights. The fog had disappeared now, and twin shafts of raindrops appeared before the roadster.

"What shall it be, darling?" he asked. "Shall we push on or turn back to Springfield?"

Delia hummed for a moment, a habit of hers while considering choices. "I could do with a cup of warm soup beside a friendly fireplace, dear. Isn't there a roadhouse somewhere along the Peltonville Pike?"

Paul's brow furrowed in thought. "I'm pretty sure there is. I've only been to Peltonville a few times, but I think I recall seeing one not far beyond the Beeton River bridge."

"Oh, let's push on then, Paul. It's such a miserable night, the ride home wouldn't be any fun at all with our clothes all clammy and cold as they are."

"No sooner said than done!" He pulled the car back onto the blacktop highway. "It's a good thing they paved over the old dirt road, isn't it!"

The roadster's tires hissed over the rain-swept blacktop. Now a few unseasonable hailstones were mixed with the drops. They clattered and bounced off the Hudson-Terraplane's hood and began to accumulate on the road surface as well. Winds pushed the lightweight car sideways but Paul Carter's skillful hands kept the roadster on a steady course. He reached to switch on the Stromberg-Carlson, but the lightning's interference and the noise of the storm, which had now struck in its full fury, made it impossible to hear anything worthwhile. Paul switched the radio back off.

He felt Delia's head resting on his shoulder and patted her hand with his own. Soon a sign appeared beside the highway, advertising Daniello's Roadhouse two miles ahead. Paul pushed on. Shortly there was another sign. *Daniello's,* it read, *Steaks, Cocktails, Dancing to Willie Moore's African Chili Seven.*

Daniello's Roadhouse was a pleasant-looking establishment built in the popular Tudor Revival style, with cream-colored stucco walls marked by half-timbered beams. At least, that was the way it appeared in the spotlights placed to illuminate its exterior. There was a neon sign on the roof, and the windows of stained diamond-glass showed an inviting amber color.

"We're here, Delia." Paul placed a gentle kiss on his sweetheart's forehead.

Delia smiled up at him sleepily, then leaned away and stretched like a contented kitten.

The roadhouse door was made of heavy wooden planks and swung heavily on old iron hinges. Stepping inside, the couple were enveloped by the pleasant odors of hot, hearty cooking. They made their way to a lounge and found space for themselves on dark leather barstools. They could hear the sound of music coming from another room. Willie Moore's African Chili Seven lived up to their name. A hot version of "Decatur Street Stomp" drifted into the lounge.

A red-jacketed bartender asked for their order. Paul ordered a hot toddy. Delia giggled and asked for a tequila sunset. The lounge was not crowded. A few couples sat at tables. The other barstools were mostly unoccupied. The bartender placed their drinks in front of Paul and Delia and remarked that they were fortunate to make it safely through the storm.

"Why is that?" Paul asked.

The bartender pointed over his shoulder. On the shelf behind him stood a cathedral-topped Capehart radio. "Can't get anything now, but earlier the news said that the bridge was out. Beeton River's rising and the bridge couldn't stand the gaff."

Paul and Delia lifted their glasses in a silent toast. Paul introduced himself and Delia to the bartender.

"Mustafa Cristopolous," the bartender identified himself. Now Paul realized that his speech was unusual, more an oddity of intonation than an actual accent. His voice was deep and sounded like a truckload of gravel. "I am half Greek, half Turkish," the bartender explained, "I was born in Izmir. I don't suppose you've ever heard of that place." His face carried the marks of past experiences. His nose had been broken more than once, an oddly appealing dimple marked the center of his chin and an old scar on one cheek had faded now but looked as if it had once been livid. The absence of hair on his skull was made up for by a huge black moustache.

"In the old country the Greeks hated me because I was Turkish and the Turks hated me because I was Greek. So I come to America. Here, everybody's everything."

"But what about the bridge?" Delia asked.

"Big storm," Cristopolous growled. "The boss don't like me playing the radio when the band is on, but I like to listen to news. I get stations from Springfield, Aurora, Littleton. News on the Springfield station says too much debris coming down the Beeton River, jammed up under the bridge, roadway cracked. They won't even have crews there till after the storm is over."

He looked toward the entrance of the roadhouse as if he could see outside. "How bad is it now?"

Paul said, "It got pretty nasty, Mustafa. Rain turning to hail."

The big bartender nodded his understanding. Paul had finished his drink now, and Delia's glass was mostly empty. Cristopolous asked if they wanted a refill but instead they left the lounge and moved to the dining room. The African Chili Seven were playing "Deep Bayou Blues." Paul and Delia found a table and a waitress took their order. Paul asked for a sirloin steak. Delia asked for chicken. Both requested soup before their entrées.

While they ate they discussed what to do next. Clearly there was no point in trying to return to Springfield. They would get as far as the bridge and have to wait for repairs to be made.

"I'm afraid we'll have to continue on to Peltonville," Paul announced.

"But then we won't get back to Springfield until tomorrow at the soonest," Delia complained. "What will people think? Mother and Dad will be beside themselves. And all our friends, Paul—do you think it's right?"

He reached across the table and took her hand. "I'm afraid we don't have much choice. Besides, people will just have to think what they choose."

"I don't know." Delia frowned. "It's not as if we were married." Then, "Do you think there's an inn at Peltonville? If we got two rooms it might be all right. And if there's a telephone, I could call Mother and Dad and explain what happened."

"A good idea, darling, but in a storm like this one, if the bridge is out, you can be sure that the telephone lines are down, too. I'm sorry. But if your parents really love you and trust you, they'll stand by you. As for anyone else—well, we'll just have to see it through."

As they were leaving the roadhouse they stopped to speak with Mustafa Cristopolous once again. Paul asked how much farther it would be to Peltonville, and whether Mustafa thought the road would be drivable now. The bartender said it was only another dozen miles, and the road was a good one.

"I'm worried about the hail, though," Paul explained.

Cristopolous shrugged his massive shoulders. "Life is risky." He paused, then added, "But you be careful. Some bad things happen in Peltonville."

"What bad things?"

"Just bad things. There is an old synagogue there, people do not go any more. Good people, I mean. Good people have mostly left Peltonville. You be careful, Paul and Delia."

Cristopolous had remembered their names. Paul found small comfort in that. He asked, "What do you mean by that—about the synagogue, I mean."

A weary smile creased the bartender's battered features. He leaned across the polished mahogany and lowered his voice. "Did I tell you, I am myself a Jew?" He looked around as if worried that he might be overheard. "One more reason I left Europe. Bad enough to be both a Turk and a Greek. Being a Jew as well—that was enough to make everybody hate me. Here in America—well, no place is perfect, is it?" He nodded toward the African Chili Seven. "They still have to struggle. But if they were in Greece or in

Turkey, they would have it far worse."

Paul was still concerned about the Peltonville synagogue. He pressed Cristopolous for information. Cristopolous told him that he had once been a member of the congregation. It was called Temple Beth Shalom—the House of Peace. But the old rabbi had been forced to leave and a new leader took control. The old rabbi, Yacoub ben Yitzak, Jacob son of Isaac, replaced by Yeshua ben Yeshua, Joshua son of Joshua.

Ben Yeshua was a kabalist. He introduced ancient Hebrew magic into the synagogue. Its name had been changed to Temple Beth Mogen, House of the Star. The old congregants had all left Peltonville, those who had not mysteriously disappeared before they could get away. Cristopolous was one of the lucky ones, he had avoided Peltonville ever since. Other Jews had come from far away to replace them and fill the ranks of Temple Beth Mogen.

"It's very bad, Paul. If you go to Peltonville, be very careful."

Once they were back in the car and Paul had the engine warming up, Delia turned toward him, the reflected light of the sign on Daniello's Roadhouse showing her worried expression. "Do you think we can make it to Peltonville, Paul?"

"There are other patrons. They didn't look too worried to me."

"But there's something else."

Paul turned and took her in his arms, comforting her. "What, sweetheart? Are you still worried about your reputation? I promise, I'll stand by you whatever they say."

"No, it isn't that, Paul. It's—remember those lights, those eyes, I thought they were. And that weird sound. They were real, you know. I could tell you didn't believe me, I know you too well to be fooled. There was something there."

"Oh, yes. A giant spider, was it?"

"I don't know. Maybe it was. Maybe something else. But there was something there, something alive. Oh, I don't like it. I don't know what it is, but I know it isn't nice at all."

Paul leaned back and looked into Delia's eyes. "If there was a monster loose in these woods, don't you think we'd have heard about it? Wouldn't there be stories in the Springfield *Courier* or reports on the radio? That's just the kind of thing they love to report. It's a nice change from weddings and Rotary Club meetings and high school basketball games. You haven't read anything about a monster, have you?"

"No," she admitted. "But still—I saw those lights and I heard that sound. You don't have to believe me but I know it was real, Paul, I know it!"

"Really, Delia—on a night like this, you were halfway asleep, we'd been listening to that spooky radio program, your imagination was playing tricks on you."

"But what about that evil rabbi? That whole story about the Jewish synagogue in Peltonville. I've been in a synagogue in Springfield. My friend Rebecca was married in a synagogue, I was in the wedding. It was a beautiful service. I don't see how it could be evil, any more than a regular church could be evil, but Mr. Cristopolous didn't seem to be making that up."

Paul shook his head. "Old world superstitions, Delia. Just look at the man. He's had a hard life. Heaven knows what terrible experiences he must have had in Europe. He was lucky to get out of there and come to America, from the things that are going on now. I don't think he was making it up either, but his head is so full of wild folktales, he could believe anything."

He turned on the headlights and backed the Hudson-Terraplane away from the roadhouse. In moments the little car was back on the highway. The storm had passed, the moon was bright and a black sky was dotted with colorful, distant stars that glittered like ice crystals in candlelight. The combination of moonlight, starlight and the roadster's headlamps showed the surface of the roadway, now white with crusted hailstones.

Paul reached to switch on the little car's radio. He twirled the tuning knob. On the Springfield and Aurora frequencies there was only hissing and crackling, but he managed to pick up a signal from Peltonville. He shook his head. "Is that music? Chanting? I can't understand a word of it. And it all sounds so weird."

Delia said, "I think it's Hebrew. The service at Rebecca's wedding was partly in Hebrew. I don't know what it means, of course, but that sounds like the service."

Paul tried to get a stronger signal but the best he could do was a faint chanting in an exotic tongue. He reached to turn off the radio but before he could do so the chanting faded into the background. Over it there came a hissing, piping, scraping noise, followed by the sound of voices exclaiming in ecstasy.

Even though the storm had passed, there was another flash of greenish lightning that seemed to come from all directions at once. The Hudson-Terraplane's engine sputtered into silence that was broken by an ear-shattering boom of thunder. Paul and Delia clutched each other's hands in alarm, then Paul managed a nervous chuckle. He grasped the steering wheel of the roadster and mashed down on the self-starter switch.

The little car's engine coughed once, then roared back to life. The orange light behind the radio's tuning dial glowed but there was no sound so Paul switched it off. He threw in the clutch, put the roadster in gear and set it to moving.

When they passed the Peltonville city limit Paul read the welcoming sign and population figures. Based on his recollection of his last visit he'd thought that Peltonville was bigger than the number indicated. Perhaps the latest census figures had shown a loss of population. Then he thought of Mustafa Cristopolous's words about Peltonville:

Some bad things happen in Peltonville . . . Just bad things. There is an old synagogue there, people do not go any more. Good people, I mean. Good people have mostly left Peltonville. You be careful, Paul and Delia.

It was hard for Paul or Delia to tell much about the character of Peltonville as the little roadster rolled into the downtown area. Every building seemed to be dark. Small houses in the style of the previous century loomed to left and right, but apparently Peltonvilliers retired early, for only the jagged silhouettes of the residences could be seen outlined against the backdrop of the night sky.

"Can you tell what time it is?" Paul asked.

Delia found the flashlight they had used earlier and shone its beam against her Elgin wristwatch. "It's 10:30," she announced. "I guess they keep going at Daniello's Roadhouse but people in Peltonville don't stay up."

After a few blocks lined by small retail shops the Hudson-Terraplane's headlamps picked out a building with a darkened marquee extending over the crumbling sidewalk. Paul pulled the car to the curb and Delia shone the flashlight on the sign.

Peltonville Inn, it read.

"Well, that's straightforward enough," Paul commented. "Let's see if they can put us up for the night."

"Paul." Delia took his arm.

He looked at her, waiting to hear what she had to say.

"Paul, you know I love you, dear. You do know that, don't you?"

"Of course, Delia. You shouldn't even have to ask. But—what's the matter?"

"Well—" She looked down. "Well, I'd really love to stay with you tonight. It would be—thrilling, Paul. But I know it would be wrong. I don't want to disappoint you, but would you mind if—if we took two rooms, dear?"

Paul shook his head. "Of course not. What sort of fellow do you think I am?"

He climbed out of the Hudson-Terraplane, walked around the car and opened Delia's door. "Come, darling, let's see what the management has to say to two poor travelers with no luggage to show for themselves!"

As Paul helped Delia from the car he realized that her breath was freezing in the air, as was his own. The wind had reversed its direction and brought the unseasonable storm back over Peltonville, or perhaps this was merely another front in a series. In any case, the wind had begun to howl unpleasantly and hail was battering both travelers.

Paul and Delia hustled to a place of shelter beneath the marquee of the Peltonville Inn. The hotel was dark. Turning back toward the street they observed that the town had not yet converted its street lamps to electric power from the older gas illumination. A few fixtures flickered feebly despite the icy wind that swept the street.

Paul searched his trousers for a coin. He found a silver dollar and used it to rap on the glass panel of the Peltonville Inn's main entrance, but to no avail. He called out but his voice disappeared into the whistling, howling gale.

Stepping to the edge of the sheltered space beneath the marquee he held Delia to him, gazing at the sky. Clouds like shreds of torn black cloth swept overhead; in the breaks between them stars glared down at the couple. Never had Paul seen them so cold and seemingly malevolent. To the east a new constellation appeared, a group of eight stars of a color he had never seen before. If he had needed to name their color he would have called it red, but it was red of a shade and quality he had never previously experienced. The stars danced. Paul shuddered. An eerie auditory amalgam, part whistle, part hiss, part scraping, sounded faintly.

"There's nobody here," he muttered. "I can't tell, Delia, either the inn is out of business or it's closed for the night. Either way, we'll find no shelter here tonight."

"But Paul," she replied. Paul looked into her face. Clearly she was struggling to summon her courage but there were tears in her eyes and the corners of her mouth quivered. "What will we do? Is there anyplace we can go? We can't just sleep in the car, we'll freeze."

She was right, he realized. The wind whipped through their lightweight garments. Even beneath the marquee of the Peltonville Inn the hailstones bounced from the sidewalk and roadway and stung them like wave after wave of angry ice-hornets.

Across the street a faint light flickered in the windows of an old, two-story building. There was a momentary break in the screaming wind and a low chanting, barely audible, drifted to their ears. Paul stepped out from beneath the marquee, shielding his eyes from the pelting of hailstones as sharp and vicious as a bombardment of granite needles.

Yes, there was a light in the building.

Paul raised his gaze. The sinister constellation had disappeared from its previous location. Now it appeared once again, swooping and gyrating above the lighted building.

"There's somebody over there," Paul exclaimed. "Come on, Delia, they'll have to let us in!"

Hand in hand they ran from the Peltonville Inn to the lighted building across the street. The building loomed above them. The light they had seen flickered through a circular stained glass window. Its pattern was regular in shape, oddly suggestive of a sheriff's badge. Paul found himself wondering crazily if there wasn't a sheriff's station or town police headquarters here in

Peltonville, if he and Delia should not have tried to find the authorities and pleaded with them for assistance against the cold and desolation of the darkness and the storm.

But it was too late for that.

Paul pounded on the heavy wooden door and found, to his surprise, that it swung open beneath his blows. He urged Delia in ahead of himself, then stepped into the shelter of the building, drawing the door shut behind them.

Clearly they were in a house of worship. The stained glass window behind them centered around a huge star formed of interlocking equilateral triangles. Paul had seen the pattern before, but there was something wrong with it this time. Each of the star's six points was surmounted by another figure, a clutching claw, a hook, or some other disquieting image. And in the center of the hexagon formed by the major triangles he saw a face such as his most horrifying nightmare had never brought to him, a face whose inhuman features were exceeded in their fearsomeness only by the malevolence of their expression, a face surrounded by dripping tentacles that appeared for all the world to writhe and clutch even as he watched.

Hand in hand Paul and Delia advanced into the sanctuary. The chamber was illuminated by a series of gas mantles mounted on pilasters. There appeared now the massed congregants, robed figures of indeterminate gender. Human they seemed, but somehow and in some incomprehensible way, *wrong*. They stood in a circle, swaying rhythmically and chanting in what had to be Hebrew.

In the center of the circle towered a massive figure, broad-shouldered, bearded, wearing a skull-cap and fringed shawl embroidered with kabalistic symbols and horrifying images. The figure raised his voice and his arms, but where Paul expected to see hands emerging from the sleeves of his robe were frightening claws that clacked angrily, wreathed by tentacles that wove and snapped like miniature whips.

The robed chanters surrounding their foul leader parted ranks. More quickly than Paul could follow they formed themselves into two rows. Those closest to Paul and Delia reached and took them by the hands. Paul's will was frozen. He stumbled forward, Delia at his side, passed from couple to couple of the frightening chanters, until they found themselves standing in the center of the newly reconstituted circle.

The leader loomed over them, far taller and more massive than any human being had the right to be. His arms were still raised, the claws and tentacles still performing their terrible gyrations. Involuntarily Paul raised his eyes, following the direction of the massive arms. Out of the corner of his vision he saw that Delia had done the same, and that even the monstrous figure before them had thrown back its head and was gazing in a state of spiritual rapture into the sky.

Yes, the sky loomed overhead. A retractable panel had been drawn back in the roof of the sanctuary. The hail had ceased to fall, but an icy wind howled through the aperture. The sound of the chanting rose, the leader began a strange and frightening dance, and in the blackness above the building, against the backdrop of faint, distant stars, the foul eight-pointed constellation appeared once more.

Only now Paul realized that the points of illumination were not distant stars but the eyes of a dreadful being, a being something like a huge spider, something like a frightening marine creature, something unholy and infinitely evil.

The eight red eyes drew nearer and the other features of the being became visible, fangs that dripped venom that steamed and sputtered as it struck the sanctuary floor, rope-like excrescencies that writhed and reached for the figures gathered beneath.

The chanting that surrounded Paul and Delia rose in pitch and urgency, the looming clergyman who stood before them lowered his arms and reached for Paul and Delia, seizing one of them in each arm, drawing them to his body that seemed to be more a chitinous shell than mere muscle and bone.

With immense and effortless strength he raised them, Paul in one horrid tentacle-circled claw, Delia in the other. Overhead the monstrous entity nodded and hissed, lowering itself toward the sacrifice that was clearly intended for it.

Paul reached for Delia, hoping in what must surely be the last moments of their lives to clasp her hand, but instead there was a monstrous crash and an icy blast as the massive doors of the building burst open and smashed to the floor. Paul was able to twist in the clergyman's grasp.

Standing in the doorway of the sanctuary was a figure he recognized at once as belonging to Mustafa Cristopolous, the Greek-Turkish-Jewish bartender whom Paul and Delia had met earlier in the evening at Daniello's Roadhouse.

But now Cristopolous was transformed. No longer bent over a mahogany surface, no longer clad in a brass-buttoned, red service jacket, Cristopolous seemed to have grown to a height half-again his previous size. His shoulders bulged with muscles. His features, the broken nose, the cleft chin, had assumed a nobility that Paul had not recognized in them in Daniello's cocktail lounge. The jagged scar on his cheek was no longer a pallid reminder of a long-ago wound, but a blazing talisman of righteous rage.

The low, accented voice that Paul and Delia had heard at Daniello's now roared its challenge in words of ancient Hebrew. Among them Paul recognized a phrase that he had previously heard, *Yeshua ben Yeshua*. The evil clergyman, startled, dropped Paul and Delia. The entity that writhed above the sanctuary hissed and writhed in rage, deprived, at least for the moment, of its sacrificial prey.

The chanting congregants parted in terror, scurrying to cower among the pews and against the walls of the sanctuary.

Cristopolous strode forward, passing between Paul and Delia as he approached the clergyman. Cristopolous reached for the other, his massive hands clutching for the other's throat. The two were of a size and well matched in strength. They bellowed imprecations at each other, both of them growling in the same archaic tongue that Cristopolous had used to issue his first challenge upon entering the sanctuary. But among the alien words of Yeshua ben Yeshua, Paul was sure that he heard the name Yacoub ben Yitzak.

The clergyman and Cristopolous clutched each other in a dreadful parody of a lovers' embrace. The clergyman was clawing at Cristopolous's face and throat; Cristopolous held the other by his waist, lifting him from the floor by main strength.

From above the writhing, seething tangle, a foul cluster of tentacles descended, dripping venom and slime. Ropelike organs wrapped themselves around the two struggling figures, then raised both, slowly, from the floor. Paul reached for Cristopolous's heavy ankles. For a moment he secured a grip on them and felt himself actually lifted from his own feet, but a burning blob of slime spattered on one of his hands. In agony he lost his grasp on Cristopolous's ankle with that hand; the other, alone, had not sufficient strength to maintain its grip.

Paul collapsed back onto the floor. Delia knelt beside him, her arms around him, her tear-stained face pressed against his. Above them Paul saw Cristopolous and the clergyman, now wholly enveloped in a cocoon of writhing, ropelike tentacles, disappear into the gaping maw of the hideous entity that hovered briefly above the sanctuary, then rose with incredible speed until it disappeared once and for all into the starry sky above.

Again a cold wind swept into the sanctuary, and again the clatter of hailstones filled the night, this time pouring unimpeded through the open roof into the ancient building.

Taking Delia by the hand, Paul made his way from the building. The misshapen congregants whose chanting had earlier filled the building and the night had disappeared. Hand-in-hand, Paul and Delia made their way back to the Hudson-Terraplane.

Together, Paul and Delia turned back for one last sight of the desecrated synagogue. The monstrous creature was nowhere to be seen; it had disappeared along with both Yeshua ben Yeshua and Yacoub ben Yitzak. But from the swirling clouds overhead a single lurid shaft of shockingly ruddy lightning crackled downward. It must have struck the gas line that fed the mantles in the synagogue. There was a deafening explosion and the building disappeared, fragments clattering down for city blocks in all directions.

"We can't stay in Peltonville," Paul announced. This assertion drew no objection from Delia. "And we can't get back to Springfield until the bridge is repaired. But we can press on. Aurora isn't too much farther, and we can find accommodations there." He paused. Then he added, "Even if we can only find one room."

Delia leaned her head against his shoulder and wrapped her arms around him. "One room is all we'll need, Paul," she murmured.

Richard A. Lupoff

When I was honored by an H. P. Lovecraft convention in Providence, Rhode Island, the organizers asked me to contribute a piece to the convention program book. I dashed off "Simeon Dimsby's Workshop" in a couple of hours, thinking that nothing would come of the story, but to my surprise it was selected by Stephen Jones for his *Best Horror Stories of the Year* anthology. Sometimes you sweat bullets over a story for weeks on end and come up with a minor piece at best. Other times the story is just *there* and all you have to do is write it down. "Simeon Dimsby's Workshop" is one of the latter.

Simeon Dimsby's Workshop

It took Regis Hardy six years to sell his first short story.

He would rise early each morning and put in an hour of mental effort, bending over his notebook, striving for the right combination of words that would elicit a letter of acceptance instead of the rejection slips to which he was accustomed. When he kissed his spouse, Helena, good-bye after a light breakfast of toast and a half grapefruit, he would ride the municipal bus to his job in downtown Elmwood, California.

The men and women around him occupied them*selves* in a variety of ways: perusing copies of the *Elmwood Daily Express-Bulletin,* listening to their favorite music on portable CD players, reading paperback novels. Often regular riders on the Number Eighteen line would greet one another and discuss the events of the world, or of their personal lives, as they traveled to work. High school students engaged in horseplay. College students took part in serious and arcane discussions of Kierkegaard, Aeschylus, or the millions of dollars they expected to make in the high-tech world as soon as they received their degrees.

Not Mr. Hardy. He lived near the end of the Number Eighteen line and always got a seat on his way to work. He would ride with his eyes closed, imagining the doings of the men and women in his stories, striving to capture just the right event, image, or turn of phrase to make his current opus the one that would carry him across the threshold of literary status from that of ambitious amateur to that of acclaimed professional.

Mr. Hardy worked at the Department of Social Services. He took his lunch each day in the department's cafeteria, notebook laid flat beside his plastic tray and yellow wooden pencil in hand, working, always working on his stories. And every night, after dinner with Helena, he would retreat to his private corner and work for another hour on his stories before joining his wife to watch the evening news.

Six years.

And then the miracle happened.

Mr. Hardy received a letter from the editor of *Mayhem Monthly.*

The editor had read Mr. Hardy's submission, "Vampire Town," and was pleased to tender the enclosed purchase agreement for the story.

The payment was miniscule and the magazine, which had rejected numerous of Mr. Hardy's efforts in the past, was a minor one, but Mr. Hardy was ecstatic. He could see a doorway opening before him. He imagined a room filled with the literary figures he had admired, almost worshipped, all his life, eagerly welcoming him to their world and to their own glamorous company.

Filled with pride, Mr. Hardy showed the letter to his wife, who threw her arms around his shoulders and planted a congratulatory kiss on his cheek.

That night, inspired by the delicious taste of success, Regis Hardy worked on his current story-in-progress for two hours rather than one. Later, lying in bed, Helena's soft breathing and warm presence filling him with marital contentment, he projected an imaginary motion picture on the ceiling, peopling each frame with characters of his own invention and creating a sound track filled with mood-inspiring music, crackling dialog and exciting sound effects.

It would be pleasant to report that Mr. Hardy, having at last achieved the mystical transformation from amateur to professional writer, was immediately greeted with nothing but editorial accolades, but such was not the case. Following the solitary sale to *Mayhem Monthly* there came a series of rejection slips from a broad spectrum of periodicals.

But Regis Hardy was not one to surrender his treasured dream, especially after having sold "Vampire Town."

Some months later came a double red-letter day. There was another letter of acceptance, this one from *Interstellar Stories*. The work in question was a novelette titled "Narcotics from Neptune." The same day's postal delivery included a brown manila envelope. The envelope contained two copies of the issue of *Mayhem Monthly* featuring "Vampire Town."

The Hardys sat happily side-by-side admiring Regis's story and the black-and-white illustration that accompanied it. To be candid, the illustration was decidedly on the crude and slapdash side, nor had the artist captured quite the flavor of Mr. Hardy's story, or the detail of his description. But Mrs. Hardy patted Mr. Hardy affectionately on the cheek, and he did feel that another milestone had been passed on the roadway to success.

As the months and years rolled by Mr. Hardy found that he was receiving fewer rejection notices and making more sales. He was able to move to higher-paying and more prestigious markets. He cracked *Image of the Imagination* and *Exciting Adventure Annual* and finally *New Modern Gangster Quarterly*.

He built a proud "brag shelf" of magazines containing his works. He admired the many black-and-white illustrations that accompanied them, and invited Mrs. Hardy out for a celebratory cocktail and dinner when *Wilderness* magazine honored him with a full-color cover painting of a scene from his story "Cannibal's Canoe."

His hair was thinning and his temples were gray now, and he suspected that Mrs. Hardy's flaming titian locks retained their brilliance only with the assistance of expensive chemicals, but he chose not to raise the subject in conversation. He had never made a living from his writing. He had kept his day job at the Department of Social Services, but he knew in his heart that the job was merely a means to the end of supporting his writing endeavors.

Only two goals had eluded him.

Despite numerous attempts he had never been able to sell a story to *Grave Yarns*. In each case the story in question had been successfully placed in another market, nor was *Grave Yarns* the highest-paying or most prestigious of periodicals, but it was a venerable publication, almost legendary in the community, and Mr. Hardy had long dreamed of winning a place in its pages. That was the first of Mr. Hardy's remaining unfulfilled ambitions.

The second was to see his stories collected into a book. He had approached a number of publishers and been turned away with the advice that he procure the services of a literary agent. He had then approached a number of agents only to be turned away by them with the advice that he write a novel if he wished book publication. Collections of short stories were virtually impossible to place, he was told.

By this time Mr. Hardy was nearing retirement age and looked forward eagerly to leaving the Department of Social Services. He would then be able to devote all of his energies to his literary endeavors. Mrs. Hardy had already taken early retirement from her own job, and offered her husband encouragement with his plan.

By the time a letter arrived at the Hardys' modest home bearing the return indicia of *Grave Yarns* Mr. Hardy was forced to don his trifocal spectacles in order to read it. But the game was most assuredly worth the candle as Mr. Hardy found that he had at last captured the proverbial brass ring on the ever-turning carousel of literature. The editor of *Grave Yarns* was pleased to accept Mr. Hardy's submission to the magazine, "Even the Dead Have Rights."

Only one goal remained now on Mr. Hardy's agenda, and that was book publication. He had not been wholly frustrated in even this enterprise, for several times his stories had been included in anthologies. These books, some colorful and some drab, some of them beautifully bound and jacketed volumes and others cheaply made paperbacks, held a special place of honor in the Hardy living room. But a collection devoted entirely to his own works was a dream the realization of which continued to elude Mr. Hardy.

And then Mr. Hardy received a letter from a publisher unfamiliar to him. Surely this was one he had never contacted, nor even read of in the trade journals to which he assiduously subscribed. The writer of the letter introduced himself as the proprietor of a new firm, Mantigore Press. He was seeking to publish the works of deserving but previously overlooked authors. He had been an admirer of Mr. Hardy's atmospheric and effective prose for some years, and if Mr. Hardy found himself in a position to place a collection of his stories with the new company, Mantigore Press was prepared to issue a contract immediately, and to offer a small but realistic advance payment against royalties to be earned.

The letter was signed, *Auric Mantigore.*

Regis Hardy was so excited that his wife had to spend the better part of an hour calming and soothing him. He then responded to Auric Mantigore's letter with a quick and enthusiastic reply in the affirmative.

Thus it was that, in due course, Mantigore Press announced the impending publication of *Return to Elmwood: the Collected Stories of Regis Hardy.*

Mantigore Press was headquartered in the city of Repentance, Maine, some 3,000 miles from Elmwood, California. At first Mr. Hardy conducted his business with Mantigore by postal means, but when Auric Mantigore informed him that the distinguished artist and resident of Repentance, Simeon Dimsby, had been engaged to create a jacket painting and interior illustrations for *Return to Elmwood,* Mr. Hardy could contain himself no longer.

Over a modest evening meal he broached his plan to his wife. "We are both now retired, Helena. Our pensions are small but adequate to our needs, and we have some savings. I would like to travel to Repentance, Maine, to meet Auric Mantigore and the great Simeon Dimsby. I intend to write to Messrs. Mantigore and Dimsby and propose such a meeting. If they are amenable to my plan, I would be most pleased to have your company on the trip, and to arrange for your inclusion in our festive gathering."

There were tears in Helena Hardy's eyes as she voiced her approval of her husband's notion.

Even before watching the evening news on that occasion, Regis Hardy penned letters to Auric Mantigore and Simeon Dimsby, broaching his plan. While similar in content, the two letters were not identical. That addressed to Simeon Dimsby included a paragraph in which Mr. Hardy expressed his admiration for Dimsby's work. Many artists had attempted to capture the essence of Regis Hardy's stories, but none had fully succeeded, at least in his opinion. But he was confident of Dimsby's ability to do so, and hoped fervently to meet the great illustrator.

Not long after writing to Mantigore and Dimsby, Regis Hardy received responses from both. Mantigore explained that he was a busy man whose responsibilities occupied him for many hours each day. Further, he was obliged by commercial considerations to spend most of each month travelling. Consequently, he suggested that Hardy and Dimsby make such arrangements as they saw fit. If available, Mantigore would join them. If unable to do so, he would nonetheless offer his best wishes.

Regis Hardy was mildly disappointed by Auric Mantigore's letter, but he was positively elated when he read Simeon Dimsby's. The artist had developed a great fondness for Hardy's stories and was most enthusiastic about *Return to Elmwood*. He had already created preliminary sketches for his illustrations and worked out what he referred to as his "concept" for the dust jacket painting. He indicated a date by which he hoped to have the final versions of the drawings in hand, and suggested that Regis Hardy come to his, Dimsby's, home and workshop on that date.

Further correspondence confirmed that Mrs. Hardy would also be welcomed at the Dimsby demesne, and that if it were convenient for the Hardys, the invitation would be so timed as to include dinner at the Dimsby home. Mrs. Dimsby was an accomplished chef, Simeon Dimsby asserted, and would be pleased to prepare her finest dishes for the Hardys.

Regis Hardy could barely contain his joy. He dispatched an enthusiastic reply, jotted the date of the proposed dinner party in his desk planner, and made a note to phone a local travel agent and book a flight for himself and his wife to the airport nearest Repentance, Maine.

It was fortunate for Regis Hardy's peace of mind that Simeon Dimsby worked rapidly, for even so Mr. Hardy found himself counting the days until his and Mrs. Hardy's flight, like a child counting days until a birthday, or Christmas, or the end of the school year. Standing before the bathroom mirror in his pajamas, Mr. Hardy took note of his lined visage, his largely naked scalp and the snowy whiteness of what little hair he retained.

He was an old man, but in his chest his heart leaped like that of an eager and joyous youth.

At last the long-awaited day arrived. The Hardys were driven to the airport by one Albert Tindle, a former colleague of Mr. Hardy's at the Department of Social Services. They boarded the huge, sleek jetliner, Mr. Hardy commenting almost involuntarily at the contrast between it and the far smaller, propeller-driven monoplanes of his youth.

Their journey was uneventful, and upon reaching Repentance, Maine, the Hardys checked into a motel. This was a locally-owned affiliate of an international chain. It was well managed in accord with corporate guidelines. The Hardys' room was comfortably appointed in a standardized and impersonal style. Mrs. Hardy remarked that they might as easily have been in Brazil, Syria, or Thailand, or even on the moon, had there been motels on the moon, for all the local character of their lodgings.

Mr. Hardy telephoned the home of Simeon Dimsby. Mrs. Dimsby took the call, reiterated the invitation to dine that evening, and even offered the services of her husband to pick up the Hardys at their motel. Mr. Hardy expressed gratitude for the offer but indicated that he and his wife would take a cab to the Dimsbys' house.

Dusk was falling when the driver pulled to the curb at the address Regis Hardy had given him. The warm autumnal afternoon had yielded to a chill breeze with the disappearance of the sun, and an early moon was rising red and menacing above the eastern horizon. Mr. and Mrs. Hardy stood side by side before the Dimsby house, gazing at the tall frame structure. A brightness flickered in the front window as if electrification had somehow bypassed the Dimsby house and its occupants relied on old-fashioned oil lamps for illumination.

An unexpected chill caused Mr. Hardy to shudder almost imperceptibly. He took his wife's hand and advanced, opening a protesting gate in the waist-high iron fence. The lawn surrounding the house had not been mowed in a very long time. The wooden stairs that led to the front porch creaked with each of Mr. and Mrs. Hardy's steps.

A search for a doorbell or knocker having failed, Mr. Hardy rapped tentatively on the wooden panel with his knuckles.

At once the door swung back. A plump woman of below-average height looked up at the Hardys. The roundness of her face was offset by the gray hair which she had pulled back into a bun. She wore a patterned housedress and cloth apron. A small birthmark above one eye evoked a mildly distasteful fantasy on Regis Hardy's part.

"You must be the Hardys. Come in. I'm Mrs. Dimsby. Eustacia

Whipple Dimsby. Please call me Eustacia."

She took Mr. Hardy's fedora and Mrs. Hardy's wrap and escorted them to a parlor furnished as it must have been a century before. "Mr. Dimsby is in his workshop. Make yourselves comfortable while I fetch him."

She disappeared down a hallway.

The Hardys exchanged glances.

A door slammed. The pendulum of a tall clock swung to and fro. There were footsteps. A figure appeared where Eustacia Dimsby had last been seen.

"I am Simeon Dimsby."

Regis Hardy rose to his feet. Dimsby shook his hand, then bowed over Helena Hardy's as would have a Regency dandy. It took an effort for Regis Hardy to refrain from flinching away from Dimsby's icy fingers. The artist was cadaverously thin, his pale countenance set off by a high-collared white shirt and heavy black suit. Waves of cold seemed to waft from him.

"Forgive me," he explained. "My workshop is below the house and I keep it cool at all times, to preserve my compositions."

"You work in oils?" Hardy asked. He knew little of artistic media.

Dimsby shook his head from side to side. "No." He offered no further explanation.

"But if you have to keep your work refrigerated, how do you deliver it to your publishers?" Dimsby did not answer at once, and Hardy filled the silence. "That is, your pictures are so fine, both your black-and-white illustrations and your paintings. Helena and I have admired them for a long time. I was thrilled when Mr. Mantigore told me you were to illustrate my book, *Return to Elmwood*. But what do you use for ink? For paint? Wouldn't it spoil?"

"Such is the wonder of modern invention," Dimsby explained. He had crossed the room and opened what appeared to be an Eighteenth Century cupboard. He turned with a graceful decanter in one hand and two round-bellied snifters in the other. "The day has taken a chilly turn, has it not? Won't you each try some brandy to warm yourselves while Mrs. Dimsby prepares our dinner."

Each of the Hardys accepted a snifter of shimmering, copper-colored liquid. As Regis Hardy held it before his face the fumes of the liquor rose with a pleasant sharpness and warmth. It was delicious on his tongue. From the corner of his eye he observed his wife sampling the beverage.

"You were speaking of technology," Hardy addressed his host.

"Yes."

"And won't you have some brandy yourself?" Hardy asked.

"I do not," Dimsby said. After a brief silence he resumed. "My compositions would, ah, *de*-compose if exposed to heat," he explained, laughing at his own play on words. "Therefore I scan them into a computer and deliver them to my publishers in the form of electronic files."

Hardy nodded. "A shame. I was hoping—that is, I had thought, maybe—once *Return to Elmwood* is completed, that you might be willing to part with one of your originals. It would have a place of honor in our house, wouldn't it, dear? Especially if we might purchase—if Mr. Dimsby would consider parting with—the jacket painting."

His wife agreed that, yes, a Dimsby original would be treasured in the Hardy home.

"Alas, I fear that would be impossible," Simeon Dimsby commiserated, "but perhaps after dinner you would enjoy a tour of my workshop. You may have some comments on the renderings I have done for *Return to Elmwood*." Before he could say more his wife returned from the kitchen and summoned them to the dinner table.

The Dimsby dining room, like the parlor, could have served as the set for a period motion picture, but there was no sense of artificiality or unreality to the room. Rather, upon entering its confines one had the impression of having stepped backward into time.

Mrs. Dimsby bustled into the kitchen and returned bearing a large platter. It was covered with a green, shimmering mass of interwoven strips the reminded Mr. Hardy of marine vegetation that he had seen on past visits to the Pacific Ocean near his home.

Mrs. Dimsby set the platter in the center of the gleaming linen cloth that covered the table.

Mr. Dimsby asked if the Hardys would object to the old-fashioned practice of saying grace prior to dining. They did not. Mr. Dimsby then folded his gray, bony hands in a manner unfamiliar to the guests. He lowered his head and closed his eyes, murmuring what Regis Hardy took to be his devotion. Mr. Hardy had no notion of Simeon Dimsby's ethnic heritage or his religious affiliation. The prayer was in a language unfamiliar to Hardy, a disquieting mixture of sibilants and gutturals. As the prayer ended the room seemed to shudder. Accustomed as he was to occasional small earthquakes in California, Regis Hardy was unalarmed by the minor temblor, despite never having heard of earthquakes in Maine.

The green substance proved to be a pre-prandial salad. Its flavor was mildly unpleasant, the dressing of an odd gelatinous consistency and its odor peculiarly marine, but Mr. Hardy managed to down a small portion of it, as did his wife.

Mrs. Dimsby removed the platter and salad plates.

Mr. Dimsby said, "The main course is Mrs. Dimsby's specialty, an old family recipe handed down ever since Colonial times here in Repentance. In fact, local legend has it that the dish was a favorite of the aboriginal inhabitants. Unlike other native peoples they neither died out nor moved away, but were assimilated by the settlers. Or, perhaps more accurately, one might say that the settlers were assimilated by the local inhabitants."

Mr. Hardy was about to ask if his host's prayer had been spoken in the natives' language, but before he could do so, Mrs. Dimsby returned from the kitchen bearing a massive iron pot. Mr. Hardy was amazed that the short woman could handle its weight, but she hefted it onto a blackened trivet. The contents of the iron pot bubbled and hissed, emitting visible columns of steam.

"I hope no one is allergic to shellfish," she announced. Receiving no objections she nodded to her husband, who lifted a long-handled implement and dipped it into the pot. Beside him stood a stack of deep bowls. He ladled a portion into one for Helena Hardy, then for Regis Hardy, then for his wife, Eustacia, and finally for himself.

Regis Hardy gazed at the contents of his bowl. Taking his clue from Mrs. Dimsby's comment, he assumed that the meal consisted of a shellfish stew or bouillabaisse. Not only bits of marine carapace but tiny tentacles, claws, and even eyestalks were clearly visible, floating in a viscid red broth. The meal must have been brought to the table while still a-boil, for bubbles rose to the surface, tentacles waved and miniscule claws seemed to snap at Mr. Hardy's spoon. He shot a glance at his wife, sharing with her his distress.

He managed to secure a spoonful of the broth and convey it to his mouth, all the while staring at a small marine crustacean that seemed to stare back at him from his bowl. The broth was hot in both senses of that word, and as it reached the back of Mr. Hardy's tongue he could have sworn that a tiny, serrated claw nipped at his uvula sending a wave of pain and nausea through him.

The Hardys managed to down a bare, polite minimum of their meal while the Dimsbys emptied their bowls and refilled them repeatedly, smacking their lips and exclaiming in pleasure at the textures and flavors of the repast. Conversation was desultory, and it was with relief that Mr. Hardy pushed his old ladder-back chair away from the table at the end of the meal, helping his wife to follow suit.

Eustacia Dimsby excused herself in order to clear the table and attend to her duties in the kitchen. Helena Hardy volunteered her assistance. Simeon Dimsby renewed his offer to Regis Hardy, to tour the subterranean workshop. Hardy attempted to beg off, pleading fatigue after the day's transcontinental travel, but yielded to Dimsby's persuasive words and the astonishingly powerful, even painful, grip on his elbow.

Dimsby insisted that Hardy precede him down a lengthy, narrow stairway. The first flight was of creaking, wooden risers and treads. Thereafter the flight plunged more steeply into what seemed bedrock, the stairs carved out of ancient New England granite.

Illumination was provided by concealed fixtures.

Mr. Hardy's breath rose coldly in visible clouds.

After an exhausting trek which left Mr. Hardy wondering how

he would ever be able to climb back to the surface, the staircase ended. He found himself in a small antechamber. A single iron door met his gaze.

Simeon Dimsby stepped past Mr. Hardy. He drew an oversized, old-fashioned key from his suit pocket and inserted it in a massive, time-blackened lock. Turning the key, he snapped the lock open and pulled the door toward himself.

Inside the chamber the temperature seemed to plunge still further. Mr. Hardy stood, surrounded by magnificent yet macabre images. At a sound he turned and observed Simeon Dimsby, who had pulled the heavy door shut behind the pair with a jarring, metallic impact.

"Let me show you my sketches for *Return to Elmwood,*" Dimsby grated. "We won't be disturbed. Only Auric Mantigore and I have keys to this door. Not even my wife, dear as she is, can enter unless we permit it."

He opened a drawer in a rough wooden table and removed a huge envelope. He undid the hasp on the envelope and withdrew one of a sheaf of renderings on stiff illustration board. He turned toward Hardy. "I hope you will be pleased."

The top drawing was Dimsby's illustration for Mr. Hardy's story "Narcotics from Neptune." The illustration for this tale in *Interstellar Stories,* created by one Barton Gorgon, had been a literal representation of the climactic scene of the narrative, in which Hardy's beleaguered space voyagers, imprisoned by amoeboid creatures from the frigid outer planet and injected with a deadly, addictive drug and forced to work in the noxious mines of Neptune's rocky moons, confronted their captors in an apocalyptic rebellion.

Gorgon had focused on the haggard, bearded faces of the enslaved earthlings. Regis Hardy had always felt that Gorgon's drawing, while not uneffective, had lacked considerably in impact.

Not so Simeon Dimsby's version.

Dimsby had dealt directly with the aliens. His rendition of them was horrifying. Dimsby had transcended Regis Hardy's own description of the aliens' physical appearance and had managed in some undefinable way to capture their overwhelming sense of monstrous power.

Hardy gasped. "How did you do this?"

A thin smile curled Dimsby's lips. "Do you like it? The medium is a substance that I manufacture myself. The primary ingredient is the ink of deep-water Atlantic kraken. And there are other ingredients as well."

Dimsby retrieved the drawing from Regis Hardy's grasp, replaced it carefully in the envelope and removed another. He looked at the drawing himself, smiled once more, again faintly, and extended the illustration toward Hardy's outstretched hand.

This time the drawing was clearly based on "Vampire Town." The tale had been Regis Hardy's first sale. Not his best work, he felt, but one for which he held a great affection because of its landmark importance in his career. The art director of *Mayhem Monthly* had assigned the story to Walter Wallace, a longtime hack illustrator who hadn't done a good drawing in thirty years, but who managed to eke out an existence on the basis of name recognition and longstanding connections if nothing more.

In contrast to Wallace's crudely gory imagery, Simeon Dimsby's night scene of the village, torch-wielding undead pursuing the last surviving day-dweller to his inevitable doom, was enough to send a shuddering *frisson* down Regis Hardy's spine.

Dimsby's images for Hardy's other stories were all powerful and frightening, but more than this they were strangely *disquieting*. As Regis Hardy looked at each drawing he felt as if Simeon Dimsby had seen past the prose of his story and penetrated into the nethermost and most fear-haunted recesses of his soul.

At last Simeon Dimsby's gray hand retrieved the last of the drawings from Regis Hardy's unsteady grasp. He returned the leaves to their envelope and the envelope to its drawer. He tilted his head on its abnormally long and flexible neck, twisted his thin lips into a suggestion of a smile, and asked, "Had you any thoughts, Mr. Hardy, regarding the jacket illustration for *Return to Elmwood?*"

"I thought you and Mr. Mantigore had already made a choice," Hardy replied.

"We have held several meetings and exchanged a number of

notions, but Mr. Mantigore felt that you deserved to be consulted before a final decision was made." He paused. "As the author, you see. Mr. Mantigore has the greatest respect for us—what he calls, 'creative geniuses.' I believe that he uses the term in an ironic sense, but perhaps I am mistaken."

He placed a bony, gray hand on Hardy's wrist. His grip was amazingly strong and his hand was frighteningly cold.

"Did you—have a medium in mind?" Hardy asked. "I mean, I'm pretty ignorant where art is concerned, but I've heard of oils, water colors, something called gouache."

"You're not as uninformed as you pretend, Mr. Hardy." The artist still had hold of the author's wrist. He leaned closer, peering into Hardy's face. In Dimsby's eyes Hardy saw distant flames dancing, yet the eyes seemed oddly ice-like, almost crystalline, and the flames emitted chill instead of warmth.

"I don't—I don't really know," Hardy managed to stammer.

Dimsby said, "Well then, let me show you some of the materials I have left from my last painting." He released Hardy's wrist and Hardy shrank back, breathing a sigh of relief. Dimsby knelt in front of a safe-like storage cabinet, He twirled the lock that held it shut, then pulled the heavy door toward himself. "A pity that Mr. Mantigore has been unable to join us," he commented.

As if on cue there sounded a grating noise from the heavy lock on the iron door to Simeon Dimsby's workshop.

The great iron door swung back.

Regis Hardy had never met Auric Mantigore, never seen a photograph of the publisher, yet even so there was no doubt in his mind as to the identity of the newcomer.

Auric Mantigore was almost abnormally short, little more than four feet tall, yet he was built as massively as the iron safe Simeon Dimsby had just opened. He might have been a blood relative of Dimsby's wife. "Mr. Hardy," he said, "I'd know you anywhere."

He strode into the room. "Your spouse was upstairs with Mrs. Dimsby. Just moments ago I had the pleasure of making her acquaintance." In the brighter illumination of Dimsby's studio, a small but disturbing birthmark was visible on Mantigore's forehead.

"Auric," Hardy heard Dimsby saying, "have you dined?"

Mantigore grinned broadly. He drew an oversized bandanna from his pocket and wiped a speck of red from the corner of his mouth. "Yes," he said.

"Well then, I was about to show Mr. Hardy the kind of materials I use for my color work."

"Were you, indeed?" Mantigore responded. "Then my timing is apt, is it not?"

He slipped his suit coat from his shoulders and laid it carefully aside, drawing a large, glistening blade from an inside pocket.

Dimsby lifted a huge iron pot from the safe. It resembled the one Eustacia Dimsby had used in her kitchen, but was larger.

Far larger.

Dimsby placed it carefully on a work table very near to Regis Hardy. The author knew even before he peered into it what he would see, but he could not keep from looking.

His impulse to retch was forgotten in the terror and pain that he felt as Simeon Dimsby seized him by the elbows, his grip like ice-cold iron.

Auric Mantigore said, "I'm so happy that I got to meet you this once, Mr. Hardy. I do so admire your work. You can rest assured that Mantigore Press will do its very best with *Return to Elmwood.* I give you my word, we're going to make your book a success. We're going to cook up something really spicy to help put it over."

He nodded as if in pleased agreement with himself. "And yet, you may rest assured, it will be in the best of taste."

Richard A. Lupoff

This is one of the rare instances in which I got a story from a dream, or rather from a series of dreams. The dreams may have been loosely based on my grandmother's stories of her childhood in Austria, well over a hundred years ago. But here is an oddity. I dreamed these dreams in Italian—and I don't know Italian. I can barely struggle through words like *pizza* and *spaghetti*. So how could I dream in Italian? A mystery to me!

Villaggio Sogno

"You'll have to pay the toll if you want me to drive into the city," the driver said, "or you could walk across the bridge and save some coins." His name was Signore Azzurro. His passengers were two girls, Margherita and Francesca. It was not clear which girl he addressed, and in fact he probably didn't care. As long as he collected his fare and a nice tip—surely these two nice girls would give him a nice tip—they were pretty much interchangeable to him.

They put their heads together and conferred, examined the contents of their purses, and decided to be extravagant.

The driver whipped up the big bay horse and clicked his tongue. The beast moved forward in a cheerful trot, the *carrozza*'s wheels rattling noisily over the rough gravel roadway. The River Fiume roared beneath the stone bridge, its foam and spray reaching the bridge, an occasional splatter of icy water reaching even to the *carrozza*. When this happened the girls shrieked in mock horror and alarm.

The city rose above white stone cliffs on the other side of the River Fiume. Buildings three and even four storeys tall, banners, noise, people speaking many languages, people whose skins were of many colors, wagons and carriages drawn by horses and horses ridden by handsome bravos and even a few actually ridden by women, barking dogs running among them—Villaggio Sogno was a place of marvels and of dreams.

Villaggio Sogno was a city of whitewashed plaster and wood. The buildings were roofed in copper and turquoise. When the sun glinted off the walls and the roofs, as it did this day, Villaggio Sogno rose to the sky like a dream. Old Allegra Chiavolini, the teaching woman, spoke of such wonders and warned the children of *il fascino,* the glamour, the magical spell that could give a repulsive old man the appearance of a handsome young wrestler, a hovel the appearance of a lovely cottage, a pig the appearance of a beautiful roe.

"You can sometimes defeat *un fascino,*" Signora Chiavolini taught them, "with this piece of music." And she whistled a tune.

The children of the town all learned to whistle the tune, and Margherita in time learned to play it as well. She had doubts about the old teacher's story, she had doubts that there was such a thing as the glamour, but it was thrilling, on occasion, to awaken late at night when the whole household was in bed and asleep, and imagine that some frightening creature was at large, disguised as a harmless animal or person. Margherita whistled the tune then, that Allegra Chiavolini had taught her, and went back to sleep feeling safe.

The two girls had been there before, brought for special treats by their respective families, but today was a special day. They were permitted to visit Villaggio Sogno without adult supervision. Their parents had fretted, Margherita's mother in particular, but twelve years old was almost grown up, or at least beginning to be grown up, and before much longer they would be going to the higher school and having parties with boys at them.

So each girl, with her savings in her purse (and with some forbidden lip-rouge and daring eye-shadow as well) was permitted to go off for the day with her best friend.

"Where shall I drop you off, young ladies?" Signore Azzurro asked over his shoulder.

The girls conferred again. Then Margherita said, "Over there. In front of the department store." This, they both knew, was not *un fascino*. Their parents had bought things for them in this emporium and they had taken them home to admire and to use.

Signore Azzurro pulled to the edge of the road and turned with his hand out. He received his payment and a tip. "When shall I pick you up for the ride home?"

Another hasty conference, even though the matter had been discussed in private and in meetings with both families, and the girls had given their solemn promise in this regard.

"When the clock in the Great Tower sounds the end of work and mechanical figures emerge to give their show."

"Very good, young miss."

The girls dismounted.

The driver watched them until they disappeared into the crowd, a wistful smile on his face. Perhaps he was a father himself, or perhaps it was simply his nature.

Margherita and Francesca stood in front of the great store. It rose three storeys into the air and its front was as long as three houses set end to end. There was a sign mounted atop the building giving the name of the establishment: *Mercato Monumentale*. The front of the store was made up of a series of show windows displaying the most marvelous clothing. The girls had seen it on their earlier visits to Villaggio Sogno, but their parents had hurried them past, intent on whatever errands occupied the minds of stodgy adults. Now they could study the contents of the windows to their hearts' content.

They could also use the polished window-glass as a mirror, and they stood side by side applying red to their lips and blue to their eyelids. They wore similar braids, Margherita's a rich, dark brown color that approached blackness; Francesca's, red. Margherita's eyes were a blue that could also be mistaken for black; Francesca's, brown.

When they had finished applying the forbidden cosmetics they inspected each other's handiwork, approved, and entered the store.

In an hour they emerged carrying packages and wearing hats. Margherita's was striped green and yellow, with a yellow feather rising from it. She wore it tilted to one side. Francesca's was a bright red beret.

They left the Mercato Monumentale and set out looking for a place to get some food. As they wended their way they passed street vendors and artisans who had set up shop on the sidewalk. They stopped to study the wares of a craftsman who made miniatures in silver. Francesca bought a tiny silver pin in the form of a book for her friend Margherita. Margherita bought a tiny silver pin in the form of a piccolo for her friend Francesca. They attached the ornaments to each other's blouses and exchanged a fond hug. Then they resumed their search for a meal.

They considered one place that smelled delicious but was filled with rough-looking men. Another seemed to appeal mainly to ancient women in their thirties and forties.

Finally they found a restaurant called Honshu Kekko Ryori.

They had a delicious meal, unlike anything they had ever eaten at home. Each dish was arranged like a bouquet. There were tender meats with delicate flavors, mushrooms of varieties new to the girls, vegetables and noodles in steaming broth. Most memorable was a bright green condiment that made both girls cry until they laughed. The meal was served by a beautiful woman of Honshu wearing a lovely silk kimono. Margherita and Francesca couldn't get over how lovely the woman was, or how delicious the food had been. They managed to eat with chopsticks, while sitting on straw mats without their shoes. It was like being in a different world. They agreed that someday they would visit Honshu and see how people lived there.

But after lunch they decided it was time to do what they had come to Villaggio Sogno to do. Margherita's father was going to have a birthday soon and the girls were here to buy him a gift. He was a big man who seldom spoke. When he was not at work he loved to read. Margherita had consulted her mother about the best gift for her father, and they decided together that a book would be the best present. Margherita thought that a beautiful new book would be the best choice, but her mother surprised her by saying that an old book would make Father happiest.

"It's the thought that counts," Mother said, "he'll be happy to be remembered and will love anything you get him. But I happen to know that he best loves books by an old writer named Jacopo Mursino. He wrote an epic poem in sixteen volumes, detailing the history of the universe from its creation to its end. Without your father's knowledge," Mother continued, "I have consulted the town scholar about Signore Mursino's poem. He says that only fifteen volumes are known to exist. The missing book is referred to in several others. Even its name is known. It is called *Lavori di Hipocrita*. By report, it tells the story of the Last Great Era, before the universe ends in volume sixteen. No copy of volume sixteen is known to survive in any library, anywhere, or in any scholar's collection."

Mother frowned in concentration.

Margherita knew her father's two great loves. One was to spend time in the bosom of his family. They walked the woodland near home taking note of every bird, animal, and flower that they encountered. They had formed a family orchestra. Father played a fiddle, Mother a miniature hip-harp, Margherita's brother Ottavio a brass horn, and Margherita herself a silver flute. The flute was the oldest and most precious possession in the family. It had been crafted by Mother's mother's father's uncle-in-law, the greatest silversmith in their town. Even after these years—generations—Alceo the Silversmith was remembered and spoken of with awe. Metalworkers to this day considered it the highest compliment to be called, "Another Alceo." The flute was said to have supernatural powers, but the only power that Margherita had evoked from it was the power of beautiful music.

The family orchestra performed in the evenings for their own pleasure, and on holidays in the town square for the entertainment of the community.

Father's second great love was his books. When he was not with his family, he was locked in his study with his books. When he was with his family he would tolerate any prank. He was a broad-shouldered man, heavy-bearded and muscled. He could lift Mother, Ottavio, and Margherita off the ground at once. As a young man, family legend had it, he and another had been rivals for the affection of the town's greatest beauty.

Father and his rival, a lad named Farruccio Farruli, had agreed to wrestle for the right to court the beauty, and a space had been selected for their match on the bank of the River Fumio. After an hour of struggle the two young men were both covered with a mixture of blood, mud, and grass, and were down to their last resources of strength. At this moment Father had charged at his rival, hoisted him bodily into the air, and thrown him so far into the river that a boat had been sent to bring him back to shore, for fear that he would drown if left to his own resources.

When Father turned back to face the beauty, she said, "You have beaten your rival. Now you may try to win my love. A good start would be to wash yourself off and put on a decent outfit."

Father pressed his suit successfully.

Margherita's earliest memories included lying on the carpet near the hearth on a winter's night, and Father lifting her as if she weighed no more than his fiddle, carrying her to her cradle and kissing her good-night. He always murmured something before he kissed her but she could never understand what he said.

Even now, almost a woman (or so she told herself), she would sometimes lower her head and close her eyes near the fire, and Father would lift her and carry her to her bed, and murmur something before he kissed her. She had yet to understand his words. He never realized that she only pretended to fall asleep.

Father's second favorite author, after the poet-historian Jacopo Mursino, was the story-writer Carla Zennatello. If Mursino's greatest (and sole surviving) work was his sixteen-volume history of the universe, the creations of Carla Zennatello were far more brief. Each "book" consisted of a single riddle, written in Zennatello's personal calligraphy, preceded and followed by pages of beautiful, colorful illustrations showing noble men, lovely women, playful children, muscular horses, swift roes, dogs, cats, and birds. Each book was bound in the tough leaves of a plant that grew deep in the woods, tanned to a strength and stamina greater than that of leather, for Carla Zennatello would neither kill any sentient being nor use the product of such a killing.

Each such book could fit into the hand of an infant. Carla Zennatello would invent a riddle and create one of her little books each time a child was born in the community, and give it to the new mother to be held in trust until the child was old enough to be entrusted with such a treasure.

Carla Zennatello never revealed the answer to any of her riddles. She told the parents of each child who received one of her books that when that child had solved her special riddle, she would know her destiny.

Now Carla Zennatello had been dead for two hundred years, almost as long as Jacopo Mursino had been dead. A few of her riddle-books were known to exist, but none of the solutions of her riddles were remembered.

Margherita and Francesca knew there was a store in Villaggio Sogno that sold new books, but they hoped to find one where they might find an old book to please Margherita's father. They walked until they heard a boy's voice crying the news. They followed their ears until they saw him, a boy somewhat younger than themselves, dressed in worn but clean trousers and blouse. He held a stack of printed sheets at his side and with the hand not so occupied he waved a single copy.

Francesca craned her neck to get a proper look at the printed sheet. Its title was *Il Popolo di Sogno*. There was a picture of a vainglorious looking man on it. He was waving to an admiring throng.

Margherita asked the boy if he knew where they might buy an old book.

The boy looked at the two girls, puzzled. "Who would want an old book?" he asked. "Better to buy a new one. Best of all, buy a copy of *Il Popolo* and get a portrait of our glorious leader for no extra money. Learn of yesterday's kicking match, learn of bodies found in alleys, learn of armies marching and of politicians arguing."

He took up his cry again.

A passer-by bought a news sheet.

Francesca tugged at the boy's elbow and Margherita said, "We want to buy an old book. Does anyone sell them in Villaggio Sogno?"

The boy said, angrily, "Go see Signore Malipiero."

"How do we find him?"

"He'll be in his shop."

"Where is that? You are not being at all helpful!"

"And you are not helping my business!" He stopped to sell another news sheet.

"Where is Signore Malipiero's shop?"

Angrily the boy turned to face the two girls. He pointed a finger and told them to proceed to the town square, to turn at the tavern displaying a sign that read *Il Ubriacone* and a giant painted mug of *birra*, to continue until they came to a dressmaker's establishment, they could not miss the dressmaker's establishment unless they were even more stupid than they seemed, to turn again (and he pointed to show them which way to turn) and they would surely see the establishment of Signore Malipiero or they could come back and he would refund their fee.

"If I am not here, merely ask for me. Guglielmo Pipistrello. Now good-bye."

He held out his hand.

Francesca put a coin in it.

Signorino Pipistrello turned away and resumed shouting the news.

Margherita and Francesca followed his directions faithfully. They stopped in the town square. A statue stood there. Its title was embossed on a copper plate, green with age: *Chaos Giving Birth to Order*. To Margherita the statue looked like a great fish or dolphin vomiting up a globe of the world. The name of the sculptor also appeared on the copper plate, and the year of the statue's creation, long ages ago. Couples strolled in the sunlight and children ran among them playing ball or eating sweets. The Great Tower stood above the square, a clock on its face and iron doors waiting to open at the end of the day.

The tavern was where Guglielmo Pipistrello had said it would be.

The dressmaker's establishment was where he had said it would be, also.

The two girls halted in the street before a shop with a wooden trough filled with old books in front of it, and glass windows so obscured with cobwebs and dust that they could not see through them. The trough of books bore a hand-written sign that gave the price of the books as a small coin for one, two small coins for three, and a large coin for an armload.

Above the door of the shop was a sign, not merely painted but carved into wood: *Ettore Malipiero, Purveyor of the Rare and Precious.*

Margherita and Francesca stared at each other.

"The boy said we could get an old book from Signore Malipiero."

"And he said that we would find Signore Malipiero's shop near the dressmaker."

"And there is a trough of cheap books outside the shop."

Margherita bent over the trough of books. She picked one up, that seemed to be promising. She had learned to read at an early age, learning to read music and learning to read words at the same time. Her earliest books had mixed pictures and music and stories.

Her mother had been her teacher. Her brother, Ottavio, could already read when Margherita was learning. It was competition with Ottavio that spurred her to develop both her skill with books and her talent with her silver flute until she surpassed Ottavio's performances with his horn.

The book looked, felt, and smelled old. Its cover was battered and the title could not be read. Margherita opened it to the title page and read, *Three Voyages in Distant Lands,* by Sylvio di Filippo. She had never heard of the author, but then, she realized, she had never heard of many authors. She knew of Jacopo Mursino and of Carla Zennatello because Father spoke of them. He had read all but one volume of Mursino's great poetic history of the universe and longed above all things to read the missing volume. In this, he had said many times over family meals, he was but one of many. He said that he wished he had been able to obtain two of Zennatello's works. They had become known as blessing books, and there was competition for the few known to survive. If he had been able to obtain two of them he would have made birth-gifts of them to his own two children, Ottavio and Margherita, but had instead laid a precious fiddle in Ottavio's cradle and the silver flute made by Margherita's ancestor Alceo in her crib, so that the children should grow up with the instruments as their earliest possessions and familiar companions.

Next to *Three Voyages in Distant Lands* Margherita found a copy of a book she already knew, Claudia Belluzzo's *Tunes and Rhymes for Little Ones.* She had loved that book, with its colorful pictures of tiny animals, birds, tortoises, and bears. Each picture was accompanied by a little poem and a simple musical lesson. Margherita had played those melodies on a miniature child's flute—this was before she was old enough to play Alceo's silver flute—and the creatures in the book had danced to her tune. Or so it seemed to her. And Mother gave her testimony that it was indeed so.

A shriek interrupted Margherita's concentration on the trough of books. It was Francesca who had shrieked. She was clutching a book to her chest. "*Minuscolo-Minuscolo!* I used to love this book! I slept with it beneath my pillow! I read my copy until it fell to pieces. Now I see another copy."

The two girls prepared to enter the store. Behind them was a narrow cobblestone street. It was unlike the broad thoroughfare where Signore Azzurro had left them, nor was there the color and bustle of the town square with its statue and great tower. Instead the street was dark. The buildings were old and their upper storeys seemed to lean toward each other, covering the cobblestones and blotting out the bright sky and warm sunlight of the day.

Something sleek in shape scurried past on one side of the street. It was a dark shade, maybe green but more probably gray-black. It appeared to be covered with a scaly or leathery skin. An armadillo in Villaggio Sogno? A snake? But it had legs, Margherita thought. Surely it moved too rapidly to be a terrapin. A small crocodile, such as the Gypsies said lived in the swamps alongside the River Nile in their homeland?

Whatever it was, it dived into a dark, narrow opening between two buildings.

An old woman, her bonnet hiding her face and long sleeves concealing her hands, scuttled by on the other side of the street, then disappeared into another street. A cart rolled past, pulled by an ox as tall as a man and as wide as a shed. The driver wore a broad-brimmed hat. His shoulders were as massive as two hogs.

Carrying the three books with them, Margherita and Francesca entered the store. As they set foot upon the doorstep they were confronted by a man so tall that he had to stoop to leave the shop. He was as thin as a stick and his height was added to by a pointed cap of purple felt. He growled at the girls and elbowed them aside, shoving between them and scurrying away from the shop.

Inside the establishment the girls confronted a boy who could not be more than fifteen years of age. His hair was the color of ground barley, his eyes the shade of the River Fiume. His ears stuck out from the sides of his head like the wings of a raven. His bones protruded through the shoulders and elbows of his dust-colored shirt. The sleeves of the shirt were too short for his arms and his wrists stuck out like two knobs.

"Signorine," the boy addressed the girls, "what can I do for you? You wish to purchase books?" He ogled the volumes that

Margherita and Francesca had brought from the trough. "Let me see your choices, please." The boy stepped behind a wooden counter, darkened by years and rubbed smooth by countless hands and books.

The girls laid their choices on the counter.

The boy turned them over, nodding his approval.

Francesca gave another shriek. Really, Margherita decided, she would have to talk with her friend about that. It was humiliating to be with someone who reacted to each little surprise as if a winged angel had suddenly appeared in the sky, surrounded by a nimbus of flame.

"What was that?" Francesca gasped.

Margherita turned in time to see a dark form disappear behind a curtain covering a doorway in the back of the store. "It is just—it was—"

"It was—" Francesca waved her hands at the level of her face.

The boy behind the counter leaned across the wood, craning his neck. "That's just Nero."

"Who?"

"Nero. The store dog. Signore Malipiero's dog. That's all. He lives in the store."

"No." Francesca shook her head. "That was no dog. It had skin like a lizard."

"No." Margherita shook her head. "It had feathers. It was shaped like a dog but it was covered with feathers. Maybe it was a—what do you call it—a gryphon."

"No such thing as a gryphon," Francesca said. "I've heard of gryphons, read about them and seen pictures. They are imaginary beasts."

"Oh, really." Margherita was annoyed. "I suppose it was a big India-bird, then."

"Not with skin like that."

"Feathers."

The boy with the too-short shirtsleeves came out from behind the counter. He stood facing the curtained doorway. "Come on, Nero. Nero, come to Peppino."

The curtain shook, then a nose appeared, or was it a beak, followed by a four-legged creature. It was a gryphon, Margherita thought, with clawed feet and feathers like a bird. She squeezed her eyes shut, then opened them again. It was an ordinary dog with short dark fur and a squarish face that it shoved into the skinny boy's hand.

Margherita turned to Francesca.

Francesca had dropped one hand and held the other to her mouth. "I thought it was a lizard," she said, "but I see, it's only a dog." She squatted on the creaking wooden floorboards and put her arms around Nero's neck.

The skinny boy reached behind the counter and brought out two bits of biscuit. He handed one to each girl. "Give him a treat and he'll be your friend."

Each girl, in turn, fed her bit of biscuit to the creature. Nero wagged his tail gratefully.

"Your name is Peppino," Margherita addressed the boy.

"At your service." Peppino made a silly bow. "Peppino Campanini. Apprentice bookseller and student of manuscripts and wonders."

Margherita and Francesca introduced themselves.

"So, you wish only these treasures from our bargain bin." The boy heaved an exaggerated sigh. "My master will be displeased with me if I cannot sell you something better than these." He lifted the three books and lifted his eyebrow and said, "But I admit that they are a good choice. Oh, you found the *Minisculo-Minisculo*. Is that what brought you in? Signore Malipiero always salts the bargain trough with a few little treasures. I think you two ladies have cleaned us out today. *Minisculo, Tunes and Rhymes, Tre Viaggi*—everything else outside is trash. Surely you will not insist on buying these three treasures for a single coin."

"That's what your sign says."

"Of course, of course, but we do not count on a customer so sharp-eyed as you and your companion are."

"What else do you have?"

Peppino Campanini put the heels of his hands to his eyes as if to keep himself from crying. Then he dropped his hands. "You are too smart. I cannot deal with you."

He leaned over the counter again, impossibly far. Margherita half expected him to lose his balance and fall to the floor at the feet of herself and her friend, but he managed to hang on. "Signore Malipiero! Signore Malipiero! Customers to wait on, please."

Nero had sat on his haunches throughout the exchange. Now he stood up and trotted to the curtained doorway. He reappeared tugging by the cuff an old man, red faced and gray haired, wearing round spectacles, very dirty, making Margherita wonder how he saw through them and why he bothered to use them. He wore a pale shirt patterned with large black dots and trousers of a color so long-ago faded that it was impossible to identify. Nero had his teeth in one shirt cuff; in the other hand the old man held a tattered, oversized book. Slips of paper curled from between its pages and the old man had crooked his forefinger to save his place and his middle finger to save another.

He blinked at the skinny boy. "Peppino, why do I pay you? Why do you call me whenever there is a customer?"

Without waiting for his helper to respond, the old man turned toward Margherita and Francesca. He bowed deeply. He had a round stomach and he made a sound something like "Oof!" as he stood back up. "You wish a powder, a potion, something to help you to learn without studying, something to make your boyfriends chase you, something—"

He stopped and studied them. "My apologies. Two beauties such as you need no help to make your boyfriends chase you. You have boyfriends? You want something else? Talent? No, I can see that you both have great talent. What do you want?"

Francesca said, "My friend wants a birthday gift for her father."

The old man nodded. "Ahh."

Margherita said, "He loves books."

"Ahh," the old man said again. "Well, you have come to the right place. My name is Ettore Malipiero and this is my establishment. As you can see, I have books."

He made a sweeping gesture that included all of the store and seemed also to include Nero, Peppino, the mysterious realm behind the curtained doorway, the street outside and very likely all of Villaggio Sogno.

"And what are your names, young *signorine?* And what does your father wish to receive for his gift? You must ask yourself,

What will make my beloved father happy on this day?"

"He loves old books," Francesca said.

"Very old books," Margherita said. "And other old things, but best of all, old books."

"Good, good," the old man said. "The old books are the best books."

Nero snuffled at Margherita's hand. He was looking for another biscuit but she had no more. She bent to apologize to the dog, and as she did so she could detect Signore Malipiero from the corner of her eye. There was something strange about him, something that did not agree with his cheerful and friendly manner. She straightened but he was just an old man, smiling at two girls and his dog. And from the corner of her eye, Margherita caught another glimpse of Nero, and he was not a friendly dog but something else once again, something that he ceased to be when she looked more closely at him.

"How much money do you have?" the old man asked.

Margherita and Francesca conferred. They had started the day with their savings but they had paid Signore Arruzza for the ride into Villaggio Sogno and had tipped him to make sure that he would return for them at the end of the day. And their meal at Honshu Kekko Ryori had cost them a pretty penny and then some. And they even bought a news sheet from Guglielmo Pipistrello just to get him to pay attention to them long enough to get directions to the bookstore.

To Ettore Malipiero, Francesca said, "Not very much."

"Not very much, eh? Then why did you come to my store? Don't you know this is the finest establishment in Villaggio Sogno for the purchase of rarities of this type? Perhaps your father, Signorina, would like a powder instead. How old is he? Do you think his powers are waning? Something to restore the strength and energy of a man of some years. I can make you a very good price, and your father will be grateful. As will your mother, I assure you."

"No, a book."

"Ah, well." Signore Malipiero scratched his head. Margherita was almost certain that she saw sparks fly from his hair when he scratched, and the sound that accompanied them was unlike anything she had ever heard before.

"Perhaps," he said, "a new book would please your father. There are many talented authors even today, Signorina. Does your father read Cesare Zampieri? Very fine, his writings inspire the reader to deeds of courage and nobility. I even knew a man who had been unhappily married for many years but did nothing save put up with a nagging wife and a demanding daughter, pardon my candor, Signorine, I am an old man, you must forgive me, until he read a copy of Zampieri's fine book, and then he set his mind to awaken him one night after the entire household was soundly sleeping and—"

He stopped and smiled as if ashamed of himself. "I am so sorry. This matter is too delicate for the ears of two such young ladies as yourselves. No, I would not recommend Zampieri. Perhaps a better choice would be the meditations of Oreste Ronga. Yes, I think Ronga might be the perfect gift for the father of a lovely young lady like yourself." He turned to Francesca. "I think your friend's father would enjoy Ronga. Do you know Oreste Ronga? A very talented writer. No? You do not know Ronga? There is a store not far from here that sells new books. I send customers there every day. *Libri e Libretti*. Just step outside my shop and turn—what is it, Signorine?"

They were both frowning.

"An old book!" Margherita said.

"An old book!" Francesca echoed.

The old man sighed. "If you insist. Well, come with me, I will see if I can find something, perhaps a codex whose binding is lost, water-stained, foxed, tilted, missing a signature. I'll try and find you something."

Something scratched Margherita's hand and she looked down and caught a glimpse of a clawed foot moving away. But it was only Nero. "I think he wants another biscuit," she told Peppino.

"It's almost his dinner time," the boy said. "I don't know if it's such a good idea."

Nero stood on his hind legs. He was tall enough to reach the counter and he scratched its surface, leaving a row of parallel tracks. For a common dog he had very long, very sharp claws, more like those of a hunting bird than a house pet.

Signore Malipiero said something softly to his assistant and the boy grew pale. He reached under the counter for a biscuit and tossed it to Nero.

"Come." Ettore Malipiero stood in the curtained doorway to the second room. "Come with me, young ladies, and we will see what we can find to make a suitable gift for your father's birthday gift. You are sisters?"

Francesca said, "No, we're neighbors and friends."

"Ah, good." The man led them into a second room. Like the first, it held many, many bookshelves. It was a very odd room, with five walls instead of the customary four. Two of the walls were filled with books from floor to ceiling; two, from ceiling to floor; and one, starting at the level of Margherita's blue eyes, was filled in both directions, to the ceiling and to the floor.

There were a number of cabinets in the room, each with many small drawers. The cabinets were of wood. The drawer-pulls, by their appearance, were of rare ivory. If this were the case, the ivory would have been imported from distant Abyssinia.

The center of the room was clear, save for two wooden chairs.

Oil lamps and candelabra stood on the cabinets. When they entered the room only a single lamp was burning, casting dark shadows in the room. The flickering flame of the lamp made the dark room seem doubly dark, but Signore Malipiero lit a straw from the burning lamp and used it to light more lamps and candles.

"Sit yourselves down," Signore Malipiero told the girls. "I will bring you some books. Oh, I have been in this business for a very long time, young signorine. I have been buying and selling books and other things for more years that you can imagine. I do know my stock. Oh, yes."

He went to one wall and stood studying the bookcases, one hand to his chin, which had clearly not seen the glint of his razor for some days, the other upraised tentatively as if he were about to reach for this book—no, this one—no, this. At last he gave a satisfied sigh and pulled a volume from the shelf. He did not carry it to the two girls, but instead walked to a wooden cabinet and laid the book on its back so that the light of a candelabrum flickered across its reddish cover.

Margherita noticed that the flames of the candles and the lamps were wavering as if in a breeze, and in fact she did feel a chilly flow of air passing over her face and her shoulders. She looked at Francesca and saw a wisp of her friend's hair flutter in the current of air.

Signore Malipiero crossed the room and knelt to reach the bottom row of books. He pulled a volume in a brown cover from the shelf, studied it for a time, then slipped it back into its place. "No, no," the girls heard him mutter, "that one will never do. Not for one's father, not for one's father's birthday." He pulled another volume from the shelf, one with a yellow cover that bore the signs of great age. "Ah, this one, this one will please such a man as could be the parent of such a daughter."

He laid the yellow book on the cabinet beside the red one.

Once more he crossed the room. At the wall where he now stood, a ladder rose. Margherita's gaze had followed the old man since they entered the room. Now she watched him climbing the ladder. It appeared to be old, everything in the store appeared to be old except for the helper, Peppino Campanini.

Margherita watched the old man climb the old ladder until it disappeared into darkness. How tall was this room? Margherita wondered. How high did the bookshelves rise? How high would Signore Malipiero climb?

Sounds of scuffling and of grunting came from high above. The ladder shook. Margherita feared that it would fall, that Signore Malipiero would tumble from the heights and break his neck when he landed. What would happen then?

But eventually the old man's feet reappeared covered in scuffled and worn boots, then his legs, then his torso, then the back of his head. When he reached the floor he turned to face Margherita and Francesca. He was covered in dust or soot, it was not possible to tell which. He held clutched in his arms a huge volume, its binding hiding his entire torso. In fact, it reached from his knees to his shoulders.

Signore Malipiero staggered beneath its weight, struggling to cross the room and lay the huge, black-covered volume, on the cabinet.

He bent and opened a drawer in the cabinet, removing from it an old pair of bellows. He closed the drawer once again, then walked to the far side of the cabinet where directed the bellows at the three books he had pulled from the shelves. He pumped the bellows once, twice, thrice; at the red book, the yellow book, the black book.

A cloud of dust arose from each of the books and was carried on an air current to the center of the room. Margherita was startled and gasped in surprise, not a wise thing to do, for she found that she had inhaled the dust. She heard Francesca gasp as well, and realized that her friend had also inhaled the dust. It had formed a cloud, the three colors blending and whirling about one another, and in the cloud Margherita saw another place, a terrible place.

It was a room larger than any she had seen in her life, a room the ends of which she could not see. The floor was of stone, the stone covered with a deep layer of gray dust. Pillars as large around as the largest tree rose from the floor only to disappear in darkness above. Row upon row the pillars stretched in all directions, so that Margherita turned about, unsure whether she was in the bookstore or in this other place, trying to get her bearings. Instead she felt her head beginning to whirl. Everything about her was gray, fading in the distance to blackness. The air was cold and left a stale odor in her nostrils and a foul, choking flavor in her mouth.

She turned her face and peered upward. She could not see the tops of the pillars, nor the roof above her. There was only blackness. Something cold and very light landed on her face; she brushed it away and found a tiny smudge on her fingertip, as if she had brushed away a small snowflake made of floating soot rather than frozen water.

Rows of blocks stood between the pillars, each as tall as her waist, as long as a wagon and as wide as a bed. Something lay atop each block, covered with what appeared to be a soft cloth.

Everything was gray.

Ettore Malipiero was there, but he was not the kindly, gruff-mannered man of the bookshop. He was something different, something frightening and evil. He was the creature she had seen from the corner of her eye. Nero was at his side, but it was not Nero the friendly hound but Nero the terrible animal she had glimpsed so briefly.

She tried to reach for her friend Francesca's hand but a cold lethargy had stolen away her power of movement.

The creature who was Ettore Malipiero loomed over Margherita and Francesca, the three books balanced in his arms. Even Signore Malipiero was seen through a film of gray, but the books retained a suggestion of their colors. He dropped the red volume on Francesca's lap and the yellow volume on Margherita's. He still held the black book himself, but instead of a feeble old man who could hardly manage to balance the huge volume in his arms, he had become a giant. He was bigger than Margherita's brother Ottavio, bigger than Margherita's father. His skin was not that of an old man, but he was manlike enough to hold the book open before him as easily as a child holds her first reader.

His face was not that of a man. It was more like that of a lizard, and when he opened his mouth to reveal rows of gleaming teeth his tongue flicked out, a tongue forked like that of a snake, and his voice was half the voice of a man and half the hiss of a snake. He turned away and opened cabinet drawers, and Margherita wondered briefly how cabinets had appeared among the great columns, but her attention was drawn back by the sight of this changed Malipiero hooking ivory pulls with curving, razor-like claws. He scooped powder from a drawer and half-spoke, half hissed words while he dropped powder into the burning candles of the candelabrum. As he did so colored columns mushroomed up from the candles, yellow and red and black in this new gray world.

He took a shallow bowl and filled it with powder and stood over Margherita and Francesca and blew the powder at the girls. His breath was cold and stank of rancid oil.

Margherita tried not to breath the powder that the creature that was Signore Malipiero blew at her, but it swirled around her head while she held her breath until finally she could hold her breath no longer and had to inhale the powder. She felt herself lifted. She could not tell if she was floating into the cold, stale air or if Signore Malipiero was lifting her in his scaly arms. She felt a pressure inside her head as if her brain was going to explode. She shut her eyes and tried to think only of Mother, Father, Ottavio, Francesca.

When she opened her eyes she knew she was in that other

world, the gray world of huge columns, rectangular blocks, dust-covered stones and distant blackness. Now she could see the ends of the giant room. Far, far from her the pillars came to an end, as did the rows of blocks; beyond them was blackness and a few very distant stars. A few flakes of the gray, unclean snow drifted from the heavens.

The creature that was Signore Malipiero bent over a block. The cloth that lay over it moved as if lifted by a wind, but Margherita felt no wind. It moved as if what lay beneath it was moving feebly. Signore Malipiero lifted the cloth and lowered his face over what lay on the block. Clearly Margherita saw that the block was of stone, but Signore Malipiero's form prevented her from seeing what lay beneath the cloth.

She raised her eyes. The cloths on other blocks moved as if stirred by the wind or by what lay beneath them. The silence of the great place was nearly complete, but there was some sound, Margherita was certain of this, some faint and strangely sorrowful sound.

The shapes of the things beneath the gray cloths were similar to the lizard-snake Malipiero, yet some of them were smaller than he, and in a strange way made Margherita think that they were the shapes of girls. She shut her eyes, trying to understand what had happened, but when she opened them again she understood no more than she had before. Malipiero moved to another block, drew back another cloth, bent sorrowfully over another girl-lizard-snake.

This was a world of death, she thought, and these were the daughters of the creature she had seen as Ettore Malipiero. Monster though he was, he was a father. He wished to save his daughters. He wished to bring his daughters into Margherita's world.

This must be the meaning of the powder, the yellow and red and black powder. She had been deceived by *un fascino,* a glamour. There was no Signore Malipiero, no human Signore Malipiero. There was only the horrid snake-lizard creature of this world of the dead, and the two snake-lizard daughters of the creature. Somehow, Margherita realized, the father had managed to cross from this dead world into her own, into Margherita's beautiful living world. But he could not abandon his two daughters. He was not a human father but in his own horrid way he was some kind of man, some kind of father.

With a start, Margherita realized that she felt a terrible pity for the snake-lizard Malipiero and an aching kinship for his two snake -lizard daughters. They were girls, unlike Francesca and herself and yet like them, too. What had become of their mother? Did she occupy another block of stone, did she lie beneath another gray cloth? There was no way that Margherita could know. And what would become of Margherita and her friend Francesca now?

The snake-lizard Malipiero loomed over Margherita and Francesca, and over the blocks where lay his two snake-lizard daughters. He held something that might be the great black book and bowl that must contain the colored powders that he had burned in the bookshop. If it was a bookshop! What if the whole shop had been a glamour? What if it was a deceptive extension of this world of death into her own world?

With a whir of wings more faint that that of an insect approaching on a summer's night, a tiny speck appeared. It moved through the distant blackness, through the dark night and the dusted snow beyond the farthest pillars. It moved toward Margherita and the others, growing as it approached, walking upright like a man or a snake-lizard thing, but it was neither.

The thing that was Ettore Malipiero rose to its full height and stood facing the newcomer. The newcomer halted. He smoothed the cloth over one girl-figure, then the other. He placed his hand on Ettore Malipiero's shoulder and drew him toward himself. Margherita thought that the newcomer was trying to comfort Malipiero, but Malipiero seized him in his great claw-tipped hands and hurled him against the nearest pillar.

The newcomer collided with the pillar and crashed to the floor sending up a cloud of gray, choking dust. He leaped to his feet but Malipiero was upon him, slashing with his claws, biting with his rows of shining teeth. The two rolled on the floor, wrestling as Francesca's father and his rival had wrestled so long ago for her mother's favor, but this struggle was for something other than love.

What would happen to Margherita and Francesca once the two

struggling figures had settled their dispute? Margherita decided that Signore Malipiero had found a way to bring her and her friend to this world and was determined to leave them here to spend eternity lying on blocks of stone, covered with heavy cloths, while slow layers of cold dust drifted down upon them. He would return to the world of Villaggio Sogno with his own girls, giving them the places of Margherita and Francesca.

The two fighters, Ettore Malipiero and the newcomer, rolled and thrashed in clouds of dust.

Margherita grasped Francesca by the arm. She pursed her dry lips and tried to whistle the tune that old Allegra Chiavolini had taught the children of the town long ago. Her mouth was dry and tasted of dust and death. All that emerged was a meaningless *whoosh* of air. She wished desperately for her silver flute, the wonderful flute of her ancestor Alceo, but that was at home in her own room. In a flash she reached for the decorative piccolo she had pinned to Francesca's bodice. With trembling fingers she retrieved her gift and placed it against her lips.

Was it a real silver flute, however tiny? Could she draw a tune from it? The finger holes were dreadfully close together but they were placed properly. She blew through the mouthpiece one time, then gave her all to playing the tune that Allegra had taught the children, the tune that the aged woman claimed would dissolve any glamour and reveal the truth behind it.

She managed to evoke Allegra's tune, shrilly and softly, but each note emerged from the instrument accurately and danced away through the cold air.

The dead world disappeared.

The massive pillars, the stone blocks, the shrouded figures, the distant blackness and stars and snow-of-dust disappeared.

Margherita was back in the shop, Francesca at her side. Or was she? She blinked. She was not seated in the five-sided room of *Ettore Malipiero: Purveyor of the Rare and Precious*. She was seated beside Francesca in a shop where dummies stood with half-finished gowns held in place by pins. Pictures of clothing of various sorts adorned the walls. Two, no, three seamstresses sat in a circle chattering busily as they tended to their work. An older woman, clearly the owner of the business, stood with a customer, showing her samples of cloth.

Margherita could not help but take note of the work of the three seamstresses nor to overhear the conversation that took place among them. Each was working on a lovely gown, each gown of a different color. One was yellow and gay; one, red and daring; one, a somber black but brightened with a pattern of glittering diamonds and onyxes.

The first seamstress was saying, "I trust that Signorina A. will be pleased with this golden gown, to wear on her honeymoon journey. I know she will be happy with her new husband."

The second seamstress said, "I hope that Madonna B. will approve of her crimson gown, to wear on her triumphal tour of the concert halls. I know it will draw the attention that a great diva craves."

The third seamstress, smiling, made her contribution. "I know that *La Duchessa* C. will be pleased with her so-dark gown. So young and energetic a woman, to be married to *Il Duca,* so aged and fragile a man. She ordered the gown herself, giving orders that *Il Duca* was not to see it or even know that *La Duchessa* was thus preparing for the inevitable."

Margherita clutched the hand of her friend and tried without success to stifle a giggle.

The older woman looked around, startled. "Who are you two girls? What are you doing in my shop? I didn't see you come in."

She spoke to the seamstresses, calling them by name. "Did any of you see these two girls come in? Do any of you know them?" The seamstresses all shook their heads. No, Madonna. No, Madonna. No.

The woman spoke angrily to Margherita and Francesca. "Did my rival send you here? Have you come to spy on me, to see my new patterns, to steal them from me?"

The girls started to protest but the woman did not wait. "Get out! Get out of my shop! Get out of here or I'll call my son Peppino and have him beat you with a broomstick! Go back where you came from and tell her to get patterns of her own if she wishes to compete with me!"

Chased by the angry woman, Margherita and Francesca stood outside the shop. The sign above the door was carven and painted. It read, *Eleanora Pampanini: Purveyor of Lovely Gowns and Useful Garments.*

Margherita and Francesca clutched each other and set out to retrace their footsteps to the town square. As they turned one corner and another they came upon an establishment called *Libri e Libretti.* Inside they inquired, without much for hope, for Murcino's *Lavori di Hipocrita* or for one of Carla Zennatello's riddle books. The merchant smiled a wry smile. "Not in all my years selling books, young ladies. Not in all my many years." They purchased a new book instead, as a gift for Margherita's father, and left the shop.

As they did so, a very tall figure who had been concealed in a shadowed nook followed them. In the street outside, strangely, he managed to place himself ahead of them in their path.

The two girls halted, gazing up into the face of the very man who had brushed past them as he left the shop of Ettore Malipeiro. He smiled down at them from beneath his pointed cap.

"I could not but hear your request at *Libre e Libretti.*"

"Please, Signore, we are on our way home."

"Of course, of course, Signorina, I would not wish to inconvenience you. But if you seek the books of Signore Mursino or the great Donna Zennatello, I might be able to help you." He bowed and introduced himself. "I am called Ragno Distruttore."

The tall man seemed to arch over the heads of the two girls, like a willow tree arching over a pond.

Francesca said, "Do you have such books?"

"Alas, Signorina, not just now. But books come to me from time to time, as do many other rarities and wonders. If you would care to visit my establishment, I would gladly guide you there right now."

Francesca made to follow the man, but Margherita placed her hand on the arm of her friend. "Look at the sky. It's late. Signore Azzurro will leave without us."

"Yes, yes." Francesca said, "I'm sorry, Signore Distruttore, we cannot."

"Well then, may I extend an invitation. You will find my place of business as well as my home in the Piazza Campo Sereno."

"I do not know that place."

"Ah, surely you can find it. Ask anyone at all. If they do not know the piazza, surely they know it by the monument to the great soprano Lucrezia Spina di Rosa, the famous singing statue of Villaggio Sogno. Once there, you will find my house, as tall among its neighbors as I am tall among other men. Come by day or night. I suffer, you see, from an inability to sleep. You will see the lantern flickering in my window to all hours. It is the burden I bear."

"Come, Francesca! We must go!" Margherita was tugging at her friend's sleeve.

"But, Margherita, Signore Distruttore—"

"We must go!"

"But—"

"Signore Distruttore, addio!" Margherita dragged her friend away from the sticklike man. He reached a long, skinny arm and long, clawlike fingers after them, but Margherita dodged from his grasp, dragging Francesca along with her. Ragno Distruttore pursued them, his long legs covering ground in great strides, but he seemed to tire quickly and soon fell behind. The girls ran until they were out of breath, then stood, feeling more secure in the midst of a crowd of jolly women and men.

By this time the sun was surely setting. The streets of Villaggio Sogno were as busy as ever, but now they were filled with workers making their way home and with celebrants arriving for an evening of revelry. The two girls stopped outside a music hall. From within they could hear musicians tuning their instruments and singers preparing their throats for the evening's performance.

"Why did you drag me away from Signore Distruttore?" Francesca demanded.

"I do not trust that man. He frightened me."

"But he said he might help us find the books."

"We have a book already. Father will have to do without Mursino or Zennatello. I do not know what Signore Distruttore had in mind, but I'm sure we would have been sorry if we had gone with him. You are too trusting, Francesca. Far too trusting."

Francesca snorted. "After this day, I will not be afraid of

anything. "We escaped from monsters, Margherita. I would not be afraid of a mere skinny man."

Margherita felt the need to change the subject. "I feel sorry for Signore Malipiero."

Francesca agreed. "And for his daughters," she added. "Especially for the daughters. I wonder if they had names. I wonder what became of them." She shook her head. "Surely, they died. Their world was nothing but a world of death. Their father was trying to rescue them, trying to make an exchange."

"Us for them," Margherita said.

"Yes, us for them. But instead, it was them for us."

They stood for a few moments, crowds of men and women passing them on all sides, busily heading for whatever destination they had chosen for themselves.

On their way back to *Mercato Monumentale,* Margherita and Francesca passed by Guglielmo Pipistrello, still peddling copies of *Il Popolo di Sogno.* He smiled at them this time. They raised their noses in the air and walked past him.

Signore Azzurro was waiting for them in front of the great department store. "You are ready to go home?" They climbed into the *carrozza.* He whipped up his horse and whistled and the carriage creaked and rattled away from the curb, toward the high bridge, toward the River Fiume, toward home.

"I wish I could have found the missing Mursino volume that Father longs for," Margherita said, "or one of Carla Zenatello's riddle books." The present she had found for her father at *Libri e Libretti* lay in her lap, brightly wrapped and tied with a birthday ribbon.

"Now do you think we should have gone with Signore Distruttore?" Francesca asked.

Margherita shook her head. "Absolutely not!"

"You say that now," Francesca said. "You say that now. But we will return to Villaggio Sogno. I would like to see the statue of the great Lucrezia Spina di Rosa. Surely you agree with me."

"Perhaps."

As the *carrozza* left the high bridge over the River Fiume and turned toward home the girls glanced back at Villaggio Sogno.

The sun had disappeared behind the walls and spires of the town, the sky had darkened and stars were shining from the heavens. Other lights twinkled in the piazzas and in the buildings of the town, where families were gathered at dinner, players performed comedies and tragedies upon the stage, couples exchanged gifts or courted over meals served with wine, ale, or mead. One of them might even be the lantern in Signore Distruttore's window. Someday, Margherita thought, she would leave her family home and make her own way, perhaps in Villaggio Sogno, perhaps in the great world beyond. She might even see the land of Honshu with its soft-spoken people, its lovely costumes and its strange ways.

Margherita felt herself growing sleepy. She knew that Signore Azzurro would deliver her and Francesca safely to their families, and dropped her head to her best friend's shoulder and dozed.

Richard A. Lupoff

Seamus "Splash" Shanahan was inspired unabashedly by one of my childhood heroes, Lance O'Casey, a comic book hero whose exploits were often scripted by my friend Otto Binder. Lance was a fairly simple individual, a happy-go-lucky adventurer who sailed the South Seas encountering pirates, pearl divers, and lovely Polynesian maidens month after month. My protagonist is a far more complex character with a somewhat checkered background. I introduced Splash in a story called "Secret of the Red Robe Men." "Tangaroa's Eye" is Shanahan's second adventure. There may be more but I make no promises.

Tangaroa's Eye

The walls of the shack were of rough-hewn, undressed timber. The roof was crudely thatched with palm fronds and local grasses, backed with scrap tin. In theory the tin kept the shack dry in the rainy season and the thatch provided insulation against the brutal heat of the tropic sun. Neither worked very well, but that was the theory, anyway. And the thatch made a nice home for the rats who built their nests inside it.

A short staircase led to a little-used verandah. The shack might once have been whitewashed but years of weathering had removed all visible effects of that effort, and a series of owners had never got around to renewing the coating. Someone, however, had gone to the trouble of carving a sign which was mounted over the entrance. In large capitals it read, FRISCO JIM'S. Beneath these bold words, in smaller lettering, had been added, *American Bar.*

It was early afternoon and the place contained only three or four male customers, barefooted, unshaven, old beyond their years. There were even a couple of females, long past their prime, exchanging occasional angry glances. Each might have fancied herself younger and cleaner and more desirable than her rival. Why did the males, each sunk in his woozy world of alcoholic dreams and regrets, not pay the women tribute?

Such was the steady clientele of FRISCO JIM'S *American Bar.* Over this little population of regular customers Frisco Jim himself presided, a monarch in his own kingdom, from his place behind the mahogany.

There was one more customer in FRISCO JIM'S *American Bar.* He sat in a corner of the room, his elbows propped on a rickety table, a glass of rum in front of him. If he had raised his eyes he would have seen Frisco Jim and the other customers of the establishment, female as well as male. He did not, however, raise his eyes. He sat with his gaze focused on the liquor.

It was not very good rum and it had not been served in a very clean glass, but that did not matter to the man. His name was Seamus Shanahan, known as Splash. He wore a captain's cap that had once been white, a striped shirt, faded dungarees and lightweight deck shoes.

This was the situation when the uproar broke out.

Shanahan, it should be added, was an alcoholic. Shanahan would not have called himself that. He was a plain-spoken man, a New Englander who had served aboard the submarine *Cichlid* during the Great War. When a German cruiser's depth bombs destroyed the sub Shanahan was the sole survivor, thanks to the self-sacrifice of his best friend. Guilt and grief had sent him to the bottle after the war, and it was only when he had hit bottom that he had climbed out of the bottle and worked his way back to a degree of self-respect.

Now he lived on board a tiny sloop, the *Goby*, eking a living by trading among the islands of the Western Pacific. His experiences had left him with a hatred and fear of the sea. He had chosen his occupation with deliberation, forcing himself to confront his demons every day as a way to preserve his manhood. And when the liquor-craving got strong he would head for the nearest saloon and buy himself a glass of rum and stare into it, defying it to make him drink, until he felt strong enough to rise to his feet and walk away, leaving the rum behind for someone whose need was greater than his own.

A sound like a gunshot broke Shanahan's reverie.

He looked up, startled. The room was abuzz with anger and consternation.

Frisco Jim had started around the bar. "Here now," he ground, "get out of here, you! What's the matter with you! Can't you read, *American Bar?* No, I guess not. Well I'm telling you, no kanakas in here! This place is for Americans!"

The sound like a gunshot had been made by a shiny silver dollar slamming against the table top inches from Shanahan's face. He looked up in time to see the new arrival whirl and confront Frisco Jim.

"Americans, hey? I'm as American as anybody and more so than most!"

"I said, *no kanakas!*" Frisco Jim repeated. He reached back, ducking his arm under the bar.

"Don't do that!" the newcomer shot. A Navy Colt revolver had appeared as if by magic in the newcomer's hand and was pointed at Frisco Jim. "Just come on around the bar as you were," the newcomer ordered. "Move carefully. I don't want to hurt anybody. You others—" she gestured with the heavy Colt "—just sit back down and drink your drinks. I have no quarrel with you."

Half-turning toward Shanahan, the newcomer said, "It's you I have business with. You are Seamus Shanahan, aren't you?"

Shanahan said, "I am."

He looked up at the stranger. As tall as he was, dressed in a cotton plaid shirt and dungarees that looked newer than his own. A holster on one hip and a foot-long scabbard on the other. Shanahan looked down. Boots, and he was certain there was another weapon or two therein.

He looked back up at the stranger's face and body and arms. A woman, with black skin and strong hands, one of which held the Colt unwaveringly while the other hovered near the handle of her mighty knife.

Shanahan said, "I'll get you a chair, Miss. We can sit together with our backs to the wall."

She nodded and he did what he had offered to do.

Frisco Jim was frowning. "You don't talk like no kanaka."

"I told you," the woman said, "I'm American. I was born in Boston."

"I detected that in your voice," Shanahan put in. "I'm from Providence myself."

"So I've heard."

"Really," Shanahan replied. "And from whom did you hear that, may I ask?"

"Your old friend in San Francisco. Fisherman called Pops Piacenza."

Shanahan grinned. "Thought you were from Boston."

"I said I was born there. Don't make assumptions, Shanahan."

"And don't take liberties. Try Mister Shanahan."

"Fair enough. I'm Mrs. Preston."

"Okay, then. Seamus. Or Splash. Take your pick, Mrs. Preston. And where is Mr. Preston?"

"Seamus. I'm Lydia. Just so long as we're on equal terms. And he's dead."

"I'm sorry."

"So am I. That's why I'm in this slum. By the way, what are you doing in a dive like this? You don't look like these other dregs."

Shanahan shook his head. "Too long a story, Missus, uh, Lydia."

She looked around the room. The male drinkers had gone back to their drinks. The females had gone back to staring daggers at each other. Frisco Jim had gone back behind the bar. He looked very peaceful now.

"Maybe we could find a better place to talk than this dive, Seamus."

"Room to sit aboard my boat. Or we could just walk on the beach."

"Let's start walking. Then we'll see." She picked up her dollar and slipped it into her dungaree pocket. She strode out of the saloon. Shanahan followed her. She didn't look back. Either she was confident that nobody would attack her from the rear or she was too arrogant to consider the possibility or she trusted Shanahan.

Take your choice.

"How long has that shack been there?" she asked.

He rubbed his hand over his chin. The stubble was getting bristly, he'd probably take a shave one day soon. "Ever since the last one was knocked down ."

"And when was that?"

"Let me see. I think Frisco Jim built it in 1922."

"That recently?"

"Big typhoon that year. Tsunami, actually. Knocked down the old place. At least, that's the story. I was back on the mainland then. Story is, every time a big storm comes along and knocks the place down, they put it up again. Time before that was the Yoshimama tsunami. That was in '96. Time before that was '83 when Krakatoa blew."

"You're quite the folklorist. Frisco Jim didn't look that old to me."

"He's just the latest in a long line of Frisco Jims."

"You picked a lovely group of friends back there," Lydia Preston changed the subject. "Can't you do better than that?"

Shanahan laughed. "Not around here." He shook his head. "But they're not such a bad bunch. Mostly harmless, actually."

"Really?" Lydia Preston sounded unconvinced.

"Don't turn your back on them, if that's what you mean. But this island isn't exactly the Cote d'Azur."

"I didn't think it was."

The air was heavy and a warm breeze sent waves running up the strand to mutter and bubble before retreating, leaving behind a line of luminous foam that gradually faded time after time. The moon was huge and hot, the ocean on one hand blue-green and hissing and the jungle on the other green-black and whispering.

The settlement housed a few dozen traders, Americans, English, German, Chinese. FRISCO JIM'S *American Bar,* Shanahan knew, was actually open to any whites. The name was a joke, of sorts, chosen after the original owner returned from a trip to Paris. As for the present owner, nobody knew his actual name. He was just Frisco Jim, the latest in a series. Nobody on the island had to give his legal name, and few there were who did.

A hundred yards away from the nearest building, Shanahan stopped walking, his hand on Lydia Preston's arm. As he touched her he felt her tense, then relax. He sensed that she could easily have pulled her knife from its scabbard in the blink of an eye, had she decided Shanahan was hostile.

From the corner of his eye he saw her tip her head backward to catch a glimpse of the southern sky, its tropical constellations blazing against the infinite blackness. Her hair was long and glossy and an errant breeze whipped a strand against his skin with a delicious sting.

"What a glorious world!" she exclaimed. Her voice was softer than it had been in the bar. Her manner was different.

"Lydia," Shanahan shook his own steel-gray head, "that's all very fine but you didn't pick me up in Frisco Jim's to stroll on the beach like a couple of high school sweethearts."

"No," she admitted. "I didn't."

"Then suppose you tell me what this is about."

"All right. Let's sit."

Shanahan assented.

"I want to hire you."

He turned to face her. Lydia had her knees pulled up beneath her chin, her hands clasped around them. The nightlight glinted off her dark eyes.

"I'm in business," Shanahan said simply. "You have to tell me what you want to hire me for. Mainly, I sail around these waters trading. A few bales of copra here, a basket of pearls there. Some trade goods. Knives, medicine, anything the local populace wants to trade for. And of course news from home and trade goods for the whites. There are Europeans and Americans scattered all over these islands."

"Are there, Shanahan?"

He ignored the question. "Some of 'em come out here for a few years, then go back to the home office if Chicago or New York or London or Hamburg. They can tell stories about the islands for the rest of their lives. They get up in the morning and scrape the whiskers off their cheeks and ride the trolley cars to the big office buildings downtown and don't see the sky or breathe fresh air for the next ten hours. Then they ride home and sit beside the radio listening to dramas of the great world, or reading cheap magazine stories about adventures in the jungles of Africa or the plains of the West or the mountains of Mars."

"Do they, Shanahan?"

"And at nine o'clock they put out the cat, tuck in their children, and climb into bed with their wives."

"Doesn't sound so bad, Shanahan. Does it to you?"

He heaved a sigh. He was seated beside her on the amazingly white sand of this island in the Western Pacific. "I don't know," he said softly. "Maybe not. Maybe not. But—"

He pushed himself to his feet, reached back and lifted Lydia Preston, Mrs. Lydia Preston, widow lady, to hers. He knew she could have pulled a knife from her boot if she chose, or shoved that big Navy Colt between his ribs, but he knew, somehow, that she would not.

"Do you think they ever dream that they're back out here, Lydia? In their dreams, do they ever hear the palm fronds rattling in the trade winds? In their dreams do they ever taste the salt spray as a dugout canoe skims across the water? Do they ever think of the brown-skinned girls they might have met in Ponape, the fisherfolk of Kwajalein, the volcano gods of Kazan-Retto?

How can any man with red blood flowing in his veins go back to Louisville or Liverpool or Leipzig after he's seen this world?"

He swung his arm in a gesture that took in the sea before them, and as he completed his turn he locked eyes with Lydia Preston and felt a rush of embarrassment.

"Don't pay any attention to me," he said. "I get foolish sometimes."

"So I've heard."

Suddenly he was angry. "You've heard, have you? You've heard of Splash Shanahan, sole survivor of the *USS Cichlid?* I've got a reputation, I suppose. But I don't know anything about you, Lydia Preston. I don't know a damned thing about you. So suppose you tell me just who you are what you want to hire me to do for you. If it's legal I'm your man. And if it's not, we can talk."

"All right, Shanahan. I'll tell you."

They were walking along the beach, now. Not far ahead a small wooden wharf extended out into the water. Two or three small craft were moored there. The moon seemed to have grown larger than ever, or closer, perhaps, to the earth.

"My people came from Africa in the seventeenth century. They were free crew on clippers that traded all over the world. Men and women, sailors and cooks. We had our own communities in America, even before the colonies won their freedom. A lot of people think the only Africans in the country were slaves until the great sachem freed them. Well, that was good of him. You might even say, mighty white of him. But we were here before most of the whites ever arrived from Europe, we owned our homes and businesses, ran schools, held public office. Did you know that, Shanahan? Before the War of the Southern Rebellion, we were citizens of the United States of America. Did you know that?"

"I'm afraid my education was lacking on the point."

"A lot of people's education is lacking on a lot of points, Shanahan. Did you know that things are worse in the South now than they were in slavery times? Hard to believe, but it's so. All the progress that was made after the War of the Southern Rebellion has been lost. My people's land was stolen from them, we were run out of public office, denied every right. And if we protest we're lynched. Sometimes they lynch us just for fun. And in the North things aren't much better. It's getting harder and harder for blacks to live in the land of the free and the home of the brave. That's why we need a place of our own."

They were close to the wharf now. It stretched out into a natural harbor, surrounded by two small outcroppings of coral and sand. A number of small craft were moored it. Somewhere in the lush greenery a monkey chattered and its mate replied.

"I appreciate the history lesson," Shanahan said, breaking the silence that had descended on them. "But you're still not telling what I need to know. What do you want me to do?"

"I want you to take me to an island."

"You're on one now."

"Another island. I'll give you the bearings once we're at sea. Not before then."

"What about a chart?"

"The only chart you'll need is in here." She raised a slim hand and tapped the side of her head with a long finger.

They had reached the foot of the wharf and started out on it.

Shanahan said, "You want me to run a private passenger service, is that it? Just take you to—your secret destination?"

"You could put it that way."

"Why me? There are plenty of other sea-tramps in these waters. What about my pal O'Casey? The *Brian Boru* is a trim little craft. Lance is a terrific guy. He's saved me from more than one jam in the past few years."

"I know Lance," Lydia said. "And I know you've pulled his chestnuts out of the fire a few times, too. I also know where he is right now."

"You're ahead of me on that score."

"And I can't wait for him to get back."

"What about Shannon and Duval? *Bold Venture* is a good vessel."

"You don't keep up with the news, do you, Shanahan? They're holed up in some hotel in Havana. They're on the other side of the world. And don't even mention the *Sea Hound*. Too big, too many people involved."

"I guess I'm your last choice, then."

She mentioned a price. "Should take us less than a week."

"What then?"

"Then you lay up for a few days, refit if you need to, and bring me back here."

"Here's my boat," Shanahan said. "The *Goby.*"

"A modest name."

"She's a modest craft. I'm a modest man."

"Before we go on board, I need to get something." She didn't wait for his response, turning back toward the beach and striding across the sand on long, lean legs.

Shanahan started after her, trotting to make up lost distance. "What's this all about?"

"You'll see."

She led him to the edge of the greenery, paused to sight on a pair of tall palms and a distant mountain peak.

"Here."

She knelt and used her heavy knife to scrape away soft sand, then rose to her feet again, a shovel in her hands. She counted off a series of steps and started to dig.

Shanahan asked, "You want me to do that?"

"No thanks. This keeps my muscles hard."

Within minutes Shanahan heard the shovel strike something hard. She dug some more, then fell to her knees and lifted a wooden chest not much bigger than a good sized cook-pot from the ground.

"We'll need this."

"How long has that been there?"

"Not long. I brought it to this island with me. I didn't want any of the local citizens to see it."

Shanahan grinned. "Lady, you are full of surprises. It's a good thing you're paying me because I'm having so much fun I'd take you on board for free just for the pleasure of your company."

She smiled back. "It is heavy, though. If you want to play the gentleman, you might carry it on board for me."

"I shall be delighted."

Once back at the *Goby* he put the chest on wharf. It was bound with metal straps and securely locked. He held out his hand and gallantly helped Lydia Preston climb down onto the deck. He had the feeling that she didn't need any help. They were like two characters in a play, trying to remember their lines and their stage directions. He turned back and lifted the chest and stowed it aboard the sloop.

The *Goby* was fitted with twin bunks separated by a gap of a couple of feet. Shanahan watched as Lydia Preston lowered herself gracefully, sitting on one bunk. He sat on the other, facing her.

"We live pretty simply aboard the *Goby*. And there won't be much privacy once we cast off."

Lydia Preston smiled. "I'm not worried. And I'm not shy. Can I trust you to keep your distance, Shanahan?"

Shanahan laughed out loud. It was a low, friendly sound. It was the first time he'd laughed in a long time. "Scout's honor." He held up his hand, fingers raised in a salute he hadn't used in a decade in a half.

She laughed back.

After he'd showed her around the *Goby*—it didn't take long!—they ate a light supper on the beach and slept under a billion burning stars, not touching, cool southern breezes fanning their dreams.

They cast off before dawn. Shanahan sculled the *Goby* away from the wharf. Once past the outcropping of coral and sand the sloop's sails caught a soft breeze and the craft moved steadily away from the island. He pulled the scull on board, lowered the keel and stationed himself at the tiller.

"All right, Mrs. Preston," Shanahan said. "We're at sea. What about our destination?"

"Are you familiar with the islands of Viti Levu and Vanue Levu?"

"I know of them. Never been there. They're pretty far off the beaten path. No white settlements, no trade goods that I know of."

"But you can take me there, can't you?"

"I can do it. Sure, I can take you there. Think of the *Goby* as a taxicab. I'm the driver. Anywhere you want to go, just pay the fare. But—why Viti and Vanua?"

"I don't really want to go to Viti or Vanua, Shanahan. I want to go to Maiduguru."

Shanahan wore a captain's cap, a minor vanity that he'd allowed himself ever since he took up the freelance sailor's trade. He shoved it toward the back of his head by snapping his thumb against the cap's visor. "Now you've got me stumped, Lydia. That's a new one to me."

She shook her head and smiled. The early morning sunlight glinted off her teeth. "We try to keep it quiet."

"What is it?"

"It's a small island, between Viti and Vanua. You might even call it a nation."

"All right, I wasn't very good at geography back at Saint Anselm's in Providence."

"That's all right. You won't find Maiduguru in any geography book or any atlas. Hardly anybody knows about it. We want it that way."

"Right. You're a real mystery woman, you know that? Who is—*we?*"

"My people, Shanahan. I told you things are getting worse and worse for us in the United States. Woodrow Wilson despised us. President Hoover isn't much better. None of the states are willing to do anything. White haters are becoming more numerous and more powerful. Blacks were good enough to go to Europe and fight the Hun. I was there myself. I was a nurse. We thought once we came home we'd get decent treatment but it was back to the same old oppression. Worse. So a few hundred of us got together and pooled our funds and bought an old tub. We set out for our own promised land, and we found it. We call it Maiduguru. That's where our people originated. In Africa. It's a white man's colony now. There's no going back there."

"Wait. I've heard of something like that. Are you Marcus Garvey people?"

She shook her head. "Marcus wants to go back to Africa. The European powers have sliced up Africa like a roast pig. England gets a haunch, France gets a shoulder, Belgium gets a rack of ribs, Italy gets some juicy chops. It's been going on for two hundred years. The Kaiser got his share, and when the Great War ended the others just took it away from Germany and split it up among themselves."

"But—a tiny island? There must be thousands and thousands of blacks in America."

"Millions."

"All of them going to Maiduguru?"

"No, Shanahan. Just a few hundred. We can't save the world, we can't save everyone. It's enough if we can save ourselves."

"Okay, okay. That'll do for now." He directed Lydia Preston to retrieve the sloop's charts from the binnacle. Once she had done so he spread them on the deck and located Viti Levu and Vanua Levu. He studied the sloop's compass, scribbled some computations with a stub of pencil, and had Lydia place the charts back in the binnacle.

They didn't talk much until afternoon. Shanahan had broken out some sea rations and they took a light meal. He brought a sextant out of the binnacle and took their position. He grunted satisfiedly.

"Something bothers me," he said.

Lydia looked at him, waiting for him to go on.

"I'm not one of your people." He held up a callused hand. The skin on his arm was darkened by sun and wind, the fine hairs bleached to near invisibility. "Why me?"

"We had a craft at Maiduguru. We try to keep communication with the rest of the world to a minimum, Shanahan. The island is self-sufficient. There aren't very many of us, anyway. We have some fields for grain, we bought seed from the mainland and we plant every year and reap every year. It's hard work but the soil is rich and the crops are good. And we have some livestock, some chickens and pigs."

"Sounds like something they're trying in Russia."

"Maybe, maybe not. It's a hard life but it's our own. If the world found out about us—we don't know what would happen. Somebody would probably decide that we were an offense to their dignity. We don't want to wake up one morning and find a flotilla of ships from Italy or Japan or France coming to bring us the benefits of civilization. Still less would we like to be invaded by freebooters. But every so often, we need to trade with the outside world for something we don't have on Maiduguru. One thing we do have is a short wave radio and a small office on the mainland. When our little ship set out a few months ago it disappeared. We don't know what happened. Maybe it ran aground, maybe—I don't know. When there was no word for—too long—my people radioed to the mainland. That's where I was working. I have to get back to the island. That's why I hired you."

"And the chest?"

"Never mind that. Just get me to Maiduguru."

For three days they beat westward. They dined on hardtack and fresh-caught fish broiled over *Goby's* spirit stove, carefully rationing their supply of fresh water. Each night they set a sea-anchor to prevent the sloop from drifting too far off its plotted course.

Lydia Preston denied prior experience as a sailor. Splash Shanahan doubted her claim but conceded it was possible that she was simply a fast learner. At any rate, he was discovering that it was easier to manage the *Goby* with a mate on board than it had been alone. And Mrs. Preston made good company. The days were busy with tending the sloop's lines and sails, keeping her on course, and bringing their meals of fresh-caught fish on board.

But the nights were filled with talk. Shanahan told his passenger of his childhood in Providence, his service in the navy during the Great War, the sinking of the submarine *Cichlid* and his survival thanks to the sacrifice of his best friend, Albert le Fleur. He told her of his rescue by the German cruiser *Regensburg,* his long interrogation by its kapitän, Franz Wilhelm von Schachleitner, and his internment until the end of the war.

It was the sinking of the *Cichlid* and the death of his friend that had given him a hatred of the sea and a fear of it, that had led him to a hopeless life of vagrancy and drunkenness which he had conquered only by confronting the sea, by becoming a sailor.

Lydia Preston told her own story. She told Shanahan of her childhood in Boston, of her genteel upbringing by a family of well-educated and well-to-do black gentry and the shock of discovering the real life faced by her people in Twentieth Century America. She told him of her marriage, of her husband's quixotic mission to the American South in hopes of awakening the black people there. She told him with bitterness of the day she received news that her husband had been lynched by hooded night-riders, hung from an elm tree and left to swing like carrion.

It was then that she had joined the covert movement to Maiduguru.

Each morning they were awakened by the sun, rising above the horizon like a ball of brilliant flame. Each night they ate their dinner of hardtack and fresh broiled fish, retiring to the *Goby's* snug cabin to sleep in bunks separated by a few feet that might as well have been as many miles.

Midmorning of the fourth day Lydia Preston spotted a distant peak that Splash Shanahan recognized as Mount Fatmalapa. By afternoon they had beached the *Goby* and crossed the beach to the village of the Ni Vanuatu where Shanahan was known. He used the native pidgin to introduce Lydia Preston to old friends who marveled at her black skin and glossy tresses, comparing their own brown pigmentation and fuzzy hair to hers with grins and exclamations.

Shanahan left Lydia Preston and a crowd of Ni Vanuatu women comparing notes and becoming fast friends with gestures while Lydia took a lesson in pidgin. Shanahan made his way to the combination trading post and saloon operated by the island's sole permanent white resident, the Dutch Rip van Roosevelt.

"Ach, Mijnheer Shanahan," the trader greeted him. "Such a long time away you have been." Unshaven and unwashed, van Roosevelt exuded an oily *bonhomie*. "And what have you brought me this time?" He led Shanahan into the stale-smelling shade of his establishment.

Shanahan described the light cargo of trade goods that he had stowed in the *Goby's* lockers. Van Roosevelt placed a bottle and two glasses on the table between them and poured himself a sizable portion of spirits. Shanahan politely declined to join the Dutchman. He was finding it easier to resist booze with each passing year but he did not trust himself to sample the liquor that nearly killed him not many years before.

Once they had worked out a barter of knives and cooking implements for ship's stores, Shanahan prepared to take his leave but van Roosevelt was curious. "You are bound where, friend Shanahan?" he asked.

"Westward," Shanahan replied.

"Westward, eh? Westward lies a great deal. Many islands, continents, not?"

"I'm carrying a passenger," Shanahan said.

"There are liners, no? A passenger alone hires you to deliver him somewhere?"

"No accounting for taste," Shanahan said.

"Well, I have some good news to share," van Roosevelt said. "Look here, I have saved this to show you now." He rummaged through pockets in his ragged shirt and trousers, finally emerging with a sepia-tone photograph, its crinkled edges bent and fingerprinted.

"Eh, look here," he repeated, holding the photo for Shanahan's inspection. It showed a family group, a man, woman, and cluster of children. The woman bore a striking resemblance to Rip van Roosevelt.

"Who's this?" Shanahan asked.

"*Ach, mijn zuster*—in English, to say, my sister. Trudel she is called. With her husband, Zeeman, and their children. A trading station they start on Vanua Levu. You have been there, Shanahan?"

"Never."

"Well, some time, perhaps. If you are there, tell them you are my friend. They will treat you well, I promise this."

Shanahan rose and gathered the packages he had bartered for. As he started for the door, the trader stopped him once more.

"A lot of traffic I have had lately. A steamer on the horizon passed. All I could see was dark smoke. But a big one it was, I could tell. And then a friend of yours here came, Shanahan, after that. The red-hair, what is his name? You Irishers are all the same."

Shanahan held his silence.

"*Ach, ja!* O'Casey, that was who here was. He left behind some papers, you would like them maybe." He retreated behind a seldom-used bar, returned with a pile of newspapers. "You would like them maybe," he repeated.

They cost Shanahan a frying pan and a spatula that he was not pleased to part with, but curiosity overcame him. He hadn't seen O'Casey in a year or longer. Shanahan and the red-hair, as van Roosevelt called him, had crossed paths more than once and had become fast friends. O'Casey knew that Splash stopped at Vanuatu from time to time. He'd probably left the newspapers with van Roosevelt as a gift for Shanahan but van Roosevelt would never pass up a chance to squeeze some profit from any exchange.

Aboard the *Goby* Shanahan shared the newspapers with Lydia Preston. They were tattered and yellow. They were a motley selection. There was a Boston *Globe,* a Chicago *Tribune,* a San Francisco *Call-Bulletin.* The dates were as scattered as the cities of publication, but none was newer than a month or two. A month or two, Shanahan thought. He didn't know the date, didn't care. It hardly mattered nowadays, not to a man living the way he lived.

Nor did the events on the mainland or in the rest of the world mean much to Shanahan. Alfonso XIII, Most Catholic King of Spain, had been forced to abdicate and the nation became a secular republic. The Vatican retaliated by beatifying 498 Spanish Catholics who had died defending the kingdom. The Japanese Imperial Army occupied the Chinese province of Manchuria. A daring thief had made off with a ruby, believed to be the world's most valuable, from a museum in Chicago. Gang lord Al Capone was sentenced to eleven years in Federal prison for evading income taxes.

The news reports gave Shanahan and Lydia Preston something to talk about. Somehow the Vatican news brought their conversation around to religion, the last thing that Shanahan would have expected to find himself discussing with a beautiful woman in the middle of the Pacific Ocean. Shanahan had been raised a Catholic in Providence but his experiences in the Great War and the death of his fellow submariners aboard the *Cichlid* had turned him against all religion.

Lydia Preston heard him out but had little to add until he asked if the people of Maiduguru had brought Christianity with them. Lydia shook her head. "Why should we? We had our own gods in Africa. What did the Christians bring us, and then the Muslims? Slavery. Slavery, Shanahan, and rape and death. We brought our own gods to America with us. Then we brought them to Maiduguru."

It was late in their second day out from Vanuatu. Shanahan had set a sea anchor. Lydia Preston was cooking fresh fish, its white, tender meat stuffed with fruit they had brought with them from the island. The sun was about the dip beneath the horizon. Its reflection was a highway of gold leading across the water to the west.

"Lots of African gods, Shanahan, lots of African gods. My favorite—you'll see him in Maiduguru—Uwolowu. Of course we couldn't worship African gods openly in America. But Uwolowu is the greatest god. He created everything. He created all the other gods, in Africa and everywhere else."

Shanahan shook his head. "Sorry. Never heard of him."

"That's all right. I have a sneaking suspicion he wasn't a he anyway. Males are much better at destroying than creating. But whether he's a boy or a girl, Uwolowu gets around. I think they call him Tangaroa in the islands."

"Oh, Tangaroa I've heard of. He rules the seas all right. I always thought he was the local version of Neptune."

By the time they finished their meal the conversation had drifted to other topics, then lapsed. Lydia Preston went on deck to rinse their crude cooking implements. Shanahan sat on his bunk watching her. He'd had few encounters with women, none in a long time. The most powerful relationship he'd ever had was with Fenchy le Fleur's sister, Antoinette, who had sworn to kill him in vengeance for her brother's death.

Briefly he watched Lydia Preston, silhouetted against a brilliant constellation, then turned his face toward the bulkhead and squeezed his eyes shut.

They spotted Viti Levu and Vanua Levu late in the afternoon. Shanahan was at the tiller. The twin islands rose abruptly from the sea, each crowned by a lazily smoking volcano. He called to Lydia Preston. "There are Viti and Vanua. I don't see your Maiduguru anywhere."

"You won't. Not until we're closer. It's mostly lowlands. A few hills. No peaks like the twins."

Shanahan was doubtful of making landfall before dark, and he didn't want to navigate for so small a target at night. He set a sea-anchor, Lydia Preston prepared a light meal for them and they turned in for the night.

In the morning he raised the *Goby's* sails and caught a breeze that moved them briskly toward Viti Levu and Vanua Levu. An hour later he heard Lydia Preston exclaim in surprise. "There's smoke—and not from the volcanoes!"

She was right. Shanahan had seen smoke rising from many volcanoes from Hawaii to Papua and never was it like the dense, black smoke that was rising ahead of them. He handed the tiller to Lydia Preston, ran to the binnacle and brought out a seldom-used glass. One glance was enough to send a chill through him.

"Shanahan, what is it?"

"It's a steamer. Rip van Roosevelt said he'd seen a steamer from Vanuatu not long ago. This may be it."

"It can't be. No one knows about Maiduguru."

"Somebody does."

After a stunned silence that seemed far longer than it was, Lydia Preston said, "They picked up our boat. We were always afraid that would happen. Our man must have been picked up by the steamer, or word got out and they captured him in port somewhere."

Shanahan studied the steamer through his glass. "Looks like a tramp. I can't tell much. There are ships in this part of the ocean, nobody keeps track of them."

"Can we—can we sneak past them, to Maiduguru?"

"We can try." Shanahan lowered the glass and relieved Lydia Preston at the *Goby's* tiller. "We're small and I don't think they'll be looking for us."

It was a plan. It was a plan, and it worked. Shanahan plotted a course and sailed the *Goby* quietly to the south of Vanua Levu, then approached Maiduguru from the direction opposite the tramp steamer. As Lydia had said, Maiduguru was a low-lying island. Its few hills rose barely a hundred feet above the lush greenery that surrounded them.

There was a natural harbor. He sailed the *Goby* carefully into it, raising the sloop's cast-iron keel and beaching the craft on white sand. It wasn't the only small boat present.

There were bodies scattered on the beach. Most of them were black, a few looked like Europeans.

The steamer was called the *Schwert von Mann*. Splash Shanahan and Lydia Preston stood facing the steamer's captain, armed crewmen standing by threateningly. They had been treated roughly. Lydia Preston had used her Navy Colt and her heavy knife to good effect, but the *Schwert von Mann's* shore party had outnumbered and surrounded them, struck them down and dragged them onto the steamer's small boat and transported them to the ship.

The captain studied them in silence, nodded, approached Shanahan and stood eye to eye with him. Then he smiled.

"I know you, fellow."

The captain's choice of English words was flawless but his enunciation was distinctly accented. Shanahan had heard it before. He blinked in recognition. "Yes, you do."

"Wait," the captain said. He retreated behind a massive desk. They were in his stateroom. Daylight streamed through opened portholes along with fresh air tainted with foul-smelling smoke. "Do not tell me. I take pride in my powers of recollection."

He leaned forward and gazed at Shanahan once again. "Yes, yes, you are the American sailor. You were my guest once before, fellow. Don't tell me your name. Some funny English word, I think. Shingles, shenanigans—no, I have it! Shanahan, that's it! I never forget. Yes, the American torpedo man, I remember filling out reports with your name. Seamus Shanahan, torpedo man third class, *USS Cichlid.* We talked for a long while but you didn't tell me anything useful, Shanahan. But that was another time, another war. This time, you will tell me more."

"This is not war, Captain. We're all civilians now. You have no right to hold us."

The captain smiled. "Do you remember me, Torpedo man Shanahan?"

"Von Schachleitner."

"Ja, ja," the German lapsed briefly into his own language. Then, once more in English, "In those days I was *Korvettenkapitän* Franz Wilhelm von Schachleitner of the Kaiser und König's Imperial Fleet. Lieutenant Commander, you would call me. Now, alas, I am merely Herr Schachleitner. Or Kapitän Schachleitner of the steamship *Schwert von Mann.* And you and your charming companion are my guests."

He paused, then resumed.

"Torpedo man Shanahan—or plain Mister Shanahan now, I suppose—you will forgive, please the slightly ungentle treatment that you and your companion received from my sailors. And you would be so kind as to introduce your friend to me?" He bowed toward Lydia Preston, a touch of irony in the movement.

"My name is Lydia Preston," she said, not waiting for Shanahan to speak. "Missus Preston to you, Captain. You and your men are criminals. You're murderers. You'll pay for what you've done. You're beasts. Killers!"

Out of the corner of his eye, Shanahan saw Lydia Preston begin a move toward her boot. Her revolver and broad-bladed knife were gone but not her concealed knife. Shanahan lunged at von Schachleitner but four of the captain's crewmen caught both Shanahan and Lydia Preston by their elbows before they could accomplish anything. Von Schachleitner nodded toward another of his minions, an unshaven, heavyset individual in dirty sleeveless shirt and faded dungarees.

The latter bent to pry at Lydia Preston's boot. He was greeted by a knee to the jaw that sent him sprawling across the cabin to crash against the far bulkhead. A second crewman caught Lydia

Preston's ankle and with massive hands extracted her slim-bladed knife and threw it on the captain's desk.

With a burst of laughter and a single backhanded swing of his hand, von Schachleitner delivered a stinging blow to the faces of both his captives.

He glared at Lydia Preston. "You are not a Polynesian, *fräulein,* are you? *Nein.* This is very strange, very strange. And you, Herr Shanahan, in the company of this woman—is she not an African? How very strange. We found another of her kind, a man, not so very long ago. He did not like to chat with us. We wanted only a little information from him but he did not like to talk."

Von Schachleitner nodded sadly.

"He did agree to talk with us, finally. He told us about this island of yours, this little piece of African paradise in the middle of the ocean. So strange a place. What did he call it? *Ach, ja,* I now remember it. Maiduguru, is it not? Or, should I say, was it not. The tenses of your English verbs are so irregular. Such a language."

He shook his head.

"Well, your Maiduguru is no more, I'm afraid. You saw what happens to lesser peoples who resist us, *Fräulein.* A pity. Fortunately they had no firearms. They fought my men with spears and arrows like the savages they was. No, they *were, ja?* Such a language! But we now have a lovely little island for ourselves. We have equipment in the hold of this ship. Shortly this island will have a new name. A new population. It will be part of a new world order. But what to do with you?"

He picked up the knife that his subordinate had drawn from Lydia Preston's boot. He studied its blade, turned it so that a ray of bright tropical sunlight flashed across the cabin and the faces of his captives.

"What are you going to do with us, von Schachleitner?" Splash Shanahan demanded. "Kill us? We have friends. They'll look for us. You'll be found out. You Huns tried to conquer the world once in this century and you failed. You'll fail if you try again."

"I do not think so." Von Schachleitner seemed to be enjoying the repartee. "My country now, *ach,* a sad place it is. The liberal fools in Weimar and the corrupt degenerates who pollute Berlin will not last. The Republic is on its last legs. Soon we will have a leader again. The Kaiser und König from exile will return, I think. Or perhaps some other leader will come to power. This time things will be different, you will see, Shanahan. If you live, you and your African savage companion, you will see."

He was striding up and down now, stopping to stare into Shanahan's face, then Lydia Preston's. He raised a hand and touched Lydia Preston's cheek with it. To Shanahan the gesture looked like an assessment more than a caress. Lydia Preston spat into von Schachleitner's face.

Von Schachleitner sent a fist crashing into her cheek, then another into her belly as his subordinates restrained her. He retreated behind his desk and threw himself into his wooden captain's chair.

"You know, Torpedo man Shanahan, you are not quite as stupid as your African friend. I'm going to let you go. Oh, both of you, yes, Shanahan, you and your African queen. You can go. I doubt that you will survive long, but I will have my men bring your little, *ach,* there is a good English word for it. I must remember. *Nein, nein,* do not help me. *Ja, ja,* now I remember. Your little cockleshell. Such a good word."

He grinned with self-satisfaction.

"My men will bring your little cockleshell here and you and your savage friend can sail away if you wish, and if you tell anyone about our friendly encounter, and if they come to this island, why, what do you think they will find? What do you think, eh? They will find men hard at work building a coaling station for passing ships to use. That is all they will find. And if you tell them wild stories about what you think you learned today, they will laugh at you."

His face changed from a mask of irony to one of iron command. He shouted a string of orders to the men filling the cabin.

Shortly a prize crew, if such a term can be applied to a handful of brutal sailors, had returned to the beach and retrieved Shanahan's sloop, the *Goby.* Von Schachleitner accompanied Shanahan and Lydia Preston to the rail of the *Schwert von Mann* and watched as they were lowered to the *Goby*.

"Good-bye," the German captain called after them as the *Goby* drifted away from the *Schwert von Mann*. "Perhaps we will meet again, Shanahan. In the meanwhile, watch out for your companion. They are cannibals, you know. You might make a nice meal for that savage."

Shanahan tried to shout his defiance at von Schachleitner but his voice was drowned out by a sudden roaring. Shanahan felt Lydia Preston gripping his arm, saw her lips move, shook his head, unable to hear a syllable. She leaned toward him, brought her mouth close to his ear, shouted, "What is it, Shanahan, what is it?"

The roaring increased. It was the sound of a freight train, its steam engine bellowing at the top of its voice, its whistle screaming and its brakes screeching on the rails, all of it multiplied a million times over.

Shanahan looked up at the dark bulk of the *Schwert von Mann*. Sailors were running around the deck in panic. The sky behind the ship was even darker than its hull, as if a titan were sweeping a paintbrush of midnight pigment across the horizon. The *Schwert von Mann* rocked and loose gear from her deck flew overhead to splash into the water behind the *Goby*. A black form came spinning from the freighter, spinning like a pinwheel, followed by another and another as sailors were carried from the freighter's deck and sent hurtling through the air.

A torrent of rain drenched the *Goby* and threatened to swamp her little craft. A wall of water appeared beyond the *Schwert von Mann* and with a horrifying rending crash that was audible even above the roaring of the sea the freighter broke into pieces, the stern fragment and then the bow going end-up, then sinking with another roar beneath the water.

A wall of green-black brine swept beyond the *Goby*. Clearly, it was the bulk of the *Schwert von Mann* that had saved the tiny sloop from being smashed to flinders.

Shanahan didn't need to answer Lydia Preston's question. He knew and she knew that a tsunami, the dreaded killer wave of the Pacific, had destroyed the *Schwert von Mann* and spared the *Goby*.

Lydia Preston took Shanahan's arm and pointed. The great wave was gone, the black freighter was gone and—the island of Maiduguru was gone. Viti Levu and Vanua Levu remained visible, the twin volcanoes sending their slow, steady streams of gray-white smoke into a once more clear Pacific sky.

Without a word, Shanahan and Lydia Preston made their way below decks and began the process of pumping out the *Goby*. It was a long and exhausting task.

When it was completed Lydia Preston retrieved the wooden chest she had brought aboard the *Goby*. From a pocket in her trousers she extracted a key and opened it. Since boarding the sloop, Shanahan had honored Lydia's wishes. He had neither attempted to open the chest nor interrogated her as to its contents.

Now he watched as she raised it lid, swung it back on its hinges, and lifted from a bed of pale velvet a magnificent, glittering ruby. She climbed from the cabin of the *Goby*, Shanahan following, fascinated. She held the huge gem to her bosom, facing westward, the sun's rays suffusing the stone with an almost supernatural glow that spread from the gem to the woman herself. She made her way to the bow of the sloop.

"It is his eye," she said. "Or—hers."

She held it over the edge of the sloop, over the once more clear water of the Pacific. "It is yours, creator of all things, yours, father-mother. It is yours."

She released the ruby and it fell into the water, disappearing into the depths.

Shanahan said, "We can make for Vanua Levu. We can be there before nightfall. I don't think the damage was as great as it was in Maiduguru. I'll have an introduction to some new friends there named Zeeman and Trudel."

Together he and Lydia Preston set the *Goby's* sails, then he took the tiller and the sloop moved gently toward the shining green island.

The late Tiffany Thayer once wrote that an anthologist or the author of a collection should open and close his book with his two strongest stories. If you start well, Thayer argued, the reader is set in a good mood that is likely to carry through the rest of your book. And if you end well, the reader will carry away a favorable feeling about your efforts. "Snow Ghosts" has been one of my most popular stories, and it is one of my own favorites. I hope it lives up to what I have come to think of as "Thayer's Law."

He pushed at the heavy door with all the strength of his frail frame. He couldn't budge it. From inside the Garnet Saloon he could hear the music, something by Mozart, a relief from the jinglelike Christmas carols and canned cheer that went with the season. And he could see the decorative lights within, a few annoying red and green bulbs but mostly the Garnet's traditional pleasant amber and ruby.

It was cold, and the snow sifted down the collar of his mackinaw. He looked around to see if anyone was approaching, but there was only the occasional pair of headlights moving cautiously through the center of town. Not many people out on December 24. They were home with their families or celebrating with friends.

He felt in his pockets and found a coin. He rapped with it against the small pane in the Garnet's door. Inside, the bartender moved around the end of the bar, headed for the door, and pulled it open for him. He gathered his strength to step across the threshold, but the bartender had already taken him by the arm and was half lifting and half pulling him inside.

"You shouldn't be out, Old Timer." She smiled at him, but her face showed concern. "You'll catch your death!"

He mumbled something, thanking her for letting him in. He tried to climb onto a barstool.

"Come on, Old Timer. Can you make it? Rather sit in a chair?"

"I was balancing on one of those things before you were born, Jen."

"I know, Old Timer. I know you can handle it. But you might be comfier by the fireplace."

He let her lead him to a captain's chair near the hearth. A wood fire was burning, and its warmth felt good on his face.

"Coming down pretty hard, is it?" Jennifer asked.

"Little bit."

She didn't wait for his order but poured hot water into a glass and then dumped it out again. She lifted a bottle of Bushmills and poured some of its contents into the glass. She filled it the rest of the way with coffee and then spooned whipped cream on top. She brought it to him. "This will warm your insides, Old Timer."

He took the glass and studied it without speaking. After a little while he sipped. They were making the drinks weak nowadays. In his heyday he would have swallowed his Irish without the coffee, but everyone thought was feeble now and had to take care of him. Well, maybe they were right. Not everybody made it to ninety. In a small town like this, on the edge of the lake, hardly anybody. The winters were too cold, the air too thin, life too demanding. But he'd made it through nine decades. And now he was alone.

Jennifer looked into his face, patted him on the shoulder, and started away. "Let me know how you're doing."

He nodded.

The Garnet wasn't as empty as he'd expected. Two or three tables were occupied by couples. They looked amazingly young, eyes shining, skins glowing. They touched hands, exchanged glances. Occasionally one of them would look at him surreptitiously. He smiled and they looked away.

The Mozart was pleasant. Time was when the Garnet wouldn't have played anything more classical than Hank Williams, but they'd gone upscale and put in a CD player and concealed speakers to make the big-spending skiers from San Francisco happy. He couldn't place the piece, but it was familiar, peaceful. Maybe one of the German dances. At the far end of the bar, he could see a huge TV screen and on it a colorized version of *It's a Wonderful Life,* happily sans soundtrack. Jimmy Stewart and Donna Reed were dancing at the high school gym, and he knew that they would shortly fall into the swimming pool. How many times had he seen them do that?

There were a few drinkers at the bar. They were hunched over; unlike the couples at the tables, they were serious about their alcohol.

Jennifer looked at him, came out from behind the bar again, and squatted beside his chair. She was a full-figured woman, her generous bosom filling the button-down shirt that she wore whenever she was on duty. "Are you okay, Old Timer?"

He nodded, ignoring the TV images, peering instead into the

dancing oranges and reds in the fireplace.

Christmas Eve, alone in a saloon. Ninety years old, and all alone on Christmas Eve. He looked up at Jennifer, tried to nod reassuringly to her. She was a good woman, a kind woman. If he were a few years younger, he thought . . . then almost laughed. Some few years! Fifty or sixty would be more like it.

"I'm okay," he managed.

"Want me to freshen that up a little?" She took his glass without waiting for an answer. Had he finished his drink already? Or was she just taking it away from him, afraid that he'd drop it on his lap?

He looked at her and she seemed blurred. He had good eyes, he was proud of that. But they were watering a little. The cold and wind outside, the heavy flakes of falling snow, and then the warmth inside the Garnet, and the drink, and the fire—that must be it.

Jennifer could almost be her granddad, Jack McGyver, wearing the same white shirt and the same black bow tie. Of course, Jack didn't have the bosom that Jen did, but he'd been a hearty, beefy man all the same. And beyond Jennifer, seated at the bar, a tall, gray-haired fellow swung about and held his glass high in a friendly gesture, almost a Christmas toast.

Seated in his chair by the fire, he tried to return the toast but discovered that he didn't have his glass any longer. He looked around for Jennifer. She'd gone to refill his glass, hadn't she? He could use another Irish coffee.

Seated at the bar, the gray-haired man saw the bartender returning. "The old fellow all right?" he asked.

"He'll be okay," Jack said. "Ninety years old, and alone at Christmas. Christ, I feel for the old man. I hope I never get that old."

"Beats the alternative," Shelton said.

"I'm not so sure."

"Doesn't he have anybody? Not anybody?"

"Old Timer's wife died years ago. They had a daughter, career army nurse. Served in Vietnam, working in a field hospital. Vietcong smuggled a porcupine mine into the place and—*wham!*

—that was that. Didn't think the old fellow was going to navigate for a while after that, but he came out of it all right."

Shelton shook his head pityingly.

Jack McGyver took a few steps, reached up, and turned the knobs on the 17-inch Magnavox. Even though it was Christmas Eve, the local station was showing an old Humphrey Bogart-Lauren Bacall movie. There were few Christmas decorations scattered through the Garnet, but the atmosphere was gloomy. The dominant feature was a huge black wreath framing a hand-tinted portrait of John F. Kennedy.

"Sure don't feel like Christmas," Jack said.

"No." Shelton looked into his shot glass. He shoved it across the mahogany. McGyver reached for the Bushmills and refilled the glass. "You're the only Scotsman I've ever met who'd rather drink Irish."

"To you, Jack." Shelton hoisted his shot glass and saluted first his living friend and then the portrait of the dead president.

"You think Johnson can do the job?" McGyver asked.

Shelton sipped thoughtfully at his drink. "I don't know, Jack. He's a smart one, but I don't know."

"He wouldn't have pulled that boner at the Bay of Pigs, you can bet on that."

"Maybe not."

"Neither would Nixon. They're two of a kind, Nixon and Johnson. Don't know how Johnson got mixed up with Kennedy, but things work out funny sometimes."

"They do that."

"You think he'll bring the troops back from Asia?"

Shelton shook his head. He'd had a blurry moment. Not exactly as if his eyes were blurry, and not exactly dizziness, either. But one moment he'd been looking at the old fellow near the fire, and the old fellow was ninety, he knew that, and the female bartender was bringing him a drink—there was a female bartender, wasn't there?

But—he peered up at the Magnavox. There was a Buick commercial ending, the camera lingering on the chrome-rimmed decorative portholes above the front fender, and then it was replaced by a jingle and a pack of dancing Old Golds.

"Kennedy said something about pulling out by Christmas," he

said.

"Sure he did," Jack McGyver said. "And he said we're going to the moon, too."

They shared a bitter laugh.

The door of the garnet swung open, and a draft of cold air brought a flurry of snowflakes with it. Shelton swung around on his barstool, catching a glimpse of the codger still warming himself at the fireplace.

The man who entered the Garnet wore a fedora pulled down over his forehead and a tweed overcoat with its collar turned up. A woolen scarf swathed his features and thick gloves covered his hands, so that only his eyes were visible.

"Close it!" a chorus rang out.

Scotty Shelton shoved the door shut and crossed the barroom to the coat tree beside the fireplace.

Young Jack McGyver, the bartender, said, "You manage to park okay, Scotty?"

"Slipped a little bit, but it's okay."

"You going to keep running that old Hupmobile?"

"Don't have much choice, do I? Won't be any new cars, now we're in the war."

"Won't be much chance to buy gas or tires, either."

"Well, I don't suppose I'll be here long, anyhow. Going to get back in my old outfit."

"Come on, Scotty. They don't want duffers like you. War's a young man's game! Why, they put you up against one of Adolf's storm troopers or a squad of those little Jap monkeys, they'd take you to pieces."

"I haven't seen you rushing to enlist, Jack."

"I know better. You must love getting up at five o'clock in the morning and marching around with a rifle on your shoulder. Heck, Scotty, rifles are for deer-hunting, that's my motto."

Behind McGyver, a Philco radio was playing a transcription of the Andrews Sisters singing "The Pennsylvania Polka." The song ended and the announcer said, "It's 10:30 P.M. Pacific War Time. That's 22:30, you GI's on leave. And in a minute we'll have Der Bingle to lend a little Christmas cheer, but first, have you thought about your teeth lately? You know, in wartime, we can't afford to neglect our health. Uncle Sam needs our doctors and nurses in the armed forces—and, yes, the dentists, too! So the makers of Ipana tooth powder and paste urge you . . ."

"Turn that thing off, will you, Jack?"

Instead, McGyver turned the volume down.

"You really want to go back in, don't you?" the bartender asked.

Scott looked around the Garnet. An aged man sat huddled near the fireplace. Another aging citizen with silver-gray hair had apparently left his place at the bar and was walking slowly toward the oldster, drink in hand. Scott Shelton swung back to face the waiting Jack McGyver. Again he pushed his shot glass toward the barkeep. "Want to? No, I don't want to. But this one, well . . ."

"But you served in the last one."

"I know. That time they drafted me. What did I know? I was just a young kid."

The bartender snorted. "Don't flimflam me, Scotty. I remember how you went jumping up and down when you got your notice. Just 'cause I was too young to go, you acted like Lord High Muck-a-Muck. But you did your share, Scotty. Let the kids go this time, too."

"The kids don't know anything. They don't know why they're fighting. Put 'em in a uniform, hand 'em a gun, and they'll go anyplace, fight anybody. They think a set of khakis and some polished brass and they can get drunk, get laid, go off on a great adventure, and come home heroes. It isn't like that, Jack. I've been watching this Hitler character for a long time."

"I read the papers, too. Is he any worse than Stalin? What's the difference between a Nazi and a Bolshie? Or that man in the White House, for that matter?"

"Don't say that, Jack."

"Don't say what?"

"About FDR."

"Aah, you Democrats are all alike." McGyver reached behind him and picked up a day-old *San Francisco Call*. He spread it on the bar between himself and Scott Shelton. There was a war situation map on the front page, and the two men put their heads together over it.

"God, it looks bad there in the Philippines." McGyver rubbed his heavily stubbled cheeks. "Those poor bastards don't stand a chance. If I could just get my hands on that slant-eyed Tojo and his buck-toothed boss Hirohito . . ."

"You can join up, Jack. You didn't go last time, go now."

"Can't do it, Scott. I've got a wife and baby to think of."

"Me too, in case you haven't noticed."

The Philco was playing Bing Crosby's record of "White Christmas." The front windows of the Garnet were draped with thick blackout curtains to prevent any Jap bomber flying over the Tahoe region from zeroing in on the landmark.

"Well, I'm just an in-betweener," McGyver said. "I was too young for the last war, too old for this one. I think you're a fool to go, Scott, but I can't stop you."

"That you can't, Jack." Scott Shelton lifted his glass. "Well, to Christmas, anyway." He turned from the bar toward the crackling fire. He took his glass with him and climbed from his stool.

The elderly, gray-haired man was standing behind the ancient character, and they both seemed hypnotized by the dancing flames. Scotty moved toward them.

There was a rapping at the door, in a complex pattern. McGyver came out from behind the bar, stood by the door, and yelled. "Who's there?"

"It's me. Open up, Jack."

"Who sent you? What's the governor's middle name?"

"Will you cut that out and open the door! I'm freezing my hind end off out here."

McGyver slid the latch-bolt back. The door swung open and a rattle of hailstones clattered across the hardwood floor. A young man, hardly into his thirties, stood in the doorway.

"Well, close the damned door before we all freeze," the bartender commanded. He was even younger than the newcomer, his hair slicked down and his cheeks smooth.

"Sorry, Jack." The man in the doorway took another step into the Garnet and shoved the door closed behind him. A few hailstones that had somehow clung to his long coat and battered fedora bounced on the floor and then lay still, beginning to melt.

The newcomer surveyed the bar, his eyes passing over the old man at the fireplace and the two younger ones standing near him.

"Let me have a double, will you, Jack?"

"A double what?"

"Irish."

"Scott, you know we don't serve illegal booze here. You can have a mug of coffee, a glass of fruit juice. How about a nice hot cup of tea on a cold, dark Christmas Eve?"

"Come on, Jack, cut it out. You've been paying off the sheriff ever since Prohibition came in, and you're not about to start worrying about it now. Besides, Roosevelt's going to repeal it. The country's going wet. At least that will be something to cheer about."

"Okay, okay. You have any luck yet, Scott?"

Scott shook his head.

"You want this on your tab, then."

"What do you think?"

"I think you're into us for a lot of money, old son."

"Is that my fault?"

"I'm working, Scott."

"Your father owns a saloon, Jack. How many people you know have jobs today?"

McGyver dropped the conversation, placed a glass on the mahogany, and poured a double Irish for Shelton.

Shelton downed half the drink and then lowered the glass. "Thanks, Jack. You know I'm good for it."

"I know you're no deadbeat, Scott. But if you don't have it, you can't pay me, can you? What are you going to do, rob a bank?"

Shelton laughed. The line about robbing a bank was a standing joke. The banks were broke, too. "Maybe Roosevelt will do something."

"I doubt it."

Behind Jack McGyver the amber dials of an Atwater-Kent radio glowed warmly. In some distant studio a pair of musicians were playing "Adeste Fidelis" on a scratchy violin and an off-key cornet. The Atwater-Kent's reception was uneven, and the music was barely louder than the superhet hum, but it was remarkable that they could hear the station at all, up here at the lake.

"Well, Hoover's had three years to work on the Depression, and things just keep getting worse."

"Give the man time, Scott. He didn't cause the crash, you know."

"Who did, then?"

"That's easy. Red agitators. Open your eyes, man. Don't you see, there's a hunch of Rooshians running around this country, stirring things up, making trouble, them and their dupes. They *wanted* the Depression. They *love* it!"

"Oh, come on, Jack."

"They did. They had to get rid of Hoover, and now they're about to put Roosevelt in the White House. You know, that isn't even his real name. His real name is Rosenfeld, and he's descended from a family of Dutch Jews. I just read it the other day in one of those little news things. *Lightning,* they call it. It's a real eye-opener."

Shelton shook his head in disgust and turned away from McGyver, moving from the bar toward the fireplace. He didn't neglect to bring his half-full glass with him.

The door swung open and a young man—hardly more than a boy—charged into the Garnet. Behind him the night was cold and the December constellations blazed like points of flame, almost as brilliant in the reflective waters of Lake Tahoe as in the black winter sky above the Sierra Nevada.

"Mr. McGyver! Is Jackie here?"

"He's cleaning out back, Scotty. What's the excitement?"

"I got it! It came in the afternoon mail!"

"I see." The elder McGyver leaned on the bar, his white-shirted elbows rubbing on the polished mahogany. "What came in the afternoon mail, Scotty?"

"It's here, she can't stop me now!"

The barkeep laughed at the youngster's enthusiasm. He called his son from the back room. "Your friend Scotty's here, Jackie. Come on out and talk to him before the boy has a conniption fit."

Jackie emerged from the back room. He was three years younger than Scotty, but he was big for his age and the two boys were very nearly of a size.

"Look at this!" Scotty waved the letter. "My mom wouldn't let me enlist when I wanted, but she can't stop me now! It's my draft notice, Jackie! Kaiser Bill, watch out! The Yanks are coming!"

Proudly he held the letter for his friend to see. "See this? I have to go to Truckee to report, and then the train down to Sacramento. I bet I'll see San Francisco, New York, Paris—every place!"

"You lucky dog! I wish I could go."

"Maybe the war will last and you will, Jackie. But don't bet on it! Oh, I can hardly wait."

Behind him the door of the Garnet swung open, and a huge man in a bowler hat entered. He kicked the door closed behind him. He held a bundle in his arms. Balancing it carefully on one elbow, he hung his bowler on the rack and smoothed his heavy mustache. "Here he is, my lads!"

He advanced across the hardwood floor and laid his bundle on the bar. The bartender gazed at the tiny boy. "He's a fine one, Joseph."

The proud father beamed. There were Christmas wreaths and berries throughout the saloon, and a fire roared on the hearth. A fragile-looking, aged man, thin almost to the point of transparency, sat beside it in a captain's chair, warming himself. Several others stood at points between the old man and the mahogany bar.

"His name is Scott Shelton," the big man announced. "Scott so he'll never forget the land of his ancestors. It's a joy—having a new son to go with this new century, Mr. McGyver."

"And what does the missus think of your taking the little one out on such a night?"

"It's warm enough in here, Mr. McGyver! And besides, didn't the little Lord Jesus lie in a chilly barn on this very night?"

"He had the animals to keep him warm."

"Aah, I won't argue theology with an Irishman!"

"Nor I with a Scot! He's a lovely baby, Mr. Shelton. Long life and happiness to him! And convey my best wishes to his mother, will you?"

The big man nodded, grinning still. "And aren't you and your own missus going to start adding to the population?"

The bartender reddened. "We'll get to it, Mr. Shelton, rest assured. In good time, we'll get to it." There was a brief, uncomfortable silence. Then, "Let me pour you a big one, on the house," the bartender said. "And while I take care of that, Mr. Shelton, perhaps you'd do an act of kindness."

"Eh?" The big man raised a thick eyebrow.

"You see the old gentleman sitting by the hearth?"

"I do that."

"He seems very sad, Mr. Shelton. It must be hard to be so old, and all alone on Christmas Eve. I think it might cheer him a bit to have a look at the little one. if you think the missus wouldn't mind, of course."

The big man thought about that and then nodded. He turned away from the bar and carried the baby carefully to the old man sitting beside the hearth. He stood with his back to the fire, towering over the fragile oldster. In a semicircle behind the old man, hardly moving, stood others. A man with gray-white hair, another in an odd soft-crowned hat and dark overcoat, another with a face that looked younger but seemed filled with despair, and still another, this one hardly more than a schoolboy, his face filled with an energy and excitement that the big man could remember from his own past.

They all seemed to be concentrating their gaze on the fireplace. All except for the very old man.

The man holding the baby in his arms loomed above the oldster. After a moment he knelt, slowly, and with great care he placed the infant in the old man's arms.

He thought he saw the old man look at the infant, and almost imperceptibly nod, and then for the briefest instant raise his eyes to those of the infant's father. Then the old man's eyes fell shut.

SECRET HOURS
MICHAEL CISCO

AVAILABLE TO ORDER

www.mythosbooks.com

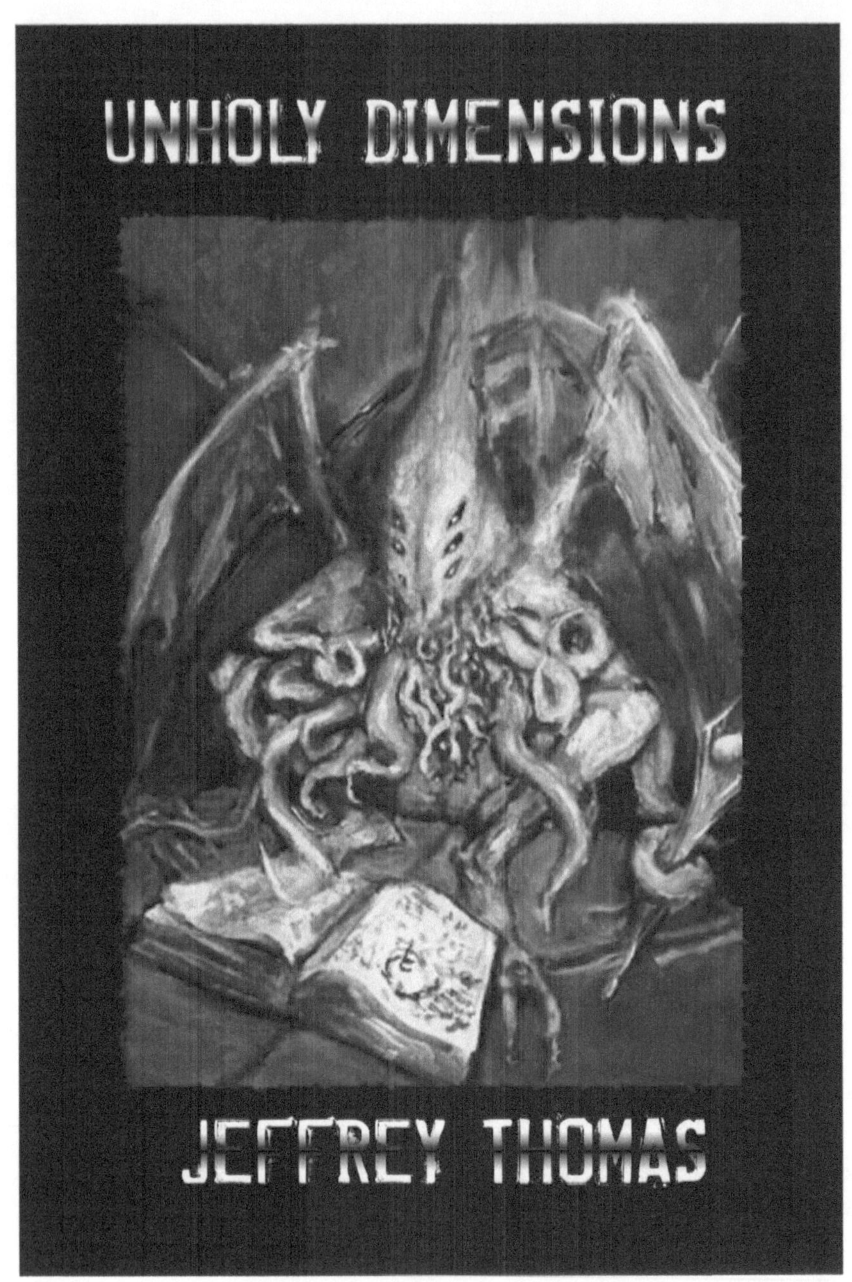
UNHOLY DIMENSIONS
JEFFREY THOMAS

www.ingramcontent.com/pod-product-compliance
Lightning Source LLC
Chambersburg PA
CBHW030808310726
48980CB00006B/427/J
* 9 7 8 0 9 7 2 8 5 4 5 4 2 *